The Land of God

The Two Daggers – Book 2

Elizabeth R. Andersen

The Land of God, Haeddre Press, 2021

Cover design by More Visual Ltd.
Map designs by Theodor Jurma.
Layout by Polgarus Studios.

ISBN: 978-1-7374544-1-0

For Jordan, who read three first drafts.
Now that's love!

Sign up to receive updates on books, news and more at
www.elizabethrandersen.com

CYPRUS

TRIPOLI

MEDITERRANEAN
SEA

DAMASCUS

TYRE

ACRE   *Sea of Galilee*

Jordan River

JERUSALEM

Dead Sea

CAIRO

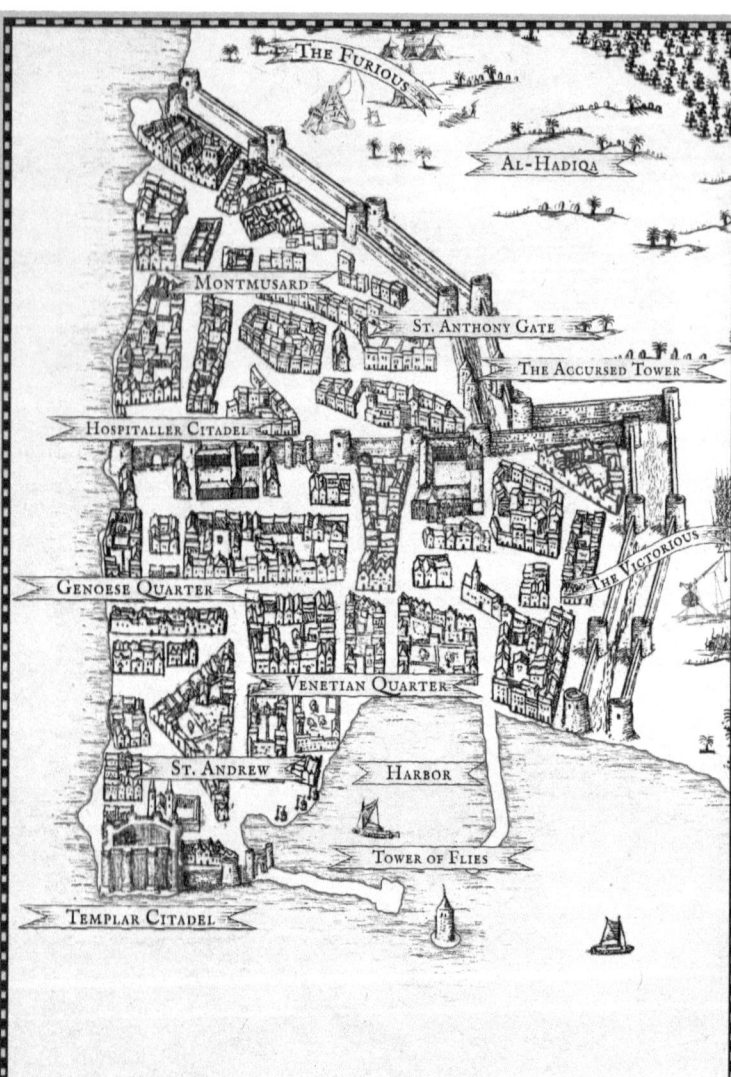

THE FURIOUS

AL-HADIQA

MONTMUSARD

ST. ANTHONY GATE

THE ACCURSED TOWER

HOSPITALLER CITADEL

THE VICTORIOUS

GENOESE QUARTER

VENETIAN QUARTER

ST. ANDREW

HARBOR

TOWER OF FLIES

TEMPLAR CITADEL

ACRE 1290

Prologue
December 1293
Palestine

Abdul planted his feet in the sandy ground and grunted, straining to shift a large limestone block. It had not looked difficult to move the stone when he was standing above it on the ruins of a pillar, but now that he had attempted it and the palms of his hands were raw, he was about to give up. And yet, he couldn't. He knew that there were riches beneath this stone, and so far, Abdul's senses had never failed him. Some said he could smell gold. He certainly could smell something, but the strong wind blowing in from the jewel-blue Mediterranean sea snatched the scent away before he could identify it.

"Jalal!" he hollered, hands on his hips as he evaluated his challenge. "Come help me."

He heard the scrape of Jalal's sandals as he leapt from stone to boulder and occasionally tiptoed along a shattered timber toward him.

"This stone is too big, Abdul. Come, I found a cache of pots behind the hammam. Still intact, although the oil inside of them is rancid."

"No, Jalal," Abdul rubbed his stinging hands together, "this one. I have the feeling about it."

Jalal argued no further. He knew his little brother better

than anyone, and everyone knew that Abdul was blessed with intuition, given by God himself. He nodded, then put his hands on the edge of the stone. Abdul braced his shoulder against the other side and counted down.

"Wahid… itnan… talata!"

Jalal heaved, Abdul pushed, and the stone shifted and toppled onto its side with a great muffled thud.

"Oh, God and His angels!" Jalal clapped a hand over his mouth and nose. Staggering backwards, he fell onto a pile of broken stones, retching loudly. Abdul pulled a corner of his wool keffiyeh over his nose and peered into the shallow hole that the stone had covered. The stench of flesh, sealed and rotting in the cool, damp darkness for two years, rose from the hole, and no amount of fresh sea air could carry it all away. But who cared? In the white-hot sunlight, gold blinked back up at him, alive with a rich yellow glow. Abdul reached into the hole and tugged at a glittering necklace, which was clutched in a bony fist. He tugged again. Sometimes the dead refused to relinquish their riches without a fight.

Drawing his curved shamshir from its sheath on his belt, he hacked at the brittle bones of the wrist until the hand and the necklace came out of the hole together. Tossing this into the sand next to him, he felt around the head. Yes, this was a woman – the skull was small, and he could feel an earring hanging onto what was left of her earlobes – now just a slimy black mass of putrefying flesh. He pulled out her second earring and noted without emotion that there were long blond hairs snagged in the clasp.

"Jalal! Come, I need your help before the others notice." He cast a concerned glance at the ragged scavengers who picked through the cracked stones and collapsed houses.

After two years, it was unusual to find anything of high value here, despite how large the city had been. Thirty thousand people, all gone – dead or fled – their homes destroyed with such violence that it was hardly possible to tell there was ever a city here at all. Everything that the citizens could not take with them now hid like cockles under the sand and rock, and as each treasure was unearthed, the seekers became more and more desperate.

Abdul did not fancy a fight today. His leg still ached from the place where another scavenger had slashed him in a brawl over a cache of rusting blacksmith's tools a few weeks ago. Jalal crawled back to his feet, looking pale.

"I do not like this, Abdul. There are ghosts here. You remember what happened to Mustafa."

Abdul handed Jalal a rock. "Break the fingers off this necklace and be quick about it. Act casual, or else the others will come." He did not want to think about Mustafa.

"A dead Franj walked into Mustafa's tent, Abdul. A holy warrior no less – tall and yellow-haired and dressed in white. He said we would all go to hell!"

"Shut up!" Abdul hissed, grabbing Jalal by the front of his loose brown thawb, which he had tied up around his knees for easier mobility over the stones. "Mustafa is a liar and a simpleton."

"But he has not left his tent since, and Omar hears a woman screaming every night from under the sea. Khalid hears her too!"

"Shut up, *shut up!*"

From a distance, Abdul heard a shout. Several of the other men were tripping and sliding over the broken houses toward them. Abdul plunged his hand back into the hole, right into the woman's rotting abdomen. After scavenging the ruins of the destroyed city for over a year, there was little that could turn his stomach, but the repugnant feeling of his hand inside the soft, rotting flesh made his head spin. He

3

pushed her corpse aside. Underneath it was a smaller body and skull. Her baby. Many of the women under these stones were found with their bodies curled protectively around smaller skeletons.

He shoved the baby aside as well and smiled. A soggy leather sack was there. He pulled it out and peeked inside. A few tarnished silver cups with pearls embedded in them glowed dully. He stuffed this in his sack along with the necklace and the earrings, quietly thanking the woman for giving up her treasures.

Whatever atrocities happened to you before Acre fell, I am sure it was terrible. And I am sure you deserved it.

Three years earlier…

Chapter 1

November 1290

House of Yusuf al-Hikma Ibn Shihab, Cairo

Yusuf Ibn Shihab sighed and rolled over on his cotton-stuffed mattress, stretching an arm out beside him to the empty indent where Abreshmina had lain only hours before. She left sometime during the night and retired to the women's quarters, no doubt to consult with her seer and her lady's maids about her prospects of bearing another son. Although she had already given him two healthy boys, he knew that she was ambitious, and he had willingly granted her request to try to produce more heirs. Still, he wished that she would not leave every night. Perhaps he could convince her to wake up with him. What would it be like to see her eyes opening as the sun rose?

He sighed again, blinking at the cream and gold mosaic of his bedchamber wall. He and Abreshmina genuinely enjoyed each other's company, especially in the marital bed, but he sought her out more often than she sought him.

The sun was still below the horizon, but he could see a greenish glow from his window where it would soon crest the edge of the featureless desert. He propped himself up against his horsehair-stuffed bolsters and watched the black ribbon of the land solidify beyond the rooftops of the houses on the outer edge of Cairo. If he unfocused his eyes, he could sometimes pretend the city's rooftops were the craggy crowns of the Caucasus mountains. His mountains. He used to roam there before that day when the Mamluk army roared through his village and took him away.

He rubbed his eyes and stared into the darkness of his high-ceilinged bedchamber. When he was a boy, he had looked up at the underside of a horsehide tent, his uncle snoring loudly nearby in a drunken stupor. Sometimes Yusuf, whose name had been different in his youth, did not sleep at all, sore as he was from the bruises his uncle regularly bestowed upon him. Every day, Yusuf thanked Allah for bringing the Mamluks into his life. For bringing him a future as a statesman instead of as a goatherd.

Ahead of him was another day of prepping for the invasion of Acre, which meant hours spent in council with the amirs, arguing and persuading them to remember their place and do the sultan's bidding. As Qalāwūn, the aging sultan, declined in health, Yusuf also prepared the amirs to swear loyalty to prince al-Ashraf Khalil. The time to switch rulers would be here soon.

The room was chilly, and he pulled the silk coverlet to his chin, burrowing back into his mattress and pillow. He would sleep for a while longer. A gentle knock sounded at the door, and Hakizimana, his eunuch, slipped inside. Because Yusuf's household was still small, Hakizimana was the only eunuch Yusuf owned. The household eunuch was responsible for serving the women's quarters during the day and rousing his master from his sleep in the morning.

"My lord amir," Hakizimana whispered, hesitating at the door. Yusuf could see that the slave had wound his headdress hastily and that his robe was rumpled. "A rider pounded at the gates this morning before the sun rose. Prince Khalil demands your presence at his tent in al-Salihiya at once."

8

Yusuf groaned and stretched his feet, wiggling each toe. His friend Khalil was a demanding companion. Due to his father's rapidly failing health, Khalil's anxiety about inheriting the throne was reaching an intensity that taxed Yusuf's patience and allowed few in the royal palace complex a peaceful night's sleep.

"I was told to join the march in a month's time with reinforcements from the garrisons on the borders of Nubia. What can he want at this hour? Please lay out my clothes and then go find me something to eat."

Hakizimana busied himself about the room, filling a deep basin for washing and laying out a robe of indigo silk with a pale blue linen tunic underneath and a pair of black sirwal pants that tied at the ankles. Yusuf splashed the water on his face and gave himself a quick wash with a woven cloth, then pulled on his tunic and pants, winding his calves snugly with fine strips of purple silk, and sliding his feet into his tall leather boots. A servant entered the room bearing Yusuf's armor, and he slid into his mail and scale cuirass, which buckled at his sides and back, while Hakizimana wrapped the leather straps of his boots for him. Centering his conical metal cap on the crown of his head, he arranged a blue silk turban around his temples, securing the cap firmly. Hakizimana hurried back from the kitchen with a cold meat pie and handed it up to Yusuf as he mounted his horse.

Because of the heat, people rose early in Cairo to work in the cool morning air, and the streets already bustled with commerce and porters who preferred to carry their loads before the land became tolerable only to snakes and scorpions. Holding his pie with one hand and the reins with the other, Yusuf navigated the narrow, pre-dawn streets toward Bāb al-Barakīyyah – the gate in the eastern wall – before spurring his horse to gallop toward al-Salihiya.

At the camp, a guard directed Yusuf to Qalāwūn's tent, and he immediately noticed something amiss. At least two dozen of Qalāwūn's Mansuriyya guards stood shoulder to shoulder around the tent, creating a wall of spears and shining armor. Yusuf approached cautiously, but the guards did not move to let him pass.

"In God's name, move out of the way!" A voice bellowed from inside the tent. "I told you to allow Amir Yusuf inside!" Two guards stepped aside, and Yusuf entered into a blaze of lamps and braziers. In the center of the room, Sultan Qalāwūn lay gray-faced and cold upon his bed. Nearby, a Sufi mystic hummed and rocked back and forth, and a physician packed his tools and bottles into a small box. Khalil paced nearby with a far-off look on his face.

"What has happened?" Yusuf breathed. "Is my lord Qalāwūn dead?"

The physician nodded his head sadly. "He ate stewed sheep's brains with dill herb for his dinner last night, which I did not advise, for both of those foods induce upset of the stomach and sickness for those with cold temperaments, like the sultan, may Allah preserve him. His heart could not take the strain of it."

"Apparently, my father was only to be eating insipid foods, but being an old man and a stubborn one, he did what he pleased," Khalil commented to Yusuf. The physician bowed and left the tent, and Khalil pulled Yusuf onto a cushioned seat next to him. Yusuf looked nervously at Qalāwūn's body, which was only an arm's length away.

"My friend, there is not much time. My father did not officially name me as his heir, and I fear that Turuntay will try to take the throne. Stop looking at the body and look at me!"

Yusuf snapped his gaze back to Khalil, whose face flushed with urgency.

"The other amirs will arrive soon, and we will be unable to contain the news after that. Al-Shuja'i is on my side, which counts in my favor the most, but I distrust Lajin. And you, my friend, I must know if I have your loyalty. I wish to have you at my side."

Yusuf clasped Khalil's hand and kissed it. "You did not even need to ask for my loyalty, my lord, for you must have known you always had it. I will support you in your bid for the throne, but you should work quickly. Do not allow Turuntay to rally his supporters. The man is foul and hated by most of the amirs, but he was your father's wazir for many years."

"Allow me to deal with Turuntay." Khalil rose with nervous excitement and began again to pace about the room. Yusuf stole another glance at Qalāwūn. A fierce warrior in his youth and diplomat in his old age, Yusuf's beloved sultan seemed so exposed in the middle of his tent. Small. Alone. As powerless as any other mortal man. As Khalil talked of his plans, he hardly seemed to notice his dead father, but Yusuf could look at nothing else. He had lost his father and mother the day that a tribe of Seljuks attacked his caravan. The day that he went to live with his uncle and understood true cruelty. *If I could have stayed with my dead father and mourned, I would have done so until the sun set, and beyond,* he thought. Khalil did not understand what it was to be torn from your family.

"Take down a letter, Yusuf. I will have it read across Cairo before tomorrow is over."

Yusuf rummaged in one of the dead sultan's trunks, pushing down the feeling that he should apologize to the cooling corpse lying conspicuously in the middle of the room. Khalil cleared his throat.

"I, al-Malik al-Ashraf Salāh ad-Din Khalil ibn Qalāwūn,

take my father's throne and his household as his son and heir. As well as assuming the rule of Cairo and all of the conquered lands secured by my father and his predecessors, I also withdraw the army from marching across the Sinai. We will attack Acre, secure our flanks against the Mongol scourge, and take back what belongs to the Believers – not now, but when we are ready to win."

Chapter 2

November 1290

The House of Sir Eirik Einarssen, Acre

When he opened his eyes the first time, Henri of Maron-en-Ruergue saw only the wavering light from an oil lamp burning on a table near him. Someone placed a cool cloth behind his neck, and he closed his eyes again. The cloth felt like heaven.

The second time he opened his eyes, the lamp no longer burned, and the darkness disoriented him. He lay on his stomach with his head on his hands. Lifting his head caused a stinging pain in his neck, and shifting his shoulders sent white-hot knives of agony along his spine. He gasped and then moaned as barely healed wounds on his back cracked open in the darkness and began to ooze.

The flogging. The crowds. His sister screaming. Henri's breath came shallow and rapid, and he reached his hands out in the darkness for something solid to reassure him that he still lived after his brutal beating by the Templars in the city square.

"Peace, my lord." He heard the voice of Ibrahim, his steward, in the dark. A glowing coal was plucked from a brazier with a pair of tongs – a red comet in the black room – and the wick in the oil lamp flickered to life. He lay on a thick mat of woven reeds on a stone floor. Ibrahim slept, wrapped in his cloak, next to Henri's pallet. He didn't recognize the room, but it was finely furnished, with rich tapestries draped from ceiling to floor on the walls and polished furniture that glowed in the dim light. He was in the house of a wealthy knight or a merchant.

"Ibrahim… Blanche…" was all he could say through his dry, cracked lips.

"Your sister is at al-Hadiqa," Ibrahim whispered. "You must drink, my lord. You have been lying on your stomach for a day and a night, and we did not dare to shift you." He filled a shallow bowl with ale and held it out.

Gasping again with the pain, Henri gingerly raised himself to his knees and slurped the ale, spilling half of it down his front. He was naked but clean – the dried blood and remnants of his humiliating cart ride through the city scrubbed from his skin. Reaching up, he touched the back of his head.

"You cut my hair!" he croaked.

"Madame Einarssen felt it was best. Much of it had been ripped out. She said you looked like a fox with a damaged tail. She did not remove all of it, my lord, and you do resemble a member of the knightly order now."

"So, I am at the house of Sir Eirik?" And as if to answer his question, he heard a baby snort and then screech with displeasure in another room.

Ibrahim sighed. "You were lucky to be unconscious, my lord. Even the young heir of Sir Einarssen could not rouse you."

"Does my mother know what happened?" Henri asked, dreading the answer.

"I do not know. I delivered Mademoiselle Blanche to the house and then returned to you before I could talk with Lady Nasira," Ibrahim responded quietly. "I am sure that either your sister or Master Mafeo has informed her by now."

Henri sank slowly back to his stomach. He tried to recall the last thought he had before he lost consciousness. Hazy memories of screaming.

A fist pounded on the door of the house, and Ibrahim looked up with alarm.

"*Helvete*!" they heard Sir Eirik shout, followed by the sound of a sword being withdrawn from a leather sheath as he stomped to the heavy cedar door. "Who the devil hammers on my house at this hour in the nighttime! *Gå vekk*!"

"My lord, why do you smile?" Ibrahim asked.

"That will be Brother Philip at the door, here to finish me off."

"No, it cannot be, my lord, for I told no one where we took you!"

"And yet, he beat me as if he intended to kill. I doubt that he will be pleased to hear I am still alive."

Footsteps clapped against the stones in the hall, and Zahed's dust-streaked, sweaty face appeared in the light of the oil lamp. "Lord Henri, praise be to God that I found you!"

Henri stared at him, his hazy thoughts clouding over and his eyelids sliding open and shut. "Well met, Zahed... is Mafeo already plotting how to spend my fortune once I am dead?"

Zahed, a former Mamluk soldier, was the slave of Mafeo di Orsini, Henri's stepfather.

"My master does not know I am here, my lord. But I must speak to you about him."

Henri smiled lazily, then winced. "I like talking to you, Zahed. But not now. I think I will try to sleep again." He closed his eyes and the voices in the room slipped away.

But sleep eluded him. The pain in his back throbbed with each pulse of blood through his veins. When he tried to stand the next day, a wave of dizziness struck, followed by another of agonizing stinging, and he fell to his hands and knees, vomiting water and bile.

Another day passed and a fever set in. The wounds on his back became redder and hotter with each passing hour. When he looked around the room, all he saw were shapes that changed as if they were made of water and air. Voices buzzed around him like a hive of bees. He wanted to roll onto his back, but hands held him down on his stomach until he screamed to be released. Someone placed more cloths on his neck, his arms, his buttocks, and legs. He shivered violently, thrashing the strips of linen away, then begged for them again as his fever rose and his skin shone with sweat. He dreamed of the cool shade of his citronnier. He dreamed of being burned at the stake, the flesh sizzling and melting from his limbs like the fat of a pig.

He was drifting, swooping away on ocean waves. Each wave that came had a face, and each face was that of the scribe, Master Tamrat, the man he had killed.

Or had he?

He swam away from the waves, but they crashed over him, and the old scribe's voice pleaded for death as Henri raised his arm again to stroke through the water, to stroke the ragged tails of a whip on the man's back.

Hands grasped his shoulders – strong, young hands. Their touch pulled him back from the waves. They pushed his shoulders down onto the bed and massaged his aching head until he fell asleep again. Once more, he swam in the waves. This time they roared in the voice of Brother Philip, the Templar, "*Quiet, your lordship. QUIET, YOUR LORDSHIP!*"

Then someone was pouring liquid onto his hot, throbbing

back. The liquid stung like the juice of a lemon, and he immediately arched and screeched.

"Yes, Lord Henri, it hurts," a woman's voice said quietly, "but it will destroy the pestilence. Let it hurt."

It was difficult to determine who was speaking. Henri tried to open his eyes, but his lids remained fused together. "Please… please stop," he begged.

"If I stop, you will die. Sir Eirik, I must bind him around his waist."

He was gently lifted to his knees by a pair of brawny, orange-furred arms, and he could feel strips of soft cloth being wrapped around his entire torso, with the cool wet of a poultice on his back. Then he was set down on his stomach, and sleep took him.

***

"Drink this, little Hamza," a dry voice rasped.

Henri jerked his head up. The blurry forms of two people sat before him. One of them forced a bowl of bitter liquid between his teeth. He gagged and tried to spit it out, but a claw-like hand clamped over his mouth.

"Swallow it!" came the command. Henri swallowed, then whimpered like a child.

"There we are. My, you have grown into quite the strapping young thing, hmmm?" He heard a cackle. "Of course, this I knew. I am told of everything and everyone in this city."

Henri felt like retching. He heard more talking, but his eyes could not focus on the speaker.

"I will return tomorrow. If the lad continues to have pain, the girl said to give him a tea of this willow bark boiled in water and honey. If he lives through this night, he will likely recover." A pause. "Also, take a pomegranate and stew it in

17

the broth of a two-year-old goat with pure white hair and hang it over the bed by his head, see? Do not take it down. When the pomegranate skin has dried out, crush it into a powder and make him drink it in a bowl of new ale. The girl will tell you otherwise, but I swear I have cured many sick men this way."

Then the sound of the voices fuzzed, and he drifted off again to dream of waves and torture.

***

Henri's eyes were crusty with dried sweat, which caked in his lashes when he tried to open them. Moonlight glowed through an open window in his small room, and Ibrahim's mat was empty. His thoughts were clear for the first time in... he had no idea what day it was. He stood on weak, shaking legs, wrapped a woven qamash around his waist, and crept through the house, searching for signs of life.

Eventually, he found Zahed on the roof, lying back on a dusty rug and gazing pensively at the stars. Henri lowered himself to his stomach next to him.

"Lady Nasira came to see you, but you would not wake," Zahed said without glancing at him.

"Was it she who poured fire on my back?" Henri asked, his voice breaking.

"No, it was a pretty maid who attended you," Zahed said, his forehead knit with thought. "Also, a seer woman who said that she was your mother's midwife. She says she brought you naked into this world and would help you leave it if she must – also naked. But it was the girl who saved you. She would not tell us her name, but every day she came with physicks and poultices. It was some kind of liquor that she poured on your back, and then she gave you milk of the poppy, and you giggled like a drunk prostitute before falling asleep for a day and a night." He looked sideways at Henri. "One of your friends?"

"I do not know any women who possess that kind of knowledge," Henri mused.

"Well, she had hair like a wild saltbush, and she dressed like a Jew."

Henri was quiet a moment. "How long have I been here?"

"Eleven days."

"Have you been here for all this time? Who is keeping the beetles out of Mafeo's wardrobe and powdering his bottom for him?"

Zahed grinned. "I have the night watch. Ibrahim or your sister stay here during the day."

"My sister?"

"Yes." Zahed turned to look at Henri. "She wanted to be near you, and your mother, well…"

"Mafeo would not let her come, am I correct?" Henri knew he should not complain about his new stepfather, for he had arranged the match himself, but Mafeo's true nature revealed him to be crude and abusive.

Zahed nodded, then his shoulders slumped, and he sighed. "My lord, Mafeo is very determined to have an heir. Lady Nasira could be in, well, danger if she does not bear him a son soon."

"My father has been dead only a few months – can he not wait a little longer? She is still grieving."

Zahed looked at him pointedly.

"I know." Henri dropped his head into his hands. "I married her off only a month after my father died. I wish she had stopped me. I wish that anyone had tried to stop me."

"Would you have listened?" Zahed stood. "Mafeo does not wait for anything. Now you must go back to sleep, my lord. You will need your strength back."

Zahed had intended to tell Henri more. Ever since young Lady Blanche had seen her brother beaten nearly to death in a public square, Mafeo had hovered around her, claiming fatherly concern, but Zahed knew better. Although he had no proof of wrongdoing, he knew his master's nature. Still, Henri looked pallid and shaky. It could wait a bit longer.

Chapter 3

November 1290 Fajar,
The Hills of Idmit

"Tamrat ben Moshe!" the messenger yelled. He stood near the well in the small, dusty village of Fajar, holding a sealed and folded square of paper above his head. "I have a message for Tamrat ben Moshe, the scribe!"

"The old man is dead," a woman with a hard face said as she lifted the planks that covered the well. "You have traveled in vain to the most forgettable village in Palestine."

"I was told only yesterday that the scribe Tamrat lives in these hills. A Franj gave me this message. He said I would be paid," the man insisted.

"Carry this water to my house for me, and you shall be paid," the woman snorted. "You can take my worthless husband back with you and sell him in the market for a very small profit."

Sidika bat Tamrat was feeding the chickens when she heard her father's name called. Dropping her grain on the ground, she flew from the stable, her six hens greedily rushing to the sudden bounty. She dusted her hands on her apron as she ran to the well and bowed quickly to the woman, adjusting her slipping headscarf nervously.

"Good morn, sayidati Karima. Would you like me to

carry your water for you today?"

Sayidati Karima glanced archly at Sidika. "I suppose I should let you since you never have to carry water of your own anymore."

Sidika willed herself to keep silent. Against her wishes, Fakri, the village potter, delivered a fresh goatskin of water to her door every morning, which raised eyebrows with the other women and set gossiping tongues wagging. Still, she accepted these offerings. The time she saved dragging the water up the hill to her house meant more hours for her work – writing and illustrating manuscripts in her deceased father's name. She told the villagers that she was creating dye and ink powders, which was not entirely a lie. She was indeed making these supplies… for her own use.

She turned to the messenger.

"I am the daughter of Tamrat ben Moshe. I will take your message." She reached into the dainty embroidered bag dangling from her girdle for a few coins, but Fakri, attracted by the noise, strode confidently to the messenger and snatched the paper from his hand.

"I will take this. Tamrat's business was not for women," he said, filling his voice with gravity and respect that he did not possess.

Sidika crossed her arms. "Fakri, give me the message."

Fakri smiled. "Sidika, you do not need to do this to yourself. Let me take care of this for you. It is not correct that a woman receives messages from strange men."

"Fine." Sidika lifted her chin. She handed the messenger three copper coins. "Take the message and handle it, Fakri – as soon as you have deciphered how to read it."

Fakri slipped the paper into his robe. "I will take it to Jafar."

Sidika felt the side of her mouth twitch and suppressed

her laughter. "Very well, take it to Jafar, only you must take me with you."

***

Jafar lived a short distance away in a larger village at the base of the foothills. The elder of his village, Jafar served as the keeper of stories and match maker, with a strong belief in his own wisdom and infallibility. Because there was no church or priest in this village, he also considered himself the spiritual ruler of his tiny kingdom, and the locals of the nearby villages, who practiced their own form of Nestorian Christianity, held him in awe. When Fakri appeared in his doorway – with half the town trailing curiously behind him – Jafar nodded his head with the sagacity of a mystic and motioned for the potter to sit. Sidika followed him inside.

"Get out, woman!" the old man snarled, waving his stick at her. He was sitting in his usual place – cross-legged on a dusty rug in the middle of his unlit mudbrick house, like a sultan. He wore an equally dusty taqiya on his head, and though his chin hid under a straggly gray beard, it receded so dramatically that he always reminded Sidika of a tortoise.

Sidika stomped outside and waited next to the door. She knew that Jafar was able to write his name and recognize a few simple words in Arabic, which elevated him to an educated man in the villagers' eyes.

Rahat, Sidika's only friend, looped an arm around her waist, giving her a squeeze. "Do not fret, Sidika. Fakri will sort this out for you."

Sidika set her mouth in a hard line.

Eventually, Fakri emerged from the house, his face pale and his eyes wide. Handing the letter to Sidika, he turned to the expectant villagers. There was no question of trying to hide the contents of the letter – they had come for entertainment.

"It says," Fakri raised his voice, "that Tamrat ben Moshe owed an enormous sum to the miller of Jafar's village for grains threshed and delivered but never compensated." He swallowed and turned to Sidika, who was scanning the letter incredulously.

"Sidika, I know that you have the money to repay this debt. Jafar says that he will ensure the miller receives payment and your father's name is restored," Fakri whispered to her.

Sidika stormed into Jafar's house. Behind her, the villagers crowded the old man's door, blocking the light and whispering with expectation. Sidika thrust the letter in front of Jafar's rheumy eyes and poked a finger at one of the words.

"What does this say? This word here – what does it say?" she demanded.

"You do not need me to translate every word for you, Sidika bat Tamrat. You heard what Fakri told you." He pushed the paper away. Sidika whirled and faced her audience.

"This," she held the letter up, "is written in Latin. It is the language of the Franj, and the messenger said that it was a Franj who sent it. Jafar does not know how to read more than his own name. This letter merely says that my father is requested into the city of Acre to discuss the creation of a shipping manifest with one of the local tradesmen."

The villagers looked back at her blankly.

"Why would a Franj send a letter written in Latin demanding that my father pay the village miller, who is Jafar's son-in-law?" she asked the silent crowd.

"Franj," the common term that local Palestinians used to refer to the Christian occupiers from Francia, the Italian peninsula, the Holy Roman Empire, or any other kingdom of the West, was part colloquialism, part insult.

"Sidika, do you accuse Jafar of lying?" Fakri was aghast.

"I accuse him of lying and also of trying to steal from me!"

"Young woman, your father owed my son-in-law for grain, and he did not pay that debt. It matters not what that devil letter says!" Jafar smacked his stick on an unlit brazier, sending up a puff of ash. Sidika turned back to him.

"You are correct, elder Jafar; my father did not pay that debt to your son-in-law because he was murdered before he could pay it. I settled the bill after your daughter came to my house demanding money."

"Do not lie to me, young woman!" Jafar waved his stick at her threateningly. "Do you think I will take the word of an unmarried foreigner over the word of my son-in-law? You owe him five bezants!"

Sidika turned, shouldered her way through the crowd of scandalized neighbors, and walked briskly up the hill toward her village with Rahat chasing after her.

"Sidika," Rahat panted once they reached the house. "Do not despair, my dear. Fakri has said he will marry you, and he is the most prosperous man in the village. Let him take care of this debt for you. Marry him, and you will have his protection from accusations such as this!"

"Fakri was more than happy to stand by and allow Jafar to extort me, Rahat. I will not marry such a buffoon just to avoid more false accusations. I will manage my own affairs."

"But Sidika," Rahat glanced behind her at the villagers who straggled up the hill. "Do you know what people say about you? The women think that you meet with their husbands in the hills and that you use witchcraft to keep yourself from getting with child."

Sidika glared at her friend. "I have never bedded anyone, Rahat, which is why I have never gotten with child."

"But…"

"I care not what people say about me as long as they leave me alone."

"They will never leave you alone while you are living sinfully and unmarried, Sidika. I say this as your loving friend."

Sidika softened and looked at Rahat. Her friend was seventeen – only a year older than her – but the last year had put lines on her face. Rahat had already born two still babies and worried that if the child now in her womb did not live, her husband would seek a lover to bear his heir. Already she had approached Sidika for a spell or a potion to keep the child in her womb.

"Rahat… I thank you for not asking me again. As I have said, I do not know any witchcraft. All I can do for your child is pray, and I do – every day and twice on Shabbat."

Rahat nodded miserably. "Sidika, you would tell me if my husband approached you, would you not?"

"I would tell you right after I told him to sew his robe shut and run home to you," Sidika smiled. "He would not do such a thing, I am sure." Sidika kissed Rahat on the cheek, assuring her that she required no protection. Then she ducked into her house and slammed the bars across the door and the window shutters. She put her weight against the rope pull that her father had strung through a wheel in the ceiling and slowly winched their skylight cover back to reveal the dim, November day. Slowly, she flattened the letter on her table. Although Fakri and Jafar had cracked the seal, she recognized the image of two knights astride a single horse in the remnants of brown wax. The seal of the Knights Templar.

> *Sidika bat Tamrat, the blessings of Jesu Christi be upon you. I request a contract of work from you that must be fulfilled in all haste. Please meet me at the olive press owned by the Brethren at Le Touron, and*

we will discuss the details there. Do not tell anyone where you are going and do not delay in coming, for I will not wait long.

~ Beaujeu

Chapter 4

December 1290
The Road to Mt. Hermon

"Brother Philip, how much further? We shall not make it back to Acre by nightfall if we continue, and I dislike our proximity to Qal-at al-Subeiba right now," Brother Languedoc called out from astride his horse. Ahead of him, Brother Philip de Fons Bleudi searched the ground at the side of the cart track that they traveled.

"You are acting a coward, Languedoc," Philip said. "Women and priests travel this road with less fear than you show."

"I am not a coward; I am sensible. Surely there are many Mamluk patrols out on the roads this close to their fortress. It would be a shame if Acre were to lose two skilled knight commanders at the same time."

"Aye… a shame indeed, although I care not if that foul city and its inhabitants disappear into the sea," Philip muttered under his breath. Then he straightened in his high-walled saddle. "Ah! Here it is!" he called out.

"Remind me why it was necessary for me to come with you to find this person?"

"Because you are my brother in Christ, and it is your mandate to stand by me in a time of danger."

"What danger? I thought we were to meet with one of Beaujeu's informants and collect a scroll?"

"Ah, but you yourself said that there are patrols, and we are indeed perilously close to Qal-at al-Subeiba."

Brother Languedoc glowered from his saddle. Next to him on a smaller mount, his sergeant-squire, Marcus, continually scanned the tops of the hills for movement or a flash of color. Philip could not convince Brother Languedoc to leave Marcus at the Templar citadel in Acre, which posed a problem. He had told Buqu that he would only be bringing one knight with him, and he doubted that the mercenary would be capable of handling a Templar and an experienced squire on his own. He gave quiet thanks that he had decided to pay someone else to have Brother Languedoc murdered, for the man was a stern and formidable warrior.

Philip certainly had not developed an aversion to killing, but he had spent enough of his years repeating liturgy and listening to sermons to develop a real fear of the repercussions of murdering one of his own brother-knights. Some things were just too risky. He wasn't sure that anything could wash away the stain of murdering a man who had been cleansed of sin by God.

They turned off the road, following Philip into a narrow, rocky canyon between two low hills. It was winter, and the horses' hooves made sucking sounds in the sticky muck on the canyon floor. In the mud, Philip saw evidence of fresh tracks. Good – Buqu was here. Ahead he saw the tree that he had felled days earlier and carefully laid across the canyon at an angle. It was possible to go underneath it, but only if the rider dismounted and ducked, and this is what Philip was counting on.

"Wait here, I need to shit," he said lazily and slid off his horse. "I will join you shortly."

"Since when have you been shy?" Brother Languedoc laughed.

"I feel a slight unease of my stomach. By all means watch me, if you wish to see the contents of my bowels."

Brother Languedoc put up both of his hands. "No, I certainly do not. Come with me, Marcus, and cover your nose."

The two men dropped from their mounts and led them by the bridles underneath the tree. As Brother Languedoc ducked beneath the shriveled boughs, there was a rustle and then a shout.

"God, no!" Brother Languedoc shrieked just before Buqu's axe buried itself between his shoulder blades.

Marcus's horse reared and kicked at the attacker but only succeeded in kicking Brother Languedoc violently to the ground, where he lay still, his back broken, his mouth bleeding. Marcus drew his sword, but Buqu slapped it away with the flat of his axe and chased Marcus back underneath the tree.

"Brother Philip! Brother Philip, we are under attack!" Marcus screamed.

Philip stood in the middle of the canyon next to his horse, arms crossed over his chest. "Indeed."

Marcus paled and dodged, unable to hide in the high-walled canyon. Buqu raised a bow and fired a single arrow into Marcus's back. The squire stumbled but kept running.

"Go after him!" Philip shouted.

But Buqu shook his head. "You not tell Buqu of two men. Only tell of one man!" He held up his index finger aggressively. "You give more gold!"

"Listen, you useless deserter." Philip reached out to grab Buqu by the front of his dirty linen deel, but Buqu put a hand on Philip's wrist and wrenched his arm back. Philip felt the wet edge of Buqu's still bloody axe blade against his throat.

"You give more gold or Buqu kill. Send you to Tamu."

Philip smiled nervously. "Well, I was a mercenary once. I suppose this should not surprise me. Very well, I give more gold."

Buqu took Philip's sword from its leather sheath and threw it behind him. Philip reached into his robe, pulled out a sack of gold, and emptied it into Buqu's hand. Satisfied, the mercenary tucked it into his deel and released his grip.

Philip strolled to where Brother Languedoc lay. He was unconscious, still breathing. Philip turned the injured knight onto his back and ripped his muddy robe open, exposing a powerful, scarred chest. Tucked into the folds of his sash, the handle of a jewel-crusted dagger glittered.

At last. Now only one remains.

Philip slipped the dagger into his belt. "This man is not dead," he called to Buqu.

The mercenary strolled to where Brother Languedoc lay and severed the neck with one quick stroke of his axe. Then he looked over his shoulder and gestured in the direction that Marcus had fled.

"Man not live long. Arrow in back. He die soon. Far from water. Die soon."

Philip nodded and fingered the dagger. "Yes. Die soon."

Chapter 5

December 1290
Templar Citadel, Acre

The wounds on Henri's back healed into a wicker of thin raised scars that prickled and ached. A month after his public flogging, he received a summons to sit on the city council at the Templar citadel, and as he rode toward the city, he noticed the increased presence of knights guarding the road. *It starts again*, he thought with resignation. His lemon and cinnamon groves had only recently begun to produce at a mature rate after the last band of Bedu raiders burned half of his trees while his father still lived.

He hadn't been back to the citadel of the Templars since his imprisonment and subsequent beating for killing Tamrat ben Moshe in defiance of Brother Philip. Instead of orderly rows of white-robed men practicing combat drills, this time he found a press of knights and horseflesh, a forest of lances, and black-robed sergeants running back and forth in the bailey. He dismounted and walked around the perimeter, looking for a familiar face with his horse, Raven, following obediently.

Brother Gregoire, tall, yellow-haired, and dressed in spotless white robes, saw Henri walking close to the walls and hailed him.

"Here to sit on the council, Henri? I heard that the Hochmeister of the Teutons even deigned to come – although he waited until the Holy Father in Rome forced him," Brother Gregoire chirped. "I do not envy you, Maron. I would rather just go out and fight. Sitting on a council sounds like dull work to me."

Guillaume de Beaujeu, the grand master of the Templars, quietly walked up behind Brother Gregoire, accompanied by two white-robed knights, his secretary, and Sir Jean de Grailly.

"What sounds dull, Brother Gregoire? I hope you are not still bragging about that sermon that you gave to the initiates last week."

Brother Gregoire blushed, muttered an excuse, then left in haste. Beaujeu's gray eyes twinkled. "Back for more, Lord Henri?" He turned to the other men standing with him and they chuckled. "Are you ready for this, young man?"

Henri nodded. "Yes, my lord."

"Right then, come with us. Let us get this over with."

Henri and the four other men followed as Beaujeu led them to the great hall – a large, rectangular room with a towering ceiling of honey-colored stone that glowed in the light of the many glass and metal oil lamps in the room. As a sign of their austerity, the stone remained unplastered, although it had been honed and polished to look smooth and soft. At a large table in its center sat ten of the most influential citizens of Acre, along with the Patriarch, Prince Amalric of Cyprus, and the grand masters of the other knightly orders – the Hospitallers, the Teutons, The Lazars, and the Knights of St. Thomas.

Henri felt relieved to see that he was not the only man on the council who had not yet reached the age of twenty. Amalric, one of Henri's closest friends, was a serious warrior, but at nineteen years old, he looked out of place and young. Next to him sat an older man that Henri didn't recognize. He wore the white robes of the Order of the Teutonic Knights, adorned with a slim black cross, but he did not have the look of a warrior. Jeweled rings twinkled on his hands, and his eyes were hooded with boredom.

Beaujeu called the meeting to order. "Let us start this council so we can send a messenger with our answer at first light tomorrow. You all know Burchard von Schwanden, Hochmeister of the Teuton Brothers?" he said, indicating the bejeweled Teutonic knight. The men at the table nodded respectfully, and von Schwanden inclined his head, accepting their acknowledgment like a monarch at a banquet.

"Before we start, Guillaume, I wish to know your reason for asking young Lord Henri of Maron to sit on this council. Has he not been found to be disloyal to the city?" drawled Jean de Villiers, the grand master of the Hospitaller Order.

"Lord Henri is here because, after Lord Amalric, he has the highest title in the city and owns the most land," Beaujeu said calmly.

"But surely that should not matter in this case," interjected Lord Jacques de Conques. "The young man was just publicly whipped for insubordination to a knight of your own order, and there are rumors that he assisted a Mamluk spy. If he is on this council, no one will accept our word as truth!"

Henri clenched his fists under the table but willed his expression to remain indifferent.

"Lord Conques." Beaujeu appeared to be searching for a tactful way to proceed. "You have been in Acre for only a few years and have also made your intention to return to Francia well-known. Henri was born here. His father and his grand-père fought to protect the Kingdom of Jerusalem and settled the land in the name of the Church. His father even fought alongside King Louis in Tunis and witnessed his death. If I am not mistaken, Lord Conques, your father declined to take the Cross when he was invited, did he not?"

Lord Conques began to protest again, but Amalric stood up.

"Lord Rogier of Maron and my father were comrades at arms, and I have known Henri since we were boys." At this, a few of the older men at the table exchanged exasperated glances. "I trust his judgment and the honor of his forefathers. Let us have no more discussion about this. We are here to determine whether or not our actions will cause a war with the Mamluks, not to quarrel amongst ourselves."

Lord Conques reddened and crossed his arms over his chest.

"Now," Beaujeu said, as if addressing a group of small children, "can we begin, or would anyone else like to launch a personal attack on the other members of this council first?" He took a deep breath. "I am sure you are all aware of the situation: King Henry and I requested additional support from the Holy Father in Rome because Sultan Qalāwūn began to act as if he were preparing raiding parties in June. What we received instead was a disgraceful hoard of un-trained Sicilians who did not even come here to fight for Acre. They came to enrich themselves. Although my men attempted to control them... and the Hospitallers also helped" – at this comment, Grand Master Villiers rolled his eyes and snorted – "there were nearly two thousand Sicilians, and we were unable to watch them all constantly. Several groups of men roamed the streets killing Arabs due to rumors of a domestic affair that they had no business involving themselves in."

"So?" asked Signore Tiepolo, "I heard that those killings

were justified. What would you have us do, Beaujeu, punish Christians for killing Muslims?"

"I did not say they were Muslim. I said they were Arab," Beaujeu responded icily. "The men killed were Christian, Jew, and Muslim. The Sicilians attacked men with beards."

The Patriarch steepled his fingers and cleared his throat. "Brother Beaujeu, what did Qalāwūn specifically ask for in his letter?"

"He asked that we turn the murderers over to him for punishment."

"And you have these men in your custody?"

"Indeed, your holiness."

"And you would hand them over to Qalāwūn to be slaughtered in cold blood?"

Beaujeu's face grew hard. "Lord Patriarch, I mean to avert a war if I can."

"You are a warrior of the Temple, Beaujeu. I have trouble understanding why you think that we would fail in this endeavor. God is on our side."

Henri stood from his chair, and fifteen hostile glares turned on him. "I agree with Grand Master Beaujeu. If you were to let these men go free, the Mamluks would take offense and surely attack the city."

"No one asked for the opinion of a Saracen and a child," muttered Lord Conques.

"I agree with Lord Henri, although I do feel that if these Mamluks attacked, Acre would withstand," Amalric said. "After all, the city is well-fortified."

"We lost Jerusalem, Lord Amalric," Henri said. "Antioch, Caesarea, Tripoli... Acre is the only great city left to us. If we require reinforcements, who would come to our aid? We are an island surrounded by a sea of enemies, and the only way for us to maintain control of this city is to keep good relations with our neighbors. The Sicilians murdered citizens of Acre with whom they had no quarrel. I say that we turn them over to Qalāwūn. We sacrifice those few to save thousands."

Beaujeu watched this impassioned speech keenly. "Lord Henri, you speak of compromise. You seem to say that you are not a bloodthirsty man, and yet you advocate to turn these prisoners over to certain death."

"I am a man first, a warrior second," Henri replied. "A man does not kill another man without just cause. A warrior in the heat of battle kills anyone he can."

"Maron is just worried about his own lands, and his faith is weak," Lord Conques said with a wave of a bejeweled hand. "I knew your father well, boy. He served the Cross as a true pilgrim until his injuries. How did you manage to become so vapid and cowardly? I hear that you have more interest in women than your trade."

Henri's temper flared. "Am I cowardly because I want to protect the lives of my family and the hundreds of families living in my villages and in this city? And are you going to bring up women when it is so obvious that they care little for you?"

Lord Conques jumped to his feet, prepared to strike, but everyone looked around at the sound of a loud snore. The Hochmeister of the Teutonic Order appeared to be dozing in his chair.

"Alright, Lord Henri, sit down." Beaujeu focused his cold gray eyes on the faces of the other men. "Does anyone else have any information about this situation? We must consider all of the facts."

"The fact is," said Lord Conques, "that a lusty Saracen was caught in an affair with a Christian woman of this city. Her husband killed the man, as was his right, and these

Sicilians also took up the cause on behalf of the injured husband. They did not verify that the men they killed had any relation to the adulterer, but honestly, Beaujeu, if those Arabs cannot keep the hems of their robes down below their knees, then I see no reason why we should allow them to go on seducing our women unpunished."

"Whose wife was she?" Henri asked.

"The young wife of Puglisi, the silk merchant."

Henri nodded. Signora Puglisi, sixteen years old, had recently moved to Acre from Firenze to wed the aging tradesman, who had flatulence and rumored "unnatural" sexual tastes. He was nearly fifty-five years old. The young signora, by contrast, was dewy-skinned and willowy, with golden hair that fell to her waist. She had certainly caught Henri's eye.

"What did Puglisi do to them?" Amalric asked.

"He caught them in each other's arms," said Villiers. "*En flagrante delicto*. He struck the Saracen on the head with an iron candlestick and beat his wife with it. While they were unconscious, he doused them with lamp oil and immolated them both."

Henri swallowed and tried not to picture that long golden hair shriveling and eaten by flames.

"And then he had the Sicilians go out and murder any Arab they could find?" he asked.

"We have no proof that he ordered them to murder, but they claim they did it on behalf of Signore Puglisi," said Villiers.

The men sat silently around the table.

"We could…" Beaujeu considered his words and continued. "We could send Qalāwūn the Acrean citizens in our dungeon who are already condemned. After all, they will die for their crimes regardless of who administers the punishment. We might as well allow the sultan to manage this undesirable task for us while also making him believe that he has avenged the dead men."

Several of the lords stood from the table and started talking at once.

"It is an outrage!" Lord Conques yelled. "We cannot allow these men to die at the hands of those infidels!"

"But gentlemen, we will surely start a war if we do not give Qalāwūn what he desires!" Beaujeu raised his voice and was met with a chorus of insults and hand gestures from the room.

"Beaujeu, you coward! You did not even take King Louis' side when it mattered!"

"Do you hate Sicilians, Beaujeu? I will wager my horse that you would not hasten to throw the Venetians to the infidels so quickly!"

"Are you a Christian, Beaujeu, or an infidel in disguise!?"

Jacopo Tiepolo, a wealthy man who had recently traveled to Acre, crossed his arms. "Beaujeu, you are so mired in intrigue that I would not vote for your scheme even if it did make sense. How are we to discern if you are not taking us down a road to a resolution that most benefits you? My father, the Doge, always said that you were a snake."

Across the table, Grand Master Villiers rolled his eyes. Signore Tiepolo couldn't resist the temptation to summon the name of his powerful father, the Doge of Venice.

"I am trying to avert war!" Beaujeu shouted, pounding the table with his fist. Hochmeister Schwanden's eyes jerked open, and he sighed heavily.

"Hush now!" Somehow the Patriarch's aged, papery voice rose above the rest. "There, you have all the facts. Let us take a vote. Who of you favor turning the imprisoned Sicilians over to Qalāwūn?"

Henri raised his hand. He looked around the table. Beaujeu's hand was also up, and so was Amalric's.

Reluctantly, Grand Master Villiers also raised his hand and shrugged. "I do not wish to vote the same way as Lord Henri of Maron or as Beaujeu, but they make a strong case. We are isolated here. If this Mamluk army should penetrate the city walls, we would be without support."

"All in favor of declining to give Qalāwūn satisfaction?" Beaujeu asked in a resigned voice. The rest of the hands at the table went up.

"Let us send a clear message to Qalāwūn that the Muslims who instigated this violence received the punishment that they deserve," Brother Matthieu de Clermont, a marshal of the Hospitallers, smacked his fist into his hand as he spoke.

Henri stood from his seat again. "But Brother Matthieu, these were also Christians who died, and Jews! And have we not cordial relations with the Muslims as well? Those men did nothing wrong – they were simply in the wrong place at the wrong time! This is unjust!"

Brother Matthieu eyed Henri. "Ah yes, your newly developed sense of 'justice' is well-known in this city. Perhaps, Lord Henri, you need a Hospitaller to administer more lashes this time. It seems that you are still defying your elders."

"It is settled, then. I will send the message to Qalāwūn, although Lord Patriarch, elders of the city, and my Lord Amalric, I must again insist on my extreme reservation about this verdict. It will surely start a war," said Beaujeu, rising from his seat.

"We will be victorious. Acre is the headquarters of the three largest orders of knighthood. It is the seat of the Kingdom of Jerusalem. Qalāwūn has sworn an oath of peace with us, and now he is breaking it. Please deliver the message…" the Patriarch said haltingly, "and send along some gold as well."

Henri felt ill. War was coming, and Arabs were being slaughtered in the streets. Muslims and Jews were no longer safe in the city, regardless of how much money in taxes they were forced to pay above their Christian neighbors. He left the citadel without lingering and hurried back to al-Hadiqa, his sprawling estate in the countryside.

"Ibrahim! Durant!" he bellowed, dismounting in the courtyard without waiting for a groom to take Raven to her stable. The two men appeared from the great hall.

"We must prepare. War is coming to Acre."

Chapter 6

December 1290
Le Touron, The Plain of
Acre

The olive press and abbey at Le Touron perched on a modestly sized mound that rose above the expansive plain of Acre, affording the occupants a view of the city against the mirror-bright sea. The locals called it al-Fukhar, referencing its past as a pottery works in antiquity. Now, gnarled groves of ancient olive trees surrounded the buildings, stretching their dusty-green fingers to the sky.

I must purchase a donkey when I am in Acre, Sidika thought as she stopped to dig a pebble from her doeskin shoe, *else I will ride the goat next time I have to make that infernal trek*. She had passed patrols of knights along the road and saw armed men peering down at her from the crenellations of their fortified homes, but their presence did not provide peace of mind. Franj men were tall and loud, and they took whatever they wanted. Like all non-Christians, Sidika avoided them.

At the gate, a taciturn monk in a brown robe greeted her and led her to a basin of water to wash her face and hands, then into a small, sparsely furnished hall and told her to wait. The hall was cool, and the swish of her frock echoed in the empty room. Limbs aching from her long walk, she sank onto a bench with relief, only to jump up again as the door to the hall slammed open.

Grand Master Beaujeu stalked quickly into the room, his white, split robe snapping around his shins. Behind him followed a frowning and battle-scarred knight – the man who had flogged Lord Henri in the square only weeks prior. Although Beaujeu looked at her with recognition, the tall knight kept his eyes focused on the wall behind her, his mouth pressed into a disapproving line. Beaujeu sat at the long table in the hall and folded his hands.

"Please sit, for we have much to discuss," he began without pleasantry. "Does anyone know where you are, young woman?"

"No, my lord."

"Good. Brother Anselmo told me that you walked here from the hills. Do you not own a horse or a donkey? I expected you here sooner."

"My lord, our beast fled when my father was killed." Sidika could not help but let her voice carry an edge of the anger she still felt. Lord Henri might have used the knife against her father, but it was Templars who forced him to do it. Next to Beaujeu, the knight's frown deepened. She knew that he had been there when Henri killed her father. Did he participate in torturing her father before Henri gave him mercy?

"Yes, well, it was most unfortunate that your beast could not be found and brought back. I have a task that I require of you, but before I tell you this errand, you must promise me that you will do it. If you cannot make that promise, you may return to your village."

"But my lord—"

"You do not need to ask me a question – just tell me that you will do exactly as I say when you hear it," Beaujeu interrupted her. The other knight made an agitated movement, and Beaujeu looked up at him. "Do you have something to say, Brother Philip?"

"My lord," the man dropped to one knee, "a girl is not fit for this task. Let us instead send one of the confreres, or contact one of your Saracens in Damascus."

"None of the amirs that I am on friendly terms with are currently in Damascus." Beaujeu turned to Sidika and appraised her. "It is for her to determine if she is fit for the task." He leaned forward. "Young woman, are you prepared to take on a task that Brother Philip thinks only a knight can do?"

"Well," Sidika said slowly, "what tasks can only a knight do that a woman cannot? A knight can kill with a sword, but a woman can kill with sharpened words. A knight can raid a man's house and occupy it, but does not a woman do this when she marries a man?"

Beaujeu chuckled, but Brother Philip spun toward her. "A brother-knight can pray in true holiness. He can experience the fullness of the spirit of Christ and have a heart that is truly chaste!"

"Cannot a woman also pray and be chaste? Does not Acre contain convents and cloisters stuffed with nuns?" Sidika shot back.

"A devil-worshipper like you cannot understand," Brother Philip started, but Beaujeu held up his hands.

"Peace, both of you! Mademoiselle Sidika, I require your answer now. Do not waste my time."

Sidika was silent for a moment.

"You will be compensated," he continued. "Twenty bezants."

"I will do what you ask, but for compensation, I only wish that you bring me my father's bones so that I may bury him next to my mother and my brother."

Beaujeu's eyebrows shot up, and he motioned for Brother

Philip to sit. "Do you speak any Turkish? Your father once told my secretary that he found you in Damascus. I assume you realize that you were adopted?"

"I remember but little of my native tongue, although I still recall the names of the streets in Damascus," Sidika replied. As an urchin, the streets in Damascus were her territory, and she would remember the layout of the city, its smells and hidden nooks, until the day she died.

"Well, that is something, at least," Beaujeu said. "I require you to go to Damascus to collect information for me. I have been trying for months to get a spy close to al-Shuja'i, Khalil's governor and trusted amir. He is a paranoid man, and I thought it impossible until last week. You must go to him and find out if he is building siege weapons for an attack on Acre. My contact in Cairo has told me as much, but the citizens' council is unwilling to address the threat without more proof."

Sidika could hardly conceal her surprise. "But my lord, if you cannot get your knights close to him, why would you think that I could come within a mile's distance to such a man?"

Beaujeu smiled. "Brother Philip was at Toron a week ago, discussing the security of the roads with Lord Amaury. While they were on one of those roads, some Bedu raiders attacked a group of travelers and gravely injured them. One of those travelers bore a message, which he handed to Lord Amaury just before he died. The message was addressed to your father, from the house of Alam al-Din Sanjar al-Shuja'i al-Mansuri, the amir of Damascus."

Sidika blinked, confused. "I know of no times that my father took a commission from an amir of Damascus."

"When al-Shuja'i was wazir to Qalāwūn many years ago in Cairo, he possessed a book that your father created, and he admired the work greatly. He sent the message to beg your father to come to Damascus to discuss the commission of a manual on siege weaponry. He says that the words are written, but he requires an artist to complete the work. This is the opportunity that we have needed. It has been handed to us by God!" Beaujeu beamed.

"Young woman," Brother Philip towered over her. "You will go to al-Shuja'i and complete these drawings. You will make copies of what you see and present them to us when you return."

Sidika felt her knees begin to quake. The thought of returning to Damascus, where she had spent her young years as a pickpocket before Tamrat found and adopted her, shot fear through her entire body.

"Damascus is a far distance to travel alone, and what if they will not see me because I am a woman?"

"You are the daughter of Tamrat ben Moshe, the scribe. You will tell them that he has fallen ill, and you shall stay to do the work as your father's emissary. They will not refuse you, for the Muslims freely allow their women to study, paint, and even compose poetry and songs," Beaujeu answered. "We will furnish you with clothing, ink, and supplies, and you will travel north with a caravan of Saracen merchants that leaves the day after tomorrow."

Sidika rose, woodenly. "My lord," she asked, "what will happen to me if the amir suspects or if he refuses to let me leave?"

"So, you will do it?"

Sidika nodded.

Beaujeu scrutinized her silently for a moment. "If he does not allow you to leave, then you will remain in Damascus. It is possible he may execute you, but most likely, the amir would make you a concubine. We will send no rescue, so do not let him suspect you, mademoiselle, unless you wish to spend your days as his bed warmer until he tires of you. Then Brother Philip would surely be correct by suggesting that you are unchaste."

Chapter 7

December 1290
The Citadel of Salah ad-Din, Cairo

It was hot outside of Cairo's towering walls, even in the shade of the great citadel of Salah ad-Din – the square mountain, some called it. Here, the breezes were usually fresh due to the citadel's coveted high position, but on this day, Yusuf and the royal entourage stood in the foulest of places, where the citadel's sewers emptied, and the cesspools stagnated. Although he sat cross-legged on a raised dais away from the clouds of flies that buzzed around the fetid water, and even though Khalil had brought ten young eunuchs with fans of hawk's feathers and censors of burning incense, the stench still staggered Yusuf's senses.

He was not even supposed to be in the city on this day. His planned trip to Damascus was delayed by a day because Khalil wanted all his amirs to bear witness to the punishment for treachery among his courtiers.

The object of today's lesson was Husam ad-Din Turuntay, the late sultan Qalawun's wazir. Turuntay's gaze slipped and rolled, his purpled eyelids barely open, as he knelt at the edge of the dais in the dirt. His chin was a swollen mass of blood and blisters where Khalil had ripped his beard out. Khalil had just finished washing the blood from his hands in a gilt basin when he looked critically at the man.

"What is wrong with him? Why do his eyes roll around like a drunkard?" He turned to the *na'ib*, a thickly built man of medium height in his middle years who served as the officer of the sultan's prison.

The *na'ib* bowed slowly, buying himself a few minutes of time to run through the possible explanations.

"It is the heat, your eminence, and thirst. This vermin has not had a drop to drink since the morning." Behind them, the sun was setting, its pink light shimmering in the heat against the walls.

This was annoying. Turuntay had been tortured already for a day and a night. The muezzins would begin the call to Asr prayer very soon, but Khalil seemed to be getting a good deal of satisfaction from dragging Turuntay's execution out as long as possible. Yusuf didn't have the stomach to participate in execution and prayer in the same hour. The words of an imam from years ago drifted into his consciousness.

The Qur'an says, "My mercy embraces everything." Do you think that only applies to your friends? To your allies and your family? If Allah has mercy on the entire world, then that also means your enemy, no?

He understood how the dynamics of power worked in their young sultanate. Mamluk rulers rarely lasted for long on the throne, the exceptions being Baybars and Qalāwūn, who both kept their authority in place by swiftly executing their rivals and would-be assassins. Turuntay made it no secret that he intended to claim the throne when Qalāwūn died, and when Khalil took it first, the wazir did not bother to appease his new master. They had apprehended him at Bāb al-Barakīyyah, attempting to flee with his riches and his wives, and dragged him back to the citadel. Turuntay had accepted his fate with relative poise. He knew the risk that he had taken.

Khalil waggled a finger at Turuntay with barely perceptible movement. "Give him some drink. I want him refreshed and fully awake."

The na'ib roughly shoved the throat of his water skin into Turuntay's now toothless mouth, and the man gagged, spitting bloody-pink water down his front.

"Stop," Khalil commanded. "Give him cool wine to drink and mop his head. Wake him up."

A eunuch handed a gold ewer of wine to the na'ib, which had been sitting in a larger, copper vessel filled with ice wrapped with straw. The ice was grimy and small, but the amirs and wealthy ayan of Cairo hoarded it carefully to cool their drinks and their heads when the sun heated their city like a clay oven.

Turuntay took a tentative sip, then gulped the chilled wine, spilling it down his chin. The na'ib wiped Turuntay's forehead with a tepid cloth, and the prisoner closed his eyes with relief. When he opened them, Khalil had stepped down from his dais, away from the incense and fans, and into the stench.

"You poisoned my father," he spoke menacingly as he approached, "and I shall avenge his death."

"No," Turuntay whispered. "You will murder me, but I will go to my grave saying I did not kill your father."

Khalil stopped in front of the prone man. "Prop him up and hold his hands behind his back."

Turuntay began to mutter a dua, tears squeezing from the edges of his swollen eyes. "Inna illahi wa inna ilayhi raji'un…"

"You. Na'ib." Khalil commanded. "You are to strangle this man until the light leaves his eyes."

Tutuntay let out a little sob as the na'ib casually approached him. His eyes bulged and his skin mottled, first red, then purple, when the na'ib squeezed. He twitched and thrashed, but his hands were bound fast behind him, so he flopped like a fish on the end of a hook. The na'ib's face was also red with exertion, and he tightened his grip until Yusuf could hear Turuntay's windpipe crackling.

When Turuntay's thrashing began to slow, Khalil's dagger flashed in the dying light of the sun and ripped into the taut flatness of the stomach, spilling his rival's blood in a red curtain to the ground. The edge of a smooth, pale intestine slipped out lazily. Yusuf forced himself to keep his expression passive, but the smells, the heat, and the violence caused his gorge to rise.

Then the muezzins inside the city walls began to call the Believers to prayer for Asr. Yusuf's head spun. This was not holy. This was not right. It did not bring glory to Allah. It did not bring anything to Islam, it only brought more power to Khalil. To one man.

His body longed to perform the movements, the ritual of the prayer, to comfort himself in the act of worship, for he felt shaken.

Already, the flies that hummed around the sewage began to land on the glistening wetness pooling around what remained of Turuntay's bowels. The na'ib picked up the corpse and threw it next to a sweltering cesspit, and Yusuf swallowed, lest he gag at the sight. He must not show his horror, he must distract his mind.

In the name of Allah, the Most Gracious, the Most Merciful: All Praise is due to Allah, Lord of the Universe, the Most Gracious, the Most Merciful...

The words soothed him. Surely this was necessary to secure safety and freedom for Allah's people. Surely.

Chapter 8

December 1290
Al-Hadiqa, Palestine

As the sun rose and gilt the tops of the lemon trees, the residents of al-Hadiqa awoke not to the usual sound of the roosters greeting the day from the roof of the well-house, but Mafeo's enraged yells. Henri sat up in bed, blinking blearily. The drapes had not yet been opened in his room, and it took him a few minutes to shake off his confusion in the darkness.

"Where is my wife?!" Mafeo shrieked, and Henri leapt to his feet, pulling a robe around his shoulders before yanking his door open and running out onto the colonnade that surrounded the courtyard below.

Mafeo stood naked in the semi-darkness, his finger jabbing at Madame Habiba, Lady Nasira's maid.

"Where is Zahed! Someone fetch Zahed immediately. And you," he turned on Madame Habiba again, "you will spend the night in the thieves' hole if you do not tell me where my wife went!"

"Mafeo di Orsini!" Henri said sharply. "Cease your yelling. We do not even have a thieves' hole at this house. What troubles you?"

Mafeo pointed to Madame Habiba again. "Ask her. She helped my wife leave under the cloak of night. And my two step-daughters with her!"

"My mother is allowed to travel outside the estate if she wishes, and it is not likely she would leave her daughters here without her."

"So, she is your wife now?!" Mafeo snarled. "I am her lord and master, and she is not allowed to leave except with my blessing. I told her that she is to stay here!"

Henri tightened the sash of his robe around his waist and stood as close to Mafeo as he dared. "So, she did not tell you she wished to spend some days in the city? How interesting…" he looked at the man sideways. "Seems she needs a bit of space, Mafeo. My father was confident enough in his marriage to let her go to the city when she pleased. This is one of the reasons why we have a house there – so she can stay comfortably and visit friends, which is what she is doing now."

Mafeo's face mottled purple with outrage. "Would any of those 'friends' be trying to put a bastard into her? A woman is not to leave the house without her husband's knowledge!" He spun around as Zahed ran up the stairs two at a time onto the colonnade, his prayer rug still tucked underneath his arm. When he saw his master's nakedness, Zahed dropped the rug and hurried into Mafeo's darkened chamber, emerging with a robe and sash. Mafeo snatched the robe, grabbed his slave by the front of his tunic, and shook him.

"Where were you this morning, you heathen?"

"Praying, my lord."

"Praying, were you? On your knees!"

Zahed hesitated, then slowly sank to his knees as Mafeo pulled the robe on, then kicked his slave in the stomach. Henri saw Madame Habiba flinch, but Zahed remained stoic – upright and empty-eyed.

"You spent all morning bowing to your heathen god,

well, now you will bow to me, pig! Lick the ground like the swine that you are!"

Zahed took a deep breath but remained erect, looking sightlessly ahead. Mafeo pulled his foot back to kick him again, but Henri lunged forward.

"That is enough!"

"Heretics," Mafeo said harshly, "all of you in this house are soft-shelled heretics and infidel lovers. I should never have taken a wife in this family." He turned and slammed his door to his room.

"On that, we all agree!" Henri shouted at the door, then offered Zahed a hand up.

Madame Habiba sniffled and wiped her eyes. "Oh, master Henri, what is to be done about him?"

Henri ground his teeth, still looking at Mafeo's closed door. "Something, Madame. Something must be done."

***

Zahed strolled across the courtyard, his arms swinging lazily at his sides with practiced nonchalance. One of the maids smiled at him, and he nodded in greeting, keeping his face neutral and pleasant. Rounding a corner toward the tunnel that led to the citronnier, he looked left and right and then ran down the cool, dark corridor into the gloom of an overcast winter's day, his soft sandals slapping on the smooth stones. After a brief check that no one else was among the lemon trees, he darted to the corner farthest from the house. There was a small stone chapel of some kind here and a cool, shadowy niche between the chapel and the wall where Zahed would often go to find respite from his master.

He fell to his knees in the shade and then to the ground, curling up in the clammy grass with his knees pulled to his chest.

Allah help me, I held it all in. I did not kill my master. Merciful God, please release me from this man! his mind screamed.

"Please release me!" he shouted, pounding the ground with his palms. He tore at the grass and howled his frustration into his clenched fists. Zahed was not sure exactly how old he was, but he thought he must be twenty-one or twenty-two, which meant that he had spent exactly half his life as a slave. Half of his life was given to someone else. No, not given. Taken. He groaned again and then let out a scream of rage, pounding the ground until his knuckles bled.

"Stop! You will hurt yourself!" a young voice spoke behind him, and he whirled around.

Lady Blanche was looking down at him, her hands clasped with worry. Zahed scrambled to his feet, conscious that his turban had unwound at some point, and he had grass and mud on his clothes. He bowed quickly, as low as he could, with his palms at his forehead.

"Forgive me, my lady. A thousand apologies for my behavior. I thought the citronnier to be empty." His heart sank as he spoke. One word of this behavior to Mafeo, and he would be beaten or humiliated again.

Blanche took Zahed's bleeding hand away from his forehead, inspecting it. "You must not do this, you know." She clucked her tongue and reached into her delicately embroidered aumônière, which hung from its drawstrings at her wrist, and drew out a silken handkerchief as delicate and blue as a spring sky. She wrapped the cloth around Zahed's bleeding fist and tied it securely. "There. And now you must see Mother's physician for a poultice to prevent this from festering."

Zahed lowered his eyes. "Thank you, my lady…" he mumbled. He was a dead man. Mafeo would have him bound and thrown into the sea to drown like an unwanted puppy.

Lady Blanche was looking at him, her brown eyes full of concern. "I will not tell my mother's husband about this, if that is what worries you."

He couldn't meet her eyes while she was being kind to him. He did not want to see any pity on her face, but she continued to stare at him until he felt compelled to look up.

"He treats you very poorly, Zahed. Mother has tried to speak to him about it, but he does not care to listen to her. Please see the physician about your hand, because there is nothing else that we can do to help you. Your master, well, he treats us poorly too, only in a different way."

Her eyes were solemn, not pitying. They were deep with sadness.

"I promise I will see the physician when he comes, Lady Blanche."

"Very good," she smiled, and he helped her to her feet.

"I am the only family member who comes to this chapel. I am here at nones on most days, but otherwise, you may be sure to have it to yourself unless the workers are tending to the trees. I shall tell no one of your sanctuary."

"Allah's blessings be upon you, my lady. You have a kind heart." He bowed again, and she turned to leave.

For the second time in his tenure at this house, a Maron of Acre had surprised him.

Chapter 9

December 1290

House of Amir al-Shuja'i, Damascus

It had not been a difficult journey. The Templars equipped Sidika with a fine wooden box filled with more mineral dyes and parchments than she had ever been able to afford in a year. There was also a well-tailored gown of garnet-red linen and a blush-colored scarf of fine muslin to drape over her hair and face. The grand master himself presented her with a copper brooch to fasten her dress modestly at her throat. It bore the likeness of a large-eyed owl – the symbol of Athena. A scribe, he said, should not look like a pauper. Not when she is about to approach the governor of Damascus.

The streets of Damascus were the same as she remembered – resplendent on the surface with tidy houses and graceful mosques, filthy and tragic when one looked closer at the poor and the ill who lived in the shadows and alleys. As she moved through the city with her caravan toward the amir's house, she could see small children in ragged clothes reaching into the robes of the merchants and wealthy citizens. Although the beautiful buildings of the city towered over her, she only had eyes for the hovels and lean-tos that clung to the walls of the great houses like barnacles.

After a brief argument at the front door, the amir's

Mamluk guards ushered her into a small, private courtyard occupied by several men who eyed her with hostile curiosity. They sat on low benches around a cluttered table, littered with rolls of paper, books, and trays of nuts and dried fruits. The grand master had instructed her to approach the governor and his men with the authority and confidence of an educated woman. Sidika did not know exactly what that meant, and so she genuflected respectfully but rose to her feet, forcing herself to look up at the men, even though her eyes wanted to slip comfortably to the ground.

"My lords, I am sent here by my father, the scribe Tamrat ben Moshe, to learn of the commission you request of him. He sends me as his trusted emissary due to his illness."

The men absorbed this news in silence for a moment, scowling, but the youngest of them, a handsome man in a fine split tunic of black wool and neatly wrapped black turban, had eyes that sparkled with good humor, and a smile tugged at his mouth.

"I did not request the assistance of an emissary and a woman. I requested ben Moshe," replied one of the men, the oldest and most lavishly dressed. "Return to your father and bring him here. I will provide a camel for him with a palanquin that can transport him comfortably."

Sidika bowed again. "Gracious lord, my mother and brother recently died, and my father is sick of the heart and body. He does not wish to travel, but knowing of your great name, he would be pleased to provide you with what you seek. I am a trained scribe and illuminator."

The younger man rose to his feet and laughed incredulously. "So, he sends us a shaykha! And a Jewess, no less! Tell me, little owl, have you taken commissions for your father before?"

Sidika touched her owl brooch unconsciously, taken back

by the familiar way in which the man spoke to her, but she forced herself to look straight at him. "My lord, I am currently assisting him on a physician's manual for the sultan in Cairo and recently completed an illustrated book of cookery for the guild master of the Sicilians in Acre."

Al-Shuja'i snapped his fingers in irritation. "Be seated, Yusuf! I want the best scribe to illustrate this text, not some snip of a girl. If ben Moshe will not come, then I will use one of our illuminators here in the city."

"If you wish for the best illuminator, then it is me that you want, my lord. Because I have a smaller hand than my father, it is I who often illuminates his more important works, such as the sultan's book." Sidika felt her heart thudding in her chest. She wanted to run away from these strange, hostile men into her little mudbrick house. She wanted to sit by the window, reading or drawing – anything but this.

Yusuf, ignoring al-Shuja'i's order to sit, paced gracefully around a nearby fountain with his hands clasped behind his back. "Come here," he beckoned to her. "We shall put this to a test."

He led her to a nearby table crowded with miniature figurines of trebuchets and mangonels, all carefully assembled of wood and slender iron pins. "Take some time to observe these devices, girl, and then you will draw them for me without looking at them."

He called for paper and quills, and the other amirs crowded around the table as he shrouded the figurines under a piece of linen. "Please draw for me the largest of the devices that you saw on the table."

Sidika took up the quill, scrutinizing the tip. "I need a sharp knife, please. This quill tip is fine but not fine enough."

"I know better than to give a woman a knife when she is standing so close to me," al-Shuja'i grumbled, but Yusuf chuckled and pulled a gold-handled dagger from a leather sheath on his belt. For a moment, Sidika stared at it dumbly. Wrapped in hammered gold, with verses from the Qur'an etched in flowing script, it was the most beautiful, rich object she had ever held in her hand.

"Is there a default with my dagger?" he asked.

"No, it is very fine, my lord," she said shyly.

"Ha! Jews…" al-Shuja'i snorted.

Sidika felt her face glow with embarrassment. Drawing a steadying breath, she scraped and trimmed the quill tip until she was satisfied, then dipped it in the pot of ink and quickly sketched the outline of the trebuchet, talking as she worked. "This is the largest of the three machines you showed me," her quill scratched efficiently across the paper, "and this is the one that throws those vast javelins." She dipped her quill and moved on to the second machine. "Then you have this medium-sized machine here of which I know not the name."

She turned to Yusuf. "It would be helpful, my lord, if I could see the real machine so that I may draw a man near to help the reader understand its size to scale."

Yusuf grinned broadly and turned to al-Shuja'i. "Well, I think that your decision is made. The shaykha not only has a steady hand but a good memory. This little owl would make a fine addition to your stable of talentless scribes, al-Shuja'i. She might even be able to teach them a thing or two."

"You continue to be irreverent and annoying, despite your elevation to the sultan's court," al-Shuja'i growled his assent grudgingly. "Tonight, we feast to celebrate the birth of one of my sons. Will you join us, Yusuf?"

Yusuf spread his hands apologetically. "I must pay a visit to al-Musri since I intend to take his daughter to wife, and the day grows late for us to finish the negotiations. Will you be in my party when I leave for Cairo, Sanjar? We all grow tired of al-Salus and his boasting. It would be better to have you reinstated as wazir to the sultan."

Al-Shuja'i waved Yusuf away. "I prefer to rule Damascus. Your new sultan is a paranoid madman, and I do not wish a fate like Turuntay, with my guts spilled into the sand and my beard pulled out." He turned to Sidika.

"Young woman, I will take you to see the siege beasts with your own eyes, although because you are a girl, I think you will be too frightened to go near them."

Sidika set her jaw and remained silent. Yusuf kissed al-Shuja'i on the cheek and strode from the courtyard without a backwards glance. With her only advocate gone, Sidika became conscious of the other men, who regarded her coldly. They returned to their table, and Sidika remained awkwardly standing next to the model siege weapons.

"Well?" al-Shuja'i bellowed at her. "Are you going to loiter around my courtyard or get started? I will pay fifty bezants for these illustrations. It would be twice as much if your father had come, but he sent me his spinster daughter instead." He continued to grumble, summoning a servant to bring her to the siegeworks near the citadel and find a place for her to sleep in his harem. She bowed low and then retreated slowly with the servant, heaving a relieved sigh as the door shut behind her.

She had done it. She was in.

Chapter 10

December 1290
Templar Citadel, Acre

Once more, Henri received a summons to the Templar citadel to meet the citizens' council and discuss the latest developments of the impending Mamluk attack. As he and Raven trotted into the inner bailey, the usual racket of horses and men accosted his ears. In a corner, a fleet of beleaguered knights attempted their drills in the driving rain, but the rest of the bailey seethed with a chaotic scramble of activity.

"Henri, my boy!" a voice rose above the noise. "Tie up that beast of yours and join me."

Sir Phillipe de Maineboeuf, a knight whom Henri admired both for his bravery and his understanding of the Arabic language, grinned broadly and draped a soggy arm across Henri's shoulders. "Quite the din, eh?"

"What is happening, Sir Phillipe? This looks like preparations for a battle." Henri had to shout over the noise. Sir Phillipe grinned again.

"Well, very nearly so. Are you here to sit on the council? I am to take a message to the new sultan this very night. That is, if you men of consequence can find a way to tell him to shove off without seriously upsetting him. *En fait!* Henri, you should come with us! You speak Arabic perfectly, and two must be better than one."

Although news did not usually travel quickly in the Holy Land, thanks to the Mamluk postal service, word of Qalāwūn's death had reached the city of Acre only days after he passed away of sickness… or poison – no one could really be sure which. The city leaders felt that this development would bode well, since there would undoubtedly be a succession battle among Qalāwūn's amirs, which would distract them from their planned attack on Acre.

That, however, is not what happened. Al-Ashraf Khalil, Qalāwūn's second-eldest son, quickly subdued those who would take the sultanate and instructed the army to resume their preparations for war as if his father still lived. This was problematic for the Franj for two reasons: never before had the sultanate been passed successfully from father to adult son under the Mamluk regime, and reports of Khalil's sanity were mixed. There were some who said he was mad and others who described him as cunning. Either way, by all accounts, Khalil was less tolerant than his father, uninterested in diplomacy or negotiation, and unlike the son of Baybars, who failed to thrive in his short rule, Khalil was not a child.

Henri remembered Zahed's descriptions of the ferocity of the Mamluks. He wasn't sure he was interested in seeing firsthand how this new sultan would respond to a plea from the occupiers, begging permission to stay in the land that had been forcibly taken and converted at sword point.

"Ah, here comes the grand master now. I shall ask him if you may join us. The peace delegation is all knights, but I am sure another speaker of Arabic would be valuable, and you even look like a bit of an Arab!"

"That is because I *am* a bit of an Arab," Henri grumbled under his breath.

Sir Phillipe dragged Henri by his sword belt to an alcove

and shoved him toward a group of men who stood close in private conversation. Grand Master Beaujeu looked up, scowled, then his expression changed to amusement.

Sir Philippe sank to one knee. "With respect, Grand Master, I think Lord Henri should accompany Brother Bartholomew and me on our mission to speak with al-Ashraf Khalil. He has a perfect mastery of Arabic, and I know for a fact that he is a diplomatic man, else he could not be so successful in trade between Outremer and Marseille."

Henri's heart thudded. His mother always told him that intuition was God whispering in his ear. His father wrote that off as nonsense, but Henri felt sure that he did not want to accompany Sir Phillipe on his mission, nor did he deserve any accolades for diplomacy. So far, his attempts at leadership had managed to get him beaten nearly to death in a public square.

"Well, yes, Lord Henri is most impressive, I am sure," Beaujeu said, "but I do not want him on this mission. Too many people have called his loyalty into question. He is on the council as a matter of formality due to his title and property. Maron, are you on patrol this week?"

"Yes, Grand Master," Henri replied, dropping to one knee.

"Very good," Beaujeu said, "and Mainbeouf, I also wish for you to enquire and on the whereabouts of Brother Georges of Languedoc and his squire, Marcus of York. Brother Philip sent him on an errand near Qal-at al-Subeiba, but they are overdue. If the Mamluks who occupy the fortress have him in captivity there, I wish to negotiate his release."

"Yes, my lord."

"Brother Languedoc is missing?" Henri asked, "Why did no one tell me this?"

"Because it is none of your concern," Beaujeu snapped.

Henri was troubled. He disliked Brother Languedoc as much as his mother did, but the man had fought alongside his father when King Louis was defeated at Tunis and had always kept watch over Henri's family from a distance.

Beaujeu turned to the middle-aged man standing next to him. "Seneschal Grailly, please do not place Lord Henri in a patrol with Brother Philip de Fons Bleaudi. I do not wish to see this young man ascend the whipping platform yet again. I think such a sight would slay all the unmarried women of Acre." His normally flinty eyes sparked with amusement. "And perhaps several of the married ones as well."

Henri glowered. He was loyal to God and the Kingdom of Jerusalem, despite what people thought about his parentage. *I will have another chance to prove myself on this patrol, and this time, if someone ends up being beaten by Brother Philip, it shall not be me.*

Seneschal Grailly frowned up at Henri. "Are you knighted yet, young man?"

"No, sir, but I am ready to say my oath and take up my mantle."

Grailly raised an eyebrow at him. "Would that be a white mantle, Lord Henri?"

"I, uh… that is…" Henri faltered, and from the corner of his eye, he saw Beaujeu looking at him keenly.

"I think there will be time for Henri to make that decision after the council, non? Now let us go and see this finished." The grand master pushed past them into the corridor that led to one of the inner meeting chambers.

Sir Mainbeouf squeezed Henri on his shoulder. "Ah well, rotten luck, Henri. Would liked to have had you along. Come visit me when I return, and we will share our tales of battle. I would dearly like to know your side of the story concerning our sweet-tempered Brother Philip. To hear him tell it, you almost let the Mamluk spy into Acre by the main gate, ha!"

***

Henri once again found himself sitting at a table in the great hall with the heads of the knightly orders, Prince Amalric, the Patriarch, and the other influential men of Acre. The Patriarch started the proceedings.

"Eight of us have already met this week and decided to send Sir Phillipe of Mainboeuf and three others to bring a plea before the new sultan to beg for mercy upon us."

The men at the table exchanged glances. Some wanted to fight, and their expressions darkened. Many did not. Beaujeu cleared his throat.

"We will send the message along with a sizeable gift for the sultan's coffers. We brought you all here to inform you of our plans that you may be aware. There is a chance we may still avert an invasion."

"So, we are trying to buy our way out of this mess?" Lord Conques asked, incredulous.

"Yes, we are," said Grand Master Villiers, "and it worked for our fathers and grandfathers many times, so I suggest you hold your tongue, Conques, because if the sultan does not accept this bribe, your head could end up outside the city, hanging by what little hair you have left."

Henri scowled at the table, his arms crossed, and shook his head.

"There is no chance that Khalil will take this gift. My lords, this is his chance! They have nearly eradicated the Franj in Palestine!"

"Will you cease using that word, 'Franj'? It insults us. We are God's warriors. We are the men of the Cross," Amalric corrected him with obvious annoyance

"What would you do in his situation?" Henri continued. "Would you back away and allow your enemy to keep their foothold, or would you deliver the final blow to them?"

"These infidels do not think as we do, Lord Henri," Lord Conques started and then paused dramatically. "Oh, I almost forgot, you are Saracen. Perhaps your opinion is valuable after all," he sneered across the table. "Tell us, how do Saracens think when they are not busy sodomizing their camels?"

Henri jumped to his feet. "Leave my heritage out of this conversation. A man is not the blood that runs through his veins; he is the sum of his experiences and his faith!"

"Once again, Lord Henri, I must ask you to sit down, and if you continue to have these outbursts, I will remove you from the council," Beaujeu said coldly. "Lord Conques, the same goes for you. Any more personal attacks on Lord Henri during this council and I will cease to invite you. I also have my doubts that this gift and appeal to Khalil will be successful, but we must try. At the end of it all, if we did not try our best, then every single life lost will be counted as murder against us on the day of judgment. This I believe."

The Patriarch looked at Beaujeu thoughtfully but said nothing.

Chapter 11

December 1290
Damascus, Syria

Sarangerel blinked, rubbed her eyes, and blinked again. She was sober, uncomfortably so, for no one was willing to give her a copper or spare her a drink from their wineskin. She sat in her usual place near the Touma Gate in the great city of Damascus on a tattered, scratchy blanket. Her head throbbed for the need of wine, but she forgot the pain as she watched the young woman walking around the perimeter of the Touma Square. It was her girl. Her moon-child.

She could never forget the face that had first stared at her from behind a charred wagon wheel a lifetime ago on a silvery, moonlit night. She had raised the child, knew the delicate bones in her wrists and throat, and the tumbleweed of wild hair that seemed to be a living creature of its own. The girl in the Touma Square wore a fine scarlet dress, and despite the pale cloth on her head, a spiral of amber-colored hair curled around her face. But it was her eyes that Sarangerel recognized – hazel and wide-set, looking nervously around, waiting for someone to jump at her. She moved discreetly, like a rose petal that dropped from the flower, and few of the citizens in the square took notice of her. How they could not notice puzzled Sarangerel – her girl had grown graceful and willowy.

"My child…" she whispered under her breath. "You returned."

The last time she had seen Sidika, it was when that reprehensible trader in children, Bekir, was dragging the girl away. Sarangerel had bought flatbread and oil from him, and a little wine to calm her nerves, but the debts added up, and eventually Bekir took out his payment in human life rather than coppers or even silver dinars. She cursed him and his offspring, vowed to get the child back and take her own payment out on him with a bow and arrow. But Bekir's men came for her, and well, they warned her good and proper not to return. That was when she turned to the drink for solace. For forgetting.

Slowly Sarangerel rose from her pile of foul straw and blankets and took two unsteady steps forward. She sensed movement behind her and turned just in time to see an old man snatch her filthy blanket and run back into the dark shadows.

"Hi! Ismael, you cur! Those are mine! Come back here, you devil's cock-sucker!"

Eyes turned toward her, but as soon as the regulars in the square saw it was only the profane old Mongol woman, they returned to their business. Sarangerel whipped around and searched again for the scarlet dress, but it was gone. Her girl… had she only imagined it? Sarangerel looked down at her hands, which were beginning to shake. She needed a drink.

***

Sidika tapped quietly on the door of al-Shuja'i's house, and the eunuch who answered let her in and led her silently back to the women's quarters. He opened the door to the harem, and his lip curled as he glanced at her. Days before, he had made it quite clear that he felt she should be following purdah in the women's quarters during the times that she was not sketching siege weapons at the citadel. The eunuch, whose name was Baltasar, had taken his complaint to the amir himself, bowing low and airing his grievances. Al-Shuja'i waved his concerns away absently. "The sheykha is a Jewess, and if she wishes to go prowling around the streets like a trollop, that is her business. If her father cared about her honor, he would not have sent her alone."

"But my lord…" Baltasar stopped talking at the stern look from his master.

"I need her to have free access to the citadel, Baltasar. If you are so worried about her honor, then send a retinue of guards with her."

Baltasar thought of this conversation with simmering disgust. She insisted on walking about the city, which required a guard, which took one of his master's own company away from his duties to protect the amir. Who knows – the Jewess might have been seducing the guards in a dark alley as soon as she left the house. Everyone knew that Jew women worshipped the devil and craved the cock.

"Thank you," she whispered as she passed into the harem, her eyes averted toward the ground.

He slammed the gate behind her and looked up at the position of the sun. It was just beginning to lower past the tops of the tallest buildings, which cast long shadows across the street. Baltasar slipped out the front gate and walked around to the back of the high-walled governor's complex, where a few scraggly old cedars drooped.

Settling himself behind the trunk of one of the great trees, he pulled a cloth-wrapped parcel from his robe, and as he unwrapped it a few bits of delicate pastry fell in golden flakes to the ground. He bit into the treat and closed his eyes as the taste of pounded walnuts and mastic, wrapped in muwarraq dough and drenched in rose syrup flooded his mouth. Today was a rare day that he had managed to purloin a tart from his master's tray and find the time to eat it before it grew stale. So immersed was he in his enjoyment that he didn't notice the low cackling until the old woman was already starting to hobble toward him. The tart tumbled to the ground as he jumped in surprise.

"Old hag!" he snarled. "Look what you made me do!"

"I will get you another sweetie, my boy," she crowed and looked at him slyly. "Or should I call you that? What are you?"

Baltasar leveled her with a haughty stare.

"I am the servant of al-Shuja'i, the governor of this city, and you are about to be seized and thrown in his prison."

The old woman scuttled up to him with surprising agility and grabbed his wrist.

"More treats for you," she whispered, her foul breath making him gag, "if you tell me what I wish to know! I will bring an entire baker's tray to this very place and hire a pretty maid to feed them to you."

Jerking his hand back, he gave her a push and turned to walk away.

"All I want to know is why she comes here every day! The girl in the red dress!"

Baltasar stopped, and the old woman chuckled.

"You know of whom I speak." She walked toward him again.

"Why do you wish to know about her? She may be a Jewess, but she does not consort with the likes of you, of that I am sure."

"A Jewess?" For a moment, the old woman seemed surprised. "A Turk, she is. A mountain child. T'was I who

71

plucked her from the ashes in the moonlight and took her as my own when she was just a babe. My baby…"

Baltasar saw a tear slide down the woman's filthy cheek. "Do you mean to tell me that Sidika the shaykha is not the daughter of a scribe? You lie, for there is no way that young woman gained her skills in your care."

"He took her! That lying beast took her from me, and every day I watched as she did his bidding in the streets! He took her!"

"Go away, old woman. I do not know who took your child from you, but you are mistaken. I have seen Sidika the scribe's daughter at her work. She is indeed a rare talent, even if she does roam the streets like a prostitute."

The old woman's mouth split into an enormous smile. "Ahhh… you disapprove of her, I see."

"It matters not. In a few days' time, she will leave, and then my master's household can resume as normal. Never would the governor allow his wives or concubines to parade around the city unescorted like that. It is unchaste. It is against purdah."

"And where will she go when she leaves?"

Baltasar looked at the woman. Her eyes watched him hungrily, and she fingered the edge of her ragged frock in agitation. Perhaps the old crone planned to kidnap Sidika and sell her for ale money. He could certainly smell the stale wine on her breath and clothes. And if she were to do such a thing, it would justify his concerns. Al-Shuja'i would not so readily dismiss Baltasar's complaints if this brazen girl were to be taken after he warned everyone she would be. He smiled, and the old woman stepped closer.

"Acre. She leaves this house for Acre when she finishes her work for the governor. Come here every day at the same time, and I shall inform you when she goes."

Chapter 12

January 1291
Citadel of Salah ad-Din, Cairo

The four Franj men stood brazenly in the throne room of the citadel, their feet and legs filthy from travel and their sweaty heads bare. A shimmer of dust fell from their tall bodies onto the fine, red and blue carpets that had been spread over the mosaiced floor. Khalil sat comfortably in his golden chair, which had been completed by his artisans only the day before. The chair separated him from his father, who often preferred to stand, until he was too frail to do so any longer. Khalil stared down at the men from his high dais, his face blank and impassive, every muscle practiced to stillness.

"Have these men been invited to wash before speaking in this council?" he asked the room in Turkish.

The assembled amirs and courtiers looked at each other nervously. A slave rushed forward and prostrated himself to the ground. "Yes, my lord, but they did not wish to bathe until after they had spoken to you. They said they rode hard to come to you as quickly as possible."

Khalil's face remained still and unreadable, but Yusuf could guess his thoughts. Although some Franj were courtly and genteel, with knowledge of basic hygiene and manners, many were not. They were generally considered uncouth, foul, smelly, and no Mamluk – indeed no Muslim – would allow themselves to be seen in such a revolting state.

The shortest of the four, a man with a ruddy, good-natured face and a mess of dark brown hair, stepped forward and bowed.

"Honored sultan, I am Sir Philippe of Mainboeuf. We bring you gifts and a plea of mercy from the leaders of Acre. We desire peace between your people and ours, which has brought prosperity into both of our harbors during this time of truce. We ask that you reconsider your intentions to besiege Acre. Your father maintained good relations with our city, and we wish for the same with you."

Khalil frowned at this.

Today, Yusuf stood on the dais at the sultan's request in case translation was required. He wore his purple samite robe, belted with a black silk sash embroidered with verses of the Qur'an. Under the sash, the samite itched, and he willed himself to be as still as Khalil, but the urge to adjust his robes was maddening.

Khalil folded his hands over his stomach and considered the men in front of him. The silence lasted for such a long time that the Franj knights began to glance at each other, confusion muddling their sun-red faces.

"Their king did not honor my father's request to send the perpetrators of the atrocities against Believers when we asked. And they allow violence and brutality in their streets." Although the Franj had addressed him in Arabic, Khalil answered in Turkic. The faces of the Franj were changing from confidence to confusion to fear. "Therefore, I see no reason why we should return these men to Acre."

His eyes flicked to Yusuf, who bowed. "Yusuf Ibn Shihab, please explain to these men that the gold they sent will be returning to Acre, but they will not."

Yusuf dutifully translated, and when he had finished, there was a moment of silence. The knight called Mainboeuf stuttered out an explanation to his colleagues in French, and they immediately began to shout and gesticulate.

Khalil inclined his head, and five of his palace guards approached, their swords drawn.

"Please," the knight called Mainboeuf begged in Arabic, "my squire is only a boy. He has nothing to do with this business. Please send him back to Acre with the gold."

At this, Khalil stood.

"Give him mercy? How much mercy did your people show to ours when they slaughtered innocents in your streets? When they beheaded prisoners of war a hundred years ago in your very city? When they came to Jerusalem, their bellies full of the flesh of Muslims that they had consumed in their ravenous hunger? You are not men; you are animals!"

His face flushed with rage, and Yusuf could see his fists clenching and unclenching at his sides.

"Your squire will join you in chains, and I doubt that there is any gift that will be sufficient to slake my anger, which is the anger of every sultan before me! Get them out of my palace!"

He was screaming now, pointing at the door, and the five guards grabbed the Franj knights roughly. One of them, the youngest, whimpered before the door slammed behind him.

Yusuf looked at his friend, who had reseated himself in his golden chair. Khalil was spirited but always level-headed and not given to bursts of emotion or anger.

The man sitting on the throne seemed a stranger to Yusuf. An unknown.

***

When word reached Acre that a message had arrived from Cairo, the citizens' council crowded into Prince Amalric's lavish house near the harbor. As servants moved sedately among the men, their arms laden with trays of sweets and pitchers of wine, Beaujeu stood and motioned for silence, then cleared his throat.

"Well, we have received an answer from Khalil." He held up a sheaf of papers and handed them to a small man in a black sergeant's robe, who began to read.

"The Sultan of Sultans, King of Kings, Lord of Lords, al-Malik al-Ashraf, the Powerful, the Dreadful, the Scourge of Rebels, Hunter of Franks and Tartars and Armenians, Snatcher of Castles from the hands of miscreants, Lord of the Two Seas, Guardian of the Two Pilgrim Sites, Khalil al Salihi."

At this elaborate salutation, many of the men in the room murmured and began to look around at each other. Beaujeu rapped the floor loudly with the butt of his long-handled baculus, and the crowd quieted.

"To the noble master of the Temple, the true and wise: Greetings and our good will! Because you have been a true man, so we send you advance notice of our intentions, and give you to understand that we are coming into your parts to right the wrongs that have been done. Therefore, we do not want the community of Acre to send us any letters or presents regarding this matter, for we will by no means receive them."

For a moment, the room was silent. Then the messenger of the sultan stepped forward and bowed curtly, his expression hard and unsmiling.

"Your men," he began in broken French, "we have them in our cage. They stay with us," he raised his hand and closed it into a fist. "We not give them back."

Amalric stood from his chair, his silver wine cup clattering to the ground. A murmur rose from the assembled city leaders and servants as the messenger raked them with a disapproving stare. He continued.

"You broke peace. Killed innocent. No more men you send to us. No more gift. We come, and we take this city. Praise to God."

For a moment, all in the room remained silent.

"Fine," Amalric said, his eyes blazing, "let them come. The city of Acre is strong, and so are its people. If Khalil wishes to find this out for himself, we are prepared to meet him in battle."

Beaujeu stood slowly and walked from the room as his secretary translated Amalric's words into fluid Arabic. The Patriarch raised his face towards heaven and closed his eyes in prayer. Brother Mathieu de Clermont pounded the arm of his chair.

"Then let us march on this madman ourselves and end him before he can come this far north!"

"Quiet, Clermont!" Amalric snapped. "They do not need more reasons to hate us right now."

Turning to the assembled council members, he sighed heavily. "You have heard the message. Please muster your fighting men and bring any servants you can spare. We must begin to secure the city walls immediately."

Then he stood and swept from the room without looking at Henri or anyone else.

Chapter 13

February 1291
Al-Hadiqa, Palestine

January passed, and with it, Henri's eighteenth birthday. The weather became colder and colder, and by February he and his servants, spent many a punishing evening throwing tents of rough cloth over the tender green boughs of his young lemon saplings and wrapping the trunks with straw and dung to protect them from the frost.

The mornings dawned cold and clear, with shadows of raised hoarfrost beneath the trees where the sun rarely touched the earth, and webs of ice crystals that crawled up the banks of the Yasaf creek. Although his hands were raw from working in the cold, Henri looked out upon his orchards now and sighed contentedly. The saplings survived. He had done something right. Perhaps he could atone for all of his previous blunders as the lord of the Maron estate.

He walked into the great hall one morning, still rubbing the sleep from his eyes, and sat down to a meal of hot oat porridge and a bowl of *māst* – a tangy and thick yogurt swimming in honey and walnuts. He usually preferred to be alone in the morning, but the silence of the hall was melancholy on this day. Perhaps it was time for him to marry, if only he could find a woman like his mother, who had joined his father at his mealtimes.

Most Franj noblewomen preferred (or were ordered) to retreat into their quarters and eat with their lady's maids and other attendants, but Lady Nasira and her daughters had often joined Henri's father and his guests in the great hall, partaking in the conversation. Henri always wondered why his father allowed it, but now he missed their perspective, their voices. Nasira rarely said much, but she listened to the conversation with sparkling eyes, and his two sisters often commented, much to the annoyance of Lord Rogier's guests. But Rogier was proud of his women. In Francia, he told Henri, he could be chastised by his peers for allowing his daughters this much voice. Here, as settlers in the Holy Land, there were few French women at all, and less motivation to keep them quiet and cloistered.

Everyone knew that the marriage of Rogier of Maron-en-Ruergue, a fabulously wealthy noble, to the beautiful but impoverished Nasira of Galilee had been a love match – the biggest scandal in the city for years. Rogier did not appear to care, though it meant he and his children lived outside the city walls and actively partook in their trade. While other noblemen and wealthy merchants left the running of their affairs entirely up to their stewards and bastard sons, Rogier kept his little family close. He hired tutors for his daughters and loved his wife with a passion that the church frowned upon.

Henri pushed his yogurt and porridge around in his bowl. There were no women in Acre or Cyprus who were of noble enough birth for him to marry, and no one that he felt he could tolerate for a lifetime. He thought of Sidika, her eyes blazing and hair flying when she was angry with him, which was every time she saw him. *Whoever marries that shrew will have more than enough wife to deal with.*

He chuckled to the empty room, but she stayed in his

mind, staring fearlessly at him as she had done during his beating in the city square. He had always thought her homely, but that was not how he remembered her on that day. Among every other face in that crowd, hers had compassion… and of every person in the city, she had cause to hate him the most, for he had killed her father.

The door slammed open, and Henri quickly scooped a spoonful of mast into his mouth, grateful that something broke his train of thought before it led down the path to Tamrat's murder. Zahed strolled through the hall, whistling and carrying a sheath of unstrung bows. Every morning at dawn Zahed trained the estate's soldiers in Mamluk fighting techniques, and he had been so effective at it that Henri began to rotate his village militias into the estate so that they could receive the benefit of the training. Zahed dumped his bows on the table with a loud crash.

"Up awfully early, are you not, lordship?"

"Have you absolutely no respect? Remove those bows from my table while I am eating!" Henri threw his spoon down and crossed his arms.

"Respect has to be earned, but you are getting closer to having it," Zahed said absently, examining a crack in the grip of one of the bows. "All Mamluks begin their careers as slaves, and they earn the respect of their masters before they are—"

He stopped, looked up. Madame Habiba stood at the entrance to the eating hall, twisting her handkerchief in her hands, her eyes shadowed with fatigue. She looked around nervously.

"Madame Habiba?" Henri pushed his chair back. "I thought you were in the city with my mother and sisters."

Madame Habiba curtseyed quickly and then lowered her eyes to the floor. "I was, my lord. I left this morning without their knowledge. I told them I was sick." She said no more, but neither did she leave.

"Will you come sit?" Henri asked after an uncomfortable silence. "You do look ill, Madame. Shall I fetch a physician for you? How are my mother and sisters?"

Madame Habiba lowered herself reluctantly onto a chair at Henri's urging, looking at her hands. "My lord," she said quietly. "I would speak to you, but not in his presence." She glanced up at Zahed, then down at her lap again.

Henri dismissed Zahed, pulling a chair next to her. Madame Habiba took a deep breath, and her hands continued to work the fabric of her kerchief. Henri could see that a corner of it had grown gray and frayed with twisting.

"Lord Henri, I have served your family for almost as long as you have lived in this house. To me, your mother Nasira is as my own daughter – taken as she was from everything she knew – and your dear sisters are like my grandchildren, as are you," she began. "Your father, may God keep his soul, treated your mother and sisters kindly. Master Mafeo, however, does not." Here, she paused and darted a glance at Henri. When he made no move to shout at her, she continued.

"My lord, Master Mafeo has been using a heavy hand against your mother. He leaves marks on her that she tries to hide, and when she cannot, she stays in her chambers."

"I suspected as much," Henri said. "No… Zahed told me. He warned me."

Madame Habiba reached out and took his hand. "Lord Henri, something has happened. When you were recovering from your ordeal with the Templars, Mafeo, well, he…"

Henri pulled his hand back. "He what? What has he done?"

"It seems, my lord, that he became impatient with my

lady and decided to father his heir with your sister, Blanche, and not your mother." Madame Habiba looked at her lap, and Henri sat in stunned silence.

"He… he got Blanche with child?"

"Yes, my lord. My lady fled with her two daughters as soon as she found out. She has been ill with worry ever since."

"But… he is married to my mother…" Henri felt dazed. "And my mother did not tell me of this…"

"She was not certain you would disapprove, my lord."

The room moved around him. He had done this. He had brought this curse into their house. The door to the hall opened slowly, and Zahed stood in it, his face pale, his curling hair standing up wildly.

"Zahed!" Henri said sharply. "Were you listening at the door?"

Zahed jogged into the room without answering, snatched a bow and a handful of arrows from the table, then turned and ran.

"Zahed!" Henri yelled, running after him. "Wait! Stop!"

Zahed was at the top of the stairs before Henri had even left the hall. He kicked Mafeo's door, but it did not budge. Inside there was a shout and a scuffling sound.

Henri arrived at the top of the stairs and pulled Zahed back.

"How much did you hear?"

"I heard all of it! This has gone on long enough! This dog has hurt people for long enough!" Zahed shook himself free and kicked the door again.

"Wait!" Henri pulled Zahed into his mother's room, which was next to Mafeo's. Al-Hadiqa's terraces were close together, so that it was possible to jump from one to the other, which Henri frequently did when he wanted to slip away from the house without attracting attention. He sprang onto Nasira's terrace balustrade with Zahed following, leapt to Mafeo's adjoining terrace, and ripped the curtains open. Mafeo lay in his bed, naked as usual. He jumped up in alarm, pulling a robe over his shoulders with uncharacteristic modesty.

"What in God's heaven are you doing in my chamber!" Mafeo bellowed. "Can a man not have a moment of peace in the morning?"

Henri crossed the room in one bound, grabbing Mafeo by the loose robe. "What have you done to my sister?" he hissed. "Is it true?"

"Is what true?!" Mafeo screamed.

"Does she carry your child?"

Mafeo's eyes widened.

"I do not know… I do not know!"

His eyes moved past Henri and landed on Zahed, then rounded with fear. "You… I always knew you would turn on me one day. I pulled you from the slave trader's pen and saved you from a life of serving the sultan, you swine!"

"My Mamluk master treated me better. What did you do to Lady Blanche?" Zahed's voice was low and controlled.

"I did not do it," Mafeo whined, "that little bitch lied to you! She ruts with the kitchen boys and the stallions in the stable! The Maron women are lying Saracens!"

Henri shook Mafeo again. "Tell me!"

"It is your fault, you know." Spittle was flying from Mafeo's mouth onto Henri's face. "She saw you get the pulp pounded from you and needed comfort. I was just giving her some comfort! Anyone could see that you broke her spirit!"

"Giving yourself comfort, you mean! Is it not enough that you force my mother against her will every night? You promised to protect my sister! She is not your wife, and now you have ruined her! She will never make a good marriage after this!"

Zahed jumped lightly from the ledge of Mafeo's balustrade, his arrow nocked and pulled back to his cheek. Mafeo's hand shot out, and a dagger flew through the air, burying itself in the wooden lintel at the terrace door.

Then he gasped.

An arrow sprouted from the side of Mafeo's head like the slender branch of a sapling. He reached up, felt at the shaft, confused, then dropped to the floor, snorting and convulsing. Zahed slowly walked into the room from the terrace, a second arrow nocked in his bowstring.

"Fetch the physician, Zahed," Henri said coldly. Zahed's face hardened, and he pulled the arrow back further. "Zahed, did you hear me?"

The arrow flicked from Zahed's bowstring and buried itself in Mafeo's back so powerfully that it pinned him to the floor. Zahed stared at Mafeo silently, his eyes sparkling with loathing. Slowly he lifted his bow and pulled a third arrow from the quiver at his waist.

"Zahed, no!" Henri yelled, but the third arrow found its mark in the back of Mafeo's neck.

"God's bones! You could have hit me with your first shot!" Henri shouted at him. "Take care. The man is dead!"

Zahed looked at Henri. "No, I would not have hit you." He dropped the bow and walked out onto the terrace.

A fist pounded on Mafeo's door. "Henri! Lord Henri!"

"Leave us!" Henri yelled back, his nerves buzzing.

The pounding continued. "My lord! Your gates are under attack, and Mamluks are chasing the servants from their homes in the fields."

Chapter 14

February 1291
Al-Hadiqa, Palestine

From their perch on al-Hadiqa's flat roof, Henri and Zahed could see five camels loping fluidly down the frosty hill towards the house, their riders dressed in elegant scale armor and carrying spears with polished iron tips that flashed in the morning light. Already several soldiers on foot chased the terrified workers through the stubble of the harvested sugarcane fields.

Henri dropped from the roof onto the terrace and tore down the steps into the courtyard.

"Close the gates!" he cried. "Attackers in the sugar fields! Arm yourselves!"

After the first council at the Templar citadel, when it became apparent that war was coming, Henri had moved his servants and field workers behind the walls of his house and lodged them in tents in his courtyard. Children now ran playing between the groomed pomegranate trees and tidy rows of herbs, and the women filled their cookpots from his ornamental fountains. The Henri of a year ago would have thrown them out, but now he found he enjoyed sitting at the cookfires of his servants, listening to their stories and absorbing their knowledge of Palestine and his own fields, which some of them had tended for more than twenty years.

At his cry, the courtyard sprang into action. A few of the children began to whimper, but the women quickly pulled the porridge pots from their cookfires, dumped the contents into buckets, and refilled the pots with sand shoveled from a waiting pile in a corner. The trained fighting men ran to the racks of weapons and armor set up in the center of the courtyard and yanked padded gambesons and mail shirts over their heads.

"Archers, with me!" Henri yelled, grabbing his crossbow and a fistful of iron-tipped bolts. He and the archers crouched behind the short wall on the roof as the camels approached. He could see the crumpled body of one of the workers lying amongst the frozen irrigation ditches, and his head spun with outrage. *How dare these soldiers hurt one of those people. My people!*

Putting his foot in the crossbow's stirrup, he drew the bolt back and brought the stock up to his shoulder.

"Focus your arrows on the rider on the left!" he commanded, and four bolts whizzed through the air from the wall. The rider jerked from his saddle, feathered with arrows. Henri waited for a count of five as the group approached even closer. "Now, the one on the right!" he cried.

Two bolts hit the man in the chest, and he slumped forward in his saddle. The other riders wheeled their mounts and took cover behind a low hill while Henri and the archers drove them further away with more fire. Soon arrows began to fly back as the enemy approached slowly, crouching behind round shields. Henri looked to his right and noticed Zahed beside him.

"Why are you not armored?" Henri shouted.

Zahed set his jaw, drew back his bowstring, and fired. "Because it was never offered to me, my lord."

"We shall soon fix that," Henri said, turning to search for

Durant, his master-at-arms. He lurched forward as one of the estate's soldiers gurgled and fell against him, an arrow embedded in his neck.

"Take cover!" Henri yelped, pulling the man back from the wall. The soldier gasped and tried to speak, but blood seeped from his mouth and torn throat. His eyes were wild with fear. Henri grasped the man's hand and peeked over the wall. The riders were approaching the house again, this time with flaming torches. He heard a gasp and looked down. The soldier convulsed twice and died, his head in Henri's lap.

"Keep shooting," he ordered the remaining archers. Gently, he set the man on the ground and ran down into the courtyard. "They have fire with them. Everyone not fighting needs to gather water and buckets! Soldiers, with me!"

The rest of his men were buckling on leather doublets and iron caps. Durant grabbed Henri by the tunic as he ran towards the gates.

"No, my lord, wait." He slung a mail hauberk over Henri's head. Henri shoved his arms through the sleeves as Durant slapped on a leather arming cap to keep the metal armor from twisting and pulling Henri's sweaty hair, and draped a mail coif over the top.

"Durant," Henri barked, "why is Zahed not armored?

"We did not have enough armor, my lord, and I did not want to waste what we had on a slave and an infidel."

"Well then, have some made!" Henri snapped. "Put a cooking pot on his head if you must. It is cruelty to send a man into battle unarmed!"

Durant pressed his lips together with disapproval.

Henri heard the slam of an axe against the wooden gates. Two serving girls laboriously climbed the inner courtyard stairs, lugging a heavy pot of smoking sand between the two of them. Minutes later, there were screams as Zahed and the archers on the wall tipped the scorching sand onto the enemy below.

Henri ducked into his black and yellow surcoat and tied his reinforced iron polyns over his knees. Durant buckled a sword belt at Henri's waist and gave him a thump on the chest. Thus armored, he formed the men into two ranks behind him and they positioned themselves behind the gate.

They heard a cry of alarm from one of the women on the roof.

"My lord, Ibrahim has left the house!"

Henri ran up the stairs and looked over the wall. Ibrahim, his gentle, steady-headed steward, approached the attackers, bent forward in a posture of supplication with his hands raised above his head. His white robes flapped in the cold morning breeze like a flag of truce. The attackers watched warily from their camels.

"Oh, God in heaven, Ibrahim!" Henri gasped. He had seen enough. Scrambling around the courtyard, he wrenched open the little postern door.

"No one is to loose any arrows unless the Mamluk devils strike Ibrahim and me to the ground and menace the house again, do you all understand?" he asked. The fighters nodded, their eyes solemn, and he slipped out, hearing the thud of the postern slamming shut behind him and the bar sliding back into place.

Heart pounding, he jogged to the huddled attackers, who had retreated to the hill and out of range of arrows. Ibrahim and a man who appeared to be the commander of the Mamluk raiders spoke rapidly in Arabic.

As he crested the hill, Henri's heart sank. At least thirty more armed men on horses and on foot waited, some with long lances pointing toward the ground to avoid detection from the house. They carried yellow banners and round shields, and sat on their mounts in formation, looking disdainfully at Henri with disciplined stillness. The breath from their beasts puffed in clouds of cold, brilliant white as the sun moved higher above the hills.

"Henri, remove your helmet and your hood immediately!" Ibrahim commanded him in French. Henri didn't have the presence of mind to be offended that his servant was giving the orders. He removed his head protection, feeling naked and vulnerable.

"Take your hand from your sword."

Slowly, Henri willed his fingers to release the hilt of his sword.

"I am Lord Henri, son of Rogier of Maron-en-Ruergue, and this is my home that you attack," Henri addressed the commander in Arabic. "Why do you harass us? We are peaceful and have no quarrel with you."

The leader of the Mamluks raised his bushy eyebrows in surprise.

"He speaks Arabic! Better than I have seen from the other Franj lordship. Would that he could speak Turkic like a truly civilized man," and he leaned forward, smiling. Henri detected the scent of sweat, wet leather, and camel on him.

"I am the *usted* of these men. Tell me, son of Rogier, from whom did you inherit this grand house?"

"From my father."

"And him? To whom did the house belong before that?"

"His father," Henri seethed.

The Mamluk commander continued, sweeping his arm broadly to the house and the fields of sugarcane. "And from whom did your grandfather receive this land?" He smiled with exaggerated patience.

"The land was unoccupied when my grandfather built this house."

The Mamluk commander looked around, taking in the gentle hills and the meandering white ribbon of the frozen stream. "Oh, I really do doubt that. No, this is good land. Whether your Franj grandfather knew it or not, I am sure that it belonged to one of the Believers. This man," he gestured with his eyes to Ibrahim, "says you are something of an Arab."

"My grandmother and mother are Sunnis who have lived in Palestine for five generations. Her father was of the Bedu."

"Ah, a woman who turned her back on the teaching of the Prophet, married an infidel, and raised his children." He gave Henri a hard look. "So, you are half occupier, half son of the land. I do not envy you the conflict you must feel within yourself."

"I do not—" Henri started, but Ibrahim put his hand on Henri's chest.

"I ask you to show mercy to my nephew and his household. He has twenty-one servants living within his walls, almost all are followers of the Prophet, peace be upon Him, and all are loyal to Lord Henri of their own free will." Ibrahim turned to Henri, and their eyes met, deep brown and clear green, locked together.

"He treats them with honor. Please take your men and leave."

Henri continued to stare at Ibrahim.

Nephew?

"You are a loyal man, Ibrahim, and brave," said the usted, "but what will I get in return for sparing this house? My men expect to plunder. It is a long ride to Cairo, and we have come from Aleppo. We will have no food for the road and no women."

Henri pulled his eyes from Ibrahim. "I will provide your men with gold and supplies, but you must proceed directly to Cairo and leave the other villages and houses alone as you travel. No other towns may you molest on your journey. You can find women in Cairo, and I hope to God that you find them willing."

"This is well enough," the usted grunted. "I have spent many years training these slaves. I have no wish to lose them to battle or to temptation. And we need our numbers in full for when we come back to take Acre." His deep-set brown eyes twinkled.

Ibrahim retreated to the house, yelling for food supplies to be brought from the storerooms. Henri followed woodenly, ordering two servants to slam the gate behind him. Taking a lantern and a small leather sack, he kicked aside a woven reed mat in the great hall, pulled a trapdoor in the floor by its ring, and descended a stair into a cool, dark tunnel that ran beneath the courtyard. Counting each stone on the floor, he stopped at twenty-five, turned to the wall on his left, and counted up five more stones. Wriggling the fifth stone from its place in the wall, he found the carved symbol he sought: three oval lemons. From this damp nook, he withdrew a set of heavy iron keys.

The storeroom smelled musty and stale when he stepped inside, but there was no dust coating the iron-bound chests that were kept locked and chained to the walls. Every month the coins within were counted and recorded. He re-emerged with a bulging sack of gold bezants and slipped out of the gate again. Turning to Ibrahim, he spoke through the gate.

"They may yet kill me when I hand this gold to them. If the Mamluks try to overrun the house, hide the servants in the tunnels and send Zahed and Durant for help if you can. The militia may be able to survive until troops arrive from the city."

Ibrahim clasped Henri on the shoulder and then yelled to a servant to shut and lock the gate.

Chapter 15

February 1291
The Venetian Quarter, Acre

Nasira, the lady of al-Hadiqa, sat in the solar of her city house with a book on her lap, long forgotten. She stared out the window to the street below, watching a donkey braying and digging its hooves into the dust as a frustrated farmer attempted to move it and a cart of early harvest akkoub toward the vegetable souk near the harbor. When in season, the spiky blossoms were dredged in batter, fried, sold as pricey but portable street food. But the harvest was early this year, and the cooks in the great houses would surely brawl with each other for such a rare delicacy, which usually blossomed in late spring.

The donkey's ear-shattering squeals echoed across the narrow street, and Nasira smiled, delighted at how ordinary this interaction was. As a girl, she had lived in Acre's Arab quarter with her mother, and although she loved her lavish estate outside the city, she had missed these sounds of daily life in a busy city. Her mouth watered at the thought of a clutch of hot, freshly fried akkoub, sprinkled with sesame seeds and wrapped in leaves. Perhaps she could send a servant out to purchase some for her.

The faint sound of retching wafted in from another room, and reality came rushing back like a dash of cold water in the face. Her own husband had impregnated her daughter. What was she to do? How could Blanche's condition be explained to anyone? She had already gone to Madame Ardukin for a potion to end the pregnancy, but the old witch merely laughed and shut the door in her face, and no amount of money could convince her to open it again.

Her thoughts were interrupted by a knock on the heavy wooden door, and her son cautiously entered, spattered with mud. It had been weeks since she had seen him, and he had grown taller and thinner.

"Hamza!" Nasira cried, calling Henri by his pet name. "You did not tell me you were coming. Why do you arrive here in this state? Go at once to the hammam and come back to see me when you no longer smell like you have been working in a field all day." She glanced apprehensively at Blanche's open chamber door.

"But Mother, there is something I need to tell you."

"It can wait. Go clean up and return. I will have some decent clothes set out for you."

Choosing a plain tunic of creamy white wool, a wide blue sash, dark brown leather hose, and a flowing cloak of dark blue velvet that was hooded in the French style, she laid these on his bed and went in search of the cook to prepare a meal. Henri reappeared from the hammam, clean and dressed but still wearing the same expression of worry.

"You still look exhausted, Hamza. Perhaps you should spend a few nights in the city, removed from the troubles at the house."

"Mother," he said, taking her hands, "al-Hadiqa was attacked by a band of Mamluk raiders two days ago."

Nasira pulled back. "Was anyone killed? Ibrahim… is he unharmed?"

"Ibrahim is unharmed, but Mother, your husband Mafeo

was slain in the attack, along with a turcopole and one of our villagers who was helping in the sugar fields. The raiders did not harm anyone else or the house, although it cost us dearly – one hundred and twenty gold bezants."

Nasira slowly sank into a nearby chair. "Mafeo is…"

"Three Mamluk arrows struck him as he stood on his terrace. We found him hours later."

It had been Zahed's scheme. Mafeo would receive a Christian burial, but Zahed insisted on preparing the body himself. A priest, not an expert in arrow forensics, observed the preparation without suspicion.

"I… I should grieve, but I feel…"

"Relief?"

Nasira looked down at her hands. "To feel relieved at the death of my husband is wickedness."

Henri knelt in front of her. "How is Blanche?"

Nasira looked up sharply. "How do you know?"

"It does not matter. What can be done?"

Nasira stood and paced the room angrily. "What can be done? Can you roll the months back and never introduce that man to my house?" She turned and fixed her son with a stern glare.

"I am sorry," he whispered.

"Tell that to your sister. She has to bear this shame forever. Her life is over, Hamza. Mafeo may have injured me, but he has destroyed her."

"I should never have let them be in the same house with each other. She must have tempted him—"

"Do not!" Nasira stomped her slippered foot on the woven mat. "Do not suggest that my daughter is responsible for what that man did. Your father would have believed her. Your father would have protected her!"

Henri felt his mother's words settle on him like a

lodestone. "Perhaps Madame Ardukin has a potion that can relieve her," he said without conviction.

"Relieve her? This condition is not her fault, and what happens to the child is for her to decide. I think you have made enough decisions on our behalf, my son!"

"But it was you who—"

"It was I who asked to marry him so that your sister would not have to, yes. What other choice was there?" Her temper was rising, and Henri could not bear to look at her.

"I have wronged you and my sisters in a way that even God cannot forgive, Mother. Please tell me how to help?" The marriage had been Henri's idea. In his excitement and inexperience, he arranged for Mafeo to join the family immediately after Rogier's death. Now, when he looked at his mother and sister, all he felt was the weight of his shame.

"Be there for her. Protect her and find a convent that will take her now that she is bespoiled. Remember, my son, that as a man, you have immense power, which you have already abused."

Henri dropped his head into his hands and sighed.

"There is something else. Mother, can you please explain to me why Ibrahim called me his nephew yesterday?"

"He said that?"

"Is Ibrahim your brother?"

Nasira took a slow, deep breath. "No, he is my uncle."

Nasira paused. Henri waited.

"As you know, I am my mother's only living child. When I wed your father, my mother worried. We were powerless and poor. I was…" and she hesitated, taking another deep breath. It was time to be honest with her children. "I was a servant in your grand-père's house when I met your father, my son." Nasira looked down at her hands. "There is not a drop of noble blood in my body."

"I already know." Henri shrugged. "It was not as great a secret as you wish. Why do you think Amalric never invites me to his feasts when the other lords are present? Now, I wish to know more about Ibrahim. Was my father aware that he is your uncle?"

"No. Ibrahim was my father's brother – the youngest of my grandmother's six sons. Because he is the youngest, he had no inheritance and very little chance of marrying, so he apprenticed himself to a scribe and learned the ways of record-keeping and correspondence. He lived in Acre his entire life, so he already knew how to speak Latin and French.

"When we wed, your father was afraid the other servants would become jealous of my change in position and poison me, so he sacked every member of your grand-père's household and hired his own servants. He was looking for a steward to manage the estate, and I arranged for him to meet Ibrahim. I used all my powers of influence over him to accomplish this. He never knew who Ibrahim was because your father would never have allowed a member of my family to work or live at the house."

"You lied to my father."

"Oh, Henri!" Nasira stood up. "Everyone lies in marriage. Without lies, there would be no peace. Ibrahim has watched over me and you children for twenty years."

"But he failed to protect you from Mafeo when he was in a rage."

Henri watched her with a somber green gaze, and she looked back at him, piercing him with her fathomless brown eyes. "As did you, my son."

She saw his shoulders drop, and his guilt gave her a small amount of pleasure. Why should he escape the consequences of his disastrous decision to arrange her marriage?

"Your father was a fine man, Henri, but not without faults. Ibrahim and Madame Habiba have been my two confidants these twenty years. My angels."

"How am I to treat him? This man who, for my entire life, was a servant. Now he is an elder member of my family! He is deserving of my respect!"

Nasira did not know what to say. She remembered the conversation she had with Ibrahim when he first took service at her house. "You must never treat me as anything but a servant, my niece," he had whispered to her. "To do otherwise would create serious consequences for you and for me."

Henri stood. "I must go to the Patriarch and the grand masters to report what happened at the estate."

"Henri!" Nasira grabbed his sleeve. "Your sister... we must send her away. Soon her pregnancy will show, and her shame will be complete."

"Yes – it is time all of you were sent away."

***

Henri's first stop was Prince Amalric's residence near the slaughterhouse on the harbor. The servant who greeted him at the door reluctantly explained that the prince was hosting a banquet for Hochmeister Burchard von Schwanden, the latent grand master of the Teutonic Order.

"Will you also join in the festivities, Lord Henri?" the servant asked coolly, eyeing Henri's plain clothing and ring-free fingers.

"Is Guillaume of Beaujeu in attendance as well?"

"Yes, my lord."

"Very well, I accept." Henri strode into the house without waiting for a response. The first person he saw was a most unwelcome sight.

"Ah, Henri, you are looking very plebeian this evening," Sir Joscelin of Loire sneered. Joscelin and Henri had both trained at the brutal finishing school of Sir Geoffroi as children. Although he and Henri avoided each other, they still managed several dozen unpleasant encounters each year. The man swayed on his feet, spilling a dribble from his silver cup down the front of his red embroidered cotehardie.

"My name is still 'Lord Henri' to you, as it was when we were boys, Joscelin," Henri said, not bothering to slow his gait as he scanned the room for Beaujeu.

"You are still a boy. So nice for you, and convenient that you managed to inherit your fortune before coming of age. And as for your mother, well, some people earn their riches through conquest, and others through their cunts. It seems she has twice been fortunate in that regard." Joscelin laughed to himself and took another sip from his silver cup.

Henri launched at the knight, and a wave of wine from Sir Joscelin's cup spilled on his white tunic, soaking into his hose. Amalric rushed over and pulled Henri back by his belt.

"Peace, Henri," he hissed, "no need to make things even harder on yourself. Joscelin is just a drunk."

But Sir Joscelin was watching Henri with red-rimmed eyes and smiling wickedly. "Never could control your temper, could you? Someday the prince will not be around to save you from yourself, Saracen," he said, punctuating his words with a loud belch.

"What is this?" Grand Master Villiers approached, hands on his hips. "Prince Amalric invites you into his feast as a courtesy to your station, Lord Henri, and you come dressed as a tradesman and then accost his guests?"

"Grand Master, my estate was attacked by Mamluk raiders two days past. I know not why they were north of the city, but they killed three men, including my mother's husband, took gold and supplies, and left for Cairo," Henri said, turning to Villiers. "I apologize for my state of dress, but I have come to the city to warn you and the others. The commander of this raid said that the Mamluk army is gathering in Cairo to return for Acre even as we speak."

"We already know this!" Villiers snapped. "Now return to your tent and camel and let polite society enjoy the evening!" He spun on his heel and stalked to the far side of the large hall where the other grand masters of the knightly orders sat. At the high banquet table, Beaujeu watched Henri but remained in his seat.

"I must go," Henri muttered, "I know you do not like me to show my face at these events."

Amalric took his arm and led him to a servant who held a silver pitcher of wine.

"Stay awhile, Henri," he said in a low voice, taking a cup in each hand. "Two Byzantine princesses arrived with the Hochmeister. Surely you would be interested in potentially securing yourself a kingdom?"

"I have no need of a kingdom," Henri said, moving to leave again, "and I have no interest in princesses."

"What is this? Who does not find a princess interesting?" a mocking feminine voice called out.

Henri looked up as two women approached. The one who spoke peered at Henri with brown eyes that sparkled with mischief. Plump and short of stature, she looked about sixteen or seventeen years of age, dressed richly in a gown of purple silk. On her head was a boxy hat, draped with a scarf of lavender gauze shot with silver threads, and decorated with tiny seed pearls. Pearls hung from gold hooks in her ears, and adorning her throat, a collar of more gold with teardrop-shaped pearls glowed in the lamplight.

"Henri, this is Princess Isabella of Nicosia and her cousin,

Lady Keratsa of Bulgaria. Both have asked to be introduced to you," Amalric said, rolling his eyes. "Ladies, this is Lord Henri of Maron-en-Ruergue, a viscount of Acre who regularly gets into arguments at social gatherings."

"You are the most interestingly attired guest at this feast, Lord Henri. Do you wear that wine on your chest as a bold new cloth weave, or to show us that your hands shake and you are unable to grasp the cup?" Princess Isabella giggled.

"It was bestowed upon me by an inebriated goat," Henri said with a bow. "Apologies if it offends you. I had not expected to attend a feast this night."

"Keratsa, my love," Isabella whispered loudly enough to be heard by all around her, "if this is how he looks when he is out herding drunken goats, let us imagine how he looks when he actually tries to appear well-groomed!"

"I will gladly imagine that," Lady Keratsa said, watching him with a predatory smile. She was older than Isabella by at least ten years. "Tell me, Lord Henri, do you hold much land here in Acre?"

"Yes, my lady – two hundred carucas outside of the city walls, along with twenty-one settlements between here and the Sea of Galilee. My estate is located north of Montmusard and is mostly devoted to growing and distributing lemons, sugar, and cinnamon to Marseille." He glanced around, but Isabella and Amalric had pulled away and were talking at a discreet distance, heads close together.

"That sounds most pleasing. I should like to see your home sometime."

Lady Keratsa wore a deep blue silk embroidered peliote over a gauzy, floor-length shift of lighter blue. A long rope of rough-cut onyx beads draped around her throat and hung between her breasts, and she had a silver-embroidered girdle tied around her waist. Her mousy-brown hair was braided loosely, and a thin circlet of silver and sapphires held a sheer veil in place. Henri took a nervous gulp of his wine, and a servant appeared to refill his cup.

"And I understand you also have a large estate in Francia, is that correct?"

"My lady already seems to know much about me. It is true, although it is only a modest fief, and I have never visited the shores of Francia." Suddenly he was sweating. Lady Keratsa had cold, pale gray eyes that appraised him as if he were a horse for sale at an auction.

"You have a kingly look about you, Lord Henri. But not like a real king." Her lip curled. "Real kings are just indulged boys in fine clothes. You look like the kind of king that is sung of in tales. I should like to see more of you."

Henri took a step backwards. "I am quite unused to being spoken to this way, my lady," he stammered, and she threw her head back, laughing boldly.

"That is because you are used to being the aggressor. I am twenty-four years old, and I have been married and widowed already to two men who both disgusted me. I no longer have any interest in being a timid maid. I like the look of you." She reached up to touch his dark hair. "You shall come to visit me. I am staying at the house of King Henry while he arranges for my cousin Isabella to marry Amalric, and I shall stay until the negotiations are complete."

Henri's head spun. He wasn't sure how many times the servant had refilled his cup, but he kept drinking from it. He found her manners audacious, even a bit menacing, but it excited him and made him uneasy. Emine, his kitchen maid, was the last woman he had bedded, and only because there had been no Capetian lords or ladies from visiting Francia lately, with their usual entourage of lady's maids who were looking for conquests of their own during their visits to the

Holy Land. He tried not to think about how easy it would be to pull the veil away from her hair slowly, to unfasten the ring of silver around her waist.

He noticed several silk and velvet-clad noblemen of the city whispering in a corner and peering in his direction. Spending too much time talking with the princess in public could be dangerous for his safety, and her boldness in touching him would signal to the other lords that she expected him in her bed. Promising to take her on a tour of the city within a week, he made a hasty exit to the street where, although it smelled considerably worse, at least the temperature was cooler.

Above the clustered rooftops of the city, a crescent moon rose in the clear sky, painting the slender minarets and church towers with silver. In contrast, the glow of lamps and rushlights flickering in the windows of the houses twinkled across the city like warm stars. It was late, and aside from the drunken shouts and laughter escaping from Amalric's door, there was little noise in the city other than the occasional bark of a dog.

Henri's spinning head began to clear, and he set out toward his residence, grateful for the first time in his life that his presence at a banquet was not desired.

Chapter 16

March 1291
Al-Hadiqa, Palestine

M arch arrived with daily rain and fierce winds. Henri spent many nights helping the workers to dig trenches, redirecting the torrents of muddy water that overflowed from the creek and threatened to wash their fertile growing soil to the sea.

During this time, despite the looming threat of invasion, Henri felt immense satisfaction with life. Twice a week, he saddled Raven and they trotted into the city to visit Nasira and Saruca, his ten-year-old sister, and to conduct business with the Venetian merchants. Often, he would hoist Saruca into the saddle with him and take her outside the city walls to play in the fine, white sand of the shore up-current from the stinking harbor, against the protests of his mother who had other ideas about how young ladies should play.

He installed his archers in stations atop the roof of al-Hadiqa to watch for Mamluk and Bedu raiders, and every morning he and Zahed ranged the hills on horseback in a wide circle around the house, searching for tracks, campfire ashes, or scouts. Then, he and the servants set about the backbreaking business of refining the harvested sugarcane syrup into glistening brown cones to be packed in straw-filled crates bound for Marseille.

Although Ibrahim still insisted on maintaining a servant-master relationship, especially in public, he and Henri frequently found themselves seeking each other's company, and they often spent hours sitting on the west-facing terrace as the sun sank into the sea in the evening, sipping fragrant mint tea and talking of Ibrahim's family.

Henri tried to call Ibrahim "uncle," but the old steward refused. "My lord, I am your servant. It would not be well for you to call me by this title in front of the other servants. To keep the peace, let us continue as though nothing has changed."

But everything had changed. Henri did not ask anything of Ibrahim any longer and found himself searching the man's profile to see if he could spy any likeness between them. Ibrahim noticed Henri's stares but said nothing, secretly glowing with affection for his "new" family.

One chill afternoon, as Henri, Zahed, and the turcopoles practiced their blocking and recovery in the dooryard and his archers perfected their marksmanship in the harvested vegetable field, a tall destrier galloped up the narrow road, skidding to a stop near the gates.

Brother Gregoire, his white Templar robes spattered with mud, leapt down and demanded a private audience with the lord of the estate. A short time later, they sat in Henri's mosaiced study, sipping cool ceramic cups of greenish-tinged cane water. Brother Gregoire set his cup down and rubbed his eyes wearily.

"Our spies tell us that the Mamluk army have begun their march across the desert from Cairo. Once they have left that wasteland, they will move faster due to the availability of water and villages to raid."

"Have you seen them?"

"Not myself, no. My patrol got as far as Jerusalem, and

then we nearly lost our heads. Well, Brother Boisvert did lose his head, but I suppose he got what he deserved."

Noticing Henri's questioning look, Brother Gregoire continued reluctantly.

"Our vow of chastity is taken very seriously. When a man becomes a Templar, he leaves his fleshly desires behind him and commits his body, soul, and fortune to a higher purpose – to the protection of the faithful and the Holy Land. To the glorification of God. Brother Boisvert had been dallying for a while and getting away with it, but when he raped a girl in a village outside of Jerusalem, we did not stop the villagers from seeking their own justice."

"What is the purpose of making a man stay celibate, Gregoire? Surely it only presents more opportunity for sin when you create new sins to place in front of him?"

"Women's bodies are filthy," Brother Gregoire said with surprising vehemence. "They are filled with temptation and evil blood. Schemes and seduction consume their minds."

"I hope you can retire from the Order before you die, so some woman can prove you wrong. Why are you here, Gregoire? What do you need from me?"

"Will you evacuate to Cyprus, or will you stay and fight? Sultan Khalil and his army will be here in a few months, maybe even less if they push their beasts to exhaustion. The grand masters need every man, but already the boats begin to leave Acre harbor full of people instead of silks and pistachios."

"I will stay and fight. Palestine is my home."

"Good man. Will you move into the city so that you can muster quickly with the other knights? We need all men to be close at hand, and your estate is in great danger outside of the walls."

Henri looked around his study. A scroll of black and

white mosaic decorated the plaster surrounding the arched doorway. The cotton drapes performed a ghostly dance in the cool winter breeze that lazed through the tall windows. A small fire burned in the soot-blackened fireplace, and nearby a velvet-covered bench piled with horsehair-stuffed cushions provided a comfortable place to rest. He sighed. *When did I become a man who wishes to stay at home? Even Peter the Hermit was more active than me.*

"I will consider it."

"Would you also consider joining the Order, Henri? Our numbers are low. There is enough time for you to become a Templar and to learn our ways. I already spoke to the grand master about it, and he would welcome you into our ranks."

"No," Henri said quickly, and then with a wink, "I do not think it would be possible for me to forswear those filthy, scheming women."

Brother Gregoire rolled his eyes and stood, holding out a folded and sealed parchment. "Beaujeu said you would refuse. He asked me to deliver this to you." He left the room with a clink of mail and a shower of dried mud. Henri cracked the brown wax seal and opened the parchment.

> *Lord Henri, the blessings and peace of Jesu Christi be upon you. There is an errand that you must complete, not for me, but for yourself and someone you have wronged. Find me at my auberge tomorrow, and I shall tell you more.*
> *~Guillaume de Beaujeu*

***

That night, as he prepared to have the finished crates of dried lemon slices and sparkling cones of pale brown sugar transported to Acre harbor for transport to Marseille, Henri told Ibrahim about his conversation with Brother Gregoire. Ibrahim thought quietly for several minutes, then stood.

"Lord Henri. Nephew," he smiled shyly, "this war with the Mamluks will fail with great loss of life to the Franj. Will you not consider joining your father's family in Francia?"

"I will not, Uncle. I will stay and fight for my home and my land."

"Will you not consider sending Nasira and the girls to your estate in the Ruergue? Madame Habiba and I will escort them to ensure their care."

Henri nodded thoughtfully. "Yes, this is wise counsel. I shall make arrangements for them to leave Acre at once."

Ibrahim's smile broadened. "How you have grown, Nephew, from an aimless youth into a responsible man. If only your father were here to see what you have become."

Henri looked at the floor and wished that he deserved such praise.

Chapter 17

March 1291

Fajar, The Hills of

Idmit

The crockery had all been taken, along with the straw mattress and copper pot. The thieves had left a clay candlestick – although they took the candle – two tables, and a bench. Also gone were the stores of grain, dried meat, and the jars of wine.

Sidika stood in the doorway of her empty house and stared dumbly for a moment before setting her box of paper and inks on the floor and opening the windows. After months in Damascus and more days consulting with the grand masters at Le Touron, she was finally home. Even the theft of her worldly possessions could not dampen her relief at being in her own house again.

Pushing a small cupboard aside, she dug at the dirt floor with a stick until she unearthed the wooden planks covering the hole that her father had lined with stones. Her money, her father's blue and white tasseled tallit and bloodied robe, her mother's silver necklace, and her lavender hair ribbon were still there, among other things. Snatching a candle from the hole, she stuffed it into the candlestick, then went outside to light the oven with her flint.

Her shoulders dropped with resignation. The goat was gone, and the vegetable garden was picked clean. Her only consolation was the sound of her few remaining chickens clucking gently from their roosts in a nearby mulberry tree.

That night, after spending months in the luxurious harem of the amir of Damascus, Sidika crawled wearily into the stale hay in her little stable to sleep, her stomach growling angrily. She woke late the next morning, roused by the sound of a horse snorting impatiently on the other side of the stable wall.

Sidika sat straight up. No one in her village owned a horse.

Cautiously, she emerged into the early morning light, holding a stick of firewood as a weapon. Henri's back was turned to her, and he stared at the door to her house. He raised his hand to knock, then lowered it again, took a deep breath, and shuffled his feet. Sidika cleared her throat loudly, and he spun around, hand on the pommel of his sword. For a moment, they looked at each other warily.

"Ah, good, I was told you still lived here," he said in his awkward, businesslike tone, then his eyes strayed to her hair, which bristled with curls and straw. "Was I… interrupting you, mademoiselle?"

Brushing a piece of straw from her dress, she swept past him and pushed her door open. "Thieves stole my bed and all of my possessions, so I slept in the stable. See it for yourself."

He continued to look at her and not into the house.

"Lord Maron, if I were taking men to bed with me, I would not take them to the hay. I arrived home from a journey last night and discovered that in my absence, my neighbors had helped themselves to—" she stopped. He was reaching out to pluck a piece of oat straw from her hair, his fingers lingering on a stray curl. Then his face broke into a broad smile.

"You are so very undignified," he laughed. "I have never met anything like you, excluding my youngest sister." And his laughter overtook him.

Sidika regarded him coolly.

"Lord Maron, why are you here? Certainly, there are more undignified women in Acre that you could mock for your amusement?"

He stopped laughing and his expression became serious.

"I was sent here by Lord Beaujeu, the grand master of the Templars, to bring you to your father's grave."

After Damascus, she had gone straight to Le Touron, then waited a day for the grand masters and the seneschals to arrive. After handing over copies of her drawings, she was instructed to go home and wait for someone to fetch her and show her where Tamrat's bones rested. And here he stood – the one man in all the world she did not wish to take her there.

Henri looked at the ground.

"My deepest apologies. I did not come to mock. It has been many days now since anything has given me cause to laugh, and I did so improperly just now."

Sidika reached up self-consciously and felt the bits of straw in her hair.

"Well, I am sure I must look shocking. I would offer you refreshment, but I have none. They took everything."

Henri's face brightened. "I have supplies for my journey. You must be hungry," he said over his shoulder as he walked back to his horse.

Sidika peeked around the house. A short distance away, Rahat stood on her doorstep with hands on her hips, watching Henri appreciatively as he pulled an ale skin and several linen-wrapped parcels from his saddle. Sidika ran her fingers through her hair and tried in vain to disentangle the straw, but it had thoroughly worked into her curls. She snatched her pale pink headscarf and hastily wrapped it around her hair, tying it at the nape of her neck as he returned.

"I would rather we ate outside, Lord Maron," she said quickly. "The neighbors will talk."

He squinted a pale green eye at the sun.

"It will take us almost a quarter of a day to arrive at the place. How do you feel about eating while riding?"

***

His beautiful horse waited, hitched to a light, two-wheeled cart, which contained a long wooden box and a spade. They rode slowly into the mountains, speaking only when necessary, with Sidika sitting in front of him in his ornate, high-walled saddle, trying not to let any part of her body touch his. He kept the reins loosely in his hands, but seemed mostly to be guiding the horse with his legs, because he never used the bit to pull the beast in one direction or another. She found herself thinking that she would be more comfortable if she could lean back and rest her head on his chest.

This man killed your father, she remembered, and scooted further away from him in the saddle.

When it was close to midday, he reined the horse and dismounted, reaching up to grasp her by the waist and set her down on the rocky soil. Sidika flushed and made a self-conscious attempt to straighten her skirts. Henri kicked at the blackened detritus of a cold fire pit, then walked to a large stone and sank to his knees.

"Here is where it happened," he said, dragging a deep gulp of air, his eyes misting.

Sidika looked dumbly at the stone, the ground, the place where the most important person in her life had taken his last breath at the hands of this Franj. When she thought of her father's final moments, she imagined a sacred place, a beautiful place, but this was just a bland rock on an unremarkable hillside. She looked again at Henri and felt her anger rising.

"No," she said through clenched teeth, "you do not get to weep here. I am the one who is allowed to weep here, not you!" Tears burned her eyes, and she glared down at him as knelt at her feet. "Leave this place so that it will become sacred. Your false grief defiles it! Your presence here is profane!"

"It is not false grief." Tears now snaked through the dust on his cheeks. "Your father was the only person who looked at me and saw someone good. He told me there is good inside me, and then he told me to take his life. He asked me to do this awful thing after revealing that he is the one person in the Holy Land who does not look on me with disgust!"

"You did not have to obey him!" Sidika shouted. "He may have asked you to kill him, but you did not have to obey!"

"They had tortured him, Sidika. Every minute he lived was agony. Had I not listened, Brother Philip would have made your father live as long as possible. Feel as much pain as possible! His body was fevered, and Brother Philip commanded me to take up the scourge and—"

"Enough!" Sidika screamed. "I do not wish to hear what you beasts did to him!"

"Sidika," Henri started, but she put her hands over her ears and closed her eyes like a small child. He took a few shaky breaths, then stood.

"You may stay here as long as you wish. This is not the grave, but if you want to stay here and mourn, I will take Raven to the creek over the next ridge and leave you alone."

Sidika nodded silently. She sank to her knees, lowering her forehead to the dust, taking in the smell and feel of the earth that had soaked up her father's blood. Digging her fingers into the dirt, she felt the deep, aching sob rising from her stomach. It was as if every bone in her body were crying. As if her father had died all over again. Tamrat. Her second father. Her first father's charred body was another ruin in her burned village – she had seen his charred and disfigured flesh when Horse Aunty found her, shivering and alone in the moonlight. Slowly, his bones eroded into the very mountain dirt. She did not even remember her first father's name. And now, another father became dust.

Henri returned and set the ale skin and a linen handkerchief next to her, then left again. The sun moved slowly across the sky. A tiny brown lizard walked tentatively across the stone where Tamrat died and looked at her for a moment, then darted to safety. Eventually, she rose heavily to her feet and found him sitting in the shade of an olive tree.

"Please take me to where he lies," she rasped.

He found the pile of stones easily. It was a short distance away, overlooking one of the innumerable valleys in the foothills of the mountain. Sidika stared at it as Henri removed the box and spade from the little cart. Her father's grave looked small. Shorter than she remembered him.

"I do not think you wish to see this," he said quietly.

She retreated and listened to the sound of the iron spade scraping the rocks. Raven amiably nosed her, snorting curiously at her hands and skirts in search of a handful of oats or some grapes.

How could my father have begged someone to kill him? His pain must have been immense, she thought. Then she thought about Henri – flogged until he lost consciousness for defying a Templar and giving her father the mercy he asked for.

There are no heroes in this story – only my father, the wicked Franj, and the slightly less wicked Franj.

She watched as Henri exhumed Tamrat's bones and felt her anger weakening. Her grief remained, but it became something soft and resigned. It wrapped around her and encased her, but without anger, it no longer hurt.

On the ride home, Sidika sat in the bouncing cart, her hand resting on the box. "I am here, Father", she whispered. "We are going home."

They arrived in her village as the sun sank in fiery splendor into the sea. Over their heads, the cold mountain sky turned from pink to deep purple, and bats swooped through the expanse in erratic circles.

"It is dark…" Sidika began.

"I wish to help you bury him. The ground is stony, and this is a heavy burden to bear alone."

"I thank you," she mumbled, "but there is only the stable. I will ask if you may use the bed of Rahat and her husband to sleep this night."

He pulled a bedroll from the cart. "Take this and let us put some straw under it, so it is more comfortable. Raven and I will sleep in the stable tonight and keep watch over your father. Is it not a Jewish custom that the dead are not to be alone?"

You left him alone for months, she thought. She said, "I will bring you some water to wash."

When she returned from the well, she saw that he had lit a lamp inside the house and piled straw in her tiny room by the door, placing his bedroll on top of it. He had also brought his provisions inside and set them on the table, along with a sheaf of fine white paper, some delicate horsehair brushes, and a murky glass vial of precious purple dye powder derived from the snails that lived along the coast.

"An offering of peace," he said self-consciously, before retreating to the stable.

Sidika sank onto the bedroll – a heavy black and yellow wool blanket with the Maron of Acre family crest stitched into a corner. It smelled of horse and woodsmoke and the sweet, spicy cassia that she had noticed on him earlier that day. She rolled onto her back and stared out her small window at the stars until just before dawn, her mind spinning.

***

The following morning, Henri was gone from the stable. Sidika looked up at the little hill where her mother and brother were buried and saw his silhouette bent toward the ground with the sun rising behind him as he worked with his spade.

She rifled through his parcels of provisions, then gathered them up and climbed the hill. He worked in his hose, a wrinkled undertunic with the sleeves rolled to his elbows, and a keffiyeh of black cloth to protect his head. Without his mail and sword at his waist, he seemed far less intimidating – almost like a normal man. She handed him a piece of flatbread with some sweetened sesame paste which he took gratefully, and they sat together at the side of the grave, eating, each lost in thought.

"Do you know," she said hesitantly, "this is the first time I have shared a meal with another person since my father died. It is good to talk to someone again and to break bread."

"And I am often unable to eat a meal alone even if I wanted it, for I am surrounded by sycophants who wish to earn my favor, hoping that they can snatch some crumbs from my table. They bow and smile to me at every banquet and then call me a Saracen and a half-breed when I am not present."

"Is there something wrong with being a Saracen? It is

what makes you unique among your peers."

"Sameness is what counts in the aristocracy." Henri took a contemplative bite of bread. "Something I will never attain, though I spent most of my youth attempting to."

"I am sorry I said those things to you yesterday." Sidika looked at him and then quickly away. His pale eyes were difficult to avoid. Their strange, green depths made her feel birds fluttering in her chest, and this very notion horrified and angered her. It was as if her body did not know that he was an occupier and a noble.

"One should not be held to account for what they say in moments of grief," he answered.

Silence crept back, like a cushion that pushed them apart. After a few moments, he spoke.

"My offer still stands, Sidika. You are welcome to come to live at al-Hadiqa as my ward. I think you and my sisters would enjoy each other's company, and you could teach them to hunt. They could teach you to be intolerably annoying."

"Do you not already find me intolerably annoying?"

"I find you intolerably impossible to rid from my thoughts."

He had said it quietly, but the words remained between them, conspicuous and full of unanswered questions. That horrible bird fluttered in her chest again. She lowered her eyes to her lap, unable to think of what to say. He stood, shoved the rest of his bread into his mouth, and continued to dig.

Curious villagers wandered up the hill, and soon a clutch of local men assembled in a disapproving knot, waving their arms and loudly criticizing.

"Franj, you dig as if it is a luxury!"

"Do you not know the correct way to hold a spade?"

"I have seen my daughter Amina dig faster in her garden!"

"Ah, but he is prettier to look upon than Amina. Beauty should not dig!"

Henri straightened up and looked at them narrowly. "By all means, please show me the correct way to dig a man's grave. Here, I shall give you my spade," he called back, and they dispersed quickly with muttered excuses.

Eventually, Fakri swaggered over with a wooden spade of his own and jumped down into the grave. The two men lowered the box into the ground, and the thin, sandy dirt was shoveled over it. Henri retreated to the house to wash while Sidika sat on the grave with what remained of her family. Her eyes were dry. Her tears had all been shed.

Back in her house, Henri had scrubbed the grime from his face and arms and was buckling on various pieces of armor at her table.

"Thank you, my lord, for bringing my father home. It is good that he is with my mother and brother now," Sidika said awkwardly, willing herself to keep her hands still.

Henri tied on his low-slung belt and adjusted the straps that held his silver-studded scabbard at his thigh.

"Will you stay here, then? That gap-toothed potter looks at you as if you were a hare and he the fox."

"Fakri is absurd and thinks too highly of himself, but I do not believe he would do me any harm."

"I saw him hit you when I last was here," Henri said bluntly. "Has he asked for your hand?"

Sidika bristled. "I do not see that it is your business who has asked for my hand. You are not my guardian."

"I can try to arrange a match for you so that he will no longer bother you," Henri replied, reverting to a businesslike tone. "There are prosperous Jewish moneylenders in my acquaintance. Some of them are even young and fair to look upon. You would want for nothing."

Sidika snorted. "I am not ready to wed. And how could you presume to know what kind of man I wish to marry, Lord Maron? You do not know me."

"Henri."

"I beg your pardon?"

"You may call me Henri. I think we are well-acquainted enough by now. And I find this idea that you are not ready to wed very surprising. How will you support yourself? How will you keep other men away from you?"

Sidika felt the heat rising to her face. "I have done so successfully so far."

"Your house was robbed! You were gone for a month, and no one in this village knows where you were or what you were doing!"

"It is not their business or yours where I was or who I was with!"

"You are a beautiful, unmarried woman in a small village – of course it is their business!" he said, voice raised. "And mine as… as a leader of Acre and lord of the surrounding villages!"

Sidika stared at him. "Perhaps," she said with gritted teeth, "you think that this is your business because you feel I owe something to you. I have heard of your reputation, my lord. We are not in one of your villages, and you will not lure me into your bed."

Henri stepped back with surprise.

"Did I attempt to lure you last night? Have I ever behaved improperly? By God's bonnet, you are a suspicious shrew!"

Sidika wrenched her front door open and pointed to his horse.

"I think it is time for you to leave, my lord!"

"It was time long ago," he muttered as he walked briskly outside. Sidika slammed the door behind him.

Chapter 18

March 1291
Al-Hadiqa, Palestine

With Mafeo dead, Emre felt the freedom to breathe for the first time in years. He chafed at his status as a slave-soldier when he lived in Cairo with Badahir, his first captor, but Mafeo brought a different horror to the word "slave." His relationship with his Mamluk amir was more akin to a master and apprentice. Emre and the other boys from his tribe were not at liberty to leave, but neither were they maltreated. Instead of being put to work, they were rigorously trained and equipped, then granted their freedom once they had risen within their ranks. Badahir himself had been a slave. Even the sultan Qalāwūn was enslaved in his youth; so highly sought after was he as a warrior that his master paid a thousand bezants for him.

The way that the West approached their slaves bore little resemblance. Although it was possible to earn manumission, the price that a Franj master demanded was so high that few ever paid their debt. Badahir, in contrast, had wanted to make Emre his heir – the inheritor of his fortune.

With this in mind, Emre nervously approached Henri while he worked in his study one afternoon. He had taken care to dress in his nicest tunic, and his blue turban was wrapped tidily around his temples, hiding his curls. He tapped on the door and waited until he heard a muffled invitation to enter. Henri was leaning over a book, reading and copying text onto several sheets of paper. Emre bowed in respect, but couldn't take his eyes off of what Henri did.

"What do you need, Zahed? Have you made your decision?"

Emre walked a little closer and looked at the book.

"What are you reading?"

Henri stared at him.

"You are supposed to address me as—"

"'My lord,' I know it." Emre waved his hand impatiently. "It would be easier if I did not have to, though."

Henri's mouth hung open in surprise.

"Are you not the servant and I the master?"

"I would sooner be your friend, Lord Henri, which is why I have come to speak with you. I do not wish to remain here as your servant."

Henri put his quill down, his posture betraying his agitation. Emre continued.

"I will work for you, training your men, but I will join your militia, guard you when you visit your villages, train your men in Mamluk fighting skills, and keep your house secure. And I will do it as my own man. All I ask is for you to provide food, clothing, and shelter, as you do for your other soldiers."

"If you were to live with me as a servant, you would have less work," Henri said, "more free time. A weekly wage."

"I have not had free time since I was a child. The idea frightens me, and I would only squander my wages."

The side of Henri's mouth pulled up in a small smile, and Emre felt his heart skip a beat.

"I have often wondered why you do not return to the Mamluk army."

"My amir is most likely dead, and my inheritance along

with him, or taken by someone else. There is nothing for me in Cairo except questions that I do not wish to answer. I would prefer to stay here until I am ready to venture north and seek out my homeland."

Henri raised an eyebrow. "Inheritance? Are you the son of a lord?"

"Not exactly. Badahir adopted me as his heir after he killed my parents and my sister. I was born in the mountains near Cilicia and taken before my twelfth year."

Henri's smile broadened. "You really are a kidnapped child of the Mamluks? I should like to hear your tale someday, for I am sure it is worth telling."

Henri was sitting back in his chair, watching him with an easy smile on his face, and Emre felt a long-forgotten warmth spread over his entire body. It was getting harder to hide his feelings. One more smile like that, and Emre knew that he would be under Henri's power forever. He looked down at his hands and shrugged.

"Not really. It is a sad story, like a thousand other sad stories from a thousand other sad boys."

"Very well, your offer is accepted. Durant is my master-at-arms and is responsible for my training, as well as the management of the militias in the villages, but you shall be responsible for the protection of the house, the special training of my troops, and can be a bodyguard when needed. I should tell you then that a large party of guests is coming to al-Hadiqa to stay soon, although the only people who might need protection are the two grand masters of the brotherly orders… from each other."

"Thank you, my lord. And I have one other request: I would like to be called by the name that the father of my birth gave me in Cilicia, not by 'Zahed,' my Mamluk name. Please call me Emre."

"Emre," Henri turned the name slowly, and Emre felt himself falling deeper and deeper into a forbidden place within himself that he feared and craved.

"Do you have a surname?"

"No, my lord, only Emre."

"Well, here in Jesu Christi's Acre, we use two names. You shall be Emre Freeman in case anyone should dispute your version of this discussion when I am not around to verify it."

Emre grinned. "Thank you, my lord! I am most pleased with this arrangement, and I shall protect you and your house to the best of my ability. Also," he stabbed a finger at Henri's paper, "you conjugated that verb incorrectly. The proper way in Turkish is 'o seviyor.'"

Henri looked down at the papers that he had been writing on.

"What…" he started, but when he looked up, Emre had gone.

***

By the end of March, Acre's streets no longer hummed with their usual raucous trade and exuberant pickpocketing. Now the thoroughfares, although still busy, had a more subdued level of crime and commerce. The cool weather brought mild breezes from the sea that danced through alleys of the city, precluding thunderstorms and sheets of rain as clouds built up against the sloping green hills to the east.

Reports of another Acrean peace delegation brought some hope to the citizens that the sultan would be amenable to a truce, but once again, the emissaries were imprisoned and the Mamluk army pressed on. Henri's presence at the city council meetings was again requested, and the increasingly panicked council members began to assign blame on each other.

At al-Hadiqa, life maintained its amiable pace. The sugar cane grew lushly in the irrigated fields, and the lemon trees sent out new, green shoots with vigor, heedless of the oncoming march of the enemy. It was possible, out there in the hills, to forget that anything threatened them at all.

Amalric visited for a week, bringing a large entourage of servants, grand masters, and friends, including Isabella and Keratsa. Nasira left the girls in the city with her lady's maid and returned to welcome her noble guests, spending hours with the princesses and their maids, embroidering and talking in her sitting room when they were not out riding, or strolling through the groves and gardens.

In the evenings, after full days of hunting or strategizing with the grand masters about the city's fortifications, the entire party of lords gathered in the great hall for feasting and drinking. Henri tolerated his guests because it was required of him, but he found that he preferred spending time sitting near a cookfire with his servants and their families. The boorish behavior of his noble companions made him wish for the quiet of his house again.

Amalric ensconced himself in Mafeo's old quarters, and the princesses took over Blanche's chamber. The grand masters and several of the other titled knights found beds in the corners of the great hall.

"You could have let the grand master of the Hospitaller Order sleep in your bed instead of on a straw-stuffed pallet in your hall," Grand Master Villiers grumbled one morning, stretching his stiff arms. "What happened to the hospitality of the Arabs?"

"I am only half-Arab," Henri replied flippantly. "And did you not insinuate only weeks ago that I live in a tent with a camel?"

Amalric approached, a handful of sugared pistachios in

one hand and a cup of unwatered wine in the other.

"Not to worry, Lord Villiers, we will return to the city tomorrow. I need to check the progress of the new mangonels that the ingeniators' guild are creating, and I intend to send Isabella to Cyprus until the Mamluks are defeated."

Grand Master Villiers sighed heavily and stalked from the room.

"You know, Henri... Lady Keratsa will be leaving with us tomorrow as well," Amalric lowered his voice.

"Princess is too rich a flavor for me, Amalric. I do not seek a kingdom and the problems that come with it."

What Henri did not tell his friend was that Keratsa had already visited him in his chambers twice. Both times he had reluctantly rebuffed her, fearing that if he took her to his bed and put a bastard into her, he would inadvertently cause a war with Bulgaria, although his body protested otherwise.

Amalric stuffed the pistachios in his mouth.

"Well, we could all be dead by the end of this month if the Mamluks have their way, and you even sooner if you refuse to leave this little Eden of yours. Why, even now the Mamluks are taking the hill villages in the north. It is a blessing you already evacuated your settlers to Cyprus."

Henri turned to Amalric. "What did you say? What are they doing in the villages?"

"Enslaving peasants, apparently. Beaujeu's source says that the army has been forcing the men into physical labor and the women, well, forcing them into another kind of physical labor, I suppose you could say."

Henri's heart filled with dread. He had left Sidika's house in anger, and she crept into his thoughts daily.

"Excuse me, Amalric, I must be a poor host to you this evening," Henri heard himself say, "but there is somewhere

I must go tonight, and it cannot wait."

"You will be back before tomorrow?" Amalric asked as Henri busied himself about the room, grabbing a scrip and several tallow candles, flint, and tinder.

"I am not sure," he said absently.

***

A short time later, Henri and Emre galloped through the gates of al-Hadiqa, turning northeast toward Fajar. He had not provided an explanation, but Emre did not require one. It was thrilling to ride out into those hills alongside Henri, who sat upright and relaxed in his saddle. Unlike most horsemen, who dug into their horse's flanks with spurs or whipped them with the reins, Henri leaned forward and whispered words of encouragement in Raven's ear, and she flew like an arrow down the dusty roads. Emre tried to do the same to his borrowed mount, but the beast ignored him.

Behind the clouds, the sun was still high when they arrived in the small mountain settlement with its scattered collection of fields and mudbrick houses. The door to Sidika's house on the outskirts of the village was firmly shut, and the skylight closed. Henri cursed in three languages, hoping he had not ridden beyond the clutches of civilization to find her not at home.

"Zahed... er... Emre, wait out here and watch for Mamluk raiders," he said, tying Raven loosely next to the stable. "I shall not be gone for long."

Emre looked around nervously. The house was silent and dark. The whole village seemed sullen, and the few citizens that he saw slunk back into their homes when the strangers arrived.

"Hello?" Henri called out. Perhaps he could leave a message. She might have been robbed only days ago, but he knew with certainty that Sidika's house would already be littered with paper and writing tools. He tried the front door and found it locked, but the back door opened when he put his shoulder to it. Inside, the house was dark and stuffy. A rushlight burned on the large wooden worktable in the center of the room. Henri stared at it stupidly.

Why would she leave a light burning if she were not at home?

A flicker of movement at the edge of his vision caught his attention and he moved his hand up to protect his face just in time. A clay vessel flew at him, striking his arm. He yelped, falling backwards over a bench and landing in a pile of baskets, each filled with a different color of coarsely ground plant dye. Sidika was on him with a battle scream. She struck him across the face with something large and heavy, and his head slammed back against the hard dirt floor. For a moment, his vision went black, but he shot a hand out just in time to catch her wrist as she came back for more.

"Stop! Sidika, it is me!"

Sidika hesitated, panting, "What? Who?"

Emre pounded on the front door. "My lord! Lord Henri!"

"It is fine – I am well!" Henri called out loudly. "Light a lamp, for God's sake!" he hissed at her.

Snatching the rushlight from the table, Sidika held it up to his face, which bloomed with a red welt across his cheek.

"What in the name of Zeus are you doing here?" she demanded. "Did I not throw you out of my house again only days ago? How many times will it take for you to leave me alone?"

Henri groaned as he disentangled himself from the baskets. In the wavering light, he saw that she had clouted him with a semi-bound manuscript, which she now clutched to her chest. *Must be a holy book*, he thought sourly. *What else would be so heavy?*

"I came to warn you of a threat." He tried to brush a blob of white powder from his black surcoat but only succeeded in smearing it into a cloudlike pattern across his stomach.

"And you planned to warn me by robbing my house?" she demanded, raising her manuscript again, poised to strike.

"There is nothing in your house I would steal, Sidika. I had hoped to leave a message. Will you give me a drink of water? I rode my horse hard to get here."

Sidika hesitated.

"It is not proper for you to be in here. People will talk. Already they have talked of your last visit."

"Let them talk, for you will be gone by morning."

"I will not." Sidika crossed her arms. "I will go nowhere with you. I have two manuscripts to finish, and I would rather socialize with a bowl of unshelled beans than spend time in your company."

Henri finally managed to pull his feet from the last of the baskets and inspected the rainbow of dyes that painted his chest and the mail chausses on his legs.

"As you wish. A large army of Mamluks is marching in this direction, and already they enslave the local villagers. The women they are treating most cruelly for the men's pleasure." He could not look her in the eye.

Sidika sat down slowly on a bench. "But the sultan is awaiting the arrival of this physician's manual. I am sure I shall be safe from his armies."

Henri sat next to her and took her hands in his.

"Sidika, his armies would not honor this promise, for I doubt they know of it, and indeed he may not know of it either since he has only been in power for a short time. Please, you must move to the city at once."

"I will go to Cairo," Sidika said, snatching her hands back. "My brother lived there once."

"No! Sidika, you must go into Acre and even Cyprus if you can. In Cairo you would only be enslaved or taken to wife by an infidel!"

Sidika looked up at Henri.

"I mean to say, you should marry one of your own. Your kind of infidel." He hedged, rising to his feet to peer through the window toward scrubby, green hills. "I know that it was you who healed me when I was near death, and it is my fault that your honored father is dead. You will not allow me to give you protection, even though I have offered several times. Please at least allow me to warn you of this oncoming threat. I sit on the city council, and I hear of these things before others. Allow me to do this favor for your father if you will not allow me to do it for you."

Sidika looked at him.

"Thank you for the warning, and I am most grateful that you were able to honor my dead father by bringing him home. But if you think to offer your protection again, I will refuse once more. I will make my own way in this world."

"And will you listen to a warning if it is given? Do not let your pride cloud your common sense."

Sidika smiled. "These are words I would not expect to hear from you, Henri. Do they not call you *le vaniteux* in the city?"

"Can you believe me capable of change? The man I was when we first met had the pride flogged out of him."

Sidika looked at him for a long time. "Yes, you have changed. Your punishment was unjust."

"It opened my eyes to other greater injustices. For that reason, I am glad I had it." He pulled the door open. "Please seek safety in Acre if you can. If you find yourself in need of money or shelter, you may come to my house in the city. My mother and sisters are the only occupants at this time. I am still living at my home outside the walls, and you would not have to see me."

Sidika did not answer. Emre stood next to his horse, watching the door with hostility, and she watched him back, eyes wide. Never had Henri come to her house with a companion before. The man with him had tightly curled hair, which he tied back with a leather thong. He was shorter than Henri but powerfully built and dressed in the black and yellow Maron colors. His hand rested easily on the pommel of a sword hanging from his belt. The last time she had seen this man, it was in the house of the loud northman knight when Henri lay dying from his flogging.

"Sidika." Henri touched her shoulder lightly. "Please leave with us. I fear for your safety out here."

She slowly shook her head and closed the door of her house against him.

Chapter 19

April 1291
Fajar, The Hills of
Idmit

Thunk!

Sidika's eyes jerked open, and she held her breath in the pre-dawn darkness. Something had struck the side of her house. Usually, Sidika woke to the sound of the village roosters screeching at the impending sun and the morning birds trilling in the scrubby trees in the hills, but by the look of the moonlight leaking through the cracks in her shutter, it was hours before birdsong still. She rubbed her eyes and jumped as another projectile hit the wall of the small room where she slept, sending a shower of dried mud brick and plaster trickling to the floor. Shaking, she reached for her chamber pot – which was mercifully clean and empty this night – and carefully cracked the shutter open enough for her to peer through.

Outside, a small group of the village men clustered about fifty paces from the house, nervously holding a few torches. Children and women were running back and forth, gathering stones and depositing them into a pile. At the front of the crowd, she could see the firelight flickering against the craggy, slack-jawed face of Fakri, who noticed her peeking from the shutter.

"Come out, Sidika!" he shouted, "No harm will come to you!"

Sidika pulled the shutter closed and snatched her bow and a slender quiver of arrows from behind the door. Then she cracked the shutter open again.

"These men say that you have been practicing witchcraft," Fakri yelled. "The widow Nimet – she died after you visited her. She—"

"The widow Nimet had a hardness in her stomach!" Sidika yelled through the crack in the shutter. "A tumor grew within her, which is known by man but not curable. Her death was not witchcraft; it was illness!"

"You were the last one to see her. Also, Rahat's husband says that his wife will not bed him, and it is well-known you two are friends. You have poisoned her mind and her womb."

Sidika saw Rahat's husband standing behind Fakri, his features bunched into a mask of rage.

"Rahat's husband is unable to become aroused. At least, not by any man or woman. Try giving him a sheep and some time alone in the hills!" Sidika shouted back.

Rahat's husband picked up a stone and threw it at Sidika's shutter, knocking it open. Expertly, she strung her bow in the dim room and fired an arrow through the gap in the window. It was difficult to aim in the darkness, but she heard a satisfying shout as the arrow buried itself in the dust near Fakri's foot.

"Whore!" he screamed as the other men near him pelted her house with stones and pieces of dung. "How much does that pretty Franj lord pay you for time in your bed?"

Sidika's pulse thudded in her head. It was only a matter of time before they burned her house down with her inside it. She needed to buy some time and escape. Dashing to the small hole under her cupboard, she withdrew a leather bag that contained her money. She stuffed her lavender hair ribbon and her mother's necklace inside it, and a small sheaf of papers rolled around a few quills and a leather-wrapped cake of black ink.

A large stone, heaved by two men, struck the door so hard that it broke and flew open, and more rocks flew inside.

"Witch! Witch! Come out, witch!" the crowd chanted. Now they were joined by more people, and in the early dawn light, Sidika saw with a sinking heart that Rahat was there, chanting along with her husband. Sidika put her fingers in her mouth and felt the tears burning behind her eyes. She pushed the door closed and shoved a table in front of it. Her father would have gone outside and soothed the crowd with a smile and reassuring words, but Sidika hated crowds and feared them. As she paced around the room, trying to calm herself, her eyes rested on a pot of red powdered clay, and a ridiculous, impossible idea came to her. This would only work if she acted fast before the sun fully rose over the mountains.

***

At length, the crowd tired of yelling at Sidika's house, and some of the men attempted to climb on the roof to pry back the skylight, but they scuttled away when they heard a low moaning coming from within. The door slammed open, and a shrouded figure emerged from the house, screeching in a high, unnatural voice. The crowd jumped and skittered back like startled insects.

Sidika stood in the doorway, clad in an oversized, billowing black robe, her hair a scarlet mane flying wildly around her head. Her face was dark red, and her teeth were red-black in the pre-dawn light, giving the impression that she had just torn into the flesh of a live animal. She snarled and hissed at the crowd, waving a small brazier of coals in the dim, gray light.

"You are right, I am a witch!" she screamed. "I curse you with a pestilence so vile that your children's children's children shall also be afflicted! May the milk of your women become poison in their breasts, and may the penises of your men boil with blisters!"

The crowd shuffled back in alarm, and a few of them shouted and ran, but Rahat's husband picked up a rock and threw it at her.

"We will not fall for your tricks, you dog's daughter!"

Sidika laughed and threw a handful of the powdered red iron and clay at Rahat's husband, which produced a great puff of noxious-looking dust. He stumbled backwards, tripping as the other villagers scrambled out of her way.

Reaching into her father's cloak, she drew out the little powder-filled reed she had purchased during her trip to Damascus. The old Mongol man who sold it to her promised it would produce a thunder louder than the flatulence of God. The reed was full of mysterious black powder and stopped at each end by a tuft of sheep's wool. When the little twine was lit, it bloomed loudly into purple and red flowers that smelled of sulphur.

Sidika touched the twine to her brazier now and threw it against the rocky ground. It bounced and sparked in the darkness, and for a moment, she feared the old man had tricked her. Then there came a roar so loud that the noise drowned even the screams of the villagers. Sidika held her head, dazed. She had fallen back against her front door. A small scorched crater smoldered where she had thrown the packet. Ears ringing from shock, she got up and dragged herself back into the house. The villagers were gone, scattering back to their homes.

"That magic was worth every bezant that I paid for it," she said aloud to the empty house in a shaky voice.

Snatching up her sack, she tossed in a loaf of bread, a cloth-wrapped parcel of salted antelope, and her rolled-up dress and brooch from the Templars. She slung a full waterskin over her arm, and after tying the sack to her back, she stole quietly into the hills, away from the main track that ran through the village.

She stopped at a small creek to wash the clay powder from her face and hair and wring out her father's best black cloak. Her mind felt numb as she rearranged her belongings in the sack and then sat staring at the trickle of water through the reeds. From now on, she was on her own. She knew that she could ask for the viscount's house in Acre, and Henri's family would take her in. Instead, she set her jaw. It was clear that she could trust no one, and a Franj least of all.

But if you had trusted him when he came to warn you weeks ago, you would not be fleeing your house like an outcast now, her mind taunted her.

"It is too late," she said aloud to the creek. "I will not debase myself by asking for assistance from that indulged caracal!"

Tamrat and Sara had no family left in Acre, but a community of Jews could be found in every large city. She would find them, and perhaps they would allow her to work as a scribe. Despite her sadness, she felt a thrill of excitement. Adventure awaited her in Acre.

Chapter 20

April 1291
Al-Hadiqa, Palestine

"**N**ephew, it is time."

Ibrahim's voice echoed in the great hall where Henri stood looking up at the white plaster and mosaic ceiling.

"I will follow. I wish to make one last round to ensure everything is in order," Henri replied, and Ibrahim nodded, squeezing him on the shoulder before turning to leave.

First, Henri walked through the sleeping chambers and various halls. He stood for a while in his father's room, now empty except for the denuded frame of the bed where his father, and then Mafeo, had slept. He stared for a moment at the dark brown stain where Mafeo had died, pinned to the planks by an arrow. He and Emre had hidden the stain under a woven mat, but the murder seemed so inconsequential, now that the entire city was facing extinction.

Descending to the lower floor, he walked through the empty storerooms, the great hall, the detached kitchens with their iron-geared roasting spits and blackened stone tables. He strolled through the small hall where the household servants slept and into the courtyard, which had sheltered his villagers before he relocated them to Acre and Cyprus. With their tents removed, it truly looked like an army had already lived there; the dusky-leaved lavender plants had been trampled, and scorched circles dotted the ground where the women had set up their cooking fires.

My people. Henri shook his head. *If we defeat the Mamluks and return to this place, how can any of us ever go back to the way things were?*

Turning into the citronnier, he walked among the lemon trees, pulling down thrip-infested leaves and brushing the slender trunks with his fingertips. A few fruits that had survived the harsh winter still peeked through the branches, and the air smelled of resin, changing to a sweet spiciness as he moved on to the taller cinnamon groves.

He took deep, greedy breaths, like a man emerging from a long swim under dark water. Pulling out his jeweled dagger, he hewed fragrant sections of a branch from two of his trees – one lemon wood and one cinnamon. These he placed in a small leather pouch that hung from a thong around his neck. Reaching down, he chose a smooth, pale stone from the dirt beneath his feet and also put it in the little pouch.

Giving the citronnier one last long look, he strolled through the silent courtyard again, swung the wooden gates together and locked them, then heaved the great iron grate shut over that. For one wild moment, he wanted to change his mind, to increase the garrison at the house and stay. On the horizon, he could see Emre astride his horse, patiently waiting for him at the road.

Mounting Raven, he turned and lingered on the sight of the house, gleaming in the late winter sunlight. Peeking above the walls, the tops of the lemon and cinnamon trees shivered in a breeze. Henri also shivered. He could sense change coming as clearly as he could see the clouds above. Slowly taking in the house, the hills, the sky, he felt the weight of loss and the joy of the new all at once.

"Allons en ville, Raven," he said quietly. "Let us go to the city."

Chapter 21

April 1291
Acre, Palestine

The citizens of Acre stubbornly continued business and life as usual, but expressions of worry painted every face in the souks. As more people evacuated over land and by sea, the city grew quieter, except at night when the remaining residents drank away their fears and took to the streets to sing or rage. Nasira closed the paned glass shutters against the night, but they were scarcely effective at dampening the noise.

She sat with her children and Ibrahim in the main room of their city house, which was lushly appointed with mosaiced floor tiles of blue and white. Silk tapestries of blue, cream, and rose hues adorned the walls, and oil lamps blown from amber-colored glass hung from long chains, illuminating the white plastered ceiling, painted with a frieze of trees waving and dancing in a field. Her husband had told her they were beech trees, which grew in Francia, but she had never seen one with her own eyes. Several frilly palms and large-leafed plants imported from south of Nubia grew in massive stone pots, casting serene shadows on the walls from the flickering lamps.

Saruca sat primly at her ivory-inlaid table, working figures on her abacus and talking under her breath. Blanche scowled at her embroidery, slowly drawing rich silken threads through the linen backing of a tapestry, her pregnant belly a sweet little bulge under her loose gown. Ibrahim and Henri hunched over a stack of papers and several bags of coin that they had recently retrieved from a return shipment at the Court of the Chain. And Nasira paced the room, wringing her hands, her embroidery sitting idle.

"Mother, you will wear a trough on the floor," Henri mumbled without looking up.

"What is it, Niece?" Ibrahim asked, watching her with worry in his eyes. Since moving from the country and with most of the servants evacuated, there was an unspoken agreement among everyone to do away with pretense and give Ibrahim his place in the family. Ibrahim was a small, quiet man, but he seemed to grow in stature and personality with the change, and he spent as much of his time as he could sitting with Nasira and the girls or talking with Henri, trying to snatch back the years that he had lost as a servant.

Nasira left the room and returned moments later, clutching a scrap of paper. It contained a figure – a large sum of florins.

"What is this?" Henri asked.

"This," she said through clenched teeth, "is the sum of gold that Balducci asked from us to secure a boat for Marseilles."

Henri looked at the paper again. "I could purchase a hundred camels for this much gold. Does the Patriarch know that the ship captains are inflating the prices this much?"

"I do not know."

"I shall go to the harbor myself tomorrow and see what is to be done," he said, adding, "but you should know that I intend to stay and protect the city with the knights after you leave."

Ibrahim looked up sharply, and Nasira crossed her arms, setting her jaw. "You will not."

"I shall," Henri said, bending over his work again. "They may not have knighted me, but I will do the honorable thing."

"Fine. Then I shall stay too. Your sisters can go to Marseilles with Ibrahim."

Henri set his quill down. "You will go, even if I must have you bound, gagged, and thrown in the hold of the ship."

"I was born here. My father and his father were born here. I will not leave my city!"

"Your father was born in Galilee, and so was his father. You and my sisters will leave with the servants and my uncle." Henri stood to go, and Nasira balled her fists.

"You have lost your right to make decisions for me, Hamza. I shall stay here."

"Mother, I do not ask this to belittle you. It is for your safety, and—"

"And what? Am I not also allowed to defend my home? Can I not also take up a bow and fight on our walls like the other women of the city?" Nasira snapped. "I have seen them up there, fighting alongside their husbands. If you stay here to protect the city, then I stay to protect you and your sisters!"

Ibrahim watched them volley back and forth, alarmed.

"I appreciate your concern, Mother, but I do not need your protection."

"A woman's children always need her protection!" Nasira was on her feet. "All of those years, I watched as Sir Geoffroi turned you into a beast, and I was helpless to do anything!"

"You are not helpless, Mother. I would feel safer if you protected my sisters and the servants in Marseille so I can do my duty to the city. It would ease my mind greatly."

"I have only had my son back for such a short time," Nasira sobbed. "You children are all that I have left of Rogier…"

A hammering on their door stopped Nasira mid-sentence, and Ibrahim jumped to his feet. He returned a moment later leading two men; Sir Grailly swaggered into the room, and Brother Gregoire, who was not allowed to speak to women, followed him, looking resolutely at the floor. Nasira wiped her eyes and excused herself as Henri rose to clasp their hands.

"Sirs, to what do I owe this pleasure? Usually, Brother Gregoire does not come to call unless it is to summon me to some unpleasant task, like being whipped in the public square," Henri said, casually pouring himself a cup of wine from a cloth-covered pitcher.

"The scouts atop the walls have seen the smoke of the Mamluk army as it makes its way toward Acre. By tomorrow night, they will be camped outside the walls," Brother Gregoire began. "Henri, you said you would stay and fight. Do you still wish it?"

"I still wish it. Tell me what you require of me," Henri replied, taking a deep breath.

Grailly spoke up. "We require you to be a knight, Lord Henri. How many years have you?"

Henri's heart jumped. "I passed my eighteenth year only four months ago."

"Excellent. If you are prepared to take the oath, you need to take it tonight."

"Tonight?"

The seneschal huffed with impatience. "Yes. I know that it is not the normal way of things, but we do not have a day's time for you to make your peace with God. I am afraid you will have to make that peace right before you shed blood in his name and the name of the Kingdom of Jerusalem. What remains of it, at any rate," he muttered under his breath.

Brother Gregoire raised an eyebrow. "Unless you do not wish to become a knight?"

"Yes! I wish to be a knight! I am ready." Henri's heart beat faster.

"Good. Prepare yourself and then meet us at the citadel of the Templars after vespers. We will perform the ceremony there," Seneschal Grailly said, standing. "It is unusual, but, well, these are unusual times."

The men took their leave, and Henri sat in stunned silence, staring at the wavering light of an oil lamp.

"I know you are both listening," he called out, and the door slowly creaked open. Nasira and Ibrahim sheepishly walked in. Nasira took Henri's hands.

"My son, is this true what they say? You shall be knighted?"

"It is true. I must prepare." Henri rose nervously.

Nasira took a slow, deep breath. "You will fight on the walls?"

"If I am knighted, I will probably be on the ground, not the walls, although my skill at archery is greatly improved due to Emre's excellent training," he said, smiling.

"Please do not do this. Come away with us. I will go to Marseilles as you asked. Please come with your sisters and me!"

"Mother, this is my home. I cannot defend al-Hadiqa and my villages, but the servants and settlers have been evacuated, and Acre is defensible."

"It will be a slaughter, Henri," she said, the tears now rolling freely down her cheeks. "Your father barely survived the Mamluk army. Please do not stay here!"

But Henri was too excited to hear. He called for Durant.

"Saddle Raven and bring my sword. I am to be knighted this very evening at the citadel of the Templars," he ordered when the aging master-at-arms appeared in the room.

"Oh, my lord, it is a moment I have waited for since you were a boy!" Durant's eyes shone, and he hurried away to make preparations. Nasira dried her tears, composed herself, and sat quietly with her hands in her lap, head held high. Henri knelt in front of her.

"Mother, it will be well. Everything I endured at Sir Geoffroi's was to bring me to this moment. Although I am not perfect in the eyes of God, I feel that I have grown in spirit these past months. I am ready for this. It is my time!"

Nasira nodded quietly. "Every day our sons give their blood to water the earth, and their bodies to feed the fish in the oceans," tears began to roll down her cheeks again, "and our daughters lose their virtue and their souls to the conquerors, and our land is devoured by fire."

"Mother," Henri pleaded, "please do not say such things, for father always kept us safe. See, Emre is here as well – you could not be better protected than in his hands and my uncle's."

Nasira looked at him with hollow eyes. "Those were the words of your grandmother, the day the Franj burned her home, and we fled to Acre from Galilee."

Ibrahim gently took her by the arm and escorted her to her chambers. Henri knew he ought to comfort his mother, but he felt much too excited, too nervous.

Before his knighting ceremony, a young man spent the entire evening in a vigil of prayer and contemplation to ponder his new responsibilities and give thanks to God. Dropping to his knees in front of the glowing coals in the fireplace, Henri prayed inwardly.

Lord of heaven, grant me the fortitude to face what is coming as the enemy approaches, and grant me the purity to serve you as a knight in your army. I wonder who will conduct the ceremony? Brother Gregoire? Seneschal Grailly?

Jesu Christi, forgive my wandering thoughts. Please grant me the fortitude and concentration needed to serve you and protect your Kingdom of Jerusalem, which is the inheritance of all Christians everywhere.

"The inheritance of Christians everywhere."

The words rattled around in his head.

Why is it the inheritance of French Christians if we only arrived two hundred years ago and the Arabs and Jews lived here a thousand years before that?

The heretical thought jolted Henri from his prayer. He had blasphemed on the very day he was to be committed to God's service. Whose land was this? Was it his? King Henry's? The Holy Father's in Rome?

Panic swirled around him. The Mamluk usted who attacked his house months ago said he pitied the conflict Henri had within himself. Part oppressor, part oppressed. The conflict within him was always there – unacknowledged and hidden away. He rested his forehead against the cool, veined marble wall of his study and pictured the two halves of him standing side by side; a nobleman in a velvet cloak with a ring on his finger next to a villager in a keffiyeh with a prayer rug under one arm.

"I do not belong here," he whispered to the ground, clenching his fists. "I belong to no land… to no cause. Taking my vows does not mean I am a knight in the eyes of my peers. I am not one of them."

He slumped onto the cold stone floor and wept.

***

A short time later, Henri and Raven walked through the eerily empty streets of Acre to the Templar citadel. He had washed, dressed in his finest armor, and pushed his existential questions deep back into his heart. In the growing dark, he could hear the roar of the waves as they swept across the reef and slapped the limestone walls of the bulky fortress.

Dark clouds slid sulkily across the sky, which turned from a dusty pale blue at the horizon to black velvet directly overhead. A quarter moon hovered low, casting a wan light on Raven's glossy coat.

A monk greeted Henri at the citadel, escorting him to a basin of cold water to wash and instructing him to stay clothed in his family crest. After a time, the monk reappeared and ushered him into the round chapel to pray. Henri knelt at the cross and was so intimidated that he did not dare allow his thoughts to wander. The pale limestone gleamed, silk-smooth from where the Templars had knelt thousands of times before him for almost a hundred years.

Eventually, the door to the chapel opened, and several knights, some confrere and some in white robes, filed inside. Grand Master Beaujeu approached briskly.

"Well, Henri, I doubted that this day would come for you. I was so doubtful that when Seneschal Grailly informed me that he intended to knight you this evening, I insisted on doing the deed myself. I consider it an honor to have watched you transform from an irresponsible youth to an active citizen and supremely talented fighter. To think that only months ago I sentenced you to a public whipping." His gray eyes creased with amusement.

Henri reddened and hoped it was dark enough that no one could see.

"Where is your sword, young man?" The monk brought Henri's sword forward and handed it to the white-robed priest, who raised it to the tall cross in the chapel with both hands in offering and said a lengthy prayer over it before handing it to Beaujeu.

Some swords had hilts encrusted with jewels or elaborate carving depending on the knight's wealth and status. By comparison, Henri's sword was relatively simple. The hilt,

ELIZABETH R. ANDERSEN

like most, was bound with thick leather for comfort and grip. The rounded pommel glowed in the candlelight with a delicate basketweave pattern of silver and gold wires that had been flattened and smoothed to look like a fine cloth. The polished iron guard curved slightly toward the blade and was etched with an intricate mosaic. Most notable about Henri's sword, however, was the presence of a flowing stream of Arabic text, carved and filled with gold along the flat of the blade. Beaujeu paused and studied the script.

"What does this say?" he asked.

"And the angel of the Lord appeared unto him, and said unto him, 'The Lord is with thee, thou mighty man of valor,'" Henri replied. "It belonged to my father until he retired from fighting." He caught a glare from the Templar priest.

Beaujeu nodded thoughtfully.

"Henricus Jean-Rogier, son of Rogier of Maron, Viscount of Acre and Marquis of Maron-en-Ruergue, I knight you in the name of the Father God, whose words adorn your blade." He lay a hand on Henri's head and the flat of the sword on his right shoulder.

"Uphold the truth, protect the helpless, and always do good for your fellow man. Protect the innocent, no matter their creed, religion, or color." Henri could hear the tinkle of mail and armor as the knights glanced at each other. It was strange enough to have a non-Templar knighted within the citadel, but this wasn't the usual ceremony, even for a confrere.

"Your mandate is not the same as my Brethren, for you are not bound to the same mission. They are compelled to serve the Cross and Jesu Christi upon pain of ex-communication and banishment, but you are not bound in this way. Do good, not only because God commands it, but because all men should and few men do. Perhaps you can set an example for others."

Henri's eyes darted toward the priest. The man's mouth was hanging open in shock. Beaujeu continued.

"Great things are in store for you if you can live long enough to see them. Remain humble, and perhaps you can indeed become a man of valor."

Beaujeu put his hand under Henri's chin and lifted his face firmly. Then he leaned in close enough so only Henri could hear.

"No man is perfect, and you least of all. I foresee that you will suffer much. You are a Saracen and will be an outcast beyond the borders of Palestine, but because of this, you have more capacity for compassion or more cause for anger. For you, I do not know which is the correct path to take, but you will when the time is right. Do not disappoint me." With those words, he kissed Henri on the forehead, then stood and swiftly struck him across the face with the back of his hand. For a moment, bright lights flashed across Henri's vision, and his ears rang. When he put his hand to his mouth, it came back bloody. Then he heard the grand master speak the words he had longed to hear since he was a boy.

"Rise and face your peers, Sir Henri."

Henri stood. The other knights remained still and silent. Brothers Gregoire, Alaran, Lenglée, Prince Amalric, and Sir Braunhaus stood next to Sir Eirik, who grinned irreverently, his orange hair escaping the leather thong he had used to tie it into a tail. Brother Gregoire's face was solemn, but Henri thought he saw him wink in the semi-dark. Next to him stood Brother Philip, looking straight ahead, eyes unfocused, face stony with disapproval.

In the back of the chapel, lurking just outside the

doorway, Durant peeked in, not allowed to go any further. Henri grinned at his master-at-arms. He laughed, and the Templars stared at him. As a confrere, he was not bound to any rules of temperance or stoicism, and their startled reaction made him laugh harder.

"Right," Beaujeu said, clearing his throat and holding out a set of golden spurs. "Calm down now. Sir Henri, these are for you. We meet at the hour of terce to discuss the threat at our gates. Tonight, we are not Templars or Hospitallers – we are just God's men, doing what we can to keep this city and its thirty thousand souls from harm. We will prevail, for God is on our side."

"God is on our side!" The knights responded in unison.

Chapter 22

April 1291
Acre, Palestine

"Is this your first time seeing Acre, amir?"

Yusuf turned and looked at the young usted who sat comfortably next to him on his mount. He admired the man's confidence. Although his soul longed to cry out the name of Allah and rush down to claim the city, he did not look forward to the slaughter that lay before him. He dragged his gaze back to the west, over the rooftops, and across the blinding white sea.

"No, it is not the first time I have seen Acre. I have seen it many times."

Every time he had to travel between Cairo and Damascus he saw Acre, as it so happened. During his last trip, he had stopped in the city for a day to visit with his old friend Roland le Grec, who was a most worthy opponent at *shatranj* and a generally sensible man, for an infidel. Roland, a fallen priest, kept his adoration of Greek women no secret from anyone, earning him his surname when he lived in Cairo as a translator for Yusuf's master, Badahir. His exceptional knowledge of the workings of Acre's defenses and political intrigues made this an especially fruitful visit, and Yusuf had a trove of valuable information to relay to Khalil upon his return to Cairo.

Yusuf had been elated on his last trip through Acre, for he had just secured his second wife, a young woman of an influential Damascene family, who would travel to his home in Cairo as soon as the battle for Acre had ended. Yusuf planned to send fifty guards to travel with her, but he feared even that was not enough. The Christians were mostly hiding inside their double walls right now and would soon be eradicated, but the Mongols and the Bedu still prowled the roads, causing trouble for travelers.

She was much younger than his first wife, Abreshmina, had been when they married, but the girl's father assured him that was a good thing. Better to have a young wife with more energy in the marital bed and the birthing chair, and besides, Amir Sanjar al-Shuja'i's oldest son was already beginning to sniff around like a hungry dog, her father said. Her face was homely, but her manners were gentle and sweet. Yes, she might even be pleasanter to live with than Abreshmina, who sulked when she did not get what she wanted.

Yusuf blinked hard. It was the eve of battle. Staring at the tall, fortified walls of the last great Christian city in Palestine was no time to become sentimental about a wife that he had not even bedded yet. He needed to focus. Tersely, he ordered the young usted to collect a report on the city's northern flank, for the regiment from Hama was setting up their terrible machine on that side of the city just as another rose in the south. From where he stood, Yusuf still could not perceive any siege machines that seemed more menacing than the rest. Abū al-Fidā, the young usted in charge of the Hama unit, bragged much about his mighty trebuchets, but Yusuf had seen little result so far.

"Amir Yusuf?"

A youthful fursān with blonde lashes and brows slid from his horse and bowed low.

"Lord Khalil is asking for you in his tent on the potter's hill."

"You may refer to me as 'lord' and Khalil as 'his eminence, the sultan,'" Yusuf muttered. The young man looked up fearfully.

"I beg of his and your forgiveness, Lord Yusuf."

Yusuf waved him away and turned his mount toward the flat-topped hill, where Khalil's masons were assiduously pulling the walls down on what appeared to have been some kind of church with an olive press attached to it. Nearby, another group of masons, slaves taken from the hill villages, chipped the stones into projectiles for the siege engines. Nothing must be wasted.

Beyond the masons, Khalil's red tent heaved in the wind.

It was dark inside the tent, and Khalil paced with nervous excitement.

"It is a fair shame that we will not preserve this city," the sultan remarked as Yusuf entered and genuflected. "The sea breezes here are fresh in my nostrils, even though I can smell the stink of the infidels living within the walls. Stand up, for God's sake."

Yusuf rose and stood stiffly, hands folded in front of him where Khalil could see them. He kept his face pleasant, hiding his unease. Khalil's newfound authority had made him cruel. Just a few days prior, Yusuf had had to bear witness to another strangling. This time it was a eunuch who had reportedly been gossiping about Khalil's toileting habits to the other servants.

"What of the Furious and the Victorious?"

"I cannot yet see them rising above the other machines, but Abū al-Fidā swears to us on the bones of his grandfather that they will be as magnificent as we have been led to believe."

"Good. Let the Franj become lulled and comfortable before the engines are finished. We will draw out their dread."

"Wise, my lord."

"What is wrong with you, Yusuf?" Khalil swatted at a fly, and a small slave boy rushed forward to chase it out of the tent. The sultan sat down heavily on his gold chair, set up facing the front door. He looked out of the open flaps, tapping his fingers impatiently on the chair's padded arms.

"Nothing, my lord. I am fatigued from the journey."

"Then go sleep. Take a woman or some wine. Have you seen the quantity of ice that al-Shuja'i brought with him from Damascus? The residents of this city chill their fruit with it."

"I do not drink wine, my lord," *and neither did you*, Yusuf thought to himself, *until you took your throne.*

Khalil sprang from his chair and resumed his pacing. "Have you seen Lajin?"

"He was on his way to the east to assist in calming some of the fighting that had broken out within our ranks. The Kipchaks and the Seljuks have been at each other again, and two men have already died in duels."

"Ha! Doubtless, Lajin is using that as an excuse to evade me. He will be on his way over the mountains to flee to the Mongols before the day is done, mark me." His anxious fingers tapped his thigh. "You will go find him, Yusuf. Bring him back to me."

"Me, my lord? On the eve of battle? Can we not send a small troop of 'askari led by one of my trusted usteds?"

Khalil turned slowly, and Yusuf felt a spreading dread roll through his body.

"Yes, you, Yusuf. Lajin spoke ill of me before I claimed the throne, and he has been avoiding me ever since. I want him arrested."

Yusuf was speechless. He commanded one of the largest regiments from Cairo – hundreds of blue-clad furisiyya and 'askari of his house looked to him for leadership during battle. To be asked to leave at this time was madness and folly. Khalil noted Yusuf's delay with narrowed eyes, but he waited. Behind the throne, in the dark shadows of the tent's recesses, Yusuf saw movement, and his hand went instinctively to the hilt of his dagger. For a moment, Khalil stepped back, alarmed.

Shams Ibn al-Sal'us emerged from the dark, hands clasped ingratiatingly, and Khalil relaxed.

"Ah. For a moment, I thought my good friend Yusuf was about to plunge his dagger into my heart. He must have meant it for you, Shams."

The man favored Yusuf with a thin smile and bowed deeply to Khalil, touching his fingertips to his forehead.

"My lord sultan," he mumbled, "Lajin moves further away from us. If he escapes, he may try to parley with the Mongols and band against you. Is it not time for the amir to be on his way?"

Few people had any fondness for al-Sal'us, who was not even a Mamluk or a descendent of one, but Yusuf had reserved judgment until this moment. He now knew that he hated al-Sal'us as much as the other amirs did.

"I will find Lajin and bring him back, your eminence," he addressed Khalil and ignored the groveling wazir. "And if Allah wills it, I will be back in time to lead my troops into battle, where we will take the city."

Chapter 23

April 1291

Acre, Palestine

Khadir ben Schmuel answered the knock at his door, expecting to see the pockmarked face of young Yaov, the son of a renowned rabbi from Strasbourg. The boy had been sent to Acre to study the Torah closer to the home of God, and to avoid the pogroms that occasionally flared in the Frankish territories near the Holy Roman Empire. In Acre, however, Yaov's parentage meant little. Were Khadir's sister not married to the Yaov's uncle, he would have told the boy to move along, for Yaov was as rude as he was stupid.

These thoughts were in his head, and the words perched on his tongue, prepared to give Yaov the usual verbal lashing for being out past dark, but they died on his lips when instead of a surly youth, a young woman peered up at him.

"What in the name of…"

The girl curtseyed politely, and that was when Khadir noticed her large traveling sack and the dust on the hem of her dress.

"Honored master, I am the daughter of your friend, Tamrat ben Moshe. Forgive me for disturbing you after sunset. I was delayed in my travels due to the presence of soldiers on the road."

"Sidika? Tamrat's daughter! My child, why are you not in your village? Have the Muslims taken it?"

"Indeed no, Adohn Khadir. I left of my own will."

"You have left your husband?"

She looked up at him, her eyes crinkling with amusement. "I have no husband, good sir. I am seeking employment and shelter in the city with my father's kinsmen."

"Kinsmen? Ha!" Khadir snorted and then looked fearfully past her into the darkened street. "Come inside, come inside. Banat!" he bellowed. "We have a guest for the evening."

Banat, his wife, did not need to be called. She had been sullenly removing bread from the crumbling tabun at the other side of the room when the girl knocked on the door. She approached, blowing on her fingertips to cool them after handling the hot loaves.

"What is this, then?" Her eyes narrowed.

"Wife, this is Sidika bat Tamrat ben Moshe ha Shofer. You remember my old friend Tamrat from Damascus, do you not?"

"Tamrat the heretic?"

Khadir glanced nervously at the girl, whose face looked stricken.

"No, my dear, not a heretic. A visionary! Sidika will stay the night with us, and tomorrow we shall discuss options for her employment here in Acre."

Banat started in openmouthed disgust. "Young woman, how old are you?"

"Sixteen, madame."

"And why are you not with your husband? Have you left him?

"I am unmarried, madame."

Khadir huffed. Banat was just antagonizing the girl.

"And why are you unmarried? Surely your father

arranged a match for you before he died?"

"My father was unable to arrange a match before he died, madame."

The girl responded well to Banat's inquisition. Better and better. Khadir clapped his hands together. "Sidika shall bed with Rashida and you tonight, my dear, and I will sleep with Yaov and Ari."

Banat shrugged and returned to her tabun. "Rashida!" she yelled. Their seven-year-old daughter peered around the corner of the partition that separated the donkey from the house's main room. "Your father commands you to share your bed with this spinster. Make room for her."

The little girl crept from the stall and added a thin coverlet of sacking to the pile of straw where she slept. Outside, they heard the drunken slur of men singing roughly in Hebrew, and Khadir sighed. Ari and Yaov were home.

***

For a moment, Sidika thought she had overslept. In Fajar, her little rooster usually perched atop the stable roof and greeted the sun, waking her and all of the hens at the same time.

She heard a rooster, but it was far off and unfamiliar. His cry was full-throated and bold – an older bird, unlike her adolescent cockerel with his youthful, cracking voice. She blinked at the ceiling – unplastered mud brick. No skylight. She heard a loud snore and looked to her left. Khadir's son had rolled drunkenly from his straw and lay directly on the packed dirt floor, his arms flung over his head.

Sidika extricated herself carefully from the bed and stole outside. There was a well near the house, and she drew a pail full of water, splashing her face and hair. She heard the disapproving cluck of a tongue behind her. Banat, Khadir's wife, stood with two empty water skins.

"We thought you had left us. Well, I see you have gone into the street with your head uncovered, and you bathe in public. I should not be surprised, though I suppose it is not your fault, being raised by Tamrat and Sara away from the influence of your own kind."

She dropped the water skins at Sidika's feet.

"Since you are already here, you might as well fetch the water today. Do not bother being quick about it. If you stir up shit in the water and bring back skins full of mud, I will just send you back again."

She turned and stomped back to the house.

When Sidika returned, staggering under the weight of the full skins, Banat took them wordlessly and then turned her back. After a prolonged silence, she called over her shoulder. "Well, girl, are you going to sit there like a Franj and watch while I do all of the work, or are you going to help me with this meal? Today is Shabbat, and I have much to do before sundown."

All day, Sidika worked beside Banat, who only spoke to give directions or comment on Sidika's lack of domestic education. When they had finished preparing the meal, they mended Ari and Yaov's torn clothes. The two boys were out with Khadir, who, because of his language mastery, worked as a translator for the rabbi at the local synagogue.

Sidika remembered her father speaking fondly of his friend Khadir, who had a mind that quested for knowledge and a great booming laugh. However, the man of this house seemed cowed by his wife and intimidated by his wild son.

When they all came trooping back to the house before sunset, the rabbi was in tow with them. Ari and Yaov had hardly been coherent when they arrived the night before, and Sidika was out of the house before they woke. Now they both watched her with interest, Yaov, in particular, tugging on his forelocks and glancing at her over the light of the candles at the meal.

The rabbi expressed little interest in Sidika or her parentage, and so she spent the meal mostly looking at her plate, eating little, and saying nothing.

When the candles burned low, the men leaned back in their chairs and complemented Banat on the food, their full bellies pushing the sashes at their waists. Banat gave an annoyed head wag, indicating that Sidika should clear the table of the meal and dirty plates.

"But madame Banat, it is Shabbat. I mustn't."

Banat snorted. "What is the use of having a goy at the table with us if she will not even clear the mess?"

"I am not a goy."

"Ah, well," Khadir broke in, "I am sure we would never ask such a thing of a guest, goy or otherwise, would we?"

Banat looked at him balefully over the dwindling candle. Ari and Yaov both sniggered, and the rabbi seemed to be dozing in his seat.

"Rabbi, Sidika's father was Tamrat ben Moshe. You would not have heard of him since you are new to our city, but he was a fine scribe. The most talented in Acre! He was lately killed by a Franj." Khadir shook his head sadly.

The rabbi's drooping lids opened, and he raised a brow. "A pity," he yawned. "I need scribes these days. The hands of the old men at the synagogue shake so that it is getting more difficult to read their transcriptions. Perhaps young Ari, you would come to work with me?"

He looked expectantly at Ari, who squirmed in his seat.

Sidika brightened. "I am a trained scribe, honored rabbi, and I would be pleased to offer my services. I am looking for employment in Acre."

Around the table, all of the faces focused on her, astonished. The rabbi looked at Khadir, who reddened.

"The girl was raised in a mountain village, far from here. I give thanks that she has come to stay with us that Banat can train her how to behave for a marriageable young woman."

"Well," the rabbi said. "Let us hope so. Girl, is your husband deceased that you are unmarried? You look about fifteen years of age to me."

Sidika ground her teeth, but kept her countenance pleasant. "No, rabbi. There were no marriageable men where I lived—"

"You lived in a village nearby?"

Sidika nodded.

"Why did your father not seek out a husband for you in Acre? Many fathers have traveled far to find suitable matches for their children."

"Her father was an apostate, rabbi, and she his foundling. It is out of kindness and charity that my husband has taken her in. We will find a match and see her settled," Banat answered.

The rabbi nodded sagely. Khadir cleared his throat.

"Well, there are two eligible young men at this table—"

"Husband, we shall not speak business on Shabat," Banat interrupted.

Khadir smiled. "You are right, my dear, but I can converse. Come, Sidika. Are not Ari and Yaov fine-looking boys? Boys, would it not be desirable to have an educated wife who could teach your children?"

The boys stared at Sidika, and her mortification was complete. Banat stood.

"We will find her an *appropriate* husband. No son of mine will marry the daughter of Tamrat ben Moshe!"

Sidika sprang to her feet so quickly that her chair tumbled behind her. "Do not speak of my father in this way!" She could barely say the words. "My father loved me as his own flesh and blood. He spoke kindly of your husband always. How dare you say such things about him!"

She turned and ran from the house, slamming the door behind her.

"Ungrateful, wretched girl," she heard Banat calling out behind her. "Did anyone teach you not to run on Shabbat?!"

Chapter 24

April 1291

The Accursed Tower, Acre

Henri stared at the pocked, glowing moon from his perch atop the Accursed Tower. The city of Acre, roughly triangular in shape, was enclosed in a double layer of walls, with the Accursed Tower guarding the apex of this triangle where the eastern corner of the wall met the northern one. The moon's light silvered every rooftop, tree leaf, and spear tip in the city. Although the days had started to grow hot, the April evenings were still cool enough to warrant a small fire in the hearth to keep the chill away, and violent storms regularly swept in from the sea.

The city had not been idle since one of Beaujeu's spies had produced replicas of the Mamluk arsenal under development in Damascus. Siege weapons hunched in the city squares, the extensive slums outside the walls were cleared, and the fosse dredged to make it harder for an enemy to find material to scale the walls. Henri gazed out to the east, across the plains toward the hill called Le Touron – the tower hill – where the Templars kept an olive press, which they had now abandoned. Beyond it, an orange haze shimmered on the horizon; the campfires of the Mamluk army. He stared at the glow in disbelief.

His city lay besieged by the largest army ever seen in the

land, and he stood on the walls, not as Henri of al-Hadiqa or Henri of Maron-en-Ruergue but Sir Henri, a knight in God's army. The swiftness of the whole thing made everything unreal, and he worried that he would wake in his bed and it all would have been a dream. And yet, after his investiture in the citadel, Durant had clapped him on his scarred back, and Sir Eirik picked him up in a rib-crushing embrace. His status among his peers had elevated, but he felt no different.

For the nobility, the ceremony was largely the same: spend a day in prayer and receive the investiture from the king or another high-ranking noble knight. The words changed, but the philosophy was always the same. Say a prayer. Receive a resounding slap across the face to ensure that the message would not be forgotten. After that, feasting and general revelry, possibly even a parade through the streets.

The Henri Maron of one year ago looked forward to that public display of superiority more than the actual duties of being a knight. Now he only felt the hollowness of the pomp and the shallow way that men tried to use the ceremony and their lofty titles as a way to provide legitimacy to their greed and thirst for blood or status.

Nothing had gone as he imagined. He had killed men with his hands. He had made decisions that were disastrous for his mother and sister. The babe was beginning to show on Blanche's slender frame, and he could not stay in the same room with her, so powerful was his guilt. He thought back to that day when he decided to arrange a marriage to his sister, mostly out of spite. He would do anything to bring himself back, to make a different choice. Again, he wished that someone had stood up to him. He paused, realization tingling all over him. *Mother stopped me. She married Mafeo instead and protected Blanche… from me.*

"This is the most important of Acre's towers," Amalric interrupted his thoughts, "it is the weakest point that the Mamluks can exploit. Jesu Christi himself looked upon this tower and called God's wrath upon it a thousand years ago. You stand upon a holy curse!" He slapped Henri on the back with a raving laugh and strode away to check his troops along the walls.

Henri wished Emre were on the wall with him, for he could let himself talk unguardedly around his friend. Were it not for Emre's pronounced Mamluk accent and way of carrying himself, he probably would have been allowed, but Henri was afraid a Templar might try to stab him. He looked up at the sound of another footfall and drew back as Brother Philip approached and looked out upon the plain at the orange glow in the distance.

"Are you not supposed to be guarding the northern suburbs right now?" Henri asked.

"You may now have the title of 'knight,' but it does not mean that who you are has changed. Never forget that." He turned, leveled Henri with a pale-eyed stare. "You are still an overindulged minor lord who does not deserve what he has."

"I have changed much in the last year, Brother Philip, but it had nothing to do with a knighting ceremony. A man is who his actions betray him to be," Henri responded, looking back out to the plain. "Your actions betray you to be cruel and small of mind."

"And yours have always demonstrated that you care only for whoring and hiding on your little estate," Brother Philip snapped. "I can see the artifice in your newfound morality."

Henri smirked. "But I have Beaujeu's favor, and you do not." He walked further down the wall. Brother Philip followed him briskly, grabbing him by the arm.

"Listen to me, you spoiled sod. There is only one thing

that I wish to do before I die, and that is to see the light leave your eyes because my dagger is buried in your chest."

"Brother Philip, if you are so fragile that being defied by me causes you to consider murdering a fellow Christian, then you should give up the Order and become a common bandit." Henri wrenched his arm from Brother Philip's grip.

"You are not a fellow Christian, you are a Saracen, and my charter is to kill Saracens. Especially entitled thieves such as yourself!"

"Thieves?" Henri asked, blinking. "What have I stolen from you, other than the chance to take the life of an innocent man?"

"You pretend not to understand. Either you are a liar or a fool. Probably, you are both." Brother Philip turned and stalked down the wall into the darkness, his white cloak snapping in the wind behind him.

***

The next morning, and for the days following it, the Mamluk army did nothing more complicated than arrange itself into orderly regiments at a safe distance from the walls. A wagon train of timber and mangonels crawled down the sloping hills into the plain, and assembly of the wood into more siege weapons commenced. Henri wondered glumly from his perch on the walls if any of the mangonels would be constructed of lemon or cinnamon wood from his groves, and he fingered the little leather pouch at his throat. When he felt anxious, he would often rub the pale round stone he had removed from al-Hadiqa between his fingers.

He and Amalric had moved into the King's Tower on the enceinte – the lower walls that made up the first defense against invaders. From this lower vantage, the enemy seemed more numerous, the orderly dots of their tents covering the expanse of Acre's coastal plain, from the white sands of the seashore north of the city to the curving Bay of Acre to the south. Perched in the center of it all, the sultan's sprawling red tent stood out like a blister on Le Touron, its doors facing the city – an indication that Khalil intended to step out of his bed each morning to watch Acre burn.

After four days, Henri counted over twenty-five siege towers and more rising on the plain. He could not see his estate since it nestled comfortably in a shallow gully near the Yasaf creek, but his spirits sank when he considered the multitude of enemy camped on the plains. They must have taken over his house by this time.

Daily, the gates of Acre opened, and small sorties of Teutons and Hospitallers issued forth to test the enemy. Henri watched as the knights attempted to harass the attacking army while the Mamluks set up their camp. At each attack, the Mamluks dropped their tools and scrambled to their horses, some leaping atop unsaddled mounts in the way that Emre had trained him. They fought ferociously against the heavily encumbered knights, forcing the Franj back to the city.

"Do not worry, Sir Henri." Amalric stood beside him one day as Henri watched another skirmish end in failure. "This city is defensible. We have double walls, twelve towers, a deep fosse surrounding us, and all the knightly orders within the walls. And we have God's favor."

"They also think they have God's favor," Henri responded lightly.

"A false god," Amalric shrugged. "They will be humbled and turn back."

"They also think our god is false and that we worship multiple gods in the Trinity."

Amalric turned on him angrily.

"Henri, what are you on about? Now that you are a knight of the Kingdom of Jerusalem, you suddenly start speaking heresy? These words will demoralize the men, and it will earn you another beating or worse."

"Will not the sight of fifty siege weapons also demoralize the men? Amalric, we should seek a truce with Khalil." Henri willed his temper to retreat. He could not afford a confrontation with the king's brother, even if they had been boys together at the brutal school of Sir Geoffroi.

"Thank you for your council, oh wise one," Amalric said sarcastically. "Last I checked with my brother, the king, I was the constable of the Kingdom of Jerusalem, not you."

Henri hated it when Amalric reminded him who was of higher birth. It was an easy tactic to take when Amalric didn't want to admit that he was wrong. Although the two young men were friends, Amalric never let Henri forget that he was knighted younger, had royal blood, and was – at least in land – wealthier. He and his brother owned three-quarters of the buildings in Acre and vast portions of Cyprus.

"Sorry, *Constable*," Henri replied acerbically. "Will your royal brother deign to join us and defend his kingdom, or is he going to remain on his pretty little island while we all die like penned sheep at the slaughter yard?"

"I do not know why I spend so much time defending you," Amalric muttered, "you are just as disagreeable now as you were at Sir Geoffroi's."

After a full day of standing on the wall in the wind and sun, watching a sea of enemy soldiers and siege weapons surround their city, tempers were beginning to flare.

Chapter 25

April 1291

Acre, Palestine

The sun was almost up when Sidika stumbled back to the house of Khadir and Banat in Acre's sprawling Jewish quarter. She had not run far from the house after her outburst at Shabbat. The streets of a city as large as Acre were no place for a woman at night, more so now that the Mamluk army was entrenched outside the walls, for it meant that there were Franj men roaming about and looking for trouble or a warm body to slake their panic. So, she had spent several miserable hours shivering behind a haymow near a cowshed and holding her breath at the sound of every footfall. It was better than sharing a bed with Banat and her bony daughter.

She heard a scraping sound. The street sweepers were out with their twig brooms, shoveling dung and pushing bits of rubbish aside in the main thoroughfares. As the sun pulled higher above the horizon, she saw a procession of frail men and women shambling past the gates of the Jewish quarter, dressed in rags. The poor and old, begging for a spoonful of porridge from the houses and inns. As the light grew stronger, servants and goodwives emerged from darkened doorways with buckets of night soil to be emptied into the public privies. Their city may be under siege, but within the walls, all was normal.

The door to Khadir's house wrenched open, and Banat marched out with a bucket of her own. Seeing Sidika sitting on the ground next to the front door, she sniffed loudly and held the bucket out. "Empty this, then return to break your fast."

Khadir and the rabbi were just leaving when Sidika returned. Giving her a sour glance, the rabbi swept down the street without a greeting. Inside, Ari and Yaov were unwinding their phylacteries from their morning prayers, and young Rashida sat at the mending basket. The household cowed under Banat's ill-temper that morning as she slammed her spindle around and muttered under her breath.

"Gveret Banat," Sidika finally spoke. "Thank you for your generosity. I do not wish to wear a hole in your pantry, and so I will continue to seek employment. I am excited to start my life here in the city."

Banat took out a small, sharp knife, cut the thread on her spindle, and started on a new skein of wool. "Where will you go?" she asked without looking up.

"I can work as a servant in one of the great houses."

Banat snorted. "I cannot see that you would be of any use to anyone, given that you do not even know how to mend a hole in a robe."

"I can be a household scribe."

Banat put her spinning in her lap. "Enough of this talk. My husband feels sorry for you, raised as you were by such faithless parents. We will find you an acceptable marriage, and then you can move out."

"But madame, I did not ask for your husband's help in this matter."

"Silence!" Banat stood now, her wool and spindle tumbling to the floor. She was across the room in two steps, grabbing Sidika roughly by the arm. With a stinging snap,

Banat struck Sidika across the cheek. "Here is your first lesson on matrimony – do not question the man of your house! Khadir says he will help you, and that is more than you deserve."

Sidika wanted to slap Banat back. She wanted to shake the woman by her scrawny shoulders, to call the fires of heaven upon the house and burn it to a pile of charred kindling. She bit her bottom lip to keep it from trembling.

When Khadir returned to take his afternoon meal, he pulled Sidika aside and took her hand kindly. "My child, did your father ever tell you that it was I who caught you in the marketplace?"

"Yes, I remember it well, Adohn Khadir."

"I wish to see you settled. It is true what Banat says. Your father was not well liked by the Jews of Acre. Oh, he got along well with the Franj and the Muslims, the Nestorians and the Persian heathens, but he defied his father. As the eldest son, he did not continue his father's trade, and the business died. He married beneath his parents' status, and then he took his learning – the expense that his parents sacrificed! – and did he use it to teach or to copy the Torah? For a while, yes. But then he began copying other holy books. The teaching of Jesu Christi. The Qur'an. Romantic poetry, with illustrations of men and women together."

Khadir was pacing now, gesticulating.

"When the Jews of Damascus chastised him for his work, he moved to Acre, and when it happened here, he decided he did not need to be around his people. His rock of community and fellowship. That is why he moved you to the hills, my child."

Sidika sat slowly. She had known they were not a pious family, but Tamrat had never mentioned ostracism. They went to synagogue occasionally but never in Acre, and the few Jewish friends they had, while cordial, never invited the family of Tamrat to break bread.

"You see," Khadir continued, "this is why you are unmarried. But now that you are living here with us, we will help you. The others in Acre will see that you are a righteous and chaste young woman. There are some, recently arrived from Frankia and the northern countries, who do not know who your father's family were."

Her father had always told her that she could choose who she would marry. Perhaps that was not the entire truth. Perhaps he knew that she would not choose from the men of her village, and then he would not have to own up to his reputation among Acre's Jews.

No. My father did not want me to live a life like Banat's.

Khadir was still speaking.

"I have spoken to Yosi, the tanner, who moved here from England. His wife died two seasons ago, and he is looking for a good woman to raise his young children and help with the tannery. He shall come over for the evening meal tomorrow. You will help Banat prepare the meal so that you can demonstrate your cooking." Khadir smiled at her. "We will find you a better life!"

***

That evening, when Sidika offered to fetch the water, she put her mother's necklace on underneath her high-collared dress and slipped her brushes up her sleeves. She tied her small money purse underneath her skirts with her silk hair ribbon. When she walked out of Khadir's door with the two empty water skins, she didn't look back.

Chapter 26

April 1291
Acre, Palestine

L ate one evening, after his shift on the wall ended, Henri brooded over a map of the city in his study, pondering the Mamluk position in the plain of Acre and how he would evacuate his household. Ibrahim's recognizable tap sounded on the door, and the old man delivered a folded message with an unfamiliar seal.

> *Tomorrow my ship leaves Acre for Alexandroupoli. I would like to see your face, my brave knight, one last time before I must depart. I am at King Henry's house, and I await your arrival.*
> *~ Keratsa*

Henri set the note down slowly. Lady Keratsa was relentless but after days of arguing with the city leaders and interminable sessions guarding the walls of the city, his will to resist her this night was weak. He tossed the note into the fire, tucked his dagger into his belt, donned his deep blue velvet cloak, and pulled the hood over his head. Then he slipped quietly onto his small terrace, eased himself over the stone balustrade, hung for a moment, and dropped noiselessly into the street. This side of the house faced a dark alley, and he crept unnoticed through the shadows.

A short time later, he stared up at the Royal Palace, pondering how to enter without being recognized. A young boy squatted on his heels in the dust near the open door of the palace, playing cat's cradle with a piece of twine, but upon seeing Henri, he stuffed the string into a crack in the stone wall and approached.

"Gospodin Maron?" he asked, his pale gray eyes serious and still.

Henri nodded, recognizing his name but not the language the boy spoke.

"Sledvaĭte me," the boy replied, and he took Henri's hand, leading him around the back of the house where it intersected with the inner wall that separated Montmusard, the newest quarter of the city, from the central part of Acre. There, he opened a small postern door and entered a corridor as dark and yawning as an open mouth. The boy continued to hold Henri's hand, leading him carefully up a set of stone stairs in the blackness, climbing until they reached a landing lit by the anemic flame of a nearly empty oil lamp. Henri's wariness increased as they emerged into a dim, arched hall with richly carpeted walls and brass lamps swinging on chains overhead

Keratsa's determined effort to get into his bed was off-putting. With the entire Mamluk army menacing the city walls, this did not feel like a good use of his time. *Still*, he thought, *I could die tomorrow*, and in the dark, he shrugged. Better to die with his seed inside of a woman and his mind clear, even if he did not care much for the woman in question.

The boy stopped in front of a lavishly carved wooden door, knocked three times slowly, and pushed it open. Inside, candles glowed in copper basins, illuminating a suite of large rooms, the walls dressed in red and gold tapestries. The cool night air blustered into the room past the open terrace doors, ruffling the heavy crimson drapes.

The first room contained several couches of inlaid wood with plump cushions and a small ivory-inlaid table. A rich scent greeted him, and he noted that the floor mats were woven through with sweet herbs, their perfume rising sensuously with each of his footsteps. Through an open door, Henri could see an adjoining room, this one occupied by a bedstead draped with more crimson curtains. Between the heat and the red furnishings, it was like stepping inside of the warm, bleeding innards of a beast that had been opened with an axe.

The boy busied himself about the room, closing the drapes and shuttering the windows with practiced efficiency. Henri could hear sounds of splashing in the bedchamber, and he slowly walked around the corner. A massive copper tub stood near the bed, a rich cloud of steam rising from it. A sheet of red linen draped the inside of the tub, and Keratsa, her hair dark with water, watched him boldly, submerged up to her chin.

"Ostavete ni," Keratsa commanded brusquely, and the boy exited, his eyes aimed at the floor. Henri, still hooded, realized that the boy had never looked at his face, even when he approached him on the street.

"Why, Lord Henri," Keratsa said with false innocence, "you came faster than I expected. You have caught me in my bath." She swirled the water with a small, white hand. Henri pulled his hood back from his face.

"I can come back some other time if you are indisposed."

"I forbid it," Keratsa replied firmly, holding up a slender arm. Henri took her hand as she raised herself slowly from the water, wilted rose petals and buds of lavender sticking to her skin.

"Bring me my robe." She pointed to a saffron-colored silk wrap draped over a chair.

"No."

She stepped from the tub and fingered the silver and onyx clasp on his cloak.

"If you will not give me my robe, I shall have to use this, and it smells of horse. Would you have me dirty myself after I have just bathed?"

Henri unclasped his cloak and threw it on the chair, covering her robe. Putting his hands around her waist, he pulled her in close. He could feel the water from her skin soaking through his linen tunic and smell the light scent of roses in her hair.

Keratsa sighed, sinking into him.

"I have been waiting for you to come to my bed since I first beheld you. Why did you stay away until the day before I leave Acre?"

Henri couldn't speak. His desire for her was winning out over the prospect of accidentally fathering a Bulgarian heir. His breath came ragged, and Keratsa reached up, pulled his mouth to hers, and kissed him slowly, pushing her soft tongue between his lips.

"This is probably not a good idea," he breathed.

"I am sure it is not," she whispered fiercely, undoing the buckle of his belt. His dagger clattered to the floor, along with his hose, as she expertly found every button and tie holding his clothing together.

"I cannot wait any longer," she said, pulling his tunic over his head. "If you will not take me right now, I shall call the guards and have you arrested for stealing into my room."

"That would be a mistake," he murmured, "I will fight them and win."

"Then I shall bind your hands so that you cannot fight."

She grabbed his wrists and held them behind his back.

Henri broke her grip.

"Please do try, my lady."

Keratsa leaned down and grasped him between his legs, pushing his hardness against her, and Henri could have shouted with relief. He lifted her to his hips, and she put her arms around his neck, grabbing tight fistfuls of his hair. In his arms, she felt as light and insubstantial as a bird.

"What is this filthy thing?" she asked, plucking the small leather pouch by its strings from his chest and holding it as if she had a lizard by its tail.

"That contains what remains of my estate," he mumbled, breathing in the smell of her skin, kissing the warm wetness of her throat. "One stone and two chips of wood."

Keratsa pulled away.

"You have lost your estate?"

"I will get it back." His fingers delicately searched between her legs.

Keratsa was silent for a moment, then she caressed his face and laughed.

"Yes, you must get it back. For your sins, and since we only have one night together, I expect you to make your best effort to please me," she whispered.

"For this evening, I am your servant," he mumbled, walking with her on his hips to a tapestried wall and pushing her against the silk stitching, kissing her throat, her shoulders, her breasts. She moaned, and he entered her roughly, feeling relief wash over him, along with the urge to reach his pinnacle as quickly as possible. Despite the earlier protests of his conscience, his senses overwhelmed him with the release, and he groaned in his ecstasy, collapsing backwards with her on top of him onto the cotton-stuffed mattress. Keratsa laughed and ran her hands through his hair.

"Well done, my knight. Now, you may rest before I expect you to put your mouth to better use than talking."

Henri stared at the deep red canopy of the bed above him. Although his body was satisfied, he felt regret creeping upon him. What if he had put a child in her? Two more lives that he could destroy, just like his sister and her unborn. And what of Sidika? He felt somehow that he could not look her in the face again after this. *If she still lives,* his mind wandered. *I should have insisted that she come with me to the city. I should have sent Emre for her.* He did not owe her any fidelity, but the thought of her pulled at him.

"Did you hear me?" A petulant edge crept into Keratsa's voice.

"I should not be here…" he said. "I should be on the walls defending the city right now."

Keratsa crossed her arms over her breasts. "What?"

Henri sat up. "I should not have come here," he muttered, but Keratsa put her hand on his chest.

"You had satisfaction, Lord Henri, and now so shall I. Do you find me displeasing?"

"No, my lady, but I find that it is hard to concentrate on your beauty with the entire Mamluk army outside the city."

"And the entire army of Christ is facing them," she said, pushing him to his back and crawling on top of him, moving her body sinuously along his. Henri felt himself growing hard again, and his thoughts blurred.

"Ah yes," she smiled, noticing his arousal, "this is why I love young men so much. None of my husbands had more than one arrow in their quiver at a time."

Suddenly, through the closed windows, they heard a muffled roar. Keratsa sat up, pulling the coverlet to her chin. Henri jumped from the bed and ran to the window, throwing open the wood and glass screen. In the pre-dawn, drums pounded, echoing through the quiet city streets. A moment later, thousands of voices rose together in a roar, like the audience of a joust.

Henri turned to Keratsa. Her eyes were wide and frightened.

"The attack has begun," he said, "I must go."

Chapter 27

April 1291
Acre, Palestine

Henri rushed down the night-black stairwell and burst from the Royal Palace, his heavy cloak flapping behind him as he ran down the street, which now glowed gray with early morning light. The sound of the Mamluk drums thundered and echoed off stone walls and empty courtyards, filling the city with rhythmic dread. He charged through the darkened alleys and stinking slums to his house and cursed the lit candles in the windows. His mother and sisters were probably frightened, and he had spent the night dallying with the most useless princess in Acre.

He entered his house as quietly as he could, but there was no hiding.

"Hamza!" his mother cried, running down the stairs. "What in the name of God is happening?!"

His scalp prickled. Saruca was screaming in another room, her voice joining a collective cry of terror from the homes and shops nearby.

"The attack has begun," he said, crossing the hall to the stairs and climbing to his chamber. Durant was already in the room preparing his armor. The old soldier helped Henri into his padded gambeson and fixed him with a stern look of disapproval. Henri blushed and shrugged his shoulders.

Suddenly, in addition to the rhythm of the pounding drums came the deep, irregular thud of stones hitting the walls. Durant held up a shimmering mail hauberk so that Henri could duck into it, then handed him his sword and his crossbow and gave him a wordless nod. Henri quickly kissed his mother, jogged out to the stable, and hoisted himself onto Raven's back. Emre was mounted and armed, waiting near the gate. Henri shook his head.

"No, Emre. You must stay here and protect my family."

"I wish to stay with you. Together we shall defend the city."

"You will defend the city by keeping my family alive. They are the city – not these walls."

"But—"

"No!" Henri interrupted him, trotting out of the gate. "You must do this for me. You must!" He and Raven charged with an increasing flood of knights and foot soldiers towards the walls and King Henry's Tower.

"Sir Henri, where have you been?" Amalric yelled when Henri appeared at the top of the wall, but before he could answer, a stone rocked the tower just above his head, sending dust into his eyes.

"Keep your head down," Amalric said, "they have been relentlessly pelting us since the attack started. Do not worry; they cannot continue this way for long, or they will run out of stones to throw before the week is over."

The rising sun peeked over the tops of the hills to the east, and the attacking army glittered as hauberks and helmets, swords hanging from jeweled belts, and the fine trim on the saddles of the horses flashed golden in the morning light. There was a shimmer in the air for a moment as the first volley of arrows flew, and Henri recalled the small fish that would sometimes leap in their hundreds from the sea. 'Tuhliq al'asmak,' they were called. Sometimes he would catch a glimpse of them when he and the other boys swam in the sea. For a moment, he forgot about the mortal threat spread out before him, and he was frolicking in the warm waves like a porpoise, ten years old and carefree.

A scream pierced his daydream, and Henri's attention jolted back to the wall. A hundred feet away, a turcopole screeched as an arrow embedded in the top of his thigh. Another man yelped nearby, an arrow protruding from the top of his shoulder. Springing forward, Henri grabbed Amalric by the arm and dragged him back into the tower.

"Shields over your heads!" Amalric hollered, jerking himself free and running along the wall to the south.

Now some of the Mamluk arrows were lit with naft, trailing bright tails of flame, like small comets in the gloaming. Below, they could smell smoke as a thatched shelter smoldered and ignited into tongues of flame that roared in the increasing wind rising from the sea. Henri raised his shield and ran through the tower and along the wall where it turned sharply to the west.

"They are launching fire into the heavens," he shouted at the startled knights. "Shields over your heads! Move the horses under shelter! Send the women and boys for water!"

All day, as the arrows showered them and the roar of clay grenades filled with unquenchable naft rained down, the men were powerless to even look over the walls. Fresh waves of Mamluk soldiers replaced the exhausted archers at the enemy front, so that the assault never ceased. The invaders advanced patiently, sheltered behind broad shields of thatch to protect themselves from the projectiles hurled back by the Acrean soldiers from above. The air fouled with a haze of oily black smoke and ash rained down, coating every building and street with gray.

As night fell, the thunder of the drums and stones quieted, only to start again the following morning at dawn. Again, the stones of the trebuchets and mangonels pounded the walls mercilessly. Henri slept for a few hours in a stable, curled next to another knight for warmth, then ascended the tower once again only to be ordered by Amalric to defend the walls of Montmusard.

"Why do you send me away!" Henri shouted.

Amalric, his eyes red from the constant smoke of the spreading fires, whacked Henri on the back of his iron helmet.

"Calm yourself! It is not that I dislike your company, Henri, but you need to rest. I am rotating you and twenty-four other knights around the walls. Now go make sure those lazy Templars do not let anyone through, eh?"

"Fine," Henri snarled.

He stopped at his house first, and Ibrahim greeted him at the door, his face solemn.

"Your mother, sister, and the servants are all in the cellars. Nephew, what happens upon the walls? Will they stand?"

Henri began to chirp his usual encouraging reply that he used with the turcopoles – "We will win the day, for God is on our side!" – but stopped himself.

"No, they will not stand, Uncle," he said, shoulders slumping. "But there is no need to hide in the cellars just yet, I think. What news of a ship for my family?"

"A ship has been secured. It leaves three days hence."

His mother and sisters would escape. They would live. It was then that Henri felt the redness in his eyes and the ache in his shoulders from days of wearing his armor. He sensed movement and saw Emre peek around the corner of the house.

"I have barely slept," he said with a shaky laugh, "and I

must defend Montmusard. Thank you, Uncle, for taking care of my mother and sisters."

Ibrahim nodded, and another stone thudded into the church tower in the distance, the deep boom of the impact shuddering through the ground under their feet.

"I think that your bodyguard has seen battle before, Nephew. Emre is very unsettled by the drums."

"Uncle, please do not let him follow me to the walls. The Franj soldiers will turn on him."

"As you wish. Please return to the house to say farewell before we leave, Nephew. We may never see each other again," and Henri saw that Ibrahim's eyes glistened with emotion.

"I will," Henri said.

***

The double walls of Montmusard stretched from the sea in the west and around the suburb to the southeast. White-clad Templars fluttered back and forth along the top of the outer enceinte like moths, firing with crossbows through the crenellations and hurling clay grenades of naft back at the enemy with slings. Grand Master Beaujeu stalked among the men, shouting encouragements and giving orders to his commanders. When he saw Henri, he motioned him into the shelter of one of the many towers that studded the walls at intervals.

Inside, it was dark and relatively cool. Beaujeu's secretary hunched over a wooden table, scratching at a parchment with a battered quill, and the Patriarch sat on a bench drinking a cup of weak ale and swinging his short legs, his face grimy with soot from the clouds of smoke wafting over the city.

Henri stared. "Patriarch?"

"Sir Henri!" The old man stood and clasped Henri's shoulder. "Guillaume tells me that you are fulfilling your knightly role admirably and have been on the walls each day to defend the city. I am proud of you, my boy!"

Henri couldn't understand why the man was so happy. His fine linen robe was gray with soot, and his eyes puffy from lack of sleep.

"Yes, Father, thank you. Why are you here, Father?"

"I am here to provide cheer to the defenders," he said, standing, "and it is time I got back to my work." He drained his cup and tottered out of the tower, waving his arms and calling encouragements to the beleaguered Templars as Henri and Beaujeu looked after him.

"There goes a man who really does put his words into practice," Beaujeu said, "and now it's time for you to do the same." Waving his secretary away, he motioned for Henri to sit.

"You have fulfilled two of the three requests I made when I sentenced you for defying Brother Philip." Beaujeu toyed absently with a cake of sealing wax on the table. "Now, it is time for you to complete your punishment."

"You said I was to meet someone. That hardly seems punishing."

Beaujeu sighed. "Despite my expectations, you still prove to be impertinent. It will be punishing if you are to lose your head, non? I need you to venture outside the walls to meet my informant and learn how this army can be defeated. Since I cannot spare my secretary to do this job, and my other Arabic-speaking man was stabbed when he last tried to make contact, your grasp of Arabic is invaluable to me. I wish to God that Maineboeuf were not rotting in the citadel of Cairo right now." He rubbed a grubby hand across his eyes.

Henri swallowed nervously.

"Now do you understand the gravity of the situation, you naïve coxcomb?" Beaujeu was looking at him like a hawk who spotted its prey.

"When do I leave?"

"Immediately. Bring this." Beaujeu reached into a wooden chest under the table and withdrew a bulging pouch of gold florins.

"My lord, how am I to find this man? There are over fifty thousand Mamluks surrounding the city." Henri felt panic rising as he calculated the impossibility of the task.

"He is at your estate," Beaujeu said calmly, and held up his hand before Henri could protest, "so you will be able to find him easily. That was the arranged meeting place. He will stay until sundown tomorrow before returning to the army. The Venetians, who have finally decided to cooperate with us, will take you up the coast by ship and drop you into the sea. Is your horse a competent swimmer?"

Henri's mouth hung open. "You are going to drop my horse and me into the open ocean?"

"I have no time for you to be dramatic, Sir Henri. Can your horse get you to the shore or not?"

"Yes, she can swim as well as any other horse. She dislikes it."

"Well, tell her it is for the defense of her city," Beaujeu said dismissively. "When you meet the informant, you are to tell him that we agree to his master's terms with no conditions applied. He will have safe passage to wherever it is he wishes to go, but for God's sake, he must tell you how to disable this army and those trebuchets. Sir Henri, do not leave or hand him that gold until you have this information from him. And if you are unable to coax him to talk, then do not bother coming back to Acre."

"Am I allowed to know his name?"

"You are not, nor should you tell him yours or indicate in any way that you have been to your estate. Do not divulge that you are a viscount of this city or a marquis of King Philippe in Francia, for you would make a handsome profit as his hostage."

Henri nodded mutely, and Beaujeu withdrew a bundle from the chest.

"Here are your clothes. We will leave immediately."

Henri changed into a pair of loose, scratchy brown sirwal pants and a honey-colored tunic and sash. A large waxed-leather purse with a rolled top draped over his shoulder containing a flint and tinder, parchment and a nub of charcoal, a leather flask, some hard wheat crackers wrapped in cloth, and a small nosebag of oats. He was allowed to keep his dagger underneath his robe.

All along the docks, desperate citizens yelled over each other, begging for passage, waving their valuable possessions over their heads to try to entice a ship's captain to carry them to Cyprus. The Templars encircled Henri, pushing the crowd back as he boarded the Venetian ship.

"Hypocrite!" a man screamed at the Templars. "You would let this Saracen board a ship and leave us all behind?" Henri shielded his face as the man tried to spit on him.

Henri had once been by ship to Cyprus as a boy with his father and had cruised with Amalric and King Henry several years ago along the coast to celebrate the young monarch's coronation. It was not usually a gentle sea, and this day was no exception. Once out of the harbor, the ship pitched on the waves as a stiff spring wind from the west filled her sails. His innards rose with each roll of the hull until he heaved and vomited on the deck, staggering and spitting, to a chorus of annoyed curses from the Venetian crew.

Raven fared little better, screaming and kicking so that

no one could approach her. Henri lurched over to her and put a hand on her arched neck.

"Come now," he croaked, "this is unbecoming of a warhorse and a lady," then he fell to his knees and vomited again.

"Mannagia," one of the sailors muttered, "è un bambino disgustoso!" The other sailors laughed and joined in taunting him. "Bel ragazzo non è un marinaio!"

Several miles up the coast, the ship tacked shoreward and dropped its anchor. Henri mounted Raven, and the sailors strung several wide leather slings under her barrel. Then the two of them were winched into the air and slowly lowered overboard into the water, Henri still fighting a feeling of disbelief. He was going home, but what would he find there?

"What will happen if I cannot return until after sundown?" Henri yelled at the captain as the water soaked into his breeches.

"Then you can join the Mamluk army and find your own way into the city!" the captain yelled back. "And take care not to fall off your horse, or that gold will sink you to the bottom of the sea!" With a cackle, he ordered the crew to return the winch.

The rough waves washed over them, and Raven's eyes were wide with fear. Henri leaned forward and spoke quietly to her, his hands tangling in the black mat of her mane as it floated like seaweed around them. He pulled her head up to keep the waves from washing over her muzzle. Instinctively, she knew what to do, and once he had her turned toward the shore, she began to swim. When her hooves contacted the white sand of the shallows, she hoisted herself from the water and stumbled onto the beach.

Henri dismounted, opened his watertight bag, and rewarded his wet, irritated horse with the nosebag of oats. A sharp spring wind rose from the sea, and his teeth chattered with cold. Not wanting a salty, wet saddle to chafe her, he had decided to ride bareback with only a bridle, so there was no need to wait for any tack to dry out. By the sun's position, he estimated it to be close to midday, and judging by the location of the hills, he suspected that he had landed north of his house. That meant that a creek would be close.

They walked south on the damp, hard sand until they found the creek, swollen and brown from the spring rains. There, they turned inland and continued along the spongy grass of the flatland. Henri spied the ruins of a crumbling Roman aqueduct, then turned to the southeast, all the while keeping his ears tuned for the sounds of horses or soldiers. They continued until the green mist of scrubby trees lining Yasaf creek appeared on the horizon. From there, he turned into the forest and dismounted, leading Raven carefully among the low pine branches.

He knew exactly where he was now. Turning east again, they followed the Yasaf until he saw the small stone aqueduct that diverted water to his house. Tying Raven to a tree and giving her the rest of her nosebag, he crept carefully along the aqueduct, tensed on the balls of his feet, his nerves jumping. Just as he spied the walls of al-Hadiqa through the gray trunks of the pines, a branch snapped close to him. He dropped onto his stomach and waited, heart thundering in his chest.

An Arab man, tall, wearing black sirwals and a long, ornately woven black and silver tunic, walked into the brush, careless of the amount of noise he made. Henri tensed, easing his dagger from his robe.

The man's glittering sash and jeweled scabbard flashed as he dropped his pants and began to urinate on the trunk of a tree. Henri sprang from his hiding place, grasped the man around the neck, and pressed his dagger to his throat. The man swore and flailed his arms.

"What is the name of your daughter by your fifth wife?" Henri whispered the words that Beaujeu instructed him to say.

"Death! Her name is Death," the man answered with a strangled cry.

The words were correct. This was Beaujeu's informant. Henri released his grip and yelped in surprise as the man swiped at him with a short sword, slashing the sleeve of his tunic and drawing a thick trickle of blood from his bicep. The man stood tall and alert, pants hitched up one-handed, and held his sword at attention.

"What kind of beast takes a man while he is pissing!?"

Henri reached into his bag and withdrew the sack of gold. "A beast who has fifteen gold florins if you have information for me."

The man lowered his sword.

"And the terms that my amir requested for himself and for me?"

"All of them will be accommodated, provided you can give me information that will disable this army."

The man sheathed his sword, then turned.

"Let us go into the house to discuss it. I have made tea."

Every bone in Henri's body ached to walk through his house again, to drink tea in the courtyard, to look out over the groves and smell the perfume of lemon trees and hot soil, but he feared that were he to set foot inside the walls, he would never leave.

"No, we will talk here. I have no time for tea," he said, sitting on a large stone. "Now tell me; what weakness does this army have?"

"I tell you, there is none. Ours is the most powerful army

to walk in the name of Allah, *subhanahu wa ta'ala*," the man said. "Your walls will not withstand the bombardment for even five more days. You must take out the siege machines."

"We know that," Henri snapped. "But how?"

"You must send out a sortie of men in the night to fire the great trebuchets, especially 'The Furious,' which is at your westernmost gate, and 'The Victorious' at the south. They are guarded but loosely – only one sentry each while the men sleep, and they change shifts often. You should also know that tunneling started under your walls near your tower of curses. You must counter this with your own tunnel or find a way to make it too uncomfortable for the miners, else they will light a fire beneath you, and your walls will crumble like a house of sand under a wave."

"Is that the only tunnel?"

"For now, it is the only tunnel, though the sultan also talks of destroying the great fence you have built into the sea at your northwestern side."

Henri hesitated. "Why do you bring me this information?"

The man looked down at him, amused. "To secure riches for myself and my sons, of course. What a strange question to ask me."

"But you betray your army. This action by you will cause thousands of men to die. Your men."

The man stood, his hand on the hilt of his sword.

"Better them than me. Are you trying to talk me out of providing information to Beaujeu? Because I will happily take your head back with me to show the sultan if you think that would be a better tactic."

Henri tossed the bag of gold on the ground. "I will deliver your information to Beaujeu. Do you have any other message that you wish to deliver to him?"

The man plucked the bag of florins from the pine-scented forest floor and emptied the contents into his hand. The gold glowed warmly, even in the shade of the trees.

"Yes," he said, gazing pensively at the riches in his hand, "tell him that he should have left when he had the chance. You will all die in Acre."

Henri looked up. The sun was sinking toward the hills. He backed away and ran until he heard a welcoming snort from Raven. Untying her and discarding her empty nosebag, he leapt onto her back, and they headed west toward the ocean and the grueling swim back to the Venetian ship.

The Venetians taunted him again as they hoisted the sopping, angry horse from the water, but Henri couldn't muster the energy to turn their insults back at them as he climbed the rope ladder onto the deck of the ship. The spy that Henri had met at al-Hadiqa was right. This army was impossible to defeat, and the arrogance of the Christians would be their downfall.

***

Back in the city, Beaujeu assembled the grand masters, the seneschals, the marshals, Prince Amalric, and the Patriarch in the bowels of the Templar citadel, where it was barely possible to hear the drums and the thud of stones hitting the walls. Henri, still in his damp clothes from his return trip, stood in front of the table of military leaders, hands behind his back, and gave an account of his journey.

"Well, Beaujeu, who will you send to fire the siege engines?" Grand Master Villiers asked.

"Who indeed? I was about to ask you the same, Villiers," Beaujeu snapped.

In the corner of the room, Beaujeu's secretary looked up from his writing, tapped his quill into a dish of ink, and scratched at his parchment.

"Sirs, this constant bickering is counterproductive to our task," the Patriarch said with an exasperated look heavenward. "Let us have a jointly manned cadre that contains the knights from each order who are best known for their stealth and bravery. Sir Henri here seems to have won himself a place in that party due to his exploits this day."

Henri, exhausted and hungry, did not feel flattered. It was almost certainly a suicide mission. He thought of the amir's informant making tea inside of al-Hadiqa, and he burned with outrage.

Beaujeu grunted and shook his head.

"Sir Henri has done enough for one day. Let us first try the suggestion of the Pisans to attack the westernmost mangonels with their ship-mounted trebuchet, and then we shall send out a sortie." He looked sternly at Henri. "Young man, go home and get some rest."

Chapter 28

April 1291
The Plain of Acre

Yusuf sat up straight inside of his tent. It was small – easy to pack – and not as lavish as the war tent he had near Khalil's base of command outside Acre's walls. For a moment, he stared, befuddled, at the unfamiliar wool-felt canopy until his mind cleared. He was on the northern outskirts of the Mamluk army, which had filled the plain of Acre. He sought Lajin, the errant amir, on behalf of Sultan Khalil. He did not wish to be here.

"Curse me for an infidel. The attack has begun without us," he heard one of his men grumble. Indeed, it was the thud of drums that had pulled Yusuf awake, not the lessening dark of the dawn.

Outside, the twenty men he had brought with him began to stir, and their groggy morning chatter was dangerously dissatisfied. They had waited their entire lives to be a part of a historic attack such as this. Yusuf knew them to be loyal, but still would have to tread carefully. He snorted at the irony: his men deserting him to rejoin his regiment and attack the Franj. If he had not been directly ordered by the sultan to return with Lajin, he would have joined them.

The tent flap flicked open, and a young face appeared with a thin trickle of moustache around the mouth – the fursān who had been assigned as his valet on this trip.

"Amir, do you wish to break your fast?"

Yusuf stretched. "Kumis only, for me and all of the men. We must mount and grab Lajin so we can get back to the battle."

Outside, the chatter of the camp had quieted. The men were listening. When he emerged, dressed and fed, he saw his soldiers watching him with dark expressions, and he cleared his throat. All activity stopped.

"Yes, the battle has begun, and we were not there for the first charge." He met their eyes each in turn. "We seek a deserter; a coward and a usurper. His disobedience threatens our victory in this battle and those to come. This work takes us from the front line, but it will assure our continued dominance after the battle for Acre has been won and recorded for our sons and our grandsons. Remember that our strength is in our unity. The Franj fight amongst themselves, but we are stronger because we remain committed to our common purpose. You fight for Allah today. You honor the Prophet, peace be upon him, by ensuring that no member of our number, even Lajin, can sabotage us.

"Most of you are still young. Only the freedmen among you have been in a battle such as this before, and they will tell you, as I now do, that you kept your lives this day. When we return with Lajin, you will be fresh for the charge. Those who first assail the walls of Acre will probably not be so blessed."

Some of the faces still looked sulky, but overall, the talk revived them, and the men set about breaking their camp and preparing their mounts. Then they proceeded further into the scraggly northern hills. The only sound was that of the horses' shod feet against the stony soil. Two scouts, dressed in dun-colored robes, ranged ahead on smaller, quicker beasts, occasionally appearing in view on the horizon. These were the qasids, who did not have the finesse and subtlety for spying among the Franj and the Mongols in the cities, but still possessed instincts for staying concealed.

They took the road to the northeast, toward the mountains, stopping briefly to change mounts, leaving their exhausted beasts with some of the furisiyya near Safed, and they continued on. The next day, and the day after, was the same. Although Yusuf resented being sent from the battle as much as his men, he breathed the cool mountain air and exalted at the increasing greenness of the landscape. Cairo was his home now, but his soul never forgot the mountains of his birth, far to the northeast in the cool mountains of the Cuman.

Late in the afternoon of the third day, one of the scouts appeared quietly in the camp and sought Yusuf in his tent. A party of Mamluks wearing Lajin's name on their cloaks had been seen roaming in a soggy creek bed. Their camp was just over the next ridge. The following morning, before the sun rose, Yusuf and a small posse of his most seasoned men approached Lajin's tents, while fifteen of the younger recruits waited on the camp's perimeter, obscured by darkness.

"You will go into the tent after me and secure his guards," he whispered to two of his men. "I shall seek out Lajin myself. To preserve his dignity, let us have me, an amir, take him into custody and not an 'askar."

They moved swiftly in the shadows, subduing the camp guard where he sat. Then Yusuf slipped underneath the flap of the grandest tent with his two 'askari following him. Lajin sat upright on a cushion next to a dimly glowing brazier, fully dressed, his sword across his knees. He spoke.

"Ah… so it is you that he sent, Yusuf Ibn Shihab. Of course, I knew he would ask, but I did not think you would agree to hunt a fellow amir, like a man hunts a lion in the hills."

Yusuf grabbed the sword from Lajin and turned to hand it to one of his men. His two 'askari were both unconscious on the floor, with Lajin's guards kneeling heavily on their necks.

Lajin sighed. "Your scout was spotted yesterday, sniffing around my camp. I had intended to kill my would-be captor outright, but curiosity overtook me. Who would Khalil send, I wondered. Who would seek to slay Qalāwūn's close friend and advisor?"

"I had no choice but to obey Khalil, as you are aware, Lajin."

"Yes. Obey, or be strangled. That is the sultan's preferred punishment these days. And so instead, you send me to be strangled."

"You will not be strangled."

Lajin raised an eyebrow. He was a man of fifty winters, or thereabouts, but he darkened his hair and brows and lined his eyes heavily with kohl. The turn of Lajin's mouth was hidden in the dark.

"Amir Lajin, you are too well-beloved by the people and by Khalil's own court to suffer a strangulation. It is not likely he would do something so unpopular. He may imprison you for a time, but that is all."

"You try to flatter me now, while you hold my sword?"

"There are things I would say to you, but not while I hold your sword thus. I would prefer to speak freely."

Lajin glanced at his guards.

"Take those men out of my tent. Keep them bound and have Amir Yusuf's other men tied to the picket lines." He looked up at Yusuf and smiled, but there was no warmth in it. "Please, sit."

Yusuf remained standing.

"How will you help me in exchange for not killing all of your men and throwing your corpse to the dogs, Yusuf?"

"You do not need to make threats, Lajin. I came prepared to help you."

"Oh? I find this surprising. Do the other amirs not call you Khalil's fifth wife for a reason?"

"I am more loyal than his wives."

"Then why are you wasting my time, loyal Yusuf? Please, try to fight for your life so that my men can have some sport today."

Yusuf sank to the floor and crossed his legs. "Khalil will win this war, Lajin. He will be the man to free Palestine from the Franj, and to provide the security our troops need to move against the Mongols. After Acre, we have plans to move to Tyre and the outlying settlements. When he wins the hearts of the people, you will want to be by his side."

Lajin said nothing, so Yusuf continued. "Despite this, my heart is heavy because Khalil, my pious and upright friend, has become befouled by his power. He hurts men for pleasure, and he violates the message of the Prophet, peace be upon him. There is no mercy in him any more. Sometimes, it takes such a man to win the hard fight for freedom, but should he continue to rule once the fight is won? Is this the kind of ruler who should represent Allah to the unbelievers, who should lead God's people?"

Lajin leaned forward. "What are you saying, Yusuf?"

"I hardly know."

"Then I shall tell you what you are saying. You imply that you would be willing to put someone more capable on the throne for the good of the army and the Believers."

"I did not say that this man was you, Lajin."

"But it could be."

"Qalāwūn, may he rest peacefully, respected you, as did I. As did his son, Khalil, until he took his throne. But you ran, and some said it was to join with the Mongol horde to take arms against us."

Lajin sat back, his posture betraying his affront.

"I did no such thing! I fled to wait until that madman fell in battle, then I intended to return. It is Khalil who spreads these rumors of treason."

Yusuf considered the man before him. It would be easy enough for Lajin to lie, but it would also be unsurprising if Khalil did the same. Who was the lesser evil? And if Khalil found out that this conversation had occurred, likely the sultan would put his own hands around Yusuf's throat.

"I will make you no promises—"

"Then this conversation is finished," Lajin interrupted.

"I will only assure you of this," Yusuf continued, "that I will support the man who is right for Islam and right for the future of the Mamluk's success. While the Franj still exist in Palestine, that man is Khalil. But if his character does not change once the Franj are no longer a threat, I believe that man could be you."

Lajin sat perfectly still.

"You will ensure my comfort while I am confined?"

"Yes, although I cannot guarantee the same for your men."

Lajin smiled. "Well then, let us retreat to the sultan's red tent. You have a battle to win."

Chapter 29

April 1291
The Venetian Quarter, Acre

Nasira almost had everything ready. The family's silver, tapestries, jewels, and fine clothing were carefully wrapped in muslin and packed into iron-bound chests. Overhead, the sound of stones whistling through the air and pounding the walls was so familiar that it became background noise, like the sounds of people haggling in the souks. She walked down the stairs from the upper storey, which housed the family rooms, and stood with hands on her hips, surveying Henri's study. His heavy wooden table could not come with them – it was far too large. All of the books had been packed in chests, wrapped in waxed cloth, and nestled tightly in layers of straw.

She scowled, thinking of how expensive paper, parchment, ink, and all other accoutrements associated with learning and writing would be in the West. According to her late husband, paper was expensive and rarely used in Francia. It became soft in the damper climate, and insects and vermin would chew it. It galled Nasira that the French allowed such desecration of their books. She had not learned to read or write until she was nearly twenty years old, but in the tradition of her people, learning was a precious jewel to be treasured. She taught her children to treat their books, papers, and inks as reverently as if they were a trove of florins.

"Mother, there is an old woman standing outside our door."

She looked up at the sound of ten-year-old Saruca's voice.

"A woman? Perhaps she is lost."

"She asked if this was the house of the viscount Henri of Maron and I said yes, but I did not let her inside because she stinks."

"Please ask Ibrahim to deal with her. She must be begging for alms. And Saruca, you know you are not to open the doors. That is a servant's job."

"She says she is seeking the healer girl who saved Hamza," Saruca insisted.

Nasira's forehead wrinkled. "Please find Emre and ask him to meet me at the door. I will speak to her."

Outside, Nasira looked at the old woman, perplexed. Her clothes were ragged and dirty, and her hands shook, although her eyes were as sharp and alert as a bird of prey. She bowed low to the ground, always keeping a wary eye on Emre, who stood near Nasira with a blank face and his hand on his sword's pommel.

"Beautiful mistress, I seek one who might be known to you. She is a healer and a scribe who goes by the name Sidika bat Tamrat."

"Sidika bat Tamrat… a Jewess? That name is not familiar to me, old woman. If you go around to the back of the house, I will have the servants bring you a meal," Nasira said kindly.

The old woman's hand darted out and grabbed Nasira's wrist with a bony grip.

"I do not seek food. I seek Sidika! She tended to an ill member of your house, and then she traveled to Damascus, to the house of the governor. I must find her!"

"That is enough!" Emre leapt forward and pried the

woman away, then ushered his mistress into the house. Nasira climbed the stairs to the second storey and opened the glass shutters, looking down at the street. The old woman had sunk to her knees in the dust, covering her face and weeping.

"My girl!" she howled. "Where is my girl?"

Chapter 30

April 1291

The Gate of Saint Lazarus, Acre

Despite the best efforts of the Pisan marines, the ship-mounted trebuchet cracked and collapsed into the rough sea without inflicting significant damage to the enemy, although the unexpected nature of the attack shook the Mamluks, and they doubled the watch on their coastal flanks. The two largest and most destructive enemy trebuchets still stood, one at the southwestern side of the city, and the other at the northwestern side of the walls, between Montmusard and al-Hadiqa.

At the third bell of the city's still-standing clock tower, Ibrahim shook Henri awake, and he blearily crept downstairs where Durant helped him into his armor. He saddled Raven himself, draping her with a black caparison of tightly woven felt. Only her eyes, nose, and the velvety tips of her ears were not covered by the cloth armor. She shook her head and stomped her foot adamantly.

"I know how you feel," he muttered, "we will all be uncomfortable this morning, but perhaps with a little extra protection, we will live to see the sun rise tomorrow." He finished tying the last strap under her barrel and gave her a kiss on her nose. Raven snorted and whinnied loudly to be released from the infernal drapery.

Trotting through the silent streets, he met other knights and turcopoles yawning in the cold moonlight on their way to the gate of Saint Lazarus at the northwestern side of Montmusard. Gathered in a small courtyard near the roaring ocean was a mass of knights, splendid in their polished armor and bright livery. Most of the assembled were brother-knights – Templars, Hospitallers, Teutons, and the English knights of Saint Thomas. A clutch of confreres – knights unaffiliated with a religious order – stood among the sea of Brethren, keeping a distance between themselves and the leper knights of the Order of Saint Lazarus. Henri was glad that his surcoat was almost entirely black, for a full moon shone out across the city, illuminating the glowing white robes of the brother-knights like shells on the beach.

Beaujeu, Villiers, and Sir Grailly, who was responsible for the French confreres, climbed to the roof of a stable and yelled out the details of a plan as the men listened quietly. The city marshals sorted them into ranks, with the most disciplined and experienced brother-knights at the front and the confreres taking up the rear.

The iron chains and pulleys of the northwestern city gates had been greased for maximum stealth, and the portcullis rolled up smoothly as the men set out across the bridge which spanned the deep fosse surrounding the city. This close to the sea, the fosse was full of stagnant, stinking water, but near the King's Tower to the east, it was dry except during the winter rains. The horse's hooves clopped loudly on the wood of the bridge.

"Silencieux!" Beaujeu snarled. "Cease the jangling of your spurs. This is not a race. We must not let the enemy hear us coming, or we are all dead men!"

Ahead, the towering beams of their target – the massive counterweight trebuchet that Beaujeu's informant had called

"The Furious" – stood out like a strange beast against the clear, moonlit sky. As they approached it, the magnificent size of the siege engine overwhelmed their vision, and a shiver of unease rippled through the ranks.

"Mon Dieu, look at the size of this devil *machina*," a knight next to Henri swore under his breath.

"Hush," Henri snapped.

Grand Master Villiers held up a hand, signaling the men to halt and spread out around the trebuchet. Beaujeu trotted back to where Henri and Raven waited.

"Come here, Sir Henri. You are going to destroy the siege engine."

Wide-eyed, his stomach churning, Henri followed Beaujeu to where the other attack leaders huddled. Sir Grailly handed him a clay grenade.

"You are to take this, Sir Henri, and throw it at the trebuchet. It will ignite when it breaks open, and coat the wood in naft. Run back as soon as you finish and mount your horse, for surely the enemy will be upon us like locusts on a field of green wheat."

"Sir Grailly, what if The Furious does not burn? Do you have more grenades?" Henri asked, willing his voice to keep from shaking.

"No, we have one grenade, and you have one chance to get this right."

Henri's knees began to feel weak. "My lord, I do not think I am the best man to do this. Can you not select someone else?"

"Shut up and do as you are told!" Beaujeu whispered harshly.

The Furious stood behind a low outcropping of rock, and in the dark, the knights of Acre were hidden from the Mamluk guards as they spread out in a semi-circle. Most of the fires of the enemy camp burned low, and only an occasional sentry patrolled. Apparently very confident in their dominant position, the Mamluk army left their most valuable weapons sparsely guarded.

His whole body now quaking with a profound tremor, Henri approached The Furious. Against the machine, he felt as small as a child. His back to the assembled knights, his face overwhelmed by the oppressive menace of the towering weapon, he hesitated. It looked just as it had in the drawings from Damascus that Beaujeu had presented to the council, but Henri never imagined the machine would be so big; it was as if it had been constructed by gods.

Collectively, the waiting fighters behind him all held their breath.

"It will be well, Hamza," he whispered to himself. "It will be well. God is on your side. We will win this day…" His hand trembled, and he gritted his teeth. Taking a deep gulp of early morning air, he backed up and ran through the shadows toward the machine. "God is on my side—"

His boot caught on a large stone, and suddenly there was nothing underneath him but air and darkness as he felt himself pitch forward. The earth pulled him back, and he slammed hard against the ground, his bones and teeth rattling. The grenade flew from his hand into the darkness and impacted uselessly on the rocky hill, bursting into flame. Instead of burning the Furious, the naft fire quickly licked across the grass and ignited a nearby shrub. Henri rose to his knees, mouth agape in horror. Among the knights of Acre behind him, he heard a stifled cry of dismay.

Near the trebuchet, a voice called out in Turkish, "O nedir?" A pause. "Oraya kim gider?"

Henri sprang to his feet and ran blindly back to Raven, stumbling and falling again on the loose stones, scraping his hands and his elbows. The knights looked at each other and scrambled to unsheathe their swords and level their lances. A wave of noise rippled along the rows of men as metal scraped leather scabbards and bowstrings creaked taut. Beaujeu waved his hands back towards the city wildly, urging the men to retreat, but in their panic, no one looked at their leaders. The tension broke when two of the Templars spurred their horses forward with a yell that shattered the quiet of the pre-dawn.

"For Jerusalem!" one man cried.

"For the Holy Sepulchre!" yelled the other, heaving his sword into the air.

"No, you fools!" Beaujeu screamed, but it was too late. A few of the Hospitallers joined, despite the furious raging of Villiers and Brother Mathieu, and the confreres at the back of the sortie leapt forward with a shout, urging their mounts to charge through the sleeping Mamluk camp. They thundered through the orderly rows of tents, trampling cookfires and cutting down men who emerged half awake. Cries of alarm echoed through the Mamluk camp in Turkish and Arabic, and torches flickered to life across the darkened plain. Somewhere in the camp, a lone kettledrum began to throb with a frenzied, irregular rhythm.

Numbly, Henri mounted Raven and sat, staring ahead in shock. He had ruined the element of surprise. He had killed them all. The best thing for him to do now was to go forth and die bravely in battle. He urged Raven forward toward the sounds of screams coming from the Mamluk camp.

"Sir Henri, stop there!" Beaujeu barked at him. "I forbid you from going into that mayhem. Brother Philip, thank you for staying back. If any of these disobedient fools live, I shall give them all a thrashing on the morrow that will make Sir Henri's flogging look like a child being disciplined by his nurse!"

Henri hadn't even noticed Philip, but now he beheld his rival. The older knight stared straight ahead, radiating disapproval and disgust, his presence magnifying Henri's embarrassment. He wanted to die here outside the walls. Anything was better than facing the knights, should any of them live through this attack. He glanced sideways at Beaujeu, glowing in the moonlight in his white robes. He couldn't see the man's features.

"It would not have worked anyway," he heard Beaujeu say quietly to himself. "Destroying one or two out of fifty trebuchets would be as effective as drawing water from a well with a spoon."

With a shout, the knights who remained horsed raced back toward them. Many also followed on foot, their bleeding wounds seeping darkly through their surcoats.

"Retreat!" Beaujeu yelled and wheeled his horse toward the city.

As the knights galloped back toward the walls of Acre, a mounted Mamluk force led by an amir in glittering armor intercepted them, appearing suddenly in the dark. The Mamluks raised their voices in a wordless scream and charged at the knights, javelins fixed, and Henri just had time to pull his shield up when the two armies collided with a crash of steel and flesh, the cries of horses and the howls of frightened and injured men sounding like one great injured beast.

Henri's shield deflected a lance, but the force of it shoved him so far back in his high-walled saddle that he nearly lost his seat. He whipped Raven around, pulled his sword above his head, and chased his attacker, swinging his sword as the man raised an arm to parry. Henri slashed down viciously once, twice, three times, and the man shrieked, his hand dangling uselessly, blood oozing from his gauntlet.

Henri spun to the left just as another Mamluk heaved a

javelin at him. The cruel weapon landed low, penetrating Raven's caparison and sinking into her shoulder. Henri pulled back on her reigns, and she reared up, battering an unhorsed Mamluk soldier with her hooves.

"Good girl, my Raven!" Henri yelled. The javelin still protruded from her shoulder, and he reached down to pull it out. In the dark, he couldn't see how severe her wound was.

Another Mamluk on horseback pushed through the mass of struggling men toward him, lance leveled at his heart. Henri deflected it with his shield and thrust at the man's horse, sinking his sword into the animal's belly. The horse screamed and fell, spilling its owner to the ground. Henri slashed at the unseated soldier's head, but the man pushed the sword thrust away with his round shield, then grasped Henri by the surcoat and pulled him out of his saddle.

Henri slipped from his stirrups and landed on his back with a startled thud, the air forced from his lungs. His attacker kicked Henri's sword away and raised a slender lance above his head with both hands, poised to thrust.

Henri watched with detached curiosity. *Does Emre know this soldier? Will any air come from my chest when he opens me up since it seems to have entirely left my body?*

Without warning, the Mamluk soldier pitched forward violently, the back of his head exploding open as Raven bucked him with her hind legs. She was in a frenzy, kicking and biting anyone within her reach like an undisciplined mule. Henri, gasping for breath, crawled to his sword and stood up wearily.

The fight had quieted, with more Acrean knights standing than Mamluk soldiers. Slowly he approached his horse, speaking to her in a soothing voice. She stopped bucking and stamped toward him, tossing her head and snorting in agitation. In the growing dawn light, he could see dark blood glistening down her ripped caparison in three places.

With a shout, the knights of Acre slaughtered the last Mamluk, and Beaujeu hollered for everyone to retreat to the gate. The distant thunder of oncoming hooves meant more Mamluks approached from the east, and Henri knew that the knights would be outnumbered ten to one this time.

He launched himself into his saddle, but instead of using his spurs, he leaned forward and spoke in Raven's ear.

"Now, my love, we must fly to the gate. When we get home, I will stitch your wounds and give you oats. Would you like that?" He looked back over his shoulder. The enemy soldiers rumbled toward him, and the Acrean knights had already started for the gate.

"Allons-y!" he told her sharply, and she sped to a gallop. The usual, liquid-smooth rhythm of her gait felt wrong, but she still easily increased the distance between the Mamluks and her master. Henri felt an arrow hit his mail-clad shoulder and bounce off. He was just out of their range.

By now, the sky was blushing pink with the rising sun. The square at the gate of Saint Lazarus, brightly illuminated with torches, was seething with knights, turcopoles, and citizens who heard the commotion of the attack. All were milling about assisting the wounded and talking at once. Raven leapt and then stumbled clumsily as the gates slammed shut behind them, and man and horse both fell to the ground in a cloud of dust.

Henri, stunned and sprawled in the dirt, crawled to where Raven lay, her shining black flanks heaving and flecked with foam.

"Raven?" he asked quietly.

She lay on her side but lifted her head briefly at the sound of his voice. A javelin protruded from her belly and wavered with each labored breath. Henri scrambled at the straps of her caparison and cried out when he saw her left flank riddled with holes from arrows and lance thrusts. A dark pool of blood grew ominously in the dirt under her. She neighed in fear, and he put his hands over her eyes, lowering his face into her mane. She neighed again and tried to lift her head.

"Son, you need to end that horse's suffering."

Henri looked up. Brother Matthieu of Clermont, a marshal of the Hospitallers, stood over him, arms crossed. Brother Matthieu's face softened.

"Ah, it is you, Sir Henri. I saw what happened when you threw the grenade."

"Yes." Henri struggled to keep his voice from cracking.

"Then I take it this is your first battle. Would you like me to give your horse mercy for you? I know that I could not do it were it my beast laying there."

"I… she…" Henri's voice did crack this time as Brother Matthieu offered a hand and pulled him to his feet. A group of knights and citizens had gathered around them in a circle, watching solemnly.

"I will send a squire to deliver your saddle to you. Now go home, Sir Henri," he said, laying a hand on Henri's shoulder.

Henri stood, took three steps, and then stopped. Raven was watching him, tremors rolling through her body and blood draining from her side.

"I will stay here with her if you will do the deed, Brother Matthieu." Henri knelt again by her head. He thought of Salih, his groom, who he had evacuated to Cyprus. Raven's death would devastate him. Henri remembered the man's raw screams upon finding dead horses in his stable, and his own heart made that same sound now. It seemed a lifetime ago, when Henri still thought that his wealth and title gave him immunity from the consequences of his own, self-serving decisions.

Brother Matthieu drew his sword swiftly across Raven's throat latch. Her legs kicked violently, and Henri talked to her, stroking her nose until she stilled, the powerful spurts of her blood pumping from her heart and soaking the knees of his hose. Numbly, he unbuckled his saddle, and Brother Matthieu helped him pull it off, ordering several of the turcopoles to move her body to make way as more Templars arrived.

Beaujeu's secretary ran into the square, flapping his hands.

"What happened? It was too dark to see! I must record this for the grand master's treatise!" The man looked around at the solemn crowd. "I did not see the fires of the Furious as it burned. Did the Furious not burn?"

Brother Philip, leaning against a stable wall, glanced over his shoulder at Henri.

"The viscount was too scared to throw the grenade straight, so the Furious still stands," he spat into the dirt and walked away into the gloom of the dark city. One of the Hospitaller knights ripped off his helmet and lunged at Henri, striking him across the face with the back of his hand.

"You idiot! You coward! You have killed us all!"

"Peace, Brother Leon!" Brother Matthieu pushed the angry knight back. "I think Sir Henri has been punished enough for his mistake." He turned to Henri.

"Lord Henri, go home. Their blood is up, and they will throw you from the walls if you remain here."

Henri nodded dumbly, stood on shaky legs, and shuffled away from the gate of Saint Lazarus. He wandered, clutching the bloody saddle until he stood at the door of his house near the Templar citadel. Emre was hurrying down the steps, fully armored and pulling a cloak over his shoulders against the chill of the morning. When he saw Henri, he drew up short.

"My lord!" He rushed forward and took the saddle. "Why did you go to battle without me to squire for you! Where is Raven?"

"Dead." Henri's voice sounded dead as well.

Emre dashed inside the house and re-emerged with Durant, who rubbed his eyes sleepily. Henri looked at his master-at-arms.

"She was mortally injured, but she ran back into the city. She saved me…" he drifted off.

Durant took Henri's sword and shield and began to unbuckle his armor.

"Well, it is a blessing that you sent Salih to Cyprus. The loss of a loyal beast is sometimes greater than the loss of a man," Durant said, looking at the saddle, "and if you do not mind my saying so, Lord Henri, I believe that the Virgin, blessed be her, does look after those beasts who are particularly noble. In heaven, that is. Now you need to clean up before anyone sees you."

Henri looked down. The lemons of his surcoat were brown with dried blood. His hands were sticky with blood and sweat, and the knees and legs of his hose were stiff with more of it.

"I will call for a bath," Emre said, turning toward the house. They all paused as the dull thud of a stone crashing into the walls rumbled in the distance. The Mamluk army had started their daily bombardment yet again.

The Furious still stood.

Chapter 31

April 1291

The Venetian Quarter, Acre

H enri crawled wearily into his bed, his shield arm throbbing from the impact of Mamluk lances, his sword arm hanging uselessly after his morning of swinging it with cold arms. He had a black eye from where the angry Hospitaller knight had struck him in the courtyard, a lump on the back of his head, and a spreading blue bruise on his right buttock from his fall from Raven.

Emre followed him into his room, pulled the shutters closed over the windows, and blew out the candle. The sun was now rising steadily in the east, and he dragged the heavy drapes across the windows to block any additional light from seeping through the shutters. Hearing a snore behind him, he looked back at the bed. Henri had fallen asleep as soon as he lay down.

Emre slowly drew the deep blue silk coverlet over Henri's shoulders, then sat on the bed, watching him in the semi-darkness. He tentatively reached out and smoothed a lock of dark hair away from Henri's forehead and let his hand linger for a moment. Henri stirred, turned over, and clutched a cushion to his chest, and Emre pulled his hand back as if he had just touched hot coals.

No. This would not do. Day by day, it was getting too

difficult to keep his feelings hidden. It had been years since he felt stirred this way. Not since...

But Emre could not allow his mind to wander there, where dark memories lurked from his days in the meydan in Cairo during his fursān training. He would not allow himself to love again. He looked longingly at his friend and master.

"Goodbye," he whispered, then stood and strode quickly from the room.

Outside, puffy spring clouds scudded across the sky, pushed by a fierce west wind from the sea. Somewhere in the city, a burning tannery belched foul-smelling smoke that smudged the horizon. Ibrahim waited for him near the back kitchen door as they had agreed, the breeze pushing his robin's egg blue keffiyeh away from his weathered face.

Emre looked at the ground, and for a moment, the two men stood in silence.

"Do you know why I have asked you here?" Ibrahim asked.

Emre nodded, still looking at the ground. "I think I do, yes."

"Then you know how much power I have over you right now."

"You would not be the first to use this threat against me. Others who did so lost their lives." Emre's voice was stony, and he glared at Ibrahim.

"You would kill his uncle?"

For a moment, the two men looked at each other, unmoving.

"Yes," Emre replied. "I have done nothing wrong. And, I have decided not to join you. I will stay here, and if God wills it, perhaps I will escape and find my sister."

Ibrahim's face was grim, but he reached out and put a hand on Emre's shoulder.

"I am sorry that you are afflicted with this curse, young man, but I thank God for you because it will save my nephew's life. Your secret is safe with me… unless you harm any member of my family. You may stay at the house for as long as you need."

Emre reached into his tunic and pulled out a small clay bottle.

"I have procured what you seek. When the deed is done, come and find me. I shall assist you to the harbor. Have you found a way to hide him?"

Ibrahim indicated a large cedar coffin standing on end nearby.

"Very good. Pour the contents of the bottle into his wine. It should not take long."

They both jumped at the sound of a low cackle. From the shadows, an old woman emerged, hunched and dressed in rags.

"I heard you," she laughed, "you plan to poison the young lord. I heard you!"

"Shut up, old woman!" Emre snarled. "Did I not already chase you away from this house?"

The woman held up her hands in defense. "No, no! Do it! Some days my beautiful girl comes to this house and looks at it with longing. Kill the master, and she will leave. She will see me, and we will be together forever – mother and daughter!"

Ibrahim looked at the woman closely.

"A girl comes to this house and watches it?"

"Yes. They say that your master visits her sometimes in her village. Evil, evil man and his black horse! He should leave my girl alone!" She made an aggressive sign in the air. "Give us a drink, will you? I am poor and thirsty."

Ibrahim handed her his water flask. She took a drink and then spat.

"There is no sweetness in this! Are you a Muslim that you keep water and not wine in your drinking skin?"

"You may keep it," Ibrahim indicated the flask, "and you may fill it from the well at my master's house when you are thirsty." He turned to leave with Emre following.

"Yes, go!" the woman shouted. "I will wait for my beautiful one here, and soon she will see me and remember. She will love me again!"

***

After a few hours of fitful dozing, Henri gave up on sleep and emerged from his chamber. The hour of nones had just struck, the merry bells chiming a discordant reminder that only days ago, life in Acre had been normal. Henri dressed in a fresh set of white linen underclothes and covered them with a short black robe. First, he would say farewell to his family and then report back to the walls for duty.

His mother, sisters, and Ibrahim waited in the mosaiced great room, dressed in traveling cloaks against the cool April weather as the remaining servants bundled the last of the family's belongings into a cart to transport to the harbor.

"Hamza, I wish you would come with us. Will you not change your mind?" Nasira asked.

"No, Mother, I am firm. I will defend the city."

Nasira pulled Henri into an embrace, standing on the tips of her pointed slippers to kiss his cheek.

"I hope that you can forgive me someday," she whispered.

"Forgive you for what?" he asked, but she took Saruca's hand and pulled her out the door.

"Is Hamza was coming with us?" Saruca asked as Nasira led her out to the cart. "Mother, you said he was coming with us!"

Blanche moved to stand, and Henri helped her up.

"Blanche, I do not think I will live to see Francia, and I need to tell you how truly sorry I am about…" His voice broke as he searched for the words he wanted to say. Blanche had dark circles under her eyes, and she drew her cloak protectively around her midsection, hiding the little bulge at her waist. She looked at him, her eyes hard with loathing.

"I cannot forgive you yet. Perhaps I never will. If I die in childbirth and my soul drags you to hell with me, it will be less than you deserve." She stalked from the room and climbed heavily into the cart.

Only Ibrahim remained. He stood, holding two silver cups of wine, and motioned for Henri to sit.

"Nephew, let us share one last moment together."

Henri took the cup. "Uncle, after what happened yesterday, I do not think that a single cup of wine is enough. If you filled the entire city fosse with wine, that would not be enough either," he said with a shaky laugh. Ibrahim raised his cup, and they both drank for a moment in silence.

"Uncle, were you able to find the girl I asked you to secure passage for?"

Ibrahim's face fell. "No, Hamza. Emre searched for her, but her village has most likely been pressed into service of the Mamluks. Perhaps she is already in Cyprus." Ibrahim considered telling his nephew that the girl Sidika had been seen near the house, but it was pointless. It would only make things harder for his nephew.

"I hope she made it to Cyprus. God, I have failed her." Henri dropped his head into his hands.

"What do you owe this girl, Hamza? Is she your lover?"

"She is the young woman who saved me from my wounds after my flogging. The man that I slew while on patrol… he was her father. I have wronged her greatly, and I cannot make it right, no matter how hard I try."

"Then I also owe her a great debt, for she saved your life." For a moment, Ibrahim's conscience burned. No, this was right. If Henri knew the girl was still in the city, it would make Ibrahim's task harder.

"You know," he set his cup down, "I am the youngest of all my father's sons. It was never in my fortunes to marry and sire children of my own. Allah, in His grace and mercy, has blessed me, for I was there to help raise you and your sisters. You all are as dear to me as my own children."

"You speak like a Muslim just now, Uncle," Henri mused. "Have you forgotten in your old age that you converted?" He was still tired, and the weight of the morning's early battle felt like a physical thing, pulling his shoulders down, filling his head with wool.

"Converted at sword point by a Genoese knight," Ibrahim said casually, taking another tentative sip of his wine. "Even though I live a lie on the outside, I have remained faithful in my heart. Today I do not care who knows it. I believe that there is no god but God, and Muhammad is his prophet." He smiled, and his eyes crinkled at the edges.

Henri heard Ibrahim's words but did not comprehend. "I am so tired, Uncle. This war has only lasted three weeks, and yet I feel I could sleep a hundred years."

"Take some more wine, Nephew. It will help you feel better," Ibrahim urged him. Henri drained his cup.

"Uncle, you must leave soon... the ship..." Henri slumped down in his chair, his limbs numb and sluggish, his eyes half-closed as he slid toward the mosaic floor.

Ibrahim checked to make sure Henri was asleep, then summoned Durant and Emre. Together, they loaded their unconscious master into the coffin and pushed it into the cart where Nasira and her daughters waited.

Nasira looked down at him, wringing her hands. "He will never forgive me."

Ibrahim jumped up into the cart and cupped her cheek with a sun-weathered hand. "But he will live. We shall tell him it was my idea, not yours," he replied.

Durant slapped the reins against the horse's back, and they were moving. They rattled down the rutted alley toward the harbor, and Nasira looked back on her house, growing smaller as they moved away, with Emre standing alone outside of it. For five generations, her family had lived in Palestine. Her ancestors had watched as the first Franj settlers arrived, half-starved, in Jerusalem. They had witnessed as Acre changed hands between Franj and Ayyubid warlords. They were present when the Franj and English kings slaughtered the hostage warriors of Salah ad-Din a hundred years earlier, and when both Baybars and Qalāwūn had menaced the walls ineffectually. The stones in this land were the very bones in her body. She turned and looked at her uncle, her daughters, and the shape of her unconscious son, and she smiled.

She was leaving, but Palestine was coming with her.

Part 2
May 1291

Chapter 32

May 1291
Acre, Palestine

When the walls finally crumbled near the beleaguered Accursed Tower, the citizens still living in Acre knew that there would be no happy ending for them. Although mercy had been shown to occupiers in the past by noble and chivalrous sultans, such as Salah ad-Din during the recapture of Jerusalem in 1187, the new Mamluk sultan, al-Ashraf Khalil, had no such intentions. He did not wish to capture Acre for himself, nor was he interested in occupying the city or giving it to one of his sons or his amirs. Nothing but the total eradication of the Franj presence in Palestine would suffice. His father had already sacked Tripoli, but Acre's sheltered harbor was a jewel of a safe haven for the Franj occupiers, and he would see it razed to the ground, its inhabitants silenced. After that would come Tyre, and then the land would be liberated after two hundred years of oppression.

The people of Allah had suffered long enough under the boot of the colonizers, who stripped the land of its riches and enslaved its people. It galled him that these uncultured oafs had managed to dominate for so many years. Moreover, their presence created the potential for two enemies to merge into a single beast. Word of Christian priests and emissaries to the Mongols had reached Khalil, and the last thing his army needed was a fight on two fronts.

Free of the political shackles and dynastic infighting that imprisoned prior rulers in bloody and expensive wars of succession, Khalil, for the moment, had the space and energy to fight the Franj and secure himself a victory that even Baybars could not achieve.

His father had been a practical man, signing truces with the occupiers to promote trade, playing a slow game of attrition with the Franj, and eating away at their resources, both by conquering and through economic intrigue. Now in command of a vast and well-trained army, Khalil was determined to outshine his father. He would push the Franj into the sea and then beyond, back into their lands to the west, and when he had them penned there like a flock of goats, he would fill the harbors of Palestine with stones, erect gates over the mountain passes, whatever it took to keep a Franj army from finding purchase ever again.

In May of 1291, when the Mamluk soldiers pulled down the walls and spilled into Acre's crooked streets, the desperate citizens fought back behind makeshift barriers and blocked roads. After days of fighting, they had almost no arrows left, so they climbed to the flat roofs of their houses and threw rocks. When they could find no more naft, they poured boiling water or scorching sand on the enemy instead. They yelled to counteract the terror-inducing rhythm of the drums, but nothing could stand against the strictly disciplined and unquestioningly loyal Mamluks, and the citizens of Acre realized the full consequences of underestimating their enemy.

Chapter 33

May 1291

The Venetian Quarter, Acre

S idika peeked around the crumbling corner of a large city house at the desperately slow battle unfolding down the street. The overburdened Franj knights held the Mamluk soldiers back from the breach in the wall for now, but she knew the fight was pointless. The panicked Acrean knights created a wall of shields, and the highly trained Mamluk 'askari pushed back. No one could gain any ground, but there was so little space for them to maneuver in the narrow street that no one could raise a sword arm to strike a blow either, so they grunted and pushed ineffectually.

Their faces pressed close together, their sweat intermingled, Mamluk and Franj blood pooled together, creating a black, slippery batter underfoot. Occasionally, a Franj knight would lose footing in the muck and fall, gaining the Mamluks another precious few inches of ground. If it weren't so terrifying, Sidika probably would have laughed at the press of men grunting and trying to push each other over.

This would not do. She'd ventured to the harbor from her shabby inn to see about hiring a boat for Cyprus, but the Mamluks breached the walls and, in her panic, she became turned around in the serpentine streets. She had no idea which part of the city she was in now. Of course, there was always the citadel of the Templars. Grand Master Beaujeu gave his word that she would receive protection there if she asked, but she was just as afraid of the Franj knights as she was of the Mamluk soldiers.

She fled back in the direction that she had come, but the streets of Acre were a tangle of cul-de-sacs, tunnels, and last-minute additions to narrow alleys that already twisted and turned mysteriously. She ran until her chest screamed for air, and she emerged again near the heaving mass of soldiers. The streets in this city truly must be bewitched.

Sidika tried to calm the pounding of blood in her ears so she could listen for the sound of the sea, which constantly caressed the walls of the Templar citadel. Instead, she heard a triumphant roar as the Mamluks finally pushed through the knight blockade and rushed into the city.

She looked up and down the broad avenue where she stood. The city's nobles lived on this street. Every gate was closed, every window shuttered – a canyon of high walls and wealth. She ran to the nearest house and hammered on the carved wooden door with her fists.

"Please let me in!" she screamed. "I am a citizen of Acre! Help!"

There was no sound from within. The occupants were either hiding or had left the city. She ran to the next house. Again, her cries went unanswered.

A noise arose from the streets around her; terrified screams, loud bangs, and the shouts of soldiers. How close and from what direction they came, she couldn't tell. The sounds seemed to echo through the narrow alleys and twisting avenues of Acre, taking on personalities of their own. Sidika dashed down the nearest street and ran, heedless of the direction she had chosen. A strong gust of wind blew smoke through the street and brought up a cloud of stinking dust that sanded her eyes.

Ahead, a shadow, a dim silhouette slouched toward her in the street.

"My child, come!" the shadow commanded in a scratchy voice. A claw-like hand reached out and clutched at her, grasping the edge of her frock and holding tight. The other hand clamped around her wrist and pulled her with surprising strength out of the street and into an alley. In the blowing smoke, all Sidika could see was the hunched back and stringy iron-gray hair of an old woman. The screams grew closer, but the woman seemed to know exactly where she was going.

They arrived at a grand, stone staircase: Lord Henri's house. The woman thrust her heavily toward the door.

"Go inside, my girl!"

Sidika squinted through the swirling dust and smoke. The wind whistled fiercely down the street, picking up leaves, scraps of rubbish, and still-glowing embers, throwing them in her eyes. The woman slapped her on the back of the head.

"Sidika, go inside!"

Sidika pulled at the door handle, but it was securely barred from within. The old woman pushed her aside and drew something from her cloak: an old Mongol bow with a cracked grip of reindeer horn. With both her hands, she drew back and smacked the bow against the wood in a rhythmic fashion, like she was tapping out the beat to a song. Sidika blinked the dust from her eyes. She knew that bow.

"Horse Aunty?"

"Not now," the woman grunted, smacking the door again.

"Sarangerel? Is it you?"

The old woman turned, and in the dim light, Sidika saw her eyes glisten, her toothless mouth curving up into a wide, gummy grin.

The door wrenched back, and a man wearing a turban

stood there, his features darkened against the oil laps inside the house. In the streets, the nature of the screams changed. It was no longer just men who were crying out in terror and pain, the Mamluks were now entering the houses where the citizens hid, and the voices of women and children joined the collective scream rising from the city.

"Henri!" Sidika begged. "Please let us in!"

The man grabbed her by the arm and dragged her into the house, shutting the heavy wooden door and sliding a thick bar of iron across it.

"No, wait!" she yelled again, and she scrambled back to the door, straining to pull the bar up. The man's hand came down heavily on top of hers.

"Stop!" he shouted. "No one opens this door!"

"But there is a woman out there! A woman who helped me! I think… I think I know her…"

The man grabbed her by the collar of her dress and pulled her backwards.

"Sidika," he barked, "leave the door closed."

She wrenched herself from his grip and backed away.

"You are not Henri." She moved, feeling along the wall in the dim light. "How do you know my name?"

He followed her slowly, his features still shadowed.

"What is so special about you? Why do Henri and the old woman take so much interest in you?"

He dashed forward and tried to grab her, but Sidika dodged out of the way and stumbled into another room, which was darker than the first. She crouched low to the ground like a cat and watched as he crept silently around the room's perimeter, looking for her.

"You have some hold on his mind," he said to the darkness, "and I cannot see what is so intriguing about you, a village girl. A spy. Are you trying to prise information from him? Do you work for the Mamluks, Turkish girl?"

She stumbled on something in the dark. A staircase. On her hands and knees, she slunk up the steps as he felt along the walls for her, oblivious to how close she was.

"What do you want with him?" she heard the man say. "Why do you come to this house every day?"

Still on her hands and knees, she pulled herself to the top of the landing and collapsed on the platform, her heart a-thunder, hands shaking. This man was nothing like Fakri and the illiterate men of Fajar. He was tense and focused, like a lion after an Ibex; if he saw her, he would surely pounce. She slithered across the floor at the top of the stair and pulled herself toward the gray light of an open door.

"Why does he travel to your village to see you... but never stay long, whore?" she heard his voice whisper next to her ear, and she shied back. He had slipped silently up the stairs and was within a hand's breadth of her. Sidika tried to get to her feet to run, but she tripped over the skirts of her frock, cracking her knees against the stone floor. He dug a fist into her hair and wrenched her back toward him. She clawed wildly, pulling back his outer robe and straining to reach his belt. He was armed with a long, straight dagger and a smaller, ornately jeweled curved one, and she reached for them, but he slapped her hand away.

A deep, resounding *BOOM!* shook the house as a stone struck it, and for a moment, the man's grip loosened. Sidika raked her fingernails across his face, bolted into an open doorway, and slammed the door shut. There was no bar and no locks. Running to the window, she pulled the shutters open, and the hazy light of the burning city seeped like honey through the blurry amber glass into the room. In a frenzied moment, she looked around; dusty floors, a massive bedstead stripped of its hangings, some old swords in a heap behind the door, gathering cobwebs.

She wrapped her hands around one of the iron swords and hefted it. Too cumbersome. Underneath the swords, she spied a bow with a stiff, dried bowstring next to a crumbling quiver of arrows. Perhaps…

She took up the bow and dove behind the bedstead, nocking an arrow and pulling the draw back toward her cheek. Slowly, the door creaked open, and the man peeked inside. Sidika pulled the bowstring tighter, feeling the unpracticed muscles in her arms and shoulders scream with fatigue.

Another stone impacted against the house, and in her surprise, Sidika let the arrow fly. The bowstring was old and brittle, and the arrow no longer plumb, but it buried itself in the man's wrist, his bone splitting with an audible crack.

He did not cry out. Instead, he clutched the wound, biting his bottom lip until the blood dribbled down his chin.

"He is gone," she heard him say quietly in the darkness. "He has gone away, never to return to Acre. You and I must both remain here without him." He slumped against the door, leaving a smear of glistening blood against the wood. Sidika lowered her bow, and she heard him sob quietly.

"I spirited him from the city so he could live… but until the end, he kept asking about you."

Sidika stood cautiously from her hiding place. "He had no claim over me. I only came because I had nowhere to go—"

Behind her, the glass panes in the window exploded as a stone struck it, blowing inward and shattering into thousands of glittering shards. The shutter frame hit Sidika on the back of the head, and she knew no more.

**

It was the man's swearing that eventually woke her. She was in an unfamiliar room, and he was on top of her, his hand over her mouth.

"Quiet!" he whispered. "There are Mamluks outside." She could smell his sweat and feel the wetness of his blood as it seeped from his shattered wrist onto her deep red dress. Outside, she heard men yelling in Turkish and the sound of dozens of feet rushing past the house. When the voices eventually faded, he eased his hand from her mouth and pushed himself painfully to his feet. Sidika scrambled on hands and knees for the door.

"Only death will meet you that way, Sidika," he said wearily. "The 'askari are going from house to house. They will take you as a spoil of war like they did to me eleven years ago."

"You are a Mamluk?" Sidika asked, continuing to edge her way toward the door.

"No longer."

"There is no reason for me to trust a man who has only just tried to kill me."

"Not kill. Subdue."

"Subdue is enough!" she said, dashing for the stairs. Below, the rooms shook with the sound of axes shattering the outer door.

"We must hide." The man walked unsteadily toward the stairs. "In the cellars. Come."

First, he led her into the attached storerooms, where they filled their arms with water skins, stale loaves of bread, and half-burned nubs of candles. Then he staggered to a room tiled in black and white mosaic and walked to the enormous fireplace. Sidika had never seen a fireplace inside of a house and took a moment to marvel at its structure. The man kicked aside a straw mat and bent down, pulling at a metal ring in the floor until a square of the stone lifted, and he began to descend a stair into complete darkness.

"Do you want them to get you?" he hissed.

The axes were splintering the wood now, breaking holes in the thick door. "I… I am not sure which is w… worse," she blubbered, the tears burning the back of her eyes.

He reached out and grasped her by the hem of her dress, pulling her down into the blackness. She fell – she did not know how far, but she landed on top of him.

"Confound this dress," she grumbled.

In the darkness, she heard him chuckle. Then a wiry arm reached past her and pulled the trapdoor shut, closing the darkness over them.

Chapter 34

May 1291

The Accursed Tower, Acre

Grand Master Guillaume de Beaujeu had seen many battles and greeted them with bloodthirsty enthusiasm in his youth. When he was a young man, the feeling of rightness and invincibility was so powerful and penetrating that it overwhelmed him, gave him energy on the battlefield. As he grew older, he learned to temper these feelings of recklessness with political savvy, which helped him quickly rise above his other noble counterparts into a position of power and authority. Being cousin to King Louis and Charles of Anjou didn't hurt either.

Secretly, Beaujeu wondered if he deserved his exalted position, but he knew not to question it. All the men around him, from the marshals to the holy father in Rome, appeared confident and self-assured in their commissions; a man who doubted his own authority could find himself reassigned to a country abbey.

Violence justified by piety served him well when dealing with the kings and lords of the West; however, in his old age, his lust for war receded along with his graying hairline, and he found himself wishing only to die peacefully in his bed. His shoulders, though strong and gnarled from a lifetime of physical training, now ached when he lifted his sword. His left knee had never recovered from a blow by an enemy many years ago, and he could no longer run more than twenty paces before the pain in his hip became unbearable.

Beaujeu grunted as he climbed into his saddle. Despite the risk of injury, he preferred to wear his light mail, for his heavier armor caused his padded undergarments to chafe around his arms. An old man could afford to be fussy.

Steeling his features into his trademark look of stern resolve, he glared sharply at the assembled knights before him. Only twelve Templars remained. In his courtyard, the other assembled knights were a bedraggled collection of Hospitallers, Knights of Saint Thomas, Teutons, and confreres who had not yet fled by ship for Cyprus. Per his instruction, the marshals divided the men into two groups – thirty-five experienced knights in one and fifteen initiate knights in another. All wore grim expressions.

He noticed with disappointment that Sir Henri was not among them. He did not take the young man for a coward, so he supposed he must have been struck down when the Mamluks breached the walls. Beaujeu thought back to the disturbing news he had heard only that morning about Brother Philip, and he glanced at the assembled knights but did not see the man. He had not seen him at the morning prayer, either.

Perhaps it was true. Perhaps Brother Philip was an imposter and a murderer.

Beaujeu had not told anyone what he knew, for it had come in a letter from one of the Templar vineyards far to the north, containing the account of Brother Languedoc's mortally wounded squire as he gave his last confession. The man had been found wandering in the hills, his life's blood nearly gone, weeping that Brother Philip had murdered his master.

The grand master pondered these revelations and sighed heavily. Within and without of the citadel's walls, all of the news of men was bad. He cleared his throat loudly, and the knights quieted.

"The Mamluks are through the walls near the King's Tower, and they are moving their mangonels towards the weakest gates. Brother Matthieu of the Hospitallers has taken some men and gone to meet them. You all," he indicated the thirty-five solemn knights, "will accompany Grand Master Villiers and me to provide reinforcement. You are all warriors, and so you understand the odds. It is unlikely we will survive against such a force. Recall that your souls will have forgiveness for what you do today because you do it to protect the Kingdom of Jerusalem. Heaven awaits you."

The knights looked back at him solemnly. He turned to the smaller group of initiates.

"This citadel is the safest place in Acre, for our walls are thicker than even the city walls. We may need to switch our focus from defending the city to moving as many citizens within this fortress as possible. We are already attempting to make contact with the sultan to parley with him that we may arrange for a safe transfer of the survivors from the city; however, he will not be able to control his men easily. Therefore, I urge you to scour the houses and the streets and bring as many innocents as you can into the citadel. We may yet be able to evacuate them to the harbor using the tunnels."

They heard a loud crash, and one of the gilt lion statues atop the citadel walls shattered under the weight of a massive ball of Mamluk stone. Beaujeu knew the gates were shut, but he glanced at them, regardless. He turned back to the nervous men before him.

"It will be dangerous, but this is your chance to be real heroes. This city is lost. Do not sacrifice your life simply to kill one Mamluk soldier, for they outnumber us ten to one. Our only chance is negotiation, and so I say to you, protect your lives so that you may save as many as possible."

After an uncharacteristically brief prayer by a Templar priest, Beaujeu turned his horse, ordered the gates opened, and the men followed him out. The initiates spread out on foot in the streets, hammering on doors and shouting for people to evacuate their homes. Beaujeu rode at the head of his knights toward the King's Tower. No one spoke as stones continued to rain down on the houses.

It took them longer than usual to pick their way through the devastated streets, many of them blocked with makeshift barricades, to the place where the Mamluks had breached the walls. As they neared the breach, the smoke increased, and the men began to cough loudly. One of the knights cried out from behind Beaujeu in the smoke, and then another and another. Arrows were raining down on them from directly above.

"Shields over your heads!" he shouted. Ahead, he could hear the clang of metal against metal and yells of men fighting. Despite the many battles he had faced in his life, he still felt a cold slap of fear when that sound reached his ears.

"Lances lowered!" he commanded. "Be careful; our men will be at the front! Do not kill a warrior of Christ!" and he spurred his horse to a trot.

For a few moments, the Mamluk soldiers balked at the sight of thirty-five mounted knights bearing down upon them, but they quickly formed into ranks, fixed their lances, and prepared to meet the onslaught. The knights charged forward, their lances lowered, and the Mamluks threw javelins at their horses. Men spilled from their saddles as mounts screamed in pain.

Beaujeu reined his horse back. The Mamluks had locked

their shields together in the narrow alley, creating a solid wall of defense from which they could fire arrows and throw javelins from relative safety. Unlike his soldiers, these men hid and only struck when they had the opportunity. *Brilliant tactic*, Beaujeu thought with detached admiration, *there is no way any of us will survive this.*

He motioned the men back and yelled to them to charge directly into the wall of shields. They spurred their mounts to a gallop, only able to ride four abreast in the high-walled street, and crashed over the human barricade of men and shields. Immediately, the next row of enemy soldiers struck out with their lances, felling several horses, and the shield wall reformed again.

Beaujeu heard a thundering racket behind him and looked up. Knights Hospitaller were charging into the fray, their lances fixed for attack. Beaujeu raised his spear to signal his men to retreat and allow the Hospitallers a chance to charge the enemy when he felt something thud heavily on his chest. Looking down, he stared dumbly at a javelin, two fingers thick, protruding from under his arm. For a moment, all the noise and smoke around him ceased to exist.

That is not a part of my body, he thought. *Javelins are longer than that. Where is the rest of it?*

There was something foreign inside of him, and Beaujeu felt a surge of panic. If he could get away from the fighting, everything would be fine. He tried to take in a breath, but a wave of pain overcame him. Slowly, as if he were moving through honey, he turned his horse and urged the beast back down the street.

"Beaujeu! You command us to stay and fight, and yet you run away?" a knight bellowed angrily at him.

"I am not running away," he wheezed. He saw the frightened and angry looks of the men around him. Taking a deep, painful breath, he said, louder this time, "I am not running away. I am dead. Behold, the wound," and he lifted his arm briefly. The pain was blinding. He felt it deep within the core of his being. It was a pain that felt as if it had always existed in him somewhere, but he only just now understood it. He couldn't draw a breath without white-hot spears of agony radiating through his chest. He was drowning in his own blood, the air rushing from his lungs. His head drooped, the ground spun, and he slipped from his horse.

Brother Gregoire was at his side immediately, catching him as he fell. "Help me move the grand master to safety!" he shouted.

Brother Alaran ran to them and threw his shield on the ground. "Use this!"

As gently as they could, they dragged their grand master onto the shield and bore him away as the battle raged on.

"You men are not to leave the battlefield," Beaujeu gasped. "You swore an oath not to leave your brothers behind while the Templar flag still flies. You will go back, and you will fight until you die!"

"No," said Brother Gregoire, "we will not. You told us our sins would be forgiven on this day. We sin to save your life, my lord."

Beaujeu decided not to protest. Each step that the men took jostled the javelin in his lung and sent flames of liquid pain through his chest into his back.

"Alaran, we must get him inside. The enemy will surely set upon us at this pace." Brother Gregoire looked around nervously. They set the shield down.

Brother Alaran pounded on the nearest door. "Open up! It is the knights of the Temple, and we have the grand master, gravely wounded!"

The door cracked open, and the wide, frightened eyes of a servant looked out.

"Let us inside in the name of Jesu Christi, for God's greatest warrior is preparing to meet him even now," Brother Alaran yelled. The servant opened the door, and they pushed inside. Immediately the two knights began removing pieces of the old man's armor.

Beaujeu looked up. White plaster covered the ceiling, with a delicate scroll of red and blue flowers around the edges of the room. Faces hovered over him, and he breathed shallowly.

"Please," he whispered, "take me to the citadel… to my house. I would die within my own walls."

Brother Alaran and Brother Gregoire exchanged a concerned look. Outside, the sounds of battle grew louder and closer. In the room, Beaujeu's skin turned gray, and his lips paled to blue. Brother Gregoire nodded, and they loaded him onto the shield again and opened the door to the mayhem.

Chapter 35

May 1291

The Venetian Quarter, Acre

Again and again, the flint flashed in the darkness, its lightning momentarily blinding her. In each moment of illumination, Sidika saw glimpses of the man; tightly wound curls, rich olive skin, and wide-set eyes. A comely face, lined with pain as he attempted to hold the flint with his shattered hand.

Carefully, she took the flint from him and flicked a spark onto a piece of lint, which caught fire long enough for him to touch it to the wick of a tallow candle. The weak light sputtered, spitting oil and fat, but for the first time since she had entered the house, Sidika could see him almost clearly.

"You are the servant of Lord Henri," she said. "I saw you when he ailed after his flogging and at my house when he warned me to leave with him."

"I am Emre," he said simply and stood, wincing. He held his wrist tightly in his other hand as blood dribbled through his fingers and onto the ground.

Sidika looked around. A wooden ladder rose from the circle of candlelight into darkness above their heads and the underside of the trapdoor. To her left, she only saw a chasm of cold darkness. To her right, an open doorway, also leading into darkness. She looked back at Emre.

"You tried to kill me… what will you do now?"

Emre touched another taper to the first and handed it to her.

"Not kill," he said. "But I have many questions for you, mademoiselle. Namely, what is your hold over my master, for he insists that he has not bedded you, thus I can see no reason why he visits your village. I also wish to know what you were doing in Damascus at the house of al-Shuja'i."

Sidika felt herself go cold. "I was never in Damascus."

"The old woman said that you were. You are easy to recognize, mademoiselle. You should dress in a more subtle color if you wish to spy for the Mamluks. And your hair is most unchaste."

"Your hair is no different than—" Sidika started, but Emre stepped forward, put a hand over her mouth, and shushed her quietly. Footsteps clicked on the stone floors over their heads. He pulled her into the dark chasm of a storeroom and touched his candle to a cold brazier on the ground.

"Ladies Blanche and Saruca were in here only a few days ago to seek shelter from the stones." He tossed a piece of lint into the brazier and blew on it gently. "They left books and candles, unless I am mistaken."

"Books?" Sidika breathed. "Who can afford to simply 'leave' books?"

"The noble family of Maron-en-Ruerge can. Hmmm… I think we should only burn one candle, lest we eat through our supplies too quickly."

Sidika sank to her knees on the cold stone floor. "How long will they stay, the soldiers?"

"Until everyone is dead or captured. It may be days until we are able to emerge, but we should be… safe… here…" Sidika heard his voice drift as he slipped down the wall to his knees. She watched his hands trembling, brown blood crusted around the place where she had struck him with the rusty arrowhead.

If he died, there would be one less person to breathe the air, drink the water, and eat the food. And had he not already tried to kill her? It would be easy to finish him now. All she had to do was hit him over the head with something heavy.

Sidika felt delicately along the wall at her back until a stone worked loose in her hand, then she stood and walked slowly toward him.

Chapter 36

May 1291
The Bay of Acre, Acre

Henri opened his eyes and immediately closed them again as a flood of pain and nausea swept over him. It felt as if the whole room were heaving on waves of the ocean. He jerked his eyes open again. He *was* heaving on waves of the ocean, and above him lurked an angry gray sky. He sat up, immediately regretting it as his head swam and his stomach lurched. He rolled over and vomited violently, slowly becoming aware that he was cold and wet. Sheets of rain hit him sideways and stung his skin. He was in the ribbed hull of a small boat, laying on top of his armor.

"It will wear off soon, m'lord, and you will be right as bread again."

Henri pushed himself unsteadily to his hands and knees, blinking toward the voice. Durant sat in front of him, working a set of oars in the gale, his craggy face pale but determined.

"Durant," Henri slurred, "what... what?"

"Your mother," Durant's face was hard, "and Ibrahim, and even Emre conspired to kidnap you and take you to Francia, my lord."

Henri straightened and looked around. The little craft labored up the dark, rolling waves and slipped down their smooth sides into deep troughs of angry ocean. In the distance, he could see the burning skyline of Acre; its broken walls and buildings looked like a row of uneven teeth.

"I knew you wanted to stay. Told them that they should leave you in Acre to do your duty, but your mother was stubborn, and they gave you a potion to make you sleep. After the ship left the harbor, I paid a sailor to help me put you on this boat so as to bring you back. Looks like the infidels made it into the city while we were away."

"But you are…"

"I am also staying. I will fight alongside you, m'lord, as I did with your father at Tunis."

Henri looked down. Durant had tied a rope tightly around his ankle.

"The rope is in case you get swept away, m'lord. I cannot swim, but if you wash overboard, I can haul you back in, see?"

They began to climb another wave, and Durant quieted as he strained at the oars. Henri felt as if he had drunk too much wine and vomited again as they raced down the other side of the wave. He knew that the closer they got to the harbor entrance, the worse the waves would be.

"Let me take a turn at the oars," he offered. "You just concentrate on staying in the boat."

Rowing forced his mind to wake. They were drawing close to the western mole, which acted as a breakwater for Acre's elbow-shaped harbor. The waves rolled over the mole in the storm, cresting and crashing dangerously on the other side. He turned toward the south to avoid the mole, looking back over his shoulder toward the shore, trying to keep a target in sight the way that he heard the fisherman discussing in the harbor taverns. He pulled with all his strength, trying to steer them away from the beleaguered breakwater, but the little rowboat swept into a cross-current, swirling and lurching dangerously for a moment. He turned back to comment to Durant and froze.

Durant was gone.

"Durant!" he screamed. "Oh, my God, Durant!"

He saw a dark form thrashing in the water several yards away, and without thinking, he dove over the side of the boat, swimming desperately toward it. But Durant's hands only appeared briefly above the water, grasping at the air before his iron chainmail armor pulled him to the bottom of the bay.

"Durant!" Henri screamed again, trying to keep his head above the waves. He felt a tug at his ankle. The current towed the boat toward the shore, dragging him along with it.

"No, wait!" he yelled, tearing at the rope, but the water had swollen the hemp fibers, and the knot held fast. He looked back, but Durant was gone.

Pulling himself hand over hand on the rope, Henri reached the boat and clumsily fell back inside. The oars had washed away, but in the bottom of the little craft, he saw his armor and sword, neatly wrapped with rope and covered by his surcoat. Henri pulled his sword from the bundle and hacked at the simple wooden seat, ripping it from the gunnels. He plunged the plank into the water, leaning far over the bow of the craft, and paddled angrily.

Ahead of him in the harbor, he saw two ships listing to their sides, one with its mast nearly submerged. Bodies floated face down in the harbor, their arms drifting lifelessly around their heads, hair swirling in the waves.

No. He was not going to die like this, drowning within view of Acre. With a scream, he paddled harder, swallowing sea water as the waves slapped his face. On the Tower of Flies, a stinking pile of stones with a small lookout built on top, he saw men and women scrambling over the rocks like shore crabs – the refugees from the sinking ships. They yelled to him, arms lifted in supplication, but there was nothing he could do. The waves had him now, and they pushed him past the tower toward the shore.

As he approached the white sand, he saw that he had a new problem. He was drifting south of the sheltered harbor and the great iron fence that stood like a sentinel in the water, preventing enemies from entering Acre from the beach. If he could not turn himself around, he would end up outside the city with the Mamluk army. He could swim to the harbor, but he would have to leave his armor in the boat, or else it would drown him.

I have two choices: try to paddle against the waves with a plank or swim to shore and fight the Mamluks without armor or weapons, he thought desperately.

Something large drifted nearby. The bloated, stinking carcass of a dead horse bumped against the side of his little craft, legs sticking straight, bobbing and dipping like a cork.

Henri had an idea.

A few minutes later, he plunged into the waves and kicked away from the boat. His armor, tied to the carcass of the horse with the hemp rope, held steady. Throwing his arms over the beast's belly, he kicked and floundered, until the waves flung him, exhausted, against the seawall that protected one of the city's southernmost convents. He clawed at the rocks, looking for purchase, but each swell pulled him back and slammed him painfully against the slimy, barnacled stones. He positioned the horse between himself and the rocks, inching with agonizing slowness toward the point where the seawall gave way to the harbor entrance. His fingers grew numb and bloody, and his stomach, filled with saltwater and bile, soured until he retched again.

When he reached the harbor entrance, he saw the Mamluks had already been there. Bodies of men and women lay scattered on the shore, arms and legs splayed, many of them missing their heads, their corpses looted or mutilated. A short distance away, a group of Mamluks battled at a small house that hid the entrance to the Templar tunnels. After hours of fighting the waves, Henri knew he did not have the strength to lift a sword. He needed to hide and rest. Spotting a large pile of refuse – broken nets, fish bones, seaweed, shattered pottery, and leaky barrels – he freed his armor from the horse and slithered through the sand toward the pile, burying himself beneath the stinking midden. There, sheltered from the wind and the rain, he immediately fell asleep.

Chapter 37

May 1291
Acre Harbor, Acre

Henri woke feeling as if he had already been through a war. His hands throbbed, lacerated from holding onto the barnacle-strewn rocks, and his thirst was so powerful that he thought he could drink from a chamber pot – if only he could find one. Pulling on his wet, sandy armor, he cautiously climbed up from the beach onto the harbor street, which was littered with rocks, broken furniture, and the bodies of men and horses. The Mamluks had abandoned their battle at the harbor, concentrating their efforts on the convents and the citadels of the Brethren. He walked alone, bewildered and not sure where to go until he heard a shout behind him. A black-robed Hospitaller knight crouched in a doorway, beckoning.

"My friend, where are you going?" the knight asked.

"Truly, I know not," Henri replied. "Where the Mamluks are, I will go there and kill them."

The knight barked out a harsh laugh and then dissolved into a fit of coughing. Henri saw that he had a blood-crusted wound on a crudely bandaged shoulder.

"You are the viscount, are you not? Henri of Maron? They said you were dead."

"Brother, let me tighten your bandage for you," Henri

changed the subject. "The blood is starting to come through."

The knight, who gave his name as Brother Luc of Angevin, waited patiently and told of how the city succumbed to the enemy as Henri retied the man's dressing.

"The rest of the Hospitallers are with Grand Master Villiers. He is wounded, and we fear he will die like Beaujeu, and then God will truly have abandoned us," Brother Luc said, his voice saturated with despair.

Henri stopped. "Beaujeu is dead?"

"Why yes, how did you not know this? It was when Beaujeu died that all was lost. The Mamluks flooded in like a swarm of ants, and without Beaujeu, no one had the heart to fight any longer. Villiers is with King Henry and Prince Amalric at the Royal Palace right now, awaiting his death."

Henri heard the whisper of an arrow as it flew and struck Brother Luc square in the face. The Hospitaller jerked and fell forward, the arrow tip protruding from the back of his skull. Down the street, a yellow-clad Mamluk fumbled with another arrow that he had dropped to the ground. Henri ducked around a corner but crept back long enough to tug Brother Luc's water flask from his belt.

"May Jesu Christi give mercy to your soul," he mumbled, flicking the leather cap from the flask and swallowing the meager amount left in the bottle. Then he turned and ran.

The Mamluk pursued him, but this close to his city house, Henri knew the streets intimately. He ducked into an alcove and waited. The Mamluk soldier ran by, and Henri jumped out, slashing with his sword. He hit the soldier in the neck, and the man's throat exploded in blood.

Another soldier heard the noise and attacked with a long lance. Henri parried and dodged the blows, whacking the lance in half and shoving his sword into the man's belly. The

Mamluk cried out and tried to stab Henri with a short dagger. Henri thrust his sword again, and the soldier collapsed to the ground. The commotion was drawing attention, and three more Mamluks ran toward their fallen colleagues as Henri realized with rising panic that he would be outnumbered in less than ten heartbeats.

He picked up the bow and quiver from the fallen soldier. The weapon felt familiar in his hand, and he silently thanked Emre for his relentless training. Henri drew three arrows from the quiver and fired them in swift succession.

He struck the first soldier in the face, felling him instantly. The second he wounded in the shoulder. The Mamluk continued to run towards him, and he fired again, this time hitting the soldier in the chest. A third soldier charged at him, yelling, and Henri dropped the bow, pulling out his jeweled dagger. He threw it at the soldier, and it embedded in his eye. The Mamluk screamed and clutched at his face. Henri reclaimed his blade, but the soldier looked likely to recover, so he left him alive.

"Ho, Henri! Sir Henri!" He heard a shout from a rooftop. The armored figure of Sir Beauvais – a confrere and experienced fighter – waved down at him. "Well done, young man! Come to the door, and my servant will let you in!"

***

Henri fell through the front door of the house, and a white-clad slave looked down at him with hollow eyes.

"Faisal!" he heard Sir Beauvais holler from the roof. "There are five more dead in the street. Come up here and keep watch for me!" Faisal closed his eyes with a pained expression and then silently walked from the room. Sir Beauvais ran down the stairs two at a time, his armor clattering and tinkling.

"Quick, Sir Henri, you can help me," he shouted, pulling Henri outside again.

Thinking they meant to loot the bodies of weapons, Henri began to unstrap quivers and sword belts. Next to him, Sir Beauvais pulled out his ornate sword, raised it high, and severed the head of one of the Mamluks with two strikes.

"Beauvais!" Henri shouted, jumping back. "The man is already dead."

Sir Beauvais appeared not to hear him.

"Get that one," he ordered, pointing a bloody, gauntleted finger to the man that Henri had wounded with his dagger. The man was still alive, groaning and clutching at his face.

"Beauvais, this is pointless and dangerous. Let us go back into the house and conserve our strength for the living enemy."

Brusquely, Sir Beauvais pushed past Henri and swung his sword down. The Mamluk soldier cried out in fear before his head was cleaved from his body. Sir Beauvais swatted their helmets away, grabbed the two dripping heads by their hair, and ran back to the house, ignoring the pile of weapons and armor. Henri followed him, confused.

"Sayidi!" Faisal yelled from the roof, pointing urgently to the east. Beauvais slammed the door shut and secured it with a wooden bar. He picked up the heads and disappeared into another room.

Henri followed him at a distance, then stopped abruptly as the smell of decay hit him like a wave in the harbor. Beauvais walked across a stone floor that was sticky with old black blood. He placed the two heads in a niche in the wall. At least ten other heads in various stages of decomposition adorned the walls, the furniture, and the floor.

Henri backed away. "Sir Beauvais, what is this? What are you doing here?"

"Just taking a few souvenirs," Sir Beauvais said, sitting down on an ivory-inlaid couch next to a fresh specimen. "I killed all of these myself. We shall go out and get the other three later when the danger has passed. Your kills can stay here with mine unless you would like to take them elsewhere."

Henri felt the breath leave his body.

"I just… I need to go check on the threat outside…" he stammered. Slowly, he backed out of the room, then ran to the front door and yanked the bar up.

A dagger thunked into the wood at his head, and he froze.

Sir Beauvais stood in the doorway of his room of heads, and the darkness of the house seemed to gather around him. Faisal crept down the stairs and watched from the dim shadows.

"It is not wickedness," Sir Beauvais said, his voice cracking. "It is not sin because they are heathens, you see? God commands us to rid the Holy Land of them. We are assured penance for any sins we may commit – now and in the future." His hands shook, and he unsheathed his sword. "And if you are thinking of telling the Patriarch, your head shall join those in my study."

"Beauvais, your servant is terrified, and this is eating your mind. Please sheath your sword, and we will leave this house." Henri reached for his weapon, but Sir Beauvais advanced menacingly.

"My servant is fine!" Sir Beauvais yelled.

Henri looked at Faisal. Tears ran down the man's cheeks and into his beard.

"Beauvais, you need to get out of this house. Some wickedness is upon you." Henri tried to make his voice soothing, but Sir Beauvais swore and wiped at his eyes, which were ragged with exhaustion.

"They killed children, Maron! They crushed children

with their horses and raped Christian women!"

"And we have done the same to them. Surely you see that. They seek vengeance for the lives that we took, as would we if they had occupied our homeland. Beauvais, you are endangering your soul with this evil you have done on this day!"

"What is this heresy that you speak? It is true what they say. You are an infidel yourself!"

Henri ducked out of the way as Sir Beauvais screamed and ran at him. Sir Beauvais swung his sword and Henri dove behind a table. The wood splintered, and he scuttled backwards as Sir Beauvais advanced on him. The older knight stabbed viciously, and Henri rolled out of the way onto his hands and knees. He grasped the thin reed mat that Sir Beauvais stood upon and yanked it.

Sir Beauvais staggered backwards and crashed into the cold fireplace. Henri stood and threw a chair at the knight, which bought him a few heartbeats of time so he could rip his sword from its sheath. Sir Beauvais screamed again and brought his sword down over his head. Henri blocked it and pushed back, feeling the immense strength of the man. He seemed inhuman.

Sir Beauvais kicked Henri in the stomach, and he fell backwards. As the older knight yelled and ran at him, Henri slashed out with his sword, but Sir Beauvais kicked it away and it skittered, hitting a nearby wall. Henri watched in horror as Sir Beauvais let out a strangled yell of rage, his sword raised high, and swung down.

Without warning, a heavy urn flew across the room and struck the knight in the shoulder. He reeled back in surprise, and Henri struggled to his feet, took his sword and thrust it clumsily through the man's mail-clad chest. Sir Beauvais sank to his knees. "I will meet Jesu Christi soon," he wheezed, "for I have eternal penance for all my sins. I died protecting his kingdom." Blood welled from his mouth as he spoke, and Faisal approached with the wooden bar from the door and struck Beauvais across the head with it, tears still running down his face.

Henri fell back and gasped for air. "Thank you," he said, and Faisal nodded. Henri took a moment to catch his breath and calm his frayed nerves. He had just killed a knight of Acre. Would he go to hell for that? He looked up at Faisal.

"I will make for the Royal Palace and join the king. Will you come with me? You will be safe there."

Faisal shook his head sadly. "No, my lord, I shall stay here. I have seen too many horrors already."

Again, Henri entreated Faisal to join, but the man refused. He finally gave up and climbed to the roof to get a good view of the roads. The Mamluks were concentrated to the southwest near the Templar citadel, and he could see the roof of the Royal Palace. It had not burned.

Downstairs, Faisal sat on the bloody floor in the room of heads, where the stench of death mingled with the sulfurous smell of naft.

"Please leave, my lord," the slave said tonelessly. "Please go." And he struck a flint. He had coated himself and the floor around him with naft, which ignited and flashed up instantly. Henri jumped back, shouting with dismay.

"Allahu akbar!" Faisal screamed as the flames enveloped him.

Henri backed away, scrambled to the front door, and flung it open. Heedless of any enemy that might be nearby, he fled from the house and didn't look back.

Chapter 38

May 1291

The Venetian Quarter, Acre

Sidika scratched another mark into the wall of the cellar where she sat and carefully took up the book again. The *Legenda Aurea*. Some of the stories contained within were familiar, like Saint George and the Dragon. Saint George's likeness could be found carved into stone and stitched into tapestries wherever Franj Christians habituated. But some, like the stories of Saint Lucy and Saint Agatha, were unfamiliar, and she felt giddy at the prospect of reading them, even though she had already done so yesterday. Though she found their stories saccharine, it was a rare pleasure to read about the heroic deeds of women for a change.

Reverently, she brushed her fingers across the book, which was little more than a pamphlet – several dozen pages stitched together. Because illumination was so expensive, there was no adornment, but the script was delicate and exquisite. She longed for her father to see the book, for she knew that he would have pored over everything, from the quality of the paper to the straightness of the lightly outlined margins.

Reclining on a cushion near her, Emre stared at the red glow of the brazier, his eyes distant. He looked up.

ELIZABETH R. ANDERSEN

"Why did you stop reading?"

They had been in the cellar for two days. The Mamluks ravaged the house, looting anything portable before finally prying the colored mosaic tiles from the walls and the unbroken pieces of glass from the screens and shutters. Sidika and Emre crouched in the darkness, waiting for the footsteps to cease, then they waited longer. But as time passed, it became clear that Emre's wound was festering, making escape impossible. Fighting her urge to flee, Sidika took furtive trips out of the cellar to grab cloth for bandages and any dried herbs that she could find in the kitchen. She bound and splinted his wrist with a scrap of velvet she found underneath a bedstead and made a poultice of dusty old comfrey leaves that she reconstituted with some ale.

Now she read the words aloud in the book, but her mind raced around other things. Emre couldn't be moved, but the longer she stayed in the cellar with him, the greater her chance of missing a way to escape the city. She glanced up at him, and then her eyes darted back to the book. His skin was gray and waxy, his eyes half-closed. He no longer sweated with fever because they had almost no ale left to drink, so instead he lay quietly, his breath coming in rapid, shallow huffs.

"And when the provost heard that she was Christian the provost was much glad because to have power on her, for then the Christian people were in the will of the Lord, and if they would not deny their God and their belief all their goods should be forfeited."

Emre looked up at her. "Such a strange thing, is it not, that the Christians of Saint Agatha's time were compelled to renounce their religion under penalty of severe punishment, and yet they now do the same to Muslims and Jews?"

He groaned and rolled onto his side. "I was captured as a

young man and taught the Qur'an in a madrasa. Given a choice between speaking a lie and death. I chose the lie. And if I chose death, no one would venerate me as a martyr as in this book, for I would simply be one of the thousands of low-born who lived and died without being noticed by anyone. But what was once a lie has become my truth. Mafeo tried everything in his power to convert me to the way of the Christians, but I could not do it. I believe that Muhammad is God's prophet. I believe that there is no god but Allah. I no longer just say it; I *believe* it."

Sidika stared ahead, the words of Khadir's wife, Banat rattling her head. "Tamrat the heretic," she had called her father. To the inhabitants of her mostly Christian village, it had mattered little who their neighbors worshipped, so long as they kept it to themselves. The church was the center of life and politics in the city, but in the hills, it was merely a controlling group of Franj men in white robes.

She took a deep breath. "All my life, I have seen men use their interpretation of God to inflict suffering on each other. My adopted father took commissions from Muslims and Christians, always knowing that either side could kill him for working with the other, or for simply being a Jew. And in the community of Jews in Acre, my father and I are shunned because of our work. Nothing is so straightforward as people would wish, although I do not think that Allah, or Hashem, or Jesu Christi would want this violence among men."

Emre nodded slowly. "If men desire to kill each other, they will find a way to justify it so that their souls cannot feel anguish." He paused. "But I believe in the words of the Prophet, peace be upon him, and I shall speak Allah's name as I die."

Had Sidika not already spent days with Emre, she would have felt nervous. Nothing could enflame a man to murderous passion like disagreeing with his religion. She looked down at the book in her lap.

The *Legenda Aurea* was about the Christian saints, and Sidika read the stories half with fascination, half horror at the descriptions of torture and piety. She had read the great Muslim philosophers and astronomers, the Sufi poets, the medical works of Ibn Sina, and her father had once caught her reading *Le Roman de la Rose* when he worked on a copy for a local Franj noble ("Odious work of allegorical blather!" he would rant as he worked on it).

Thinking of her father made Sidika's heart heavy. What would he think if he knew his daughter was trapped underground in the cellar of Lord Henri's house with a Mamluk defector? He would probably find the whole situation amusing.

Emre looked up and listened.

"It is quiet. I hear no screams or stones. Perhaps evening has fallen. I shall go up for more water and candles."

Sidika stood. "Nonsense. You cannot even lift your head. And besides, there are no supplies left in the house – I checked yesterday."

She glanced at him anxiously. He had a day, perhaps two, before he died. She bit her lip, wondering if it would have been better to strike him over the head with a stone as she had intended instead of allowing him to suffer.

"There is a well in the square of the Venetian Quarter. I must go there to get us some more water since Lord Henri's fountain was crushed by a Mamluk stone." She looked down self-consciously, trying to ignore how badly she smelled from days of not bathing. Yes, this was better. She could not keep him and herself both alive in this cellar, and his agony would only increase as the pestilence in his arm spread. If she could not find any poisons in the house, she would wait until he slept and smother him to ease his suffering. But for now, it was important to maintain normalcy, such as it was. She pondered the irony of her situation; killing a man to give him mercy, the very thing that Henri had done for her father.

"There is no way that you will reach the Venetian Quarter without being slaughtered," Emre panted.

"And yet, that is where I will go," she said stubbornly, tying a scarf around her hair.

With his uninjured arm, Emre tugged his long dagger from his belt and handed it to her.

"Take this with you. Although you do not have the strength to overcome a fully trained ʻaskari, you may have the element of surprise."

"And what about you?"

Emre patted his side. "I have one more line of defense."

Sidika looked skeptically at the second tiny, curved dagger in his belt. It looked comically small. Perhaps its function was only for slitting throats.

Calming her pounding heart, she cautiously approached the wooden trapdoor and pushed. It stayed firmly in place. She threw her shoulder against it but still, it remained immovable. Panic rose in her. Desperately, she struggled against the door until her arms throbbed with the effort and sweat dripped from her temples.

"What is happening?" she heard Emre say hoarsely.

"It is stuck fast," she called back to him. "The stones of the house must have collapsed upon it."

A noise above caught her attention. Someone was walking upstairs. A man's voice called out, but through the heavy layers of stone and rubble above them, she couldn't make out the words. Sidika held her breath. She heard other footsteps join the first, then they all fell quiet for a very long time.

She had just convinced her frayed nerves that the danger had passed when she heard movement again. Someone was attempting to clear the rubble that blocked the trap door. Sidika's heart pounded in alarm. She scrambled to Emre's side and snuffed out their candle.

Chapter 39

May 1291

The Venetian Quarter, Acre

Henri stopped running and swept his eyes across the shattered buildings around him, trying to get his bearings. Houses had been burned to the ground or pounded with stones until the streets were unrecognizable. He could still see the spire of Saint Andrew's church through the drifting rafts of black smoke, although for how long it would continue to stand he was not sure. The church was near the Templar citadel and his house. He knew that he had a duty to find and protect King Henry, but he couldn't keep himself from trying to find Emre first.

He examined a ruined structure with three outer walls still standing. The top storey and the roof were gone, and the eastern wall crumbled into a pile of rubble, but inside he could see a familiar mosaic ceiling and floors in rooms that were in various states of disintegration.

"Emre!" Henri shouted and ran inside. A few loose stones tumbled at him, and he jumped back. Stepping carefully into what had been the main hall, he called out again, then listened, straining his ears. He heard voices a few streets over.

"Orada bir şey duydum!"

Henri couldn't speak Turkish, but he understood well enough that his shouts had been heard. He ducked into his study, hid behind the crumbling remains of the fireplace, and waited. He heard the scrape of feet on loose stones inside the house.

"Dışarı çık, küçük fare!" someone called out.

Henri quietly raised his bow and peered around the fireplace. Two Mamluk fursān stalked through the house, one motioning silently to the other to split up. A soldier stood ten feet from him, his back turned, sword raised high. Henri knelt and pulled his bowstring back, his arms straining. He loosed the arrow, and it thunked into the man's skull where the protection of his turban-wrapped helmet ended. Slowly, the soldier dropped to his knees, the tip of the arrow protruding from his gaping mouth, and fell forward.

Henri whipped another arrow from the slender quiver at his hip. The second soldier ran around the corner and Henri shot him, this time through the face. The man cried out, then staggered. Henri sprang from behind the fireplace and ran the man through with his sword.

Immediately he started to dig the rubble away from the cellar door. He could hide underground until the Mamluks left the street, then continue looking for Emre when things quieted down.

He stopped, listening carefully.

Someone groaned behind him. Easing his dagger from his belt, he inspected the soldiers sprawled on the ground, but they were dead, staring sightlessly. A slight motion caught his attention, and he noticed an arm protruding from underneath a nearby table.

"Emre!" Henri fell to his knees and dug.

But it wasn't Emre. Lying half-buried in the rubble, an old woman stirred stiffly. Dried blood crusted her clothes, and Henri could see deep gashes along her arms that looked as if she had been blocking a sword with her forearms. Her eyes cracked open, and she smiled painfully through a toothless mouth.

"Thirsty… thirsty," she croaked in Arabic, pointing to her cracked and dehydrated lips. Henri uncapped Brother Luc's flask and poured the last dribble of water into her mouth. She choked and sputtered, spilling pinkish puddles of blood and water on the tile floor.

"Grandmother, are there any others with you? A young man, perhaps?" He took her hand.

When she tried to speak, her tongue was red with blood, and the air rattled in her lungs. "My girl," she whispered, "get… her… out. Bebeğim… bebeğim… my baby…"

"Truly, there is no one else in this house. You are the only living soul left." Henri squeezed her hand, but the old woman did not seem to understand his words.

"Must… get her out!" she said more forcefully. Her eyes wandered past Henri's head toward the sky and the walls, and they rolled back. "I go… to the Great Sky," she sighed.

Henri lowered his forehead to the ground. Eleven. That was the number of people he had either killed or watched take their last breath this day.

"God…" he whispered, "there is no sense in this."

His words stirred up little puffs of plaster dust on the tile floor and he coughed. "Help us. Is this not your holy kingdom that burns around me?" He imagined God looking down on him impassively, surrounded by frowning, dead Templars.

Finally, he stood heavily, adjusted his armor, and crept from the house into the street. Emre was clearly not at the house, and it was imperative that Henri find the king. He tried to focus on listening for the enemy and not on the image of the old woman's damaged forearms or Faisal's

261

screams as flames licked up his clothing.

The words of Sir Beauvais came back to him.

"I will meet my Christ soon, for I have eternal penance for all my sins." Henri whispered the dying knight's words aloud and supposed the same was true for him.

The bishops in Francia preached that fighting for the Holy Land meant forgiveness, not just for one's personal sins, but also for the sins of others, or even for sins not yet committed. The ultimate indulgence. Sir Beauvais thought his soul was saved no matter what he did. Henri wondered what other sins Sir Beauvais had committed under this blanket of forgiveness. What were men such as Sir Beauvais like back in Francia and under the jurisdiction of King Philippe?

Using the flaming steeple of the Church of the Holy Cross as his guide, he carefully crept through the city, avoiding Mamluk patrols on his way. He passed the Church of Saint Lawrence and saw that smoke billowed from the high windows, but the heavy doors were chained shut, with several dozen Mamluk soldiers waiting outside. Henri's stomach turned. He could hear the piteous cries of people inside the church as they burned to death. There was nothing he could do against so many. Quietly he slipped past and continued on his way.

The sun had nearly set when he arrived at King Henry's modest palace on the city's inner walls, backed up against Montmusard. As he approached the heavily fortified building, several arrows flew past his head and buried themselves in the dirt near his feet.

Henri snatched a shield from a fallen knight and sheltered behind it.

"Belay yourselves! I am a viscount of Acre, come to find Prince Amalric and the king!"

No reply came from the house.

"I tell you," Henri shouted again, conscious that he was attracting Mamluk attention, "I am a friend to the king's brother, and I require shelter."

An arrow bit into Henri's shield, and he jumped back.

"God's teeth! I am a knight of Acre! Let me in! I am speaking to you in French, not Turkic, you dullards!"

The walls were silent.

Growling in frustration, Henri circled the house until he came to the postern that Keratsa's servant had used to spirit him into her room only weeks ago. It was unguarded. He put his shoulder against it and then kicked it open.

"Simpletons," he muttered, "if their hubris does not kill them, then their stupidity will." He pulled the door closed behind him and stomped up the stairs. Inside, he could hear Amalric yelling.

"Of course you should let him in, you incompetent fools! And now you have lost the viscount of Acre! Well, go and find him!"

Henri found Amalric and his older brother, King Henry, standing in the hall with two abashed-looking guards.

"Amalric," he said, and all four men jumped. "Your postern is unlocked." Henri gestured over his shoulder with his thumb.

"Well, you heard him. See to it!" Amalric snapped. The guards bowed and ran from the room.

"Walking in on the king unannounced could get you killed, Henri. I did not even know that we had a postern," Amalric said, striding over and pulling Henri into a rough embrace.

The king crossed his arms petulantly and glowered.

"I see that Henri of al-Hadiqa is just as irritating as I remember, and still showing up at my house uninvited."

Much like he was as a youth, King Henry was short and slight, with thick brown hair that fell in waves to his shorn chin. His eyes were an unremarkable brown and had a way of staring lazily from heavy lids that made him look as if he were perpetually bored. Due to his epilepsy, shadows of purple and blue bruises from frequent falls ornamented his pale arms and face.

The new king was only three years older than Henri and had recently come into his crown, and not without controversy. The inhabitants of Acre disliked the notion that their king preferred to stay confined to Cyprus and rarely visited the largest city in his kingdom. Rumor spread that the king was intimidated by the vitriolic factionalism that Acre was famous for and stayed on his island to avoid conflict.

"Well met, *your highness*," Henri allowed some sarcasm to poison his voice.

King Henry surveyed Henri coolly. "You have grown," he said, finally. "When I last saw you at my coronation, you were scrawny. Show some respect, Lord Henri. I am your king, after all."

Henri dropped to one knee and bowed his head shallowly. "Thank you for joining us, Highness. How fares Cyprus?"

King Henry rolled his eyes and stalked from the room.

"Do not antagonize him, Henri," Amalric murmured, handing Henri a cup of wine. "He has not grown milder of temper since you last saw him, and he had another fit this morning. He is always out of humor after a fall."

"He's a spoiled cockscomb," Henri grumbled.

"You would know. And as Jesu Christi said, 'remove the log from your own eye before attempting to remove the splinter from your brother's eye'. It is good to see you, Henri.

There are some who said that you abandoned the city."

Henri swallowed. "Have you seen Sir Eirik or Brother Gregoire?"

Amalric sighed. "No. Our forces scattered when the Mamluks breached the walls, and we think that many fled to the Templars because that is where the Mamluks are focusing their attention. Unfortunately, we cannot get close enough to determine whether they live or not. Beaujeu is dead, and Villiers is here in this house, sure to join him soon. If he doesn't perish from his wounds, his own Hospitaller physicians will probably bleed him to death. I wonder if those two old men will continue to quarrel in heaven as they do down here with us mortals." Amalric laughed bitterly.

"How many citizens live?" Henri asked, thinking about the two hundred villagers he had evacuated from his own settlements. Most of them fled to the city, and he feared that few had managed to escape further.

"Impossible for us to know," Amalric shook his head. "When they breached the walls, the Mamluks flooded in like water through the hole in an aqueduct, and they killed every living man they could find. The women and children they mostly carried off. My brother says that all is lost and prefers to abandon the city and retake it later."

"He would," Henri muttered.

Amalric shrugged his shoulders. "Perhaps it is a better strategy. If we cannot protect it then neither can the Mamluks. We could return and win it back before the Mamluks have time to refortify."

"We will never retake it if we surrender." Henri felt his temper rising. "How can you give up on Acre when we still have men left to fight yet? Neither you nor your brother lived in this city, but I was born here. Acre is worth saving! Let us try again to gather reinforcements from Rome and from Francia!"

"I have already petitioned the Holy Father and the kings of Christendom for more knights," King Henry declared, returning to the room with a cup of wine in his hand. "Rome is concerned with the dratted uprising in Sicily, and King Philippe has his own wars to fight in his land. French lords are wily and quarrelsome, it seems." He eyed Henri with distaste.

"I will attempt to negotiate one last time with Khalil, but if he refuses to retreat or allow the citizens safe passage, then we must leave. Why they have not torn this house down and taken us all hostage already is beyond my understanding."

"You may go back to Cyprus if your parley is unsuccessful, but I will stay here and protect the city in which I was born." Henri lifted his chin defiantly.

King Henry's mouth turned up into a wicked smile. "Yes, I think that is a wise choice, Lord Henri. You should stay and fight."

***

Henri stayed at the fortified Royal Palace, leaving daily with five other knights to harass the enemy and search for survivors. On the third day, a message arrived from Khalil, proposing to allow the citizens safe passage to Cyprus due to King Henry's "youth." King Henry, chafing at this insinuation that he was young and inexperienced, sent a refusal back to Khalil and ordered his household to evacuate, bringing Amalric and the critically injured grand master of the Hospitallers with him.

Henri felt sure that he would rather face the entire Mamluk army alone than step ashore in Marseille and face the wrath of his mother, whose plans for his extradition were foiled by Durant. He stood on the beach and watched the masts of the king's ship lean and sway as the craft pitched in the waves, heading slowly back to Cyprus. Behind him, the city smoldered. The entire Mamluk army concentrated now on looting the remains of the houses or tearing down the walls of the Templar citadel.

He could see the golden lions of the citadel shining in the sun to the south of him. If that was where the last citizens of Acre were, then that was where he would go.

Chapter 40

May 1291

The Great Blue Eternal Heaven

Ayata stood silently watching Sarangerel, his face as cool and pale as carved marble. She blinked back at him from where she stood in the blueish light of his presence.

"My lord!" she breathed in wonder. She fell to her hands and knees, pressing her forehead into the cool, short grass in supplication. She did not know how she had arrived here. The last thing she remembered was the face of the young nobleman leaning over her, giving her a sip of water in the ruins of his house.

The corner of Ayata's perfectly formed upper lip curled with displeasure.

"Get up," he commanded. Turning and walking away, he called to her without looking back. "Follow!"

Sarangerel climbed quickly to her feet and then looked down at her legs with surprise. They were young and strong, covered by a thick black woolen dress edged with silver stitching. At her waist, she wore a girdle of white horsehide, studded with milky moonstones. Ayata did not stop nor turn around, so she followed him. Her feet were bare, but the grass beneath them was soft and springy. First, she trotted, then skipped, then leapt like a young foal, laughing with joy as her body responded heartily to its forgotten youth.

Ayata had stopped at the abrupt edge of a cliff with shaggy tufts of grass flopping over its edge and waited there. Sarangerel approached cautiously.

"You have been a poor excuse for one of my subjects, earth child. The names of your ancestors are forgotten. You show no appropriate piety to me."

Sarangerel's knees began to quake, and she fell to the ground again. "Mighty lord, I am devoted to Günana, the Sun Mother. It is to her that I have given many thanks for bringing me an orphan child. For hearing my prayers!"

Ayata turned and looked down at her with cold contempt. Sarangerel saw that the fabric of his robe was of an ethereal, silvery material that flickered gently with slow shadows, as when the clouds moved across the face of the moon. An aura of glowing silver surrounded his head and hands.

"It is to me that you owe your worship, not to Günana. Were it not for the child, I would have let you move on your way to Tamu." He pointed with a long finger. "Look down."

Sarangerel looked over the edge of the cliff and gasped. At first, all she could see was swirling smoke, but as a wind pushed it away, she beheld a ruined city far below, its buildings aflame, and the tiny, sprawled corpses of its slaughtered citizens laying in the streets.

"My lord... why? Why did the Mamluk beasts do this thing?"

Ayata turned to her. "Why do you only call them beasts, earth child? Was not this very city the graveyard of thousands of Allah's people a hundred years ago? Did you not raid villages and slaughter when you lived in the high places with your tribe? All of Tengri's soul-owning creatures are beasts. Earth children are merely beasts whose mouths can worship, and hands can give sacrifice."

His voice sounded hollow, and when she tried to look at him, he seemed both tangible and insubstantial. As much as she tried, her eyes slid off his form, so she never really saw all of him at once.

"It is me that you should have worshipped, for you found the girl-child in my light. I led you to her beneath a full moon, and now she lays dying under the earth. You must bring her out."

Sarangerel sobbed. "I tried to save her, my lord! You took me too soon!"

Ayata picked her up by her braids and flung her over the slide of the cliff. "And now, I send you back!"

Sarangerel screamed as she fell, flailing and spinning toward the devastated city. The ground drew closer, the smell of smoke and decay hit, and she sat up screaming inside the Franj lord's destroyed house. Two astonished Mamluk soldiers in blue livery stood nearby, pulling their swords from their sheaths in alarm.

"Get her out!" Sarangerel rasped, swatting their swords away. "Çıkarın onu! Çıkarın onu!" She rolled onto her hands and knees, crawling, clawing the ground near the collapsed fireplace. The young Franj lord had stopped digging by the fireplace and left, but she knew her baby was down there… Ayata had said she was down there.

The stones were large, and she strained but could not move them. She was old again, with flaccid muscles in her arms and hands that shook from lack of drink. Behind her, the Mamluks were yelling in Turkic for her to stop, so she turned and grabbed the nearest one by the hem of his tunic. He pushed her hand away, so she reached up and slapped him across the face. "Aşağıda! Çabuk!"

The soldier raised his sword to slash at Sarangerel's head, but the other Mamluk grabbed his wrist, motioning for him to listen. A faint tapping sound came from below their feet.

The two men began to dig.

Sarangerel sank to her knees, then gently to her side. "I did it..." she breathed. "Ayata, I did it. Take me with you, take me—"

***

Timurhan withdrew his sword from the old woman's throat and wiped it clumsily on her cloak. He picked up the body, tossed it into the street for the slaves to remove later, then returned to help Ismael roll the heaviest stones away from the trapdoor in the floor.

"Crazy old witch," he muttered.

Chapter 41

May 1291

The Venetian Quarter, Acre

Sidika's vision blurred as the candle's fragile flame wavered and swayed with each shallow breath she exhaled. She lay on a thin coverlet spread on the cold stone floor of the cellar. Above her head on the wall were two marks that she had scratched for each day underground, but she had stopped putting marks on the wall when she could no longer open the trap door and look out to determine the day from night. Near her, Emre dozed on his cushions, still alive but never leaving his fevered delirium. The water and ale were gone, the food eaten down to every tiny crumb that fell into the floor.

As she weakened, she no longer tried to push the trap door open. Now she lay and waited for death, but she would greet death in the light. Her last candle burned to a nub of wick in a glowing puddle of tallow, and she watched it hungrily.

The house was in ruins. Emre would be dead in a matter of hours. She would die slowly with his rotting corpse in the cellar, and perhaps someone would find their bodies many years later. Perhaps her bones would lie forgotten forever underground. Dully, her thoughts slowed by hunger and thirst, she toyed with the notion that someone might discover their bones a thousand years from now and wonder why a man and woman had died in a cellar.

She heard footsteps above her. Hallucinations. She had imagined many footsteps since a man tried to unearth her trap door. She wished that he had, even if it meant that he would kill them, for now, more than anything, she wanted the oblivion of death.

If Emre dies, I could drink his blood. I am so thirsty…

Again, the persistent, dreadful thought drifted into her mind. She had battled it for hours now, and she shifted uncomfortably, her stomach turning sour at the idea, but a savage, thirsty beast within her wished to hasten his departure. It did not matter – she did not have the strength to kill him now.

"Lā 'ilāha 'illallāh…"

Emre whispered in the dark. He had been reciting the shahada for hours now in his delirium, professing his faith, preparing himself for death in his subconscious. Perhaps she should also prepare herself as well. The thought of dying deep underground in the dark, in a tomb, made her eyes burn, and if she were not so thirsty, perhaps she would have cried. "Lā 'ilāha 'illallāh…muhammadur-rasūlullāh…"

Sidika took a shallow breath.

"Glorified and sanctified be God's great name throughout the world, which He has created according to His will," she whispered, her murmurs joining Emre's. Her voice sounded strange to her ears. She didn't know if she was saying Kaddish for herself, her father, or her mother and brother. Her voice grew stronger as she spoke the words, and she sat up.

"He who creates peace in His celestial heights, may He create peace for us and for all Israel…"

Those *were* footsteps above her. Someone was in the

house. Sidika stood and swayed unsteadily. Snatching the copper ale pitcher, she staggered to the steps that led to the trap door. The effort to swing the pitcher over her head was too great, so instead she banged it against the wall. She hit it again. The footsteps began to move faster. Again and again she hit the wall until she heard the sound of talking and the thundering of stones rolling away from the trapdoor.

Finally, the trapdoor wrenched back, and Sidika shielded her eyes from the blinding light of day as it streamed into the cellar from the roofless house. Two surprised faces stared down at her from under tall, conical helmets. Mamluk soldiers. She didn't care. She had forgotten most of her Turkish when she left Damascus to live with Tamrat and Sara, but there was one word that would always remain burned into her memory.

"Yardım," she said. "Help."

They reached down and grasped her under the arms, hauling her into the light. Her hands shook so hard that her teeth chattered. She couldn't remember the Turkish word for water, so she pantomimed drinking, and one of the men handed her his flask. She let the warm, stinking liquid flow down her throat, and it was the most beautiful thing she had ever tasted.

The soldier snatched the flask back. "Yavaşla," he said, shaking his head. He was young and olive-skinned, with deep-set brown eyes. The other soldier was even younger and very fair, with gray eyes and white eyelashes and brows. Sidika blinked at them. All she wanted to do now was sleep.

Weakly, she reached for the flask again, but the brown-eyed soldier held it out of her reach. He handed her to the younger man and descended, sword drawn, into the cellar. The other soldier forced her to the dusty mosaiced floor and yanked up her skirt. Sidika weakly tried to push his hands away, but he slapped her hard across the face. The first soldier emerged from the cellars with Emre's limp body slung across his shoulders. He kicked at the blonde Mamluk with annoyance.

"Yapma," he snarled.

Sidika pulled her skirt back over her knees and gestured for more water. The soldier shook his head no, and if she had any tears left, she would have cried with frustration. Water was right in front of her, and she was too weak to take it for herself.

Eventually, an argument broke out between the Mamluks, concluding when the brown-eyed soldier threw his hands up in resignation and stomped from the house. The blonde soldier looked back at her with a smirk. Sidika's hands still shook, but the water had given her a little bit of strength – enough to scramble backwards as the soldier approached. Hidden within the fabric of her dress, her fist clutched Emre's dagger.

Chapter 42

May 1291
Acre, Palestine

F inally, the cries slowed, so Yusuf only occasionally heard the animal scream of a dying man or the pleas of a woman as a soldier snatched her children from her arms. Even though the stables and siege engines still burned, the air in the city of Acre cleared with the brisk wind coming from the restless sea. Yusuf wiped his sleeve across his dry eyes and called for his valet. *God, I hate this*, he thought as the man handed him a fresh skin of water. *I could be at my home right now, helping Abreshmina make another son.*

He thought of his new wife, Musina, who he had only ever laid eyes on for a single day in her father's house when he signed the marriage contract.

Hmm… perhaps I will make two sons when I return.

In truth, it had been a long time since Yusuf had endured any kind of skirmish that did not involve a shatranj board or a palace intrigue. The battle of Tripoli two years earlier had been the last major siege that he had partaken in, and his skills were stale. He must spend more time training at the meydan with the new recruits, for the Franj were undoubtedly going to try to retake their city after assessing their losses and gathering reinforcements from abroad.

His crotch hurt, and he shifted self-consciously, trying to find a comfortable position. He had been in his saddle in his heavy armor since sunup, leading a group of scouts through the streets, leaping over piles of rubble that blocked roads and alleys, in search of the grand master of the Temple. He felt melancholy. It would have been his great pleasure to meet Lord Beaujeu, of whom he had exchanged letters and even gifts on occasion. The man was different than the other Franj. His mind was not closed off. Now, Yusuf worried that, when Beaujeu was delivered to the sultan, he would be killed.

Khalil was growing bored with his power and always seeking more. It was disconcerting. The pious young man that Yusuf had grown to love and respect as a friend was now replaced by a paranoid and cruel ruler who was willing to ignore his beliefs to secure more wealth and authority for himself. Yusuf had spent his entire life in the presence of powerful men and become one himself. Few men to whom Allah granted power were capable of remaining good.

"The day whereon neither wealth nor sons will avail, but only he will prosper that brings to God a sound heart."

Yusuf muttered the verse from the Qur'an under his breath. Dismounting, he handed his horse off to his valet, pulled his sword from its sheath, and stalked down the street. He needed a minute to exercise his legs and let things move about freely, as nature intended.

Although everyone knew that Acre was in denial about the oncoming army, it had still been a surprise when the troops stormed into the houses only to discover that there were few signs of packing or any other attempt to hide valuables. It truly seemed as if the people were caught off their guard by the breach in the walls. Yusuf shook his head. Roland le Grec, his Franj informant, had spoken of the city's confidence in their fortifications, but Yusuf had dismissed the man's word in favor of a more prestigious and highly placed man within the merchant's guild. After all, Beaujeu was a sensible man who would protect the lives of his citizens. What Yusuf had not considered at the time was that the city leaders might not have listened to Beaujeu. The merchants and the nobles had left the city, but what could the poor do? There were only a limited number of ships available, and it seemed that, in their characteristic cruelty, the Christian infidels had left the poor to fend for themselves.

It disquieted his conscience, killing these people. Surely the poor citizens of Acre were not to blame for the city's corruption and the vile habits of the Franj nobility and clergy. He had said as much to Khalil, but his friend had looked at him coolly.

"No one must be allowed to live who does not serve some purpose to us," Khalil said as he watched his armorer sharpening the blade of his sword on a whetstone. "Every fighting man not worth training to our ways will die. Every woman not worthy of the harem or the kitchen shall meet the sword, along with her children, if they are not worth the taking. I will allow them to laze about on our land no longer."

"And what about the converts? Surely there will be some."

Khalil snorted. "Converts at the end of a sword are no true believers."

Yusuf knew that Khalil had never been to Acre before, and Qalāwūn, his father, came from the Caucasus just as Yusuf had. Who could claim this land? The Arabs? The Bedu? The Jews? Did it even matter, as long as it didn't belong to the Franj?

After days of fighting and looting, the churches and

houses were stripped of their wealth, including the very tiles from the floors. Khalil had ordered all buildings to be torn down, stone by stone, until nothing remained that would indicate that a city had once stood here. Already his masons and heavy laborers were at work, rolling great pieces of limestone and the carcasses of dead horses into the harbor, rendering it unusable to Franj ships. All around him, Yusuf watched as his soldiers destroyed the livelihoods of men – both good and bad – and tore children from the arms of their mothers to take as spoils of war.

He just wanted to go home.

"My lord amir!" A young man trotted up to him wearing the striking blue livery of Yusuf's troops. The young man bowed quickly, brushing sweat from his brow with the back of his hand.

"We found two live ones trapped in a cellar. One of them appears to have been Mamluk at once time." He pulled a small, empty scabbard from his tunic and held it out. It was made of thin hammered gold and set with sapphires that were no larger than lentils. Around the opening was inscribed a name: "Badahir, God's faithful servant."

Yusuf looked dumbly at the intricate design on the scabbard for a moment, his face growing pale. "Where is this man? What did he look like?"

"He looked dead, or nearly so." The young soldier gestured to a house with a few walls that still stood. "With hair that curls like a woman's. I do not know what happened to his dagger. We found him with a girl, and I would take her to the church with the other prisoners, but Timurhan wants to have her first. I thought you would wish to know."

"The women are not to be touched by my troops, Ismael! My men need to focus on their task!"

"There was no stopping him, my lord."

ELIZABETH R. ANDERSEN

Yusuf set his jaw, stuffing the scabbard in his tunic.

"Come with me," he commanded, signaling for more of his troops to follow.

***

"Lā 'ilāha 'illallāh muħammadur-rasūlullāh…"

Again, the lilting words of the Shahada slapped against Emre's consciousness like a wave on a seawall. For a moment, they receded, and his mind grew quiet, then they roared back, this time in Turkic.

"Tanıklık ederim ki hiçbir tanri yoktur, ancak Allah vardır ve yine tanıklık ederim ki Muhammed onun kulu ve elçisidir…"

"Lā 'ilāha 'illallāh… lā 'ilāha 'illallāh… lā…"

Someone was screaming. Emre looked around. No, wait, his eyes were still closed. With a great effort, he pulled them open, although he thought it would have been easier to lift a portcullis than his eyelids at this moment. His throbbing hand felt as large and hot as a brazier.

"Stop struggling, and this will be over quickly!" a man snarled nearby in Turkic.

Slowly, for what seemed like hours or days, Emre turned his head toward the sound. He saw shoes, Sidika's little doeskin slippers, and bare legs kicking. Too much leg. Her red dress was up around her chest, and there was a man in scale armor and a brilliant blue tunic struggling with her.

"Badahir?" Emre slurred. He once owned such a tunic – embroidered blue silk with a chain of red stitching around the hem, sleeves, and neckline, and his name, along with verses of the Qur'an embroidered on his sash. He pushed himself up onto his uninjured arm, and his head swam with fever and pain. No, this was not Badahir. The soldier shouted in surprise, and Emre heard the metallic sound of a

280

dagger clattering to the ground. Sidika must have tried to stab him.

He reached clumsily for the jambiya on his belt, but the little curved dagger was gone. With a torturous effort, he felt around on the gritty floor for the weapon, careful not to prick his hands with its deadly edge. It must have slipped out of its scabbard when the other Mamluk dumped him here. A glint of gold caught his eye. The jambiya had fallen and landed near a pile of rubble. He rolled to it, slowly, painfully, and picked it up. He had hoped to use it on himself, but the fever took him before he had a chance. His vision wavered, and he grasped the gold-plated hilt.

Badahir, his Mamluk master, had given him the dagger as a present many years ago. During his wild, flailing escape from Tripoli, Emre had managed to find the sense to bury it under a pile of rocks before the Bedu captured him. A year later, he located it again on a trip to Damascus with Mafeo.

Sidika.

The soldier had a hand pressed heavily over her mouth and nose, and her eyes rolled back in her head. He was grunting and fumbling with the strings of his sirwals. There was only one chance to get this right. Emre did not have the strength to thrust the dagger into this young, healthy soldier, but he always kept the blade poisoned, hoping that someday he could give Mafeo a little scratch.

I have not re-coated the blade since Mafeo died, his mind protested. *It surely will not be sufficient to kill this boy, and he will only turn on you and then continue to rape her once you are dead.*

Emre giggled deliriously, and the soldier stopped trying to pull the front of his pants down, turning slowly toward the sound.

"Why... why not take me instead?" Emre slurred thickly,

concealing the little jambiya in his good hand. "I have not had the pleasure of another body in over a year. Let us both enjoy this moment, since she obviously does not."

The young man jumped back from Sidika's limp form, hitching his sirwals up in his fist. With a cry, he pounced, and Emre's hand darted out, drawing a deep, long scratch down the boy's neck. The soldier yelled and jumped back out of Emre's reach for a moment, slapping a hand to the wound. Behind him, Sidika stirred, clawed her way toward the cellar door by the fireplace. Emre willed her to move faster.

"Timurhan!" a voice barked from the street. "Stay your hand!" A man in splendid gold armor darted into the house, vaulting nimbly over broken furniture and crumbling walls. Timurhan backed away from Emre, then swayed, clutching at his head.

"I said no women or children were to be touched, Timurhan! For this, you will face punishment in the camp tonight!"

"My lord amir… I feel unwell…" Timurhan murmured, dropping his sword. The gold-plated amir caught the young man just as his knees buckled and lowered him gently to the floor. The boy's tanned face flushed, and a faint purple bruise began to spread from the long scratch on his throat, which swelled under his jaw.

"Ismail!" the amir bellowed. "Take this young fool to the tent for the infirm. Tell the physician that he has been poisoned by a blade coated in hemlock."

"Yes, my lord. But…"

"How do I know? It always was Zahed's favorite poison. Now go, quickly! He does not have much time."

Ismail scrambled to his comrade, hefting him into a standing position. Timurhan's pants slid down to his ankles, and another soldier pulled them up, tying them about the boy's waist. Grasping Timurhan's other shoulder, they bore him away.

Yusuf knelt next to Emre and shook his head sadly.

"Zahed, my old friend," he whispered, "Allah has surely arranged this last meeting." He scanned the man's body quickly, noting his clammy skin and festering wound.

"Inna illahi wa inna ilayhi raji'un." Yusuf spoke close to Emre's ear, his hand on his chest.

Emre stirred and took a deep, rattling breath. "You are looking fine today, Yusuf," he gasped, "do the legs of your horse buckle under the weight of all that gold?"

Yusuf smiled. "Ah yes – the sharp-tongued brat that I remember from years ago. Have you been in Acre these two years? How did you become trapped in a Franj house by yourself?"

Emre coughed and lifted his good hand. "Not by myself."

Yusuf launched to his feet and ran out of the house toward his waiting soldiers. "There is another injured. Come! Make haste!"

Two more blue-clad Mamluks sprang forward and followed him back into the house. They gently lifted Emre onto a broken timber.

"Take him to my personal physician, and tell him Ibn Shihab commands that this man is to be cared for at all costs. He must not die of these wounds!" Yusuf shouted after them as they picked their way through the ruined walls to the street.

A slight movement caught his eye, and he whipped around, sword held ready. Someone was crawling toward the fireplace. Cautiously, Yusuf inched forward and saw a woman in a filthy red dress with a pouf of dirty hair scrambling on her hands and knees, making a clumsy dash for a hole in the ground. He slammed his sword down in front of her, and she froze. She turned to face him, and his eyes widened with recognition.

"Sheykha?!"

Chapter 43

May 1291
Acre, Palestine

B odies lay broken and sprawled outside their houses and shops, mostly citizens and turcopoles, many without their heads. In the burgeoning heat of the late spring afternoon, the bloating corpses filled the narrow alleys with a miasma of decay, the stench so strong that to inhale felt like breathing poison. Feral dogs and cats nosed at the corpses, worrying and gnawing at broken fingers and rotting ears, as clouds of black flies rose and fell again around them. All was quiet until the occasional scream echoed through the streets when another victim was discovered and dispatched.

Henri held his breath against the smell of the rotting bodies as he climbed over a makeshift barricade of furniture and stones that blocked a narrow alley. He was near the Templars, but the destroyed houses and barricades had almost completely blocked access to the citadel, which the Mamluks now surrounded. He could not get in, and they could not come out.

The barest sense of motion alerted him seconds before an arrow whistled past his helmeted face and buried itself in the wood of the barricade with a thud, sending him tumbling over it. He dove behind a pile of headless bodies and cursed quietly. There was no other place to hide.

Another arrow whispered through the air and sank into one of the bodies, passing clean through and embedding in the dirt, inches from Henri's leg. This was no Mamluk arrow – it was a crossbow bolt. Slowly, he raised his hand above the bodies.

"I am a knight of Acre!" he shouted in Latin. "Cease your firing of arrows and let us together kill our enemy! Ow!"

Another bolt grazed his wrist, penetrating his thick leather gauntlet. He heard the clinking of mail and spurs as someone strolled toward him, and he carefully drew his sword. He had dropped his shield on the other side of the barricade, so his only hope was to rush out and strike before his opponent could fire. He leapt from behind the bodies with a yell, charging forward with his sword raised over his head.

Brother Philip stood before him without his helmet, crossbow aimed at Henri's chest. Henri skidded to a stop, and a venomous smile spread slowly across Philip's face.

"I have one arrow left, little Lord Henri, and it is yours."

"Brother Philip, we both fight for one cause," Henri started to speak, but Philip pulled back on the trigger and the arrow sprang toward him.

Henri jolted as a powerful thud reverberated through his chest. He staggered, dropping to his knees. His vision swam as the pain of the arrow spread through him like the ripples in a pond. His heart had stopped. His chest had imploded. Somewhere deep within his skull was a high-pitched whining sound.

Is that an angel singing or the devil calling me? He thought.

He ripped off his helmet and wheezed, but no air would flow into his lungs. Standing above him, Philip examined his crossbow, brow knit in confusion.

Henri looked down, expecting to see the arrow's fletches protruding from his chest, but the bolt lay in front of him in the dust, its iron tip broken. He clutched at his chest, feeling the jagged barbs of broken chain mail where the arrow had hit him. And then he felt a lump – his small leather pouch which contained the pieces of lemon and cinnamon wood and a smooth, pale stone he had collected from al-Hadiqa on the day he left. The stone had shattered. He dragged in a slow, labored breath. He was still painfully alive. The devil would have to wait a while longer for him.

Philip tossed the crossbow to the ground and drew out his sword.

"I have waited for this day for nineteen years," he said through his teeth, "to see your blood spill on the ground, to watch the carefully built lies of my brother shatter like a broken cup." He advanced. "Rogier thought that giving you to Sir Geoffroi would protect you, but I have been patient." Heaving his sword above his head, Philip lunged, and the air whirred as the sword slashed down viciously.

Henri rolled away from the attack, snatched his fallen sword, and jumped to his feet in time to block a second blow as Philip advanced again. He kicked viciously and was rewarded with a loud crack as his foot connected with Philip's knee. The older knight howled, staggering backwards.

Henri lowered his sword and held out his hand in offering.

"Brother Philip, you are mistaken. Come now, let us not harm each other – it is what our enemy desires!"

"The only enemy I have is you," Philip growled.

"Why? Because I gave a man mercy to cease you from torturing him?"

Philip spat at Henri's feet. "I have wanted to take your life since the day I learnt of your birth, you unholy whelp.

Every opportunity I contrived, every man I hired to kill you, was confounded some way or another, but God has given me this war as a gift. I needed to wait for His timing to finally take what is mine."

Henri's mouth opened in surprise. "You hired men to kill me?"

"Do not play the fool with me, boy! Surely Rogier told you!"

"Told me what? Until my patrol last year, you were a stranger to me!"

Philip kept his sword raised and looked narrowly at Henri. "Rogier was my half-brother. We share the same sire, as did his reprehensible twin in Maron-en-Ruergue."

"You're my…"

"Your uncle, yes, you foul child. I am your uncle."

Henri raised his face toward the heavens and shouted at the sky. "Jesu Christi! Will there never cease to be a steady stream of men revealing themselves to be uncles previously unknown to me? This is intolerable!"

"Listen to me!" Philip barked. "Your grand-père abandoned his marriage to my mother, leaving us without property or fortune, to marry your whore of a grand-mère because she was a cousin of King Louis. He took the Cross and came to Palestine to hide the shame of what he did, refusing to honor his promise to my mother or to do his duty to his children. I am your father's senior by two years, of a legitimate marriage, and the rightful heir to Maron-en-Ruergue."

Henri staggered backwards. "My estate is…"

"Mine," Philip said, stepping closer. "Years ago, I came here to confront my father, but he refused to acknowledge me, even though I am a legitimate heir in the eyes of God. If he had not died naturally at your estate, I would have killed him myself!"

He lunged at Henri, and their swords met, the impact sending tingles of shock down both men's arms. Henri pushed with all his strength, and Philip staggered backwards.

"Rogier knew," Philip said, panting, "I revealed everything to him and the Patriarch, but the Patriarch took Rogier's side, and do you know why Henri? Because Rogier was rich. No one could do anything to unseat a man as wealthy as Rogier. He hid behind it. The coward hid instead of facing me!"

Philip attacked again, and Henri parried, smacking Philip on the arm, drawing a thin trickle of blood through his mail. Philip clutched at his bicep and looked up in surprise.

"After I kill you, it will appear as if you died in battle," Philip hissed, "and then I shall find your mother and your sisters and have them locked away in a storeroom with no key…or maybe I will take one of my nieces for myself first. I hear that young Blanche is already whoring with married men!" He ran at Henri, swinging furiously.

Henri backed away, parrying against the rapid blows. Philip was fighting in a rage, which would quickly tire him, but he was fighting brutally – like a bandit, not a Templar. Henri concentrated on not getting hit and using as little energy as possible.

"Why did you wait so long to kill me, Brother Philip? Why wait until I came of age?" he asked, stalling for time. Philip backed away a pace, breathing heavily.

"I have been trying to get to you for nearly twenty years, but a man whom I thought to be a friend betrayed me. Each time I came close, you had been spirited away."

Henri recalled the times his father would unexpectedly arrive at Sir Geoffroi's castle, where Henri apprenticed to learn his knightly skills, and take him on unannounced hunting trips. He remembered when someone abducted him when he was small, killing his older brother. Rogier and his militia had met and executed the kidnappers on the road, as if they were expecting them. He thought of his last interaction with his father before he died. Rogier had been at the Templar citadel meeting with…

"Brother Languedoc," Henri said aloud. "Brother Languedoc would come to our house and meet regularly. My father met with him right before he died."

"Ha! Languedoc paid dearly for that betrayal."

"What did you do to him, Philip? Where is Brother Languedoc?"

Philip charged. He knocked the sword out of Henri's hand with a powerful strike, sending it clanging and spinning wildly several feet away. Philip grinned triumphantly, his green eyes pale in the sunlight.

Green eyes, Henri thought. *Mother of God, can it be true?*

"How can it be? Father never told me of you!"

"Languedoc was too dim to realize that I was Rogier's brother until it was too late because instead of a Templar, he expected me as a mercenary – as I was when I left Acre the first time," Philip continued. "Perhaps I would have let him live, but he stole something from me, and it made him suspicious, because Rogerier has an identical one of these."

He pointed proudly to a dagger at his hip, and Henri gaped. The jeweled hilt was identical to the one that Rogier had given him on his sixteenth birthday. Twin weapons, commissioned lovingly by his grand-père for Rogier and his twin brother, Gaspard.

Philip rushed at him again, and Henri had a heartbeat to glimpse the broken crossbow bolt laying near his feet. He ducked under Philip's blow, grabbed the bolt, and with a yell, buried it in the man's shoulder, pushing hard until it broke through the light metal mail and hit bone. Philip screamed and dropped his sword. He charged at Henri again, slamming him against a wooden door in the alley, which broke under their weight, and they both crashed backwards into darkness.

Henri swung a piece of the broken door and struck Philip with it on the chin. Philip grabbed Henri by the front of his surcoat, slamming his head against the stone floor, and Henri saw lights flash across his vision. The men thrashed and kicked, knocking over a table, breaking pottery, and overturning a pile of stacked iron.

"You," Henri panted, "are a bastard. An unacknowledged son! How in the name of God did you become a Templar?!" By now, it had become clear to him that Philip was tired of keeping his secrets. If he could keep the man talking, he might find a way to escape.

In the darkness, Philip chuckled.

"How indeed. I am the acknowledged heir of the lord of Fons Bleaudi. Once his son revealed to me that his father was losing his mind and his younger brother had recently died, it was easy to slit the throat of the young heir of Fons Bleaudi and convince his simpleton of a father that I was his long-lost son before I poisoned him."

Philip lunged forward, crashing into a table and overturning it. Henri heard the sharp clanging of more iron hitting the floor in the dark, and he scrambled to find it. Instead, his hand closed over a tear-shaped vessel of clay stamped with an ornate pattern; a naft grenade, one of the few that remained in the city. He threw the grenade, and it shattered against Philip's foot. The noxious smell of sulfur perfumed the room.

"Once again, you prove your incompetence at throwing grenades, *Nephew*," Philip snarled, and in the light of the broken door, Henri saw him raise his sword. Henri grabbed one of the bars of iron lying nearby, raised it above his head, and struck it hard against the stone floor at Philip's feet.

A spark flashed in the dark, flying from the iron and igniting the naft. Philip yelled and jumped back, but the flames quickly raced along the trail of splattered fuel and climbed his leg and up to his torso. He dropped to the ground, thrashing his legs and slapping at them in a frenzy.

"Help me!" he screamed, "help me!"

Henri was running out the door, but the piteous cries of the knight pierced him, and he stopped. Taking a deep breath, he turned and eased back into the building. The spreading puddle of naft roared with flames which were now licking across the overturned table and casting evil shadows on the walls. Henri grasped Philip under the arms, dragging him, still flaming, from the building. Snatching up a discarded helmet, he shoveled dust from the street over Philip's legs, but the evil liquid continued to burn, eating into the man's skin, crackling and hissing until it burned itself out.

Philip's white robes were scorched up to his chest, and the mail chausses covering his legs were black and hot to the touch. The skin of his legs, charred to the fat, peeled away from his ankles and feet like sheets of vellum.

"Tha... thank you," Philip wheezed. He opened his mouth again, and his lips worked wordlessly.

"What?" Henri asked.

"P... please," Philip gasped.

Henri leaned closer. "What is it? I will take your last words or your confession."

Philip pulled Henri's face toward his, and he felt a dagger, still hot from the fire, press into his throat.

"You show too much mercy, Nephew," Philip grimaced, his back arching with pain. "I never thought that spoiled

Henri of Maron would die because he saved my life."

"Brother Philip," Henri spoke soothingly. "Uncle. Do not let your last act on this earth be murder. You endanger your mortal soul."

He pulled back with slow caution and gently began to work the arrow from Philip's shoulder. Philip continued to clutch the dagger in a shaking hand, and his pale eyes watched, unblinking, as Henri ripped a strip of cloth from the ruined white robe and bound the wound. The only sound was that of the flames as they roared from the open door of the building, grasping angrily for more fuel.

"You look like your grandfather," Philip rasped, eventually, "like my father. You have his face." The dagger fell, and Philip began to sob. "If I had a son, he might have looked like you. I loved someone once. She... she was..."

"Uncle," Henri whispered, "your dagger... it is identical to mine."

"Took it off your uncle Gaspard in Francia," Philip gasped through pale lips, and he began to tremble as the shock of his wounds set in, "after I stabbed him with it."

"You would use the daggers that my grand-père gave his twin sons to kill every last member of his household?"

"Not until you are all dead can my father's sin toward my mother be erased," Philip whispered. "I came so close..."

A shout from the end of the alley drew Henri's attention. Three Mamluk soldiers ran towards them, their swords unsheathed. Philip raised his head, pulling in a deep, rattling breath.

"Dur! Bu bir Acre Lordu! O değerlidir!"

The Mamluks lowered their swords. After a brief argument, two of the soldiers grasped Henri by the arms and began to bind his hands.

"You speak Turkish?" Henri asked, looking fearfully

293

from his captors to his uncle. "What did you say to them? Uncle, what did you say?"

Philip smiled weakly. "You are theirs now. Let us hope for your sake that you receive a speedy execution."

The third Mamluk, an amir in a blue tunic and shimmering gold armor, snatched Philip's jeweled dagger and quickly thrust it through the Templar's throat, then snapped a command to the other two men. They yanked Henri to his feet and pushed him down the alley.

"I am a noble of the city," Henri said to the amir, who walked in front, "worth a ransom if you take me to your commander."

"I know this," the amir replied, not turning to look back at him.

"You know…"

"Your companion told me as much before I gave him mercy."

"He…"

"He saved you from being skewered by my men."

"How many citizens of Acre still live? Have you negotiated extradition between Khalil and King Henry?"

The amir turned and looked at him, his dark brown eyes squinting thoughtfully. He had a handsome face – high-cheekboned and tanned, with a black, neatly groomed beard. His almond-shaped eyes were thinly lined with kohl. "You are a friend of King Henry?"

"I told you, I am a noble. I left the king's manse after he retreated to Cyprus."

"It is the holy knight I seek. Beaujeu. He alone may be capable of brokering an agreement with the sultan. I am Yusuf Ibn Shihab, and I have been in correspondence with him for many months."

"Beaujeu is dead."

The amir's shoulders slumped. "Come then." He turned and continued walking. "You will make a nice prize for the sultan."

Henri looked back at Philip lying in the street, his mind racing with questions.

Chapter 44

May 1291

Church of St. Andrew, Acre

Sidika lay on cold, hard stone, and when she woke, the darkness was so complete that it pressed on her eyes. She quickly ran her hands along her arms and legs. All accounted for. Her mind slowly churned through the last things she remembered; a candle's dancing flame, someone screaming, a face with blonde eyebrows hovering over hers.

She stood heavily, and the sound of her foot scraping on stone echoed far above her. After days in the fetid, low-ceilinged cellar of the Maron house, she was keenly aware of the sudden vastness around her in the dark and the slight tickle of a draft on her neck. Carefully, she crouched low with her hands splayed in front of her, feeling along the smooth, stone floor. She encountered something warm and squishy – a body. The body moved.

"What in the name of heaven are you doing? Go back to sleep!" a woman snarled.

Sidika staggered back in surprise, tripping over another body and falling heavily on top of a third.

"Ow! Clumsy bitch!" a woman grunted. "Why did you not use the chamber pot before the guards took the lamps away?"

"I am sorry," Sidika sputtered, "I am sorry!"

A distant flickering through a vaulted hallway caught her attention. It grew brighter as it came closer, erratically illuminating a large room full of sleeping forms, grayish and motionless in the semi-dark. Sidika alone was standing.

The light – a stamped metal lantern – cast a yellow glow on the baggy-eyed face of a man whose hairy hand reached out, grabbed her, and dragged her toward the open door, weaving through the sleepers on the floor.

"Oh please," Sidika begged, "where am I?"

"Kapa çeneni, fahişe!" came the grunted reply.

They walked into the long vaulted hall and he stopped, pulled a heavy door open long enough to throw Sidika through it, then slammed and barred it behind her. A thin slash of light glowed at the cracks in the door. This room had a woven straw mat on the floor like the Franj used in their homes, a simple wooden bench, and an empty chamber pot. When the door opened again, two guards entered, placed lanterns into niches in the walls, and waited outside. Sidika jumped to her feet as two familiar men appeared next, striding briskly into her cell.

Sanjar al-Shuja'i, the governor of Damascus and commissioner of the siege weapons manual, growled, crossed his arms, and glowered at her.

"So, it is her. It was you who convinced me to hire her, Yusuf. I hold you responsible for this."

Yusuf, wearing a rumpled blue tunic and an exhausted, harried expression on his face, looked at her sternly. "Indeed. She is talented enough as a spy to join the ranks of my qasids."

"You, of all people, should have known a spy when you saw one. Is this the quality of espionage that I should always expect from you? The sultan shall be informed."

Sidika could see Yusuf's jaw twitching, but he restrained himself from responding.

"You shall put her to the question," al-Shuja'i continued. "I wish to know what information she seduced from our leaders. She may have visited many of them and collected intelligence for the Franj."

"That would imply that she also seduced you, Sanjar." Yusuf turned to al-Shuja'i with an icy look. "Surely, it no longer matters. We have her, and we have this city. Why put the girl to the question about something so frivolous when there are knights and nobles in our prisons who have more valuable information to give up?"

Al-Shuja'i said nothing for a moment, pulling on his graying beard and watching Sidika as she stood warily in the corner of the room.

"I should not be surprised by this," he eventually muttered. "You know what your problem is, Yusuf? You are a merciful man – no wait, I am speaking!" he held up his hand as Yusuf began to protest. "Are you too soft on this girl? Yes. Why? Because you look at her and you think with your *qadib*, not with your mind. I know that you want to have me assassinated so that you can take the governorship of Damascus, just as your master, Badahir, desired. You know that your insane sultan will give it to you because you have spent the last ten years with his prick in your arse."

"Sanjar, I do not know wha—"

"Be quiet! You do not have the balls to assassinate me." Al-Shuja'i pulled Yusuf's dagger from its sheath on his belt and held it out. "Put this girl to the question, Yusuf. Show me that when you kill me someday, you will do the deed yourself, as a man. She does not deserve your mercy. Do not shame me."

Yusuf's eyes fixed on the dagger. Slowly he took it and turned it in his hand.

In the corner where she stood, Sidika held her breath.

The men were speaking Turkish, but she could plainly see what was about to happen, and she quietly prepared to give up her soul for the second time that day.

"Guard!" Yusuf shouted. A Mamluk appeared in the door. "Put this young woman back with the others. We will deal with her tomorrow." He turned to al-Shuja'i, sliding his dagger back into its sheath.

"You do not command this jail, Sanjar, I do. I have men who are, ah… highly experienced in the ways to extract a confession from a prisoner. They shall conduct the questioning while I attend to the sultan's diplomatic concerns, which, as you can imagine, are great considering he is now the man who has rid Palestine of the Franj pestilence after two hundred years. Surely this must be the work of an 'insane man,' as you insinuated."

Al-Shuja'i smiled. "A nice attempt, Yusuf. Someday you will learn that real power comes not from feigning importance but from appearing harmless."

The guard was pulling Sidika from the room. Yusuf followed them out the door, but he stopped and grabbed al-Shuja'i by the arm.

"Keep your wretched city. I do not want it."

***

Sidika slept for two days, waking only occasionally to ask for water, which was brought to her by an old Franj woman who rationed her portions and fed her salted flatbread to prepare her stomach to receive proper food. The other women of the prison told her she had dark circles under her eyes and sallow skin. "Try to look ill for as long as you can," they laughed, "and perhaps the guards will be too scared to touch you."

She was imprisoned in a church named after one of the Christian saints, near the Templar's citadel. The stripped walls, bare altars, and denuded tapestry hooks showed evidence of looting. She and the women slept and lived in the part of the church called the 'nave' – a towering, vaulted room with chilly floors and small, high windows of colored glass that the Mamluks had not yet managed to pry loose from their fixings.

Their captors did not wish to waste lamp oil or candles on the prisoners, so as soon as the smoky glow from the windows began to fade, there was nothing to do but lie down to sleep. There was a large pile of stale hay in a corner of the nave, ferociously guarded by a small gang of women who also took command of the food rations. To pass the time, the prisoners milled about, talking amongst themselves or weaving the straw into floor mats to counteract their boredom. Some sat on the floor, staring sightlessly, unable to comprehend their grief. Fights broke out over food or a place to sleep in the hay. One woman strangled another to death in the night over an old quarrel about a lover, and the Mamluks dragged her away and executed her for murder.

Murder, Sidika thought after another interminable day of tedium. *As if they have not just murdered an entire city of thirty thousand people.* A murmur caught her attention, and she looked up as a cadre of black-clad Mamluks swaggered into the room. Even their interlocking leather and metal scale armor was black. She had never seen these guards before, and their presence caused noticeable unease among the prisoners. One woman screamed and started sobbing.

"We seek the girl who came here from the cellar three days past," one of them shouted in thickly accented French. "She is a Jewess and a spy." Several of the women in the room turned and looked at Sidika, and she stood slowly.

"I am Sidika," she told them in Arabic. "Like all of the women here, I have committed no crime."

"Blameless, ha! Are you the mother of Jesu Christi? Show

me a woman who has not committed a crime, and I will show you the stone of the Kaaba," one of the Mamluks said with a laugh, pushing her toward the vaulted hallway.

Again, she was thrown into the same small storeroom. The soldier followed her inside but without a lamp. In the disorienting darkness, she felt his hand close around her throat, and he pushed her against the stone wall. For a moment, he simply held her there while she struggled, clawing at his forearms ineffectually.

"So," he said, his face close to hers, "al-Shuja'i has questions that only you know the answers to. You have until sunup, and then I will begin to search for those answers." He released her throat and pressed himself bodily against her, feeling along her back and legs with his hands, "wherever I think that you may be hiding them."

***

Emre could feel the cool hands of Yusuf's physician as he probed the hot, throbbing mass of flesh that was at one time his left hand. He was aware of the pain that each poke elicited, but also very unconcerned about it. The physician muttered something, and three assistants approached, laying their hands on Emre's arms and legs. He favored them with a lazy, lopsided grin.

"That feels nice…" he drawled.

"Good. It means that the draught I gave you is working. In a moment, it will be less pleasurable, young man," the physician answered, placing a thick strip of leather between Emre's teeth.

Emre closed his eyes and felt his body floating and drifting like a feather on a gust of wind. Something pressed on his arm, and he looked down just as the physician put his full strength behind the bone saw.

Chapter 45

May 1291

Church of Saint Andrew, Acre

It took a great deal of time for Sidika to remove the leg of the wooden bench in her dark storeroom prison. Once it was off, she hid the makeshift club in her dress and carefully balanced the bench on three legs. If she sat very still on the opposite end, it was possible not to notice the missing piece.

The door opened, and two men walked in – al-Shuja'i, and the black-clad guard. Al-Shuja'i looked at her for a moment, then sighed.

"It gives me no pleasure to inflict pain on a woman, or anyone, for that matter. Tell me what you were doing in Damascus and what intelligence you gathered, and I shall make your death very quick. Was it you who told the Assassin how to enter my house? You should know that he failed and was quickly dealt with."

Sidika blinked at him. "I do not know any Assassins. Indeed, I did not even know that their order still existed, my lord."

Al-Shuja'i crossed his arms. "I give you one more chance," he hissed through clenched teeth.

"It is coincidence that you found me in Acre, my lord. I fled to the city, as have all the people who live within the long reach of your armies!"

THE LAND OF GOD

Al-Shuja'i held out a piece of paper. "And this? How do you explain that this was found in your dress?"

Sidika looked and the paper and swallowed. It contained a receipt, stamped with the two horsemen of the Templar Order, with Beaujeu's instructions that she was entitled to shelter at the Templar citadel should she ever need it. She had received it after she turned in her sketches of the siege weapons.

"My father had many clients, my lord!"

"It seems that you have the particular favor of the most powerful warrior in Acre. This is not a coincidence. You spied on our siegeworks and reported back to Beaujeu, did you not?"

Sidika opened her mouth, but no words would come out. Damp, sticky sweat broke out under her arms and along her back, and cold fear settled over her.

They knew.

Al-Shuja'i turned and marched out the door. "See what else you can find out, Abasi." The door slammed behind him.

Abasi smiled at her. "Well, this should be interesting. The last ten confessions I have extracted were from the priest-knights. This task should be far more pleasurable. Please, sit." He gestured at the bench, and Sidika moved toward it, slowly easing herself down on the very edge.

"I like to get acquainted with my clients before we begin. It makes the process easier for everyone." Abasi unbuckled his sword belt and tossed it aside, then sat heavily next to her on the bench where she had removed the leg. The seat immediately collapsed, spilling them both to the floor.

Sidika scrambled toward the discarded sword belt, but Abasi caught the her by the hem of her dress. She pulled her club from her skirt and swung it, but he reached up and caught it, ripping it from her grip.

"Well, it seems that you are full of surprises, as I suspected," he snarled at her.

"I do not know anything that al-Shuja'i would find useful," Sidika pleaded. "He hired me to work for him and I did, that is all!"

Abasi swung the club. Sidika turned just in time, and it smacked against her shoulder. He pushed her against the ground and hit her again, this time in the stomach.

"I can make it so that you bleed inside your body and the blood comes out of your mouth instead of spit," he said, yanking her to her feet. He hit her across the cheekbone with his closed fist and then slammed her head against the wall so that she saw stars. "I can cut you so cleverly that your skin will come off in one piece, like the pelt of rabbit! When I am finished, perhaps I will give you back to the Franj, who can devise even more clever ways to make a woman suffer than I ever could!"

Sidika struggled as he tore at her dress, ripping one of her sleeves away by its laces. The lantern was almost within her reach, sitting loosely in a niche in the wall. She tried to squeeze herself closer to it, fingers outstretched, not even noticing as he slashed the rest of her dress off with his dagger until she stood in her threadbare brown chemise.

"Hmm... what are you hiding underneath this ugly garment? More sticks?" He asked, dragging his dagger down her arm and drawing a thin line of blood. "Let me s—"

Sidika swiped at the lantern with her fingertips, overturning and spilling oil down the back of Abasi's armor. Abasi screamed as flames quickly swept across his back and arms. The door opened, and another guard rushed inside. He threw Abasi to the ground and dumped the chamber pot on him to douse the flames, which were now licking hungrily across the woven mat on the floor.

Sidika picked up the discarded club and slipped out the door and down the hall.

Abasi's cries brought more guards. A soldier ran around the corner of the hall and Sidika hit him full in the face with the club. His nose cracked, exploding with blood, and he fell to the ground, gasping. More were coming. She pulled the prone man's sword from its sheath and braced her feet. She could barely hold the tip of the heavy iron weapon off the ground. Two more Mamluks ran toward her, and she swung the sword, finding strength in a scream of fear and anger. One of the Mamluks knocked it away as easily as swatting a fly, then raised his lance.

"Stop this now!" a deep voice roared from behind them.

Yusuf appeared, shoving men out of his way, and grabbed Sidika by the arm.

"On whose authority was this woman being questioned?"

The soldiers looked at each other and shrugged. Yusuf pushed Sidika ahead of him, past the door to the dark little room. Abasi was on the floor. Two Mamluks pressed damp cloths to his burned face while another gently removed his armor. In a corner, the remains of the woven floor mat still crackled and smoldered. Yusuf growled and pushed her all the way down the hall. At the entrance to the nave, he stopped and looked at her sternly.

"Well, now you have done it. I could have found a way for you to be taken as a slave if you had not been so foolish!"

"He... he was trying to r... rape me," Sidika blubbered. "He was cutting me!" Her voice was rising to a scream, but she could not control it. It had been building inside her since the day the Mamluks breached Acre's walls.

Yusuf shoved her into the nave, where the wide-eyed stares of the other prisoners locked on her. "Stay in here and

305

do not make more trouble, although it is probably too late for you."

***

"What a damned mess," Yusuf muttered to himself as he stormed back down the hall.

In the storeroom, al-Shuja'i was waiting for him.

"Well, it appears that your little sheykha has received some combat training." Al-Shuja'i's face was red with rage. "She has burned Abasi so badly that he will never be able to do his work again. He was my best, Yusuf! I will be taking one of your inquisitors as repayment for the loss of my man!"

"I did not order her to be questioned on this day. Your man was trying to rape her."

Al-Shuja'i threw up his hands in exasperation. "Of course he was! The man is an experienced inquisitor who was taught to use whatever method necessary to extract information, and as an enemy informant, she has no right to any protection! I want her executed, Yusuf!"

Yusuf stabbed a finger vaguely in the direction of the Templar citadel. "We do not do this, Sanjar; they do! We must be better than them if we are to win!"

"We have already won!"

"Remove your men and yourself from this prison, Sanjar, before I lose my temper," Yusuf said in a low voice. "I will be taking this matter before the sultan."

"Bah!" al-Shuja'i snarled. "Go crying back to your wet nurse. See how it helps you when I am sultan someday!"

Chapter 46

May 1291
The Church of Saint Andrew, Acre

The cold stone sapped the heat from Sidika's shoulders as she sat alone behind the altar. The other women had stared with open disgust when they saw her return to the nave wearing fewer clothes and more bruises. Some of them even spat at her as she walked stiffly through the room. Her head throbbed from Abasi's fists. She could feel the welts rising on her back and see the angry purple bruises on her arms.

She pulled her legs to her chest and put her head on her knees. Although she did not entirely trust Emre, she wished he were here. Their time in the cellar had been challenging, terrifying, and yet she felt a kinship with him. When they had both relaxed, she realized he was kind.

He is probably dead, she thought. *Everyone is dead.*

A shout echoed across the vaulted nave, arguing loudly in Arabic. The other women agitated and shrank away from the entrance to the church. The yelling continued – a man's voice.

"Remove your hands from me, or I will ensure that your sultan hears your name and has your head rolling on his floor during my ransom negotiations!"

Sidika sat up straight. She peeked around the altar.

"I can walk by myself without your help. Do not touch me!"

Sidika struggled to her feet. She knew that voice.

"How did he survive, and why had they not killed him yet for insolence?" she muttered to herself. She smiled, despite her pain. He lived, and although that meant little for her own survival, it warmed her.

Five heavily armed Mamluk soldiers in heavy armor and blue livery marched into the church, leading a bound and bloodied Lord Henri between them. Dried blood crusted his throat, a bruise shadowed his left eye, and both of his hands were bright red and swollen with cuts. Jagged rips marred his fine black and yellow surcoat, and he had several days of growth on his chin. The women stared and began to whisper amongst themselves; there were no male prisoners in the church. Two guards held spears at his back as he trudged through the room, and Yusuf hurried in to meet him.

Henri stopped, looking around at the women.

"What is this? Why are all of these women in here?" he asked in French.

"They are bound for the houses and harems of the sultan and his amirs, and the children into the slave markets or to be trained as new recruits," Yusuf answered calmly, his hands clasped behind his back.

"Surely the sultan and his amirs have enough women to satisfy them. Why take these?" Henri asked. Yusuf smiled. He seemed to be the only Mamluk in the church who could speak any language other than Turkic.

"Ah, but Viscount, they are... how do you Franj like to say it about our women? Exotic. Some of them we took from the convents, and we are told that they are virgins. Now that is something that interests the sultan very much."

At his words, a murmur of distress rose from the women

in the church. More guards filed in with two more prisoners, both male and of the noble class, by the look of their fine surcoats and armor. The women were all standing now, craning their necks to look. Exhausted, Henri scanned the crowd, and his gaze landed on Sidika. The guard behind him grasped his shoulder and tried to push him forward, but he shrugged the man's hand away.

"Wait," he said to Yusuf. "I wish for one of these prisoners to be included in my ransom."

Yusuf shrugged. "I am sure it is possible. Which one did you have in mind? Is she your wife?"

"Sidika," Henri called out. "Come here."

Sidika limped to him, trying not to grasp her bruised ribs as she moved. She straightened her shoulders and looked at the men defiantly.

"What have you done to her?" Henri asked, turning angrily to Yusuf. "She has been beaten!"

Yusuf paled. "Of all the women in this church, is she really the one that you wish to free? I find it hard to believe that she is your wife, Viscount, for she has been causing trouble since she arrived. Truly, she is not a gentlewoman."

The corners of Henri's mouth twitched up ever so slightly. "Yes, I am not surprised, and she will only increase in trouble the longer you keep her. She is to stay untouched by your men and placed in my ransom agreement. She will also fetch a good price, and my family will pay it."

Yusuf nodded, then spread his hands in a gesture of helplessness. "Unfortunately, Viscount, this one cannot be allowed to join your ransom agreement. She injured two guards and will suffer punishment for it. The first guard she hurt is especially keen to punish her himself once he recovers from his wounds. They believe her to be a witch, for she was able to overpower them easily."

"I said she is to come to no harm," Henri said icily, "else your sultan will surely lose many riches when he attempts to extort my family of their fortune to return me to Francia. She is not a witch; she is merely a spiteful girl who was given too much independence by her father."

Sidika looked at Henri in astonishment as he tried to buy her freedom – arguing defiantly, glaring with haughty disdain at the amir. He turned and held her with a green stare, and for the briefest moment, he looked worried.

Yusuf was shaking his head. "I am sorry, but it is not possible. Already the amir of Damascus is petitioning the sultan to have her executed for spying. The most that I can do is try to ensure that she leaves this place as a slave without having her tongue removed. Now, your fellow prisoners are in their rooms, and it is time that you went as well. I will send my physician to tend to your injuries."

Again, the guard pushed Henri forward by the shoulder, and he winced.

"Yusuf, tell your trained goat to keep his hands off my person!" He looked at Sidika, and she stared back boldly.

"Remember, Sidika," Henri said as the guard prodded him forward again, "sorrow prepares you for joy." And then he was gone down the hall.

The eyes of the women in the prison all turned to her.

"How do you know the Viscount, and why was he trying to buy your freedom?" one of the captive women demanded.

"A village slut like her can only know someone like Lord Henri in one way," another prisoner commented acidly.

"I do not know why he was trying to help me…" Sidika's mind was preoccupied, thoughts as thick as honey.

"What was he saying about sorrow?" another girl asked.

Sidika smiled slowly. "He was giving me encouragement. 'Sorrow prepares you for joy.

It violently sweeps everything out of your house,
so that new joy can find space to enter.
It shakes the yellow leaves from the bough of your heart,
so that fresh, green leaves can grow in their place.
It pulls up the rotten roots, so that new roots hidden beneath have room to grow.
Whatever sorrow shakes from your heart, far better things will take their place.'"

The women stared at her, uncomprehending.

"It is a poem of Jalal ad-Din Rumi. Lord Henri knows that I have read the poets."

"Are you lovers?" a woman whispered, her eyes wide.

"Who is Jalal al-Din Rumi?" Another asked.

"A wise Sufi, and Lord Henri must think me not wise at all, for he appears to be passing messages to you, my troublesome little witch," Yusuf interrupted them, emerging from the hall.

Sidika narrowed her eyes at him. "I do not fear you."

"That much is obvious," he grumbled. A guard approached and tied Sidika's hands behind her back.

"And I am not a witch. Where are you taking me?"

"Where I am taking you is none of your concern."

"It is my only concern, amir!"

Yusuf rounded on her, holding a threatening finger to her face. "That is enough, young woman! Know your place!"

Sidika jerked against her restraints. "My place? My home is burned, my family dead! There is no place in the world for me. If you are taking me to be executed, spare me the mystery and tell me so now!"

"If all goes well, I am taking you home. But first, we are going to see the sultan."

Chapter 47

June 1291
Marseilles, Provence

When news reached the rulers of the West that the Holy Land had succumbed to the Mamluks, anger followed disbelief, and then fingers began to point. In Rome, the Holy Father set aside his ire at the Sicilians to declare the future of all Christendom imperiled. In Francia, the bishops raged in their cathedrals. The survivors of the siege were maligned by Christians in every city as cowards and sluggards.

Slowly the refugees of Acre trickled back to their homes in the West, hollow-eyed, solemn, and suddenly poor. Many had fled first to Cyprus, a day's sail from Acre, only to find no jobs or houses, inflated food prices in the markets, and disease raging through the larger cities of Limassol and Famagusta. Some stayed, optimistic that King Henry would rally enough support to retake the city. Others who had the means chartered ships to take them further, turning their backs firmly against the idea of ever living away from their ancestral homes.

Nasira watched anxiously as her ship made its way into the long, narrow harbor of Marseilles. The enormity of what she was about to do overwhelmed her. She was fortunate, for some of the other Arab wives of the Franj in Acre had never bothered to learn French. She spoke her husband's language, and she had that in her favor. Or so she thought, until she recalled how many dialects proliferated in the region. Rogier once told her that he often spoke Provençal at home in the Ruergue, and it was the language of Marseilles, which Nasira had not learned beyond a few words and phrases that sounded amusing to her Arabic-trained ears. She never imagined that she would be so far away from home without her husband or her son.

Again, her eyes blurred with unshed tears, but she pushed them back. She had cried for two weeks on the sea. A fortnight of water in and around her. Now, as she prepared to step on dry land, she must focus on the living. Perhaps her son had not died in Acre. Perhaps Gaspard of Maron-en-Ruergue had reformed his cruel nature, and rumors of his mismanagement of the family estate were untrue. Maybe she would open her eyes and wake from her nightmare.

Marseilles rose on a series of crumbling limestone slopes dotted with dark green trees and white stone houses. The port furrowed deeply between the rocky hills, protected from the wind and the waves, but to Nasira, it felt close and suffocating after weeks on the expanse of the Mediterranean Sea. The houses looked strange to her, with baked terra cotta or thatched roofs that had shallow peaks and no canopied terraces on top of them for families to enjoy the cool evenings. At the apex of one of the hills, she saw a small cathedral, its blocky form outlined against a cloudless sky.

Ibrahim took her hand and led her down the gangway. After weeks of adjusting her gait for the rolling of the ship, she immediately felt off-balance on dry land, and she pitched forward. One of the sailors laughed.

"You must keep walking to find your legs again, madame. Otherwise, you will leave them on our boat, and they will sail back to Acre with us."

Nasira silently cursed ships, sailors, and the sea. If her homeland survived the invasion of the Mamluks, she would travel back over mountains and deserts before setting foot on another boat.

Stone warehouses and wooden structures lined the harbor, and she could see a smallish church built in a square, utilitarian style. The roads were choked with horses pulling carts, porters hauling crates and barrels, and citizens dressed in dull colors. Everything seemed drab and ugly against her memory of Acre and the Holy Land, where blue and purple dye yielded bolts of linen and silk finery in abundance.

"Lord Rogier once said the house of Monsieur Beaufort is near the abbey of Saint Victor." Ibrahim held Nasira up by the elbow. "And that is where I addressed my letters when I corresponded with them on his and Henri's behalf." He gently guided her through the crowds towards the abbey – a square spire of stone and arrowslits that peeked above the sloped roofs of the harbor buildings.

With Durant and Henri gone, Nasira and Ibrahim had agreed to seek out Beaufort and Marchand, who had been agents of the Maron family in Marseilles. The two men had visited al-Hadiqa on several occasions and had even been helping Rogier negotiate with the other nobles of King Philippe's court to find Henri a bride of sufficient standing.

After several wrong turns, they found themselves standing outside of a row of doors in a long stone building. Ibrahim knocked loudly on the nearest door, and after a short time, it was answered by a young man in brown hose and a scandalously short cotehardie of red wool. Nasira gasped and averted her eyes. The short skirt of the cotehardie barely covered his manhood, which bulged clearly against his wool breeches.

Ibrahim cleared his throat uncomfortably and asked for Beaufort. For a moment, the young man sized them up with a look of fierce dislike on his face. "Are you Jews?"

Ibrahim bowed graciously. "We are not Jews, young man. We seek your master on personal business. We have arrived here in Marseilles after a long journey."

"Right enough. I can smell you from where I stand." The young man wrinkled his nose. "Come back when you have bathed, heathen." He began to close the door.

"Listen to me!" Nasira stepped forward, throwing off her hood and putting her foot in the door. "I am Lady Nasira, the wife of Rogier, who is the Marquis of Maron-en-Ruergue. Your master serves him, and thus he also serves me. We have escaped a siege and survived a sea journey to come here. Now, fetch your master at once!"

The young man stepped back, turned, and ran up the stairs.

"And put on a modest cloak!" Nasira yelled after him.

Next to her, Ibrahim stared. "Niece!" he said, aghast, but Nasira held up a finger.

"I am in no mood to be reprimanded, Uncle."

"But to scold a man like that!"

She turned to her uncle, eyes flashing, and he held his tongue.

Beaufort trotted to the door, smoothing what little hair remained to him. He was a short man and plump, with a ruddy, round face.

"My lady! Have you fled the disastrous invasion of the infidels? I have only just heard of the siege this week, and my thoughts immediately turned to you and your dear children. Tell me, my lady, how fares young Lord Henri? Is he with you?" He stood on his toes, looking over their shoulders to the street.

"Monsieur Beaufort, may we enter?" Nasira asked wearily, "for we have a tale to tell and require your assistance."

Beaufort ushered them inside, leading them through the lower part of the building, which was used for storing goods and supplies, up a flight of sloping steps to a large room with a smoky fire burning in a stone hearth in a corner, all the while shouting orders to his servant to bring wine and bread.

"The first thing you should know, Monsieur Beaufort, is that my son did not travel to Marseilles with us. I... I do not know if he still lives." Nasira's voice choked for a moment. "There is nothing left of Acre. My daughters and I have traveled to Marseilles to seek shelter with my husband's family in Maron."

Beaufort sat completely still, his face growing slack. "You wish to seek your brother-in-law, Gaspard?"

"Indeed, he must help find husbands for my daughters, for I am not acquainted with society here."

Beaufort took her hand, patting it. "Of course. You need not concern yourself with these worries – leave them to Marchand and me. And your steward, of course." His eyes darted at Ibrahim. "When will you travel to the estate of your brother-in-law?"

Nasira sighed heavily. The room continued to rise and fall around her as if it rode the waves. She wished for a bath and a bed.

"Not for a few weeks yet. My daughter is with child, and I will not travel so close to her time. We will require lodging, Monsieur Beaufort, my daughters, servants, and I."

"Ah yes." Beaufort wrung his hands. "Well, my lady, there are many reputable inns if you journey past the harbor, or you could lodge at a convent and put your servants up elsewhere."

Nasira glanced around the room. The house was large,

although it was not nearly as grand as her city house in Acre. There was one small window upstairs, which let in the mellow Mediterranean light, but the rest of the room was dark and smoky.

"You have no wife or children, is that correct, Monsieur Beaufort?"

"I, uh… that is, well…"

"It was always such a pleasure to host you and Monsieur Marchand for those months when you would come to visit us year after year in Acre. You were the last visitors from Francia to see my beloved house in the country before the invasion forced us to abandon it," Nasira continued smoothly.

Beaufort forced a smile. "Of course, Lady Nasira, why did I not think of it sooner? You and your household must stay here with me while you wait for news of young Henri."

Nasira stood and nodded to Ibrahim, who strode towards the door. "I thank you for your generous hospitality while we find ourselves in this unfortunate circumstance, Monsieur Beaufort. Surely, Saint Victor, whose abbey guards your house, will look upon you with compassion as you help us in our time of need. I shall return to the ship and have my household and our possessions portered immediately, although…" Nasira stopped in thought.

"What is it, my lady?" Beaufort asked reluctantly.

"We brought many goods from Acre, and I am sure they cannot be safe in the harbor warehouses, for thieves may take them."

Beaufort bowed elaborately. "Allow me to place them in my warehouse here, my lady. My servant will accompany you to assist."

Nasira flashed him her most beguiling smile. "Truly, you are a saint yourself, Monsieur Beaufort. While we wait for news of my son, let us also discuss the young women you have in mind for his marriage, for I would appreciate your advice in this matter, and I know that you had written to Rogier with several recommendations."

There. That should be enough to convince him that allowing her to stay in his house was worth his while.

"Would that they were young indeed, my lady, but in this case, we must be prudent. All the eligible ladies outside of seven degrees of familial separation that we could find are over the age of thirty. Rogier's lineage is closely associated with many of the grand families of Francia. And now, you must be most anxious to return to your ship and collect your family. I will prepare for your return." He urged Nasira and Ibrahim to the door.

When they had left, Beaufort poured himself a large cup of wine and drank it with a shaking hand in three gulps, then set out to find his business partner, Marchand. The appearance of Lady Nasira in Marseilles would cause problems for them. There were goods to hide, bribes to be paid, and above all, Gaspard of Maron must be warned that his sister-in-law would be at his gates in mere weeks.

Chapter 48

May 1291

Church of Saint Andrew, Acre

"Sit down, Henri. Your pacing makes me dizzy!" Lord Melik groaned.

Henri shook his head. "If I stop walking, I will start screaming." He gripped the stones of their small cell.

"You may as well get used to it. It will be weeks before word reaches your family and then weeks again before they can deliver a ransom. We will be here for three months at the very least. Of course, my family is closer, so there is a good chance that I will leave before you." The Armenian nobleman looked at his fingernails speculatively and began to clean them with his teeth.

"Must you do that?"

"Everything that I do, I must do, and please refer to my earlier statement about being trapped together for months. It serves no one for you to be petulant and irritable." Lord Melik continued to chew on his fingers, and Henri sat on his thin straw-stuffed mattress on the floor.

"Why did I not run when I had the chance?" he whispered to himself.

"What was that?"

Henri's fingertips prodded tender, purple skin that

haloed the place on his chest where Philip's crossbow bolt had struck him.

"If I had only run sooner, I am certain that I would have escaped capture or been killed. Either is preferable to being penned like a camel."

"Were you really trying to run? I was told that you were setting a Templar on fire when the Mamluks found you."

"I was dousing the fire, not starting it."

"Why?"

"The man would have died." Henri stood and began to pace again. Seven steps to the south. Twelve steps to the west. Seven steps to the north. Twelve steps to the east.

"Better to die than to live with such injuries."

"Yusuf ensured that he received a swift end."

"So you allowed an infidel to kill him? I thought that you like to kill people for mercy."

Henri shot the man a look. He barely knew Lord Melik, who was not of French nobility or of serious consequence in Acre.

His eyes drifted to the low ceiling of the storeroom where they were being held, and he glared at the stones. Sidika was upstairs somewhere among the female captives. At least, he thought she was. The notion that Yusuf might have her executed filled him with fear.

Henri and Lord Melik estimated that they had been in the cellar of the church for ten days. Because they were worth a great deal of ransom money, the guards treated them well enough. They had beds to lay upon and plenty of food and water. Every day, a physician visited to ensure the sultan's investments didn't perish of a fever or malnourishment. Once a day, someone came to take their chamber pot, and every morning they were escorted outside for some air and exercise. Henri looked for Sidika among the women and children as they were led out through the nave, but he no longer saw her, and the guards did not answer his questions.

He heard the muffled sound of talking from outside their room, and the door jerked open.

"Come," a guard said in heavily accented Arabic. "You go." He pushed Henri against a wall and bound his hands, then threw a sack over his head.

"Tell me what is happening!" Henri yelled. "Where are you taking us?"

"Quiet, Franj!" The guard prodded him forward.

"Courage, Henri," he heard Lord Melik say, his voice strained with fear, "whatever we are about to face, we will face it with dignity."

It was challenging to walk with his hands tied and his head covered. The scratchy sack had previously been filled with grain before it became his hood, and he sneezed until his nose dribbled. The guards had taken his boots, and his bare feet stubbed and bled on the debris in the streets.

Eventually, hands guided them up a large staircase into the quiet coolness of a stone building, and the hoods were yanked from their heads. Henri blinked. They stood inside the great hall of the Hospitallers' citadel in the city. It still stood, although the plaster had flaked from the ceiling in large patches.

Yusuf, the amir, greeted them with a grin. He swept his arm toward the ceiling.

"Is this not a magnificent conquest? Now we can house you in much more comfortable quarters, your lordships."

Henri, Lord Melik, and the other captives looked at each other.

"You have captured the Hospital? But what of the patients? The sick and the injured?" asked one of the captives, a nobleman from Sicily.

"Ah yes," Yusuf's face became troubled. "Well, they were not going to survive their injuries anyway, and that brings me to mind – the sultan would like for you all to see something." He nodded to their guards, who pushed the four captives toward a door and into the courtyard. Henri and the three other men shied back as soon as they stepped outside.

Bodies, some clothed, some naked, some with their heads and many without, were stacked in a fleshy pile against the courtyard wall. The remaining Knights Hospitaller stood lined up in the sun, stripped naked, their hands bound. One of the men knelt with his head on a log and heaved with sobs. Beneath him, the ground was saturated with red.

"Mother...mother!" The kneeling knight screamed, and then the axe fell once, twice, and his head thumped to the ground.

"Merciful Virgin!" Lord Melik breathed.

"You are such a fortunate man, Lord Melik, that you were born wealthy," Yusuf commented quietly. "Had a different father sired you, your fate could be the same as theirs." He turned away as another man was pushed toward the execution block. "As long as your family pays the ransom, you shall be released. Let us hope you left them on good terms."

Lord Melik looked at Henri, his face pale with horror.

The guards led the prisoners back into the great hall and into the Hospital's prison. Now Henri understood why Yusuf removed them from the church storerooms. The Hospital was meant to keep people out... and in. The cells were larger than the storage room in the church, but the doors were set with thick iron grates. Henri and Lord Melik were assigned to separate quarters, and for several hours, the prisoners quietly contemplated their fates, each lost in his own thoughts.

"This situation is perfect, Melik," Henri said finally, hanging his hands outside of his cell through the bars in the door. "Now I can talk to you, for you are a learned man, but I no longer have to watch your disgusting habits."

"Funny thing," Lord Melik responded after a pause. "I was just thinking the opposite. You are pretty to look upon, but your conversation is intolerable." And he laughed. "Do you know any good stories?"

Henri smirked. "Have you heard the one about the knight who was supposed to burn The Furious?"

***

After a week in the bowels of the Hospitaller citadel, more prisoners arrived, bringing news that the walls of the Templar citadel had been breached. The guards taunted and jeered at the men, many of whom were still shocked and bleeding from their capture. The next day, they learned that the mighty citadel had collapsed due to the extensive undermining of the building, killing all inside, including many Mamluk soldiers. Their guards marched into the prison and expressed their grief by beating the newly arrived prisoners. Henri paced and clenched his fists at each scream, and Lord Melik huddled in the corner of his cell, covering his ears.

Two more weeks passed. The muscles in Henri's legs ached from lack of use, so he jogged in small circles for exercise. One of the injured prisoners from the Templar citadel developed a fever, and Henri could hear the man raving with delirium. Despite the best efforts of the Mamluk physician, the man died screaming in pain and fear two days later.

One day, a guard came and took Lord Melik away. He had been ransomed. Four days later, another prisoner was taken away with his ransom paid, and then another. Henri paced and paced. He recited the Bible and his lessons from Plato, phrases that he recalled from Emperor Frederick's book of falconry, poetry, and what he remembered of the Qur'an.

This last exercise amused and perplexed his guards, and one of them finally marched over to his cell in exasperation.

"The word is 'souls,' not 'children,' you dullard," the guard sneered.

"If you do good, it is your own souls you do good to, and if you do evil it is to them likewise," Henri said, and the guard nodded with satisfaction.

Henri dangled his hands through the cell door. "It seems you know the Qur'an better than me. Will you listen to me recite?"

"I am not a qāri that I should listen to you recite," the guard said dismissively, but he hesitated, casting a wary glance toward the empty stairs. After a moment of hesitation, the guard and approached Henri's door. He was just as bored as the prisoners.

"How much do you know?"

"Only the Night Journey."

"Why would you learn such a small piece of the Qur'an and not start at the beginning? It is easier to memorize that way."

Henri grinned at him and continued. "Then, when the second came to pass, we sent against you Our servants to discountenance you, and to enter the Temple, as they entered it the first time and to destroy utterly that which they ascended to."

The guard smirked and sat down on the floor outside of Henri's door. "Come, heathen. You have learned a poor translation. Let us start from the beginning."

Every day, the guard, whose name was Talbot, would listen to Henri recite. The other prisoners cursed Henri for an infidel, but he asked them if they would rather listen to complete silence or something to keep them from going mad. After that, they were quiet, and one man, Sir Thomas of Coppergate, even shouted out a correction when Henri stumbled over a verse.

After a time, Talbot started to speak of other things. He had blonde hair and blue eyes, and he told Henri that he was born of English parents but was taken as a slave when he was five years old during a raid on his father's small fief near Jerusalem.

"Do you never wish you could return to England?" Henri asked him one day as they sat playing shatranj with some colored stones and a board that Talbot had sketched on the prison floor from the charcoal end of a burned stick.

"I have never seen England," he replied, moving a stone forward. "England is a barbaric, foreign place of godlessness and women who prance about uncovered, just like your Francia."

Henri smiled sadly. "I think that they must go about more covered up and restricted in Francia than in Palestine. My mother and sisters are too stubborn to find that pleasing. Francia will be difficult for them."

"Then they are godless," Talbot declared.

"Not godless. Just different."

Chapter 49

June 1291

The Ruergue, Francia

T he village of Maron nestled in a narrow valley cut between two steep hills in the richly forested region of the Ruergue in Francia. The valley was small and ungenerous, and as the village population increased, the half-timbered houses squeezed higher up the hills until they clung to the stony slopes like barnacles on a rocky seashore. At the far end of town, a new abbey rose, stone by stone, atop the blackened carcass of the old abbey, which had burned ten years earlier.

Little level farmland was available to cultivate vegetables and grains, so the primary export of the village was sheep, who grazed on the hillsides, and tradesmen – leather workers, millers, and dyers – who took advantage of the crystal waters of the Ouche and the Dourdou rivers to run their mills.

A castle, dark and narrow like the valley, presided over this pastorale, glowering from an isolated hilltop. Every house and road below it was exposed to its stony gaze, and the villagers seemed to cower as they went about their business in its shadow.

Gaspard of Maron-en-Ruergue appreciated cowering. It granted him the opportunity to feel his importance and then feel it again when he dealt justice or compassion to his villagers. This day, as he sat in his chair in the great hall of the castle, he preferred compassion, for he had just received a letter which gave him reason to feel optimistic. The young man and woman who bowed their heads in front of him would receive mercy today, despite their disobedience.

"Well then, although you failed to seek my approval before you married a man from outside of this manor, I will allow you to remain together without seeking annulment as long as you fulfill a merchet. You are fortunate because, should I seek an annulment, you would both be guilty of the sin of carnal knowledge of each other outside of approved matrimony."

The young woman blushed deeply under her felt bonnet, and Gaspard tingled with pleasure at her discomfort.

"To complete this merchet, you will make an additional tithe to the church to atone for your lapse in judgment, say… fifteen percent this year? As well, you owe the manor three sheep for your indiscretion. Young woman, I know that your father has the animals to compensate me, and I expect them to be delivered to my herd by Michael's Mass, no later."

The couple exchanged a worried glance, then nodded, and with a wave from Gaspard's hand were escorted from the room by a servant. That was the last legal matter he had to deal with this day. He rose from his chair and stretched.

At forty-nine years of age, he was starting to feel the hardness of his chair and the chill of the room no longer left his bones when he wrapped in his fur-lined cloak. He retreated stiffly from the great hall for his study – a former storeroom that Gaspard had converted to a more comfortable space for him to work. The ceilings in this room were low and heavy-beamed, and it was dark and close, with a moldering mat of rushes on the floor that badly needed replacing and a small fire that burned in a poorly constructed stone hearth. It was nearly July, and yet the weather refused to break from a series of cold and damp weeks. Fortunately, it did not seem to damage the immediate health of livestock… nor of lemons shipped from Palestine.

Gaspard did not particularly like the taste of lemons, but the beastly little fruits had made him rich, so he championed them to every noble he encountered. Of course, in the Ruergue, which was far from Marseilles, he could not have fresh lemons due to spoilage, so he tolerated a dried citrus rind in his honey cakes or as a part of a fish sauce on occasion. This news about the fall of Acre was concerning, for if the lemons, sugar, or cinnamon ceased to flow to Marseilles from al-Hadiqa, he would be forced to do something drastic to preserve his fortune.

He sat at the table in his study and re-read the letter that had just arrived.

> *The city has fallen, and we have no word from al-Hadiqa about its condition. Your brother's wife arrived at Beaufort's residence this week, but your nephew was not with her. Please advise, as Beaufort does not wish for her to stay at his home for long. I enclose a letter that was addressed to her by the king's brother, but since she is a Saracen and a woman, we determined to send it directly to you.*
> *~Marchand*

Gaspard frowned. At one time, when he lived in Palestine with his father and his twin brother, Rogier, he wanted Nasira more than anything under God's sun. Now, her very name made his tongue sour. Nasira was lushly beautiful as a

THE LAND OF GOD

young woman, and, as usual, his brother, Rogier, took what he wanted. Gaspard's wife might not have been a beauty to look upon, but she managed to produce a son that lived to adulthood, and her fortune was an acceptable compensation for her crooked teeth and spotty skin.

He picked up the second letter on his desk and examined the wax seal. It was royal, but not King Henry's.

> *Lady Nasira, I regret to inform you that your son, Lord Henri of al-Hadiqa, has been captured in Acre. His captor, Sultan al-Ashraf Khalil, requests a tribute of 100,000 gold bezants as ransom. I have agreed to act as a mediator in these affairs, as I am well-positioned here in Cyprus to facilitate negotiations with the sultan. You may inform the Templars in Marseilles of your answer, and they will put up the funds at your request and with my oversight.*
>
> *Please do act in the greatest haste, for this new sultan has demonstrated himself to be an uncompromising man, and I am afraid Lord Henri will suffer much in the event of a delay.*
>
> *~ Amalric of Lusignan, Constable of Jerusalem, Lord of Tyre, Prince of Cyprus*

"So, my young fool of a nephew has gone and gotten himself captured," Gaspard said to himself. This news soothed the sting of the loss of the estate in Palestine and its reliable source of income.

For years, Gaspard had pondered what to do about his brother's son, who at any time could come sweeping down from the Holy Land and claim his estate in Francia. Battle mortality was high in the Holy Land, and Gaspard had hoped that his brash and arrogant nephew would simply be run through by a Saracen blade. He had to give the boy credit for living so long. The last letter he received from Marchand had informed him that the young man was alive, healthy, and not inclined to leave the Holy Land at any time soon, which was a mixed relief.

Now he had this letter, and Nasira did not know about it. Gaspard examined the remnants of the seal closely. It did not appear that Marchand had opened and re-sealed it, which meant that no one, other than Prince Amalric, knew Henri was sitting in a Mamluk prison.

"Best to wait," he said to himself. "No need to be hasty about these things." Standing from his chair, Gaspard picked up a hammer and struck a gong on his table. A servant entered quietly.

"Fetch Adrien, my son," he said, "and bring me something to drink."

Chapter 50

July 1291

Hospitaller Citadel, Acre

Without warning, the guards clattered into the Hospitaller citadel one day and took the rest of the prisoners out together, ignoring Henri's shouts for an explanation. Occasionally Talbot or another guard would check on him or bring a meal, and if their duties were dull, they would stay and practice their Arabic. Henri did not mind, for when the time between guard visits was too long, he began to forget what it was like to be around other people. The silence was maddening.

One morning, as Talbot and Henri talked, facing each other through the bars in his cell door, Yusuf padded down the stairs on pointed suede slippers. He watched with amusement for a few moments before clearing his throat. Talbot sprang to attention, his pale face reddening with embarrassment and fear.

"You do well, guard, to teach the Qur'an to our prisoners. Now please return to your post. The Viscount has been ransomed and will leave immediately for Cyprus."

Henri jumped to his feet. He gathered up his torn surcoat and held out his wrists to be bound. Then Yusuf led him up the stairs and into the light. Henri blinked and shielded his eyes from the glare of the sun. It was nearly July now – more than a month had passed since his capture.

A guard boosted him onto a horse, and the two of them walked their mounts in silence through the city's ruined streets. He scanned the tops of the buildings for familiar landmarks, but the church steeples had collapsed, and the walls of the Templar citadel were gone. The city he had known his entire life was now reduced to stones and ghosts.

"Yusuf, I asked you to include one of the women from the church in my ransom request. I trust that this happened?" Henri tried not to sound as worried as he felt.

Yusuf was quiet for a moment. "It did not happen," he finally replied. "The girl still lives, although the guards that she injured asked for her pretty head as a token to hang outside the doors of the women's prison. The sultan decided to give her to one of his amirs as a slave."

"I was most specific that she must be included in my ransom," Henri said through clenched teeth.

Yusuf shrugged his shoulders. "We could find no evidence that she is of a noble family or that she has any particular value. What is she to you that you should want her? Were you lovers?"

"I owe her family a debt," was all Henri would say.

They reached the harbor. Henri was pushed into a small cog, and Yusuf hopped in after him. A guard untied Henri's hands on the boat, and he was allowed to move about freely. The mellow, salty air filled his lungs, and he delighted at being free of the dark, stinking prison. He looked back at his abused city as the wind caught the little cog's sails and pushed her toward Cyprus.

The last time he saw Acre from the sea, it was during his desperate struggle against the waves in Durant's little boat. Now, the city skyline was lower, humbled. Smoke still streamed from a few fires, but all signs of life were gone. The

Templar citadel, which used to guard the apex of the seawall, was now a pile of broken stones. Bloated corpses bobbed in the harbor, which stank of death.

Henri slumped on the deck, his heart heavy, his stomach already churning with the anticipation of seasickness. Yusuf sat down beside him.

"Your family did not pay your ransom," he said slowly. "King Henry's brother, Prince Amalric, paid it. I am not sure what you did to enrage your family, but it seems they do not want you back."

Henri scowled. His mother would have paid his ransom, but he had no assurance that she and his sisters had survived the crossing to Marseilles. Many who escaped from Mamluk arrows drowned instead in the angry, churning seas as the waves overtook the ships that fled the harbor. He closed his eyes and willed himself not to imagine his mother and sisters floating facedown in the water, their arms waving lazily over their heads with each movement of the waves.

"You should also know that the rest of your noble prisoners were taken to Damascus at the sultan's request, to be paraded as a display of his conquest. You, I managed to spare."

Henri looked up at him. "Why?"

"Surely many would have found it amusing to see you thoroughly embarrassed, but I could not allow it. The rest of the prisoners tried to sell secrets and begged for their lives like frightened children. I am told you had the nickname, '*le vaniteux*', in your youth?"

"Why would that spare me?

"Because I do not see a vain man. I see a man in turmoil. Someone, perhaps, who is experiencing a change in himself."

Henri looked out at the ruined city, the graveyard of everyone he knew. He thought of Sidika, and his heart ached.

Yusuf was watching his face closely.

"What is this debt that you owe to the girl's family? The little witch that you attempted to ransom," Yusuf finally asked. "I am curious to know why a Franj nobleman would be so concerned with a Jewess."

"She helped me on several occasions where my life was in danger," Henri said, staring out at the pale green sea. "She is educated, skilled in healing, and…" he paused, but Yusuf continued to watch him with silent, brown eyes. "And I killed her father. I promised him as he died that I would give her protection, even though she will not let me."

Yusuf nodded quietly. "The Prophet, peace be upon him, says, 'And worship God, and do not ascribe divinity, in any way, to aught beside Him. And do good unto your parents, and near of kin, and unto orphans, and the needy, and the neighbor from among your own people, and the neighbor who is a stranger, and the friend by your side, and the wayfarer, and those whom you rightfully possess. Verily, God does not love any of those who, full of self-conceit, act in a boastful manner.'"

Henri looked out toward Acre and said nothing.

They moored at Limassol harbor. The streets were choked with people, many of whom appeared to be living out in the open. Women stared sightlessly under makeshift tents, while grubby children slept next to them or begged for coins and bread from passersby. Men in dirty, rumpled clothes leaned idly against the low walls of the harbor, waiting for work as porters on the ships.

Yusuf and three Mamluk guards led Henri to the Royal Palace, and a servant directed them into a small room consumed by a bulky wooden table and several chests with iron bands and locks on them. When they entered, a black-clad Templar sergeant with a red cross splayed over his heart stood from his seat, his pale blue eyes impassive.

"I am here for Henri of Maron's ransom," Yusuf said curtly. He did not bow, and the expressions of distaste on both their faces made it clear that the two men knew each other.

"Ah yes, the viscount at last. Please demonstrate to me that he has been unharmed," the sergeant said, walking around the table.

Yusuf ordered Henri to remove his tunic.

"See? No signs of beating or starvation, although he is a bit thin. Our physician healed him of a mild fever, which is more than what would have happened if you had tried to cure him with aught but prayers and carving crosses into his skin."

The Templar turned his empty eyes toward Henri.

"My name is Basile, my lord. Tell me, were you mistreated? You can be honest, for we are on neutral territory here."

"I was not mistreated in any way. Although my accommodations were less comfortable than I am accustomed to, I was fed and exercised daily. However, one of my requests was not met. There is a young woman of Acre who I specifically asked to be released with me."

Basile looked inquiringly at Yusuf, who shrugged.

"It did not suit the sultan's pleasure to let her come to Cyprus. We still cannot determine the validity of the viscount's claim that she is noble. Also, she is a Turk, and a Jew, which further discredits him."

Henri flushed angrily.

"I feel sorry for Lord Henri," Yusuf continued. "He has lost his home, his wealth, his dignity, and his woman, and yet he behaved with honor when he was in our care. To compensate in a small way for what he has suffered, I have two gifts for him." He reached into his cloak and withdrew a sash of rich black silk. Henri took it and noticed Arabic script stitched on it in gold thread.

Basile leaned forward. "What does that say?"

"Vision comprehends Him not, and He comprehends all vision; and He is the Knower of subtleties, the Aware," Henri read, and Basile's pale skin flushed a deep red.

"Blasphemy!" the Templar snarled.

Yusuf rolled his eyes.

"I also confiscated his sword from the sultan's armory." He turned to Henri. "It is a small gesture, but I have found you to be singular among the prisoners. I truly do wish you well. Remember, Allah commands us to be generous with each other." He bowed deeply, presenting the sword to Henri with two upraised hands.

"I will take it," Basile stepped in between them, "and give it to Lord Henri after you have safely exited the castle. He is trained to kill Mamluks, after all, and I have no wish to start another war right here in the king's house."

Henri looked at Yusuf. "I thank you for returning my sword to me. It belonged to my father. Now please tell me, what is the name of the amir that the sultan awarded Sidika to? Tell me the man's name that I may inquire after her welfare."

Yusuf hesitated. "If I were to tell you that, it could endanger the life of the sultan's man. The girl is no longer under your protection, as she has been passed to a new master. She is owned by him now."

"Sidika will allow no one to own her. Your colleague will find her challenging, stubborn, and outspoken. Best to release her to my custody since she is more trouble than she is worth."

Yusuf smiled. "That is very good to know. I wish you

well, Lord Henri of Maron. May Allah grant you peace."

He turned and walked from the room, swinging a heavy bag of gold bezants in his hand.

Chapter 51

July 1291
Limassol, Cyprus

"I did not spend one hundred thousand bezants of my brother's treasury so that you could run back to Francia like a spurned maiden, Henri. Had I known that you would flee, I would have let you rot in that Saracen prison until they took your ungrateful head off!"

Amalric's temper was up, and Henri felt his own ire rising. The two of them had been arguing hotly since the noon meal, and the servants had long since fled.

"Amalric, I will compensate you the money as soon as I can determine why my mother failed to pay it," Henri said with more self-control than he felt. "I have already written to her and told her I am coming. Now that my homes and villages in Acre are destroyed, I need to see to the matter of my inheritance in Francia, else I shall surely lose that as well."

Amalric spun angrily and stood up to him. He was shorter than Henri and stockier.

"You," he hissed through clenched teeth, "are a viscount of Acre. Acre! Not some shit-smelling town in the Ruergue! And my brother is your sovereign. If he says you are to stay and fight, then you will stay and fight!"

Henri smiled. "I have two sovereigns, Amalric, as do you, and as does your brother, who is a sworn vassal to King

Philippe." He saw Amalric clench his fists. "I am not leaving forever, and I will return as soon as I have resolved the question of succession with my uncle in Maron."

Amalric snorted. "You are only a marquis in Francia, Henri. Who cares about Maron? It is a village! Stay here and help me win Acre back, and my brother will give you the city and all the surrounding lands as a duchy."

Henri paused, then shook his head.

"If I can, I will return in six months, and we will recapture Acre. What can you do immediately anyway? You have lost almost all your soldiers. Your island is overrun with refugees requiring assistance, the knightly orders are more determined to fight each other than the Mamluks, Sidon is abandoned, and now the enemy marches on Tyre, which is without significant defenses. What could you possibly do in the next six months?"

Amalric deflated and sat heavily in a chair.

"I lost Tripoli, and now Acre, Henri. What can I do now but ponder my own failures as a man? My brother made me the Lord of Tyre, and I am sure to lose that city next."

"Losing a city because you were outnumbered twenty-to-one does not make you a failure as a man; it makes you unlucky," Henri said, "and unprepared."

Amalric rolled his eyes. "Go ahead and remind me now that you warned us this would happen."

Henri shook his head. "It gives me no pleasure to be correct. Now, do I have your brother's royal permission to leave? I am most anxious to see my family."

Amalric nodded sullenly. "Go. We will still be here when you return."

Henri boarded a ship bound for Francia the very next day.

Two weeks later, he staggered down the gangplank on

shaky legs in the long, sheltered harbor at Marseilles – thin and in need of a bath. Although he had written to his agents, Beaufort and Marchand, before he left Cyprus, there was little chance his letter would have arrived more than a few days before him. He smirked as he teetered along the wharf, unused to the feel of solid ground beneath his feet.

I wager those two thieves are panicking.

So anxious was he to see his family that he barely spared any attention for Marseilles. He paid a boy two copper bits to show him to the house of Monsieur Beaufort, which he knew to be near the harbor, and then he pounded on the door, his heart beating loudly in his ears.

A sullen-looking young man opened the door. He took in the sight of Henri, who stood unshaven, with his hood pulled low over his eyes, and immediately attempted to shut it again. Henri's hand shot out, and he grabbed the servant by the front of his scandalously short cotehardie.

"Is this the residence of Monsieur Beaufort, the merchant?" Henri asked.

The servant squirmed. "Be gone, ruffian! We are not running a poorhouse for homeless Saracens!"

There was a clatter behind the servant, and Henri saw his mother stumbling over her rich scarlet skirts down a staircase, and then she was throwing herself at him, arms wrapped around his neck.

"My son! We thought you were dead! I thought I would never see you again!"

"Hamza, Hamza!" Saruca charged down the stars next, wrapping herself around his waist. Blanche came slower, lowering herself carefully down each step, her stomach bulging like a ripe fruit under her loose dress. Her eyes watered, and she pulled him into an embrace. "I thought you

340

had died. The last thing I said to you is that I would not forgive you," she whispered.

"You do not have to forgive me, Blanche," he whispered back.

"Ah, Lord Henri! Thanks be to God that you have returned to us safely!" Beaufort gushed, but his eyes did not smile.

"Indeed, thanks be to God that the king's brother was willing to ransom me."

His mother pushed away from him, confused. "Ransom?"

Beaufort turned to the servant and cuffed him hard against the back of his head. The young man stumbled forward.

"Jacques, you nearly turned away Lord Henri, the marquis of Maron and my employer! For this, you shall suffer—"

"Please show mercy to your servant, Monsieur Beaufort," Henri interrupted, pulling his hood back, "and I shall do the same for you when you tell me why my mother never received word that the sultan had captured me."

"Hamza! Did they hurt you?" Nasira grabbed Henri's face and inspected it.

"Surely, Lord Henri, you do not think I would conceal something this serious from your mother?" Beaufort stepped back in affront. "Word never reached us of your capture. Indeed, had we known that you were in prison, Marchand and I would have put up funds for your release on behalf of your uncle—"

"Good. In that case, you owe Prince Amalric of Cyprus one hundred thousand bezants."

Beaufort swallowed visibly.

"And now I need to bathe and to rest, and by God's

341

bonnet, I would like to eat something other than hard bread and salted fish."

Nasira took Henri's hands in hers. "My son, can we return to Acre? What remains of the city?"

"Nothing remains. Acre is gone, Mother. Palestine is no longer in the control of the church."

Beaufort clutched his face and moaned. "Dreadful! God will rain the severest punishment upon the infidels for what they have done!"

"And what have they done, Monsieur Beaufort, other than remove occupiers? It is their Holy Land, too."

Ibrahim came down the stairs, his eyes shining. "Praise be to God. You live, and Palestine is free of the Franj! God is great!" He sank to his knees and bowed to the ground, touching his forehead to the floor between his hands. "Allahu Akbar, Allahu Akbar! I thank you for your blessings!"

"Please, be quiet!" Beaufort wrung his hands. "I risk much by allowing your infidel prayers inside my house!"

Henri pushed Beaufort back against a wall. "Allow my uncle to pray, Monsieur, or I shall find another agent to manage my affairs. Now, send your servant for Monsieur Marchand. We have much to plan before my homecoming to Maron."

Chapter 52

July 1291

Al-Barqiyya, Cairo

The cart rattled to a stop in a puff of pale dust, and Sidika heard orders shouted in Turkish from the retinue of guards and soldiers that accompanied her caravan. She had lost count of the days that they traveled south to Cairo, but by the smell of her unwashed body, she guessed that it had been at least five.

As the other women in her wagon stirred and stretched, Sidika peeked through a hole in the wagon cover. They were outside the low walls of a garrison, which appeared loosely fortified. Behind the walls, she saw the stone tops of several domed buildings.

Their caravan contained one wagon of women and small children and a second of boys between five and eighteen years of age. The women's wagon was quiet, but all day and night, Sidika heard the sound of weeping from the boys' wagon as the young ones cried for their mothers. They were to stay at the garrison before transport to the meydans in Cairo, where they would begin training as furisiyya – new recruits in the Mamluk army.

A fleet of eunuchs approached Sidika's wagon and removed the cover. Her legs throbbed from lack of use as she climbed down and took in her surroundings. Beyond the garrison, the rooftops of Cairo baked in the late afternoon sun under a cloud of woodsmoke and dust. In the direction they had just come, there were pavilions and large tracks for racing and training horses, and the vast desert, looking like an endless yellow smudge.

The eunuchs herded the women through the gate and directed them toward one of the domed buildings – a hammam. After a bath and a thorough inspection for lice and other parasites, they were each given a clean, shapeless frock and veil, and a meal of oat porridge and squash. When they had finished, they were sent to bed. Tomorrow, the eunuchs informed them, they would be sorted and then enter Cairo.

The next day, the eunuchs woke the women before dawn. Many of the older and visibly infirmed were separated from the rest and herded back into wagons until there was only room to stand. The wagons rattled away slowly, bound for the slave markets near the Khān al-Khalīlī in Cairo.

Sidika and a few other younger women were taken into an open-air courtyard with many iron rings embedded into the tall, stone wall. As she looked around in confusion, one of the eunuchs in a red taqiyya pushed her roughly to the wall, tying her hands to the ring. The strings that held her frock together at the throat were untied and she was stripped naked.

What followed was a careful inspection of her body – her teeth and ears, bones and toes, and a humiliating probing of her breasts and the secret place between her legs. This last part of the inspection brough tears to her eyes, and the eunuch took out a switch and smacked her on the buttocks with it until she stopped her weeping.

Again, they were sorted into smaller groups. Sidika and two other women were given proper frocks and placed in a two-wheeled cart, followed by more carts filled with furniture, coin, rugs, and other finery that had traveled from Acre with them. In front, rows of Mamluk soldiers, clad in vivid blue tunics underneath their armor, marched in formation. Bringing up the rear, a braying herd of horses, camels, and goats trotted, prodded by young boys in dusty robes. They processed through Bab al-Barqiyya, one of Cairo's many splendid gates, toward the citadel to the sound of exuberant cheering. In the street, men and boys danced and ran alongside the wagons. Women waved scarves and ululated, tossing flowers from their mishrabiyas – large wooden windows that protruded from the walls of the houses.

The remaining women in the wagon hung their heads and said nothing to each other, each pondering their futures, for the inspection and treatment at the garrison outside the city confirmed that they were bound for the houses of the amirs to be posted as domestic slaves.

Sidika sat in her usual place near the rip in the caravan cover, shaking, with her knees pulled to her chest. Occasionally, she caught glimpses of Emre as he rode ahead of her wagon on his own camel. He looked neither left nor right, his face rigid, his arm bound tightly to his chest in a sling. Unlike the captives in the wagons, Emre moved freely in the caravan. He had clean clothes and armor, and he slept in a tent with the 'Askari. The female captives were guarded closely during their journey, and the men were not allowed to even look in their direction. Thus, Sidika had not spoken to Emre since their last few moments together in the cellar of Lord Henri's house.

They pulled past the walls of the hulking citadel – the largest building Sidika had ever seen – and wound around the hill before turning through a set of arched gates decorated with blue and white tiles. Inside, she could see a small but immaculately groomed garden with limestone pathways that wandered gracefully through beds of roses and manicured trees. Servants emerged from the white-walled house and greeted the new arrivals.

In the confusion of homecoming, as wagons were unloaded and animals herded to the stables or the market, Sidika saw Emre slip away behind a stand of bay trees. She darted after him without hesitation.

He stood with his back to her in the dappled shade, gently running his hand over a name carved into a stone in the house wall.

"Who is Aktay?" Sidika asked. Emre spun and slapped his hand over the name protectively.

"No one. He is dead. And so shall you be if you are found here. You could get us both killed!"

"I am sorry. I wanted to see you and tell you that I am glad we were both assigned to the same house. It would be far more frightening if I came here alone."

Emre sneered. "I have not been *assigned* to this house. I am a guest."

Sidika took a step back. Emre's features were twisted into a deep frown, and there was no warmth in his eyes.

"Oh, I see. Of course." She suddenly felt foolish. He was a Mamluk for years before becoming a servant of Lord Henri. It made sense that he would change when he returned to Cairo. "Well, I am glad to see that you fared well." She turned to leave.

"Fared well?" she heard him say in a dangerous tone. "Look at my arm. Look at it!" He held up the stump of his handless left arm. "Were it not for you, I would still have two hands! I would not have spent days trapped in a cellar, close to death! You have ruined my future and yours as well!"

"I am sorry, Emre. I have said a thousand times, I am sorry!"

"Do not call me that. My name is Zahed once again, and your name is inconsequential, because you are nothing but a slave now." He spat the words at her.

Sidika sank to her knees, hot tears burning down her cheeks. "I know… I thought perhaps we could try to escape. Try to get back home, to Acre, and to Henri. I did not know that you hated me so."

Emre looked down at her.

"Get up. Forget Acre, and forget Henri. This is your home now."

What's next?

The story continues! Please visit www.elizabethrandersen.com to sign up for updates on book releases and to learn about the fascinating history of the 13th century (did the viscount of Acre really miss when he threw a grenade at the Furious? Was the weather really that bad during the siege of Acre? Would a 16-year-old Jewish girl really have been used as a spy for the Templars?).

I am an independent author, and your reviews mean everything to me. Please take a moment to review this book for other readers on Amazon, Goodreads, or wherever you prefer to leave book reviews.

Author's notes

When writing historical fiction, an author faces many conundrums: how much detail to include? Is it ethical to move places and dates for the sake of the narrative? These are all amusing, and the consequences of getting them wrong means that a few pedants may find an opportunity to post a correction somewhere very public. For instance, in book 1 (*The Scribe*), I agonized for weeks over whether or not I should allow Henri to have a fork when eating or just a knife and a few skewers.

The harder challenge, however, is knowing how to represent the facts in a way that conveys truth, balance, and also gets your own message across. I spent many sleepless nights wondering how to describe the fall of Acre and the subsequent slaughter in a way that did not portray the Mamluk Muslims as a one-dimensional evil, because in a battle, someone has to win, and someone has to die. Although it is easy to say that the siege and capture of Acre was purely religiously motivated, it truly was not. The Mamluk army was more preoccupied with the threat of Mongol attack than the Crusaders, who were mostly an annoyance and not considered a serious threat at that time. Still, that small threat had to be eliminated if they were to protect themselves, because the Crusaders could easily take advantage of the Mamluk army while it was preoccupied with a larger enemy.

It was also important to me that people understand that the Templar order was not a featureless cabal of evil members in a secret society. There were good men who were Templars, and there were bad men who were Templars, but mostly there were men in the order who made based on their values and information available at the time, just as we do today. History may not look kindly on us either.

Most important of all, for me, was to convey that people in the Middle Ages are not terribly different than we are in the 21st century – but they had unique challenges and influences pushing them to make decisions that we sometimes find incomprehensible. Does this excuse them from mistreating other people? No. Does this mean that everyone who lived in the 13th century was violent and never bathed? Also no. Then, as now, a young person raised in a brutal society could grow into empathy, there were multicultural cities with vibrant societies, and for God's sake, not everyone dressed in brown and gray!

There are many characters in this book who were real individuals, and their exact words were captured by their contemporaries. The description of Guillaume de Beaujeu saying "behold, the wound," are his words, some of the last spoken before he died. The text of the letter that Khalil sent to the Christians in Acre is also taken directly from Beaujeu's secretary in his account of the siege in *The Templar of Tyre*. Patrons who subscribe to my monthly newsletter receive more details about these real-life characters, and how some of them made true-to-life decisions that impacted history.

Finally, I have made some adjustments in order to help my readers. For example, although I could have used "Frankish", "Frankia", and "Franks" to describe the people who came from what is now France, I chose not to because the territory and the cultural diversity was very different from the exact region where the Maron family came from. The concept of "France" was still nascent at the time, as the French kings struggled to keep their hands around a wily bunch of counts who each ruled their own territory. Family names were just becoming more common at this time, and so instead of always referring to Henri as "Henri of Maron" or Henri de Maron" or "lord of Maron", sometimes I just called him Lord Maron. I also chose to use modern-day versions of the languages in the text (Turkish, French, Bulgarian, Arabic). Likewise, some of the views and opinion stressed by my characters are purely modern. The reality for a 16-year-old Jewish girl is that she probably would have been married. A French nobleman like Rogier de Maron would have taken a penniless Arab woman as a mistress, but he would not have married her. I have tried to use language that will educate and not confuse (e.g. in book 1 I use "castle" instead of "casale" because it might confuse, but I chose to use the little-known "caruca / carucate" to educate, since this method of land measurement was fascinating and lost to time. It's in the glossary.)

I thank you, dear reader, for staying with me. *The Scribe* was my first novel, and if you made it this far with me, you know that things continue to improve. I thank you for the time that you spent with my characters, who are as real to me as my own friends (some of them more aggravating and annoying friends than others) and I hope that you can continue on the journey with us as Henri, Sidika, Emre, and Yusuf encounter increasing challenges, both personal, and historical.

Glossary

Askari	A Mamluk who completed his training and had been entrusted with freedom. 'Askari had the opportunity to wed, own property, and even become amirs.
Assassin	A secret sect of Shi'a Muslims who were fanatically devoted to their charismatic master. Assassins were often hired by powerful rulers to covertly murder enemies and political rivals. Their sect was disbanded in the 13th century.
Aumônière	A drawstring purse, often lushly embroidered and hung from a belt or girdle.
Ayan	Wealthy, non-warrior class of medieval Muslim society.
Ayata	Moon god in the Tengri religion practiced by Mongol and Turkic nomads.
Baculus	A scepter with an octagon-carved head, used by the grand master of the Templars.

Caracal	A species of large predator cat with tufted ears and strikingly pale eyes. Native to Africa, the Middle East, and Central Asia.
Caruca	A medieval measurement of land, determined by how much a team of eight oxen could plow in a single day.
Citronnier	A lemon grove.
Confrere	A secular knight, unaffiliated with one of the Brotherly or religious orders. Although confreres were usually from the noble class it was possible to become confrere without a knighted father.
Coteahardie	An article of clothing worn by both men and women throughout the Middle Ages. Men's cotehardies became shorter and shorter as history progressed toward the Renaissance, and women's became more elaborate with the invention of the set-in sleeve. Often sleeveless, worn over a tunic or a slip, and belted at the waist.
Dua	A prayer of supplication. Dua can be recited upon many occasions, including death and mourning.
Enceinte	The outer, often lower walls of a double-walled fortress.

Fursān	A Mamluk warrior trainee, not yet considered a full faris. Fursān or furisiyya underwent brutal training, often starting when boys were as young as 8 or 9. In some cases, Turkish families would sell their young sons as fursān in order to achieve rank and glory in the Mamluk army. In other cases, the boys were bought or taken as slaves in the conquest of war.
Günana	Sun goddess in the Tengri religion practiced by Mongol and Turkic nomads.
Ingeniators	Engineers guild. Ingeniators was the original name for engineers, who were considered "ingengios".
Jambiya	A small, deeply curved, ceremonial dagger worn on the belt, often associated with the people of Yemen.
Kaddish	Prayer regularly recited in synagogues. A version of Kaddish called the Mourner's Kaddish is recited for the dead and dying.
Kumis	A salty, slightly carbonated drink of fermented mare's milk, considered a great delicacy and extremely nourishing. It is still consumed today.
Machina	Machine; in the Latin.

Mangonels	A siege weapon used in warfare since the 6th century across most of the world but invented far earlier in ancient China. Similar to a trebuchet or catapult, but with less range and power.
Merchet	A marriage fine, paid to a feudal lord as compensation for the loss of a worker when a woman married outside of her lord's village.
Mole	Not a small, burrowing creature. A mole in this context is a large berm of earth or stone that doesn't allow water to flow underneath it.
Muwarraq	A layered dough, similar to a modern-day puff pastry.
Naft	A highly combustible liquid whose fire was not easily extinguishable by water. The recipe for naft (also known as Greek fire) was so secret that it was produced by anonymous guilds. Since the production of naft was highly dangerous, it was considered a secret of the state.
Na'ib	Arabic word for jailer.
Nones	The canonical Catholic prayer at the ninth hour after dawn.

Portcullis	A heavy grate of latticed wood or iron that could be lowered within a gateway to protect from invasion.
Qadib	Arabic word for rod, staff, or slang for penis.
Qamash	Arabic word for towel or wrap.
Qāri	A man who is qualified to recite the Qur'an in a melodious and pleasing way.
Qasids	A spy in the Mamluk army. Qasids were not like Assassins, who were of a specific and secretive religious sect.
Sayidati	Arabic word for Madame or Mrs.
Shahada	A declaration of faith that is central to pious Muslim life. "There is no god but Allah and Mohammad is His prophet."
Shatranj	An early precursor to the present-day game of chess. The game pieces consisted of a king, counselor, chariot, elephant, knight, and soldier.
Tamu	The underworld in the Tengri religion practiced by Mongol and Turkic nomads. Tamu is ruled by the god Erlik.
Taqiya	A skullcap still worn by Muslim men around the world, often at daily prayers.

Tengri	The god of all creation, according to the Tengri religion practiced by Mongol and Turkic nomads.
Terce	The canonical Catholic prayer at the third hour after dawn.
Thawb	An ankle-length, loose garment with a hood and wide sleeves worn by Bedouins and Arab locals in medieval Syria and Palestine. A version of the 13th century thawb is still worn in present-day Egypt.
Peliot	An apron-like tunic covering a woman's dress, allowing the sleeves to show.
Turcopoles	A spearman, unknighted, who was of a lower class, often from the Turkish regions.
Usted	A Mamluk troop commander.

Acknowledgements

There is no way that I could have launched this book with any amount of confidence if it had not been for the kind and generous help of a multinational team of people. First and foremost, many, many thanks to Dr. Adam Ali of the University of Toronto, who helped me to understand the context of the Medieval Mamluk sultanate, their motivations, and the uniqueness of their society. I also thank him for the mountain of research papers that he gave me. I am still buried under them, but I'm enjoying it all. Huge thanks are also due to Mohammad Jawad Khaki of the IMAM Center in Kirkland, for graciously and patiently guiding me through many verses of the Qur'an, philosophy of Islam, and helping me to identify my own biases. It has always been my intention to treat the religions in this series with respect, while also staying true to the historical record. Mr. Khaki's positive view of the peace and mercy of Islam left me feeling truly happy after our conversations.

For translation help, I could not have survived without the assistance of the magnificent Vahan Dede, who helped me with my Turkish and didn't bat an eyelash at some of the strange phrases I asked him to confirm. Raanan Schnitzer has not only been a dear colleague for years but also my Hebrew translator extraordinaire. Thank you also to Iman Ayyeh for helping me with the Arabic phrases in the text.

Gratitude always to those who were willing to read the

first copies of the text: Edward Boland, who appreciated that I was willing to drag my readers through the banalities of military logistics, Debbie Roscoe, my mother, who fiercely argued that I should combine books 1 and 2 together (she wasn't wrong, but it would have been almost 900 pages long), for Matt McGinnis, who refused to allow me to be lazy with my prose (he says I also should thank Sister Margaret Mary of his school days for making him a ruthless grammarian).

Cecily Blanchard and Rachel Smith at The History Quill restored my faith in editors again, Theodor Jurma added The Furious and The Victorious to his lovely maps, and Oliver Bennett at MoreVisual created another stunning cover for me.

To the other friends, family, fans, and authors who support and encourage me, I hope that I can do the same for you someday.

Of course, mountains of thanks to Jordan and Soren, my husband and son, for putting up with hastily made meals and piles of books and papers littering their living space, and for listening to me talk *ad nauseum* about the 13th century to them.

www.ingramcontent.com/pod-product-compliance
Lightning Source LLC
Chambersburg PA
CBHW032143190726
48290CB00005BB/1384